"There is absolutely n⟨...⟩
you stick any of that B⟨...⟩

"Your little bugs—swimming through my bloodstream?! Forget it!"

"You would retain your individuality, Lieutenant, not become a member of the collective. You *couldn't* because there is no collective here." Seven of Nine stopped then and considered, realizing she was not being completely accurate. "Actually, that is not true: *we* would be the collective—a collective of two."

"You say that like somehow I'd find it reassuring. Amazing. No, Seven. Absolutely not. I won't even consider it."

"Then quite likely all these people will die."

Lowering her head, Torres hissed softly, "How long will it take?"

"Not long," Seven replied. "But it would be best if you were unconscious for the procedure. You are a very difficult person, Lieutenant. Lie down now."

"I know," Torres said, lying back on the floor. "It's just that I really don't like you at all. No offense."

Seven leaned down over Torres and unconsciously flexed a muscle in her forearm. A minuscule gap opened between Seven's wrist bones just above the cuff, and an assimilation tubule snaked out from it like a tiny black tongue. Seven touched the tube to Torres's neck, and the engineer grew quiet. "None taken," Seven said.

STAR TREK VOYAGER®

STRING THEORY

BOOK 1

COHESION

JEFFREY LANG

Based upon STAR TREK®
created by Gene Roddenberry
and STAR TREK: VOYAGER
created by Rick Berman, Michael Piller, and Jeri Taylor

POCKET BOOKS
New York   London   Toronto   Sydney   Monorha

This book is a work of fiction. Names, characters, places and incidents are products of the author's imagination or are used fictitiously. Any resemblance to actual events or locales or persons living or dead is entirely coincidental.

An *Original* Publication of POCKET BOOKS

POCKET BOOKS, a division of Simon & Schuster, Inc.
1230 Avenue of the Americas, New York, NY 10020

Copyright © 2005 by Paramount Pictures. All Rights Reserved.

STAR TREK is a Registered Trademark of Paramount Pictures.

This book is published by Pocket Books, a division of Simon & Schuster, Inc., under exclusive license from Paramount Pictures.

ISBN-13: 978-0-7434-5718-7
ISBN-10:   0-7434-5718-8

First Pocket Books printing July 2005

10 9 8 7 6 5 4 3 2 1

POCKET and colophon are registered trademarks of Simon & Schuster, Inc.

Cover design by John Vairo, Jr.

Manufactured in the United States of America

For information regarding special discounts for bulk purchases, please contact Simon & Schuster Special Sales at 1-800-456-6798 or business@simonandschuster.com.

To AnnaRita,
for all your help with the boldly going

HISTORIAN'S NOTE

This story unfolds between the fourth and fifth seasons of *Star Trek: Voyager.*

"The degree of tolerance attainable at any moment depends on the strain under which society is maintaining its cohesion."

GEORGE BERNARD SHAW

STRING THEORY

Prologue

Disaster minus 14 minutes

Mateo did not like the captain leaving the ship. True, the aliens had not committed any overtly threatening acts, but he thought that Captain Ziv was displaying unwarranted trust. As impressive as these wayfarers were, Mateo believed they were making unbelievable claims, not the least being that their tiny ship was able to attain faster-than-light velocities, but, oh, *not right at the moment* because of some as-yet-undefined, unfathomable peculiarity about local space. So fiercely skeptical was the first officer that the hair was literally standing up on the sides of his neck.

On the other hand, Mateo had not had any particular desire to leave the vessel either, which would have been his fate if the captain weren't so curious about (and so trusting of) the aliens. Traditionally, the second-in-command was the one to undertake any such diplomatic or exploratory mission, but neither Ziv nor any of his *hara* were traditional officers. Despite the fact that the captain had been put in command of their mission at the last minute and under some very peculiar circumstances (rumors of some dirtside impropriety had been circulating), Mateo both liked and trusted Ziv, and those feelings extended to the captain's closest advisors.

Mateo scanned the bridge and surveyed his own *hara*. All seemed as well as they could be, even Cho, who had been terribly rattled by their unexpected, almost disastrous encounter with the aliens. Most of the crewmen had been advised about the possibility of alien encounters (though Mateo suspected that few believed they were real), but no one had expected to meet other spacefarers so early in their journey. *How many more are out here?* he wondered.

Studying the image of the fragile-looking vessel on his viewer, Mateo wondered about its engineers' claims. "It can't be true," he muttered. A dozen of the alien ships could park side by side inside the exhaust port of his ship's drive unit. How could such a minuscule object have the power to do what they claimed? Yet Maza, as sensible and levelheaded an engineer as could be found in the service, said that he had seen their engines' specs and believed every word.

"Commander," Cho called. "The aliens' chief engineer wishes to speak with Maza again. Should I patch through the call?"

"Certainly," Mateo said. "But ask if they could have our captain call sometime soon. I'd like to hear . . ."

"Captain Ziv is hailing us on another channel, Commander."

Mateo sighed with relief and lowered himself into the captain's chair. "Very good. Complete the circuit."

The captain's image materialized on the small monitor set near the floor. Ziv looked uncommonly pleased, almost ebullient, as if a great burden had just been lifted. *"Mateo,"* he said, and waited for the gesture of acknowledgment. *"All is well?"*

"Well and truly well, my captain," Mateo said, trying to sound upbeat. "We have completed all the preparations the aliens requested. Maza says we will be under way soon and moving very quickly." He allowed a slight note of uncertainty to creep into his tone, hoping the captain would notice and respond. Unfortunately, the captain missed it.

"You have no idea, Mateo," the captain said. *"I only regret that you have not been able to see this extraordinary ship."*

Someone behind the captain spoke, someone with an oddly, even disturbingly high-pitched voice, like that of an annoyingly precocious child. *"There may still be time,"* the speaker said. *"If you permit it."*

Mateo felt a silly grin creep up over his face. *Would I like to see this alien vessel?* he wondered, and was surprised to find that the answer was yes. Very much, if only to reassure himself.

"We will discuss it when I return to the ship, Mateo," Ziv said. *"But for now, relax and tell the crew and passengers to do the same. Have you informed everyone what will be happening?"*

"Word is filtering down through the holds, Captain," Mateo reported. "It is difficult, but I think most of them have the sense that something wonderful is about to occur."

"More wonderful than even they know, Mateo," Ziv replied, and again his eyes shone brightly. *"But perhaps it would be best to keep that between us now."*

Mateo, sensing his captain's keen excitement, grinned and agreed.

"I will see you soon," Ziv finished, and both signed off.

Minutes later, a bright blue beam of light burst from the prow of the alien ship. The glow from the beam shone through the tiny portholes set into the perimeter of the bridge, suffusing everything with a sapphire radiance. Cho reported that this was the forcefield they had been told to expect. The tiny, sharp-nosed vessel began to move, and Mateo felt a slight lurch as their ship was pulled behind. He couldn't keep himself from releasing a whistle of astonishment and, yes, appreciation. All around him, Mateo heard echoes from his *hara* and other members of the crew.

Moments later, they encountered the first sign of turbulence. He punched the intercom for the engine room and asked for Maza. "Were we expecting this?" he asked as the deck rattled beneath his feet.

"Some," Maza replied. *"Their engineer claimed we would be protected from the worst by the forcefield."*

"And is this the worst?"

Mateo sensed the hesitancy in the engineer's voice. *"How can I know?"* he asked. *"Have any of us ever done this before?"*

"Then perhaps we should stop."

"If you think so, call the captain. At this point, as far as I'm concerned, we're all just passengers."

This was not the kind of response Mateo had hoped to hear. Usually, Maza was proprietary to the point of maniacal about anything that affected the ship. Hoping to evoke a more useful response, Mateo asked, "Can the superstructure take this? You're not worried?"

"It can take it," Maza said. *"And if the captain's plan works, we'll have plenty of time later to repair any damage we take. Consider what we were up against before, Commander."*

Mateo knew the engineer was right. Until a few hours earlier, their prospects for survival (let alone a successful mission) had been poor. Now, with the help of these strange beings, they might not only reach their destination, but do it in a fraction of the time they had budgeted. He had been trying to suppress the thought, but now Mateo gave a little rein to the idea that he might actually see home again someday, see his wife . . . "All right," he said. "Call me if anything doesn't feel right."

"Acknowledged."

Over the next several minutes, the surges became increasingly severe. As bad as the jostles were for him at the craft's bow, Mateo could only imagine what it must be like for the passengers in the sternmost sections. Struggling to focus past his nausea, Mateo tried to read the sensors, but the scanners were scrambled. After one particularly harsh bounce, he saw Cho tighten the harness over her chest, then watched as the rest of the bridge crew followed suit. "Another one like that," Cho said, "and I'm getting off and going home. " The joke got more laughter than Mateo thought it strictly warranted, but he was pleased to hear that everyone was still game.

The intercom buzzed and Mateo tried to answer, though it took him a couple of stabs before he could hit the button. *"Bridge,"* the anonymous caller asked. *"Are we almost through with this yet? Passengers are worried. People are getting motion sick."*

"Tell the passengers that this is a transitional phase. The aliens told us to expect it and we'll be done soon. Now clear this channel for essential . . ." But the channel was already closed down.

Without warning, the blue glow that had enveloped the ship disappeared. Blinking at the sudden change, Mateo stared around the bridge. The surges and jumps had ceased. His first thought was *It can't have been that easy.* . . . Clearing his throat, he said, "Cho, contact the captain. Ask if we've arrived."

Cho was working her console, flicking switches and adjusting dials with her long, sensitive fingers. "I'm trying, sir. Something must be wrong. . . ." Suddenly, Cho jerked back her head so sharply that Mateo heard the hardware in her harness snap against the bolts. "Commander! Alarms! From all over the ship!" Before she could finish he sentence, every light, every device on the bridge died. Mateo waited for the count of three heartbeats for the emergency power to kick in, but nothing happened. The only light came from the stars through the portholes.

Speaking very softly, struggling to be calm, Mateo asked, "What is happening?"

Cho spoke. "External sensors were sending alarms, sir. A possible hull breach . . ." These were the last words she ever spoke, the last Mateo ever heard. Her voice was lost in a strange crackling noise that seemed to be coming from the prow and was rushing toward them like an icy wave crashing into a frozen shore. The sound drowned out all other noise, even the frantic thrashing of the bridge crew struggling to undo their harnesses and reach the lockers where the environmental suits were stored. Mateo saw one of his *hara* reach a locker, but when he yanked open the door, there was nothing inside the locker except stars. All around them, the bulkheads were shattering, splintering into slivers that broke apart, then broke apart again until Mateo was staring out into the black of the void.

Remembering his training, Mateo forced the air out of his lungs and shut his eyes, but then opened them again when he felt his *hara* inside his head calling to him. Someone touched his shoulder, a reassuring grip, but then the pressure disappeared. In the last millisecond before the darkness took him, Mateo stared at his hands and was distantly, distractedly fascinated as his fingers dissolved into tiny fragments and were swept away into the void.

Chapter 1

Disaster minus 334 minutes

Tom Paris was thinking about mushrooms.

He knew he shouldn't; he knew he should be thinking about what was immediately in front of him, both tangible (that is, the flight controller's console) and intangible (the sector of space they were entering), but it was difficult to stay focused so late in a shift, especially when nothing was happening.

Not for the first time, Tom found himself recalling the first words his Academy flight instructor said on the first day of classes: "Piloting a starship," Professor Heyer had begun, "is really boring." Tom remembered the sound of twoscore styluses scratching on twoscore padds as every student (except for Tom) captured that immortal thought for posterity. Tom had merely watched the professor, who, interestingly, was watching the class. Heyer's gaze lit on him, and they locked eyes as she completed the thought. "Except, of course, when it's not."

Tom had smirked then, thinking, *Ah, well, that's the part I'm here for.*

Years had passed, but Tom had learned and relearned the lesson over and over, always more and more impressed by his teacher's wisdom: piloting a starship usually was unbelievably, breathtakingly, mind-numbingly *dull*. The trick was to stay alert, to always know that the fatally dull could instantly turn merely fatal.

"The pilot's job," Professor Heyer had continued in that lecture, "is to constantly sample the environment, to devise methods to determine when something is going to happen before it happens. If you rely only on your instruments, you will die at your post someday. Maybe not immediately, maybe not for a long time, but someday."

Cheerful woman, the professor. She had recommended that helmsmen (or "pilots," as she insisted on calling them) replicate thin-soled shoes so they could feel the deck plates underneath their feet. "A good pilot can tell an engineer when the engines need tuning," she claimed. Unfortunately, the professor had never indicated whether you should mention untuned engines to the chief engineer if you also happened to *sleep* with the chief engineer. Tom, as usual, was left to navigate that uncharted and dangerous expanse on his own.

Tom scanned the instruments, half-listened to the bridge chatter and, yes, felt for the vibration of the deck plates under his feet. With no false sense of modesty, Tom Paris knew that he was among the best starship pilots of his generation. Driving a large, powerful, maneuverable spacecraft like *Voyager* was more than he could have ever asked for back in that classroom so many years ago. If Professor Heyer walked through the turbolift door and asked to speak to the *pilot,* Tom Paris knew that he would be able to raise his hand and answer proudly, "Me. I'm the pilot."

And this was a fine thing indeed, *but* (and this was important), at the same time, Tom also knew that he needed to occupy a small corner of his mind with something else—a counterbalancing piece of consciousness that prevented the rest of his brain from spiraling down into a singularity of boredom.

Some days, he thought about his holoprograms, whatever project that currently might be. The kernel of the idea that had become Sandrine's had taken root during one particularly dull shift a few years earlier. Other days, Tom mentally scanned his ever-growing collection of films and serials from the twenty-first and early twenty-second centuries. If he were given to self-analysis, Tom might wonder why he was so fascinated with the old fantasy dramas, but he wasn't, so he didn't. All he knew was that they were simultaneously sweet and hilarious, especially the oldest from the twentieth century.

Two days ago, he had found buried deep in the library computer two chapters of a serial about a square-jawed heroic type named Commando Cody who came equipped with a jetpack, rocket ship, several robots, and a scantily clad female sidekick. (Or was she a villain? Tom wasn't sure.) Everything about the films, right down to the southwestern desert of North America doubling for Luna's surface, made Tom grin wildly. He knew he had to do something with the ideas, but he wasn't sure exactly what.

Unfortunately, Tom had not been able to find anyone who shared his enthusiasm. Even Harry was resistant to the serial's peculiar charms, and B'Elanna . . . forget about it. When Tom had shown her the second chapter, all she could do was pick it apart: "Why are there sparks coming out of the engine? Why is it smoking? Why is the smoke drifting down? They're supposed to be in space!"

Tom sighed. He loved B'Elanna very much, but every relationship had its challenges. Feeling that he had let her down in the entertainment department, Tom had cast about for some way to please his girlfriend and found his answer: mushrooms.

B'Elanna might not know fine entertainment when she saw it, but she appreciated good fungus when it was set down before her. He didn't know the entire story, but from what he could tell, Miral, B'Elanna's mother, had tried to make her daughter subsist entirely on Klingon food. Alas, B'Elanna had disappointed her, showing very little stomach for either *gagh* or heart of *targ*, much preferring less robust offerings of human cuisine, such as peanut butter and jelly sandwiches, bananas, and deep-fried breaded cheese. After John Torres had left his wife and the battle lines in the ceaseless war between mother and daughter began to be drawn, B'Elanna had made food one of the main weapons in her arsenal. Few things, she had told Tom, had delighted her as much as the reaction a dish of sautéed mushrooms and onions over risotto would provoke.

The last few months had been difficult ones for B'Elanna. News of the destruction of the Maquis had hit her hard, and though he hadn't been able to devote as much time to helping her out of her funk as he would have liked, when the opportunities arose he did what he could. On one or two occasions, food had done the trick, so, at Tom's request, Neelix had tried to find something sufficiently mushroomlike on their various resupply stops. Alas, the resourceful Talaxian had not been successful, and though replicators could do a lot of things well, mushrooms were not one of them. Then, a couple of months previously, Tom had been chatting with Tak, the Bolian who headed up hydroponics, and learned that there was a small store of mushroom spores in stores.

"Why don't we grow some?" Tom had asked.

Tak had hesitated, then had gone the dark blue Bolians do when they're embarrassed. "Compost," he said.

"Compost?" Tom asked. "You mean like . . ."

"Organic waste matter, yes."

"There are a lot of people on this ship," Tom replied. "Organic matter shouldn't be a problem."

"Acquiring the raw matter is *not* the problem," Tak said. "Processing it is. Fungus requires very precise mixtures of plant materials and organic matter. Growing spores in a hydroponics medium is difficult and time-consuming. More trouble than it's worth, really." He made a twiddling gesture with his fingers that Tom knew meant "resource conservation."

"But you have spores," Tom stated flatly.

"Sure. In cryostorage."

"Could I have some?"

"Perhaps."

Tom sighed. Shipboard economies could be so trying sometimes. Fortunately, he had something Tak wanted rather badly—holodeck time. A deal was struck and Tom got two tubes of spores. Harry, another mushroom fiend, agreed to let Tom build the racks in his closet in exchange for a percentage of the crop. Harry rated a single room and did not seem to mind the smell, so all went swimmingly. In less than five weeks, the creminis were full and plump. The portobellos were a full thirteen centimeters across and ready for harvesting and stuffing. And tonight, oh, tonight was the night. He had even managed to score five hundred milliliters of deck five cabernet, the kind B'Elanna liked so much. No early shift tomorrow, either, so magic might well be in the air. The portion of his brain that Tom Paris allowed to think about such things rubbed its tiny hands together in anticipation.

Three meters behind his left shoulder, Tom heard an alarming sound: Harry said, "Hmmm."

He looked at the chronometer on the navigation console and saw that his shift was almost over. If Harry's "hmmm" meant what it usually did, then Chakotay would insist that Tom end his shift early. "Nobody wants a tired pilot during a crisis." Even more frustrating, a crisis also meant that B'Elanna could not be pried out of engineering.

Maybe it was nothing. Maybe Harry was just clearing his throat. Maybe, maybe, maybe . . .

"Captain?"

Damn!

Tom lost the battle to not look back over his shoulder and saw that Captain Janeway was in the middle of conferring with Chakotay about some changes in maintenance rotations. She didn't even look up from her padd, but said, "Yes, Mr. Kim? Something?" A beat passed. "Eyes front, Mr. Paris. The unknown is that way."

Swinging back around, Tom wished that he had looked at Harry instead of the captain. One could determine a lot about his friend's state of mind from his posture. Risking censure, Tom quickly peeked over his left shoulder and felt mildly reassured. Harry was staring at the long-range-sensor readouts, a small, bewildered notch at the corner of his mouth. This was good: whatever it was he was looking at, Harry didn't consider it a threat. Tom noted the slight slump in Harry's shoulders, which was also a good sign. If he was alarmed, he would be standing up straight, ready to leap into action. But that wasn't what Tom saw. This was Curious Harry; Science Geek Harry had spotted something on the long-range scans that he thought the captain—a science geek of the first order—would find interesting.

"An unusual binary, Captain."

Tom felt his brow wrinkle. He suspected that if he

dared to turn and look at Captain Janeway, he would see the same expression on her face.

Before the captain could respond, another voice—clipped, dry, and devoid of any emotion except for condescension—said, "Binary stars are among the most common phenomena seen in this—or, let me assure you, Ensign Kim—any other galaxy. How is this one unusual?"

Harry glanced up from the scanner. "Hello, Seven," he said. "I didn't hear you come on the bridge." Briefly, several months earlier, Harry had attempted to initiate a romantic liaison with the former Borg drone, a fantasy that Seven had unceremoniously crushed. For a short time thereafter, Harry had felt awkward around her, so Tom was happy to see that this had passed and that Ensign Kim now understood that he was merely another one of the horde to be crushed beneath Seven's imposing high heel.

"Harry," the captain called. "You have my attention. . . ."

Harry manipulated controls, and a window opened on the forward viewer, revealing a star system chart. "Here," he said, and a small red arrow appeared beside two of the circles. "Here's an ordinary yellow star right in the middle where you'd expect it."

"Right," the captain said.

"And here's the second star—a white dwarf." The pointer moved out to a point approximately halfway between the central star and the edge of the system. The white dwarf was so small as to be invisible until Harry overlaid an image of the gravimetric and radiation fields it was producing. Also visible was a thin trail of stellar matter drawn from the larger star across the void down into the gravity well around the white dwarf—the accretion disk. Tom was slightly surprised to see a white dwarf pulling material from such a distant source, but a quick mental calculation showed that it was within the realm of possibility—barely. What, he wondered, was the big deal?

Apparently the captain felt the same way. "I'm waiting, Harry."

The pointer clicked on three dully glowing blue spots between the two stars. "These planets: I'm reading life-forms on all of them."

Tom felt everyone on the bridge pause. Some—like him—were mentally consulting their Astronomy 101 notes and realizing, that, yes, this *was* a big deal. Planets situated between a binary pair would be bombarded with exotic radiation from up and down the spectrum. On his console, Tom punched up the sensors and saw that the accretion disk around the white dwarf, though still relatively small, was chocked to the gills with lethal X-rays. The more scientifically inclined—that is, everyone else on the bridge—were no doubt already trying to figure out how this was possible. The silence stretched out uncomfortably. Even Seven seemed stymied.

Finally, as much to break the uncomfortable silence as for any other reason, Tom said, "Now, *that's* interesting."

Captain Janeway shifted her weight, cleared her

throat, then said, "When you say 'life-forms,' Harry, what do you mean? Viruses? Single-cell organisms?"

Giant radioactive cockroaches? Tom wondered, thinking back to one of the films he had watched earlier that week.

"On two of the worlds, yes, simple life-forms, all in the oceans or under the ice caps, all small."

Tom felt all the science types exhale. The universe was once again a sensible place. Harry let everyone relax for two seconds, then continued on. "But look at the third planet," he said, "the one closest to the white dwarf." The pointer blinked on the third world as the scanners zoomed in on it. Readouts danced as the circle of light grew larger and took on detail. "I'm picking up oceans, complex vegetation, animals in all the representative phyla . . ."

Tom forgot himself and looked back over his shoulder. Fortunately, the captain wasn't paying attention to him. An expression of mild incredulity creased her brow. "You're right, Mr. Paris," she said. "This *is* interesting."

Harry asked. "Worth a quick look?"

Behind him, Tom felt the war begin: Janeway the former science officer battling with Janeway the captain. Under different circumstances, Tom knew, she wouldn't have hesitated for a moment. Not long ago, she had told them all that as long as they were in a Starfleet ship, they would act like a Starfleet crew; their mission was to seek out new life, new civilizations, et cetera.

But after their encounter with Arturis and the bogus *Dauntless,* the captain was feeling wary. Some miracles, no matter how wonderful, had to be ignored or they would never get home. The captain sighed, and Tom knew that Janeway the science officer had lost. "It's tempting, Harry, but not this trip. Take readings as we pass by and send them to astrometrics. Maybe they'll be able to make sense of what we're seeing."

Harry nodded and, a little flatly, said, "Yes, ma'am." The system map disappeared from the main viewer. All around him, Tom heard the bridge crew relax and make itself ready for the end of shift. As his fingers danced across the console, securing it for the next shift, his thoughts returned to grilled mushrooms by candlelight, soft music, and B'Elanna.

"Captain, you are being too hasty."

Tom cringed. He hit a wrong key and the console blurped at him. He corrected his mistake and waited for the other shoe to drop. Anyone else—*anyone*—would have couched their concern in less hostile terms, but oh, no, not Seven of Nine.

"Why do you say that, Seven?"

The former Borg stood at the secondary science station, the one usually reserved for mapping missions, staring at the scans. Something had caught her attention, but she decided to start with a critique: "Ensign Kim did not review all the data. Look at this." Unbidden, she threw up a new overlay of the binary system on the main monitor.

"What are we looking at?" the captain asked.

"I do not know," Seven said. "Not precisely, which is

remarkable in itself. But these spikes in the EM spectrum—here, here, and here—are similar to the readings left behind by Borg wormholes."

Tom winced in pain. His mushrooms, his lovely mushrooms. He could see them in his mind's eye, all of them withering, shriveling unattended, unharvested, unloved. All because Seven got a bug up her—

"Assuming you're correct," Janeway said, "Is it your opinion that we're seeing evidence of a Borg presence?"

"No," Seven said. "I merely note that the situation is peculiar, especially in conjunction with the unexplained presence of life on the planets."

Chakotay asked, "You're recommending that we investigate?"

"I am merely making an observation so that the captain has all the available data necessary to make an informed decision."

"Thank you, Seven," Janeway said. The rustle of fabric told Tom that the captain was sitting back in her chair and leaning toward the first officer. "What do you think, Chakotay?" Rapidly opening and closing turbolift doors meant that the beta shift's crew was on deck and waiting for permission to move to their stations. Tom felt their uneasiness as they awaited the outcome of the senior officers' discussion.

"I'm inclined to up the status from 'interesting' to 'peculiar,'" Chakotay said softly. "Your decision should be based on how comfortable you are with something like these energy readings at your back. We could drop out of warp, take a quick look, then get out fast if something . . ."

Alarm klaxons blared. Emergency lights flickered on. Tom's world narrowed down to his station. Practically every indicator on his console had flipped from cheerful green to angry red. *What the hell . . . ?*

"Our warp field is collapsing, Captain," Tuvok called, then turned off the klaxon.

"Engine room!" Janeway shouted. "B'Elanna! What just happened?"

"No idea, Captain. I'll let you know as soon as I have one," the chief engineer called. *"Torres out."*

In his mind's eye, the last coal of the charcoal brazier in his imagination flickered and died. *Maybe,* Tom pondered, *maybe I'll be able to trade the mushrooms for some avocados. B'Elanna loves avocados. . . .*

Cutting the comm to the bridge, B'Elanna turned back to the controlled chaos of the engine room and watched as her technicians diagnosed the latest disaster. For a brief moment, she permitted herself to think about the thing she laughingly called her "personal life," then sighed. Tom and his mushrooms: he had been planning to seduce her tonight and she had been planning to let him. Oh, well.

"What have we got, Joe?" B'Elanna called as she headed for the warp core. Joe Carey, the assistant chief engineer and her right-hand man, fell into step beside her. Once, four years ago, B'Elanna had beat out Joe for the job of chief despite the fact that he was an Academy graduate, a good officer, and a damned fine man with a wrench. Joe's problem had been—still was—that he relied too much on precedent. Back in those days, if the solution to a problem wasn't in the all-purpose, ever-ready Starfleet Big Book of Engineering Exercises, he had been at a loss. Indeed, until they arrived here in the fun quarter of the galaxy called the Delta Quadrant, Joe hadn't believed there could *be* such a thing as a problem the book hadn't addressed.

Of course, if that were true, they wouldn't be where they were, which was sixty thousand light-years from the edge of what had once been laughingly called Known Space. B'Elanna was chief engineer because she knew that out here there was no book but the one you wrote yourself.

Fortunately, in addition to all his other qualities, Joe was a realist and, trained as an officer, understood the chain of command. When Janeway had made B'Elanna the top dog, Joe quickly fell into line. While he had never said to B'Elanna, "You were the right choice," there had been more than one disaster that never would have been averted if not for B'Elanna's quick wits and unconventional solutions. Still, despite all this, there were days when B'Elanna wished she felt like she and Carey worked *together* rather than that he worked *for* her. She was always "Lieutenant," and not "B'Elanna," or, even more preferably, "Chief."

Handing her a padd, Carey had to bark to be heard over the thrum of the core. "All the initial diagnostics have come back normal, Lieutenant," he said. "The problem isn't with the engines."

B'Elanna scanned the readings on the padd. "If we're putting out this many megajoules, why does the warp bubble want to collapse?"

"I don't know," Joe said, enunciating each word carefully. "But I'm happy to be able to say this isn't an engineering problem."

"I doubt if the captain will see it that way."

Joe grinned sardonically. "Which is your problem, Lieutenant."

B'Elanna chose to ignore the mild jab. "If you had to explain what was happening—not an engineering problem, I know—what would you say?"

Flattered, Carey became expansive. "Here's how I see it. We're producing as much energy as we usually do to move at warp six and barely managing to keep up the bubble. What does that mean? That we're not producing energy?"

Mildly exasperated by the pedantic tone, but willing to play along if the lesson would end in a concrete point, B'Elanna held up the padd. "Not according to this."

"Right. So we're pushing as hard as we can. But what if we're not pushing at the right thing? Or, put another way, what if the thing we're trying to push against isn't what we think it is?"

The idea made B'Elanna's head hurt. "We're pushing against space, Joe. That's all there is out here. . . ." But as soon as she said the words, she knew she was wrong.

Space wasn't empty. Different kinds of space had different properties, especially when you started dealing with the special composition of subspace . . . "Scratch that. I get you." She looked at the padd one more time. "But whatever else is happening, we have to get out of here. The engines won't hold up against this effect much longer. . . ."

Speak the devil's name and he will come. Her father used to say that. Say the words and they will have power over you. Tell the engines what they cannot do and, naturally, they decide you're right.

Alarms blared. Lights flashed. Vents whooshed as automatic systems dumped coolant into the core. Engineers and technicians scurried like ants under the glare of a magnifying glass. And B'Elanna, queen of the hive, could do nothing but find the biggest problem and start to work.

To say that the warp field had collapsed without warning would be a mistake. *Voyager*'s crew had received plenty of warning; what they lacked was an explanation. The streaks of blue-shifted light on the main monitor dilated into pinpoints, and Tom experienced the familiar shift as the impulse engines kicked in, deck plates vibrating under his feet.

The captain, predictably, was on the comm to B'Elanna within seconds: "What's happened to my ship?"

Voice rough-edged with resentment, B'Elanna said, *"It's not the engines, Captain. I'm not an astrophysicist, so I'm not going to pretend I understand the readings we're getting, but engines have to have something to push against. Is there something about the region of space we just entered?"*

"We're trying to determine that now, B'Elanna, but in the meantime try to get me something more definitive than 'There's nothing to push against.' "

"Understood, Captain. Torres out."

Tom looked around at the crowded bridge. The ship was still on red alert, but there did not seem to be any immediate threat for the first-shift crew to respond to. Protocol dictated that the crew on deck when the alert was called should stay at their stations unless otherwise ordered. Unfortunately, for them as for the engines, there didn't seem anything to push against. Chakotay, sensing everyone's discomfort, stood and announced, "First shift, stand down. Second shift, assume your stations."

Grateful crew members logged out of their stations, then slid out of their seats. As they always did, Tom and his relief, Ensign Clarice Knowles, spent two minutes reviewing their status and exchanging information that was not available on the status board, such as the general mood on the bridge.

"Keep your head down, Knowles," Tom muttered. "The captain hasn't had a cup of coffee in more than four hours and I don't see her leaving the bridge any time soon."

"Maybe someone should mention this to Neelix," Knowles replied under her breath.

"I'll see what I can do."

Tom turned to find Chakotay standing less than six inches behind him. *How does he do that?* Tom thought.

"Double cream in mine," the first officer said. "Bring it to the ready room. And bring a cup for yourself. We need to figure out what's going on here."

Tom sighed. "Yes, sir," he said. "Should I swing by the engine room and get B'Elanna?"

Chakotay shook his head. "No. Let her do her job. She'll report in when she has something. We're going to spend our time checking the navigation logs to see when this effect started."

"All right. I'll be ten minutes."

"Make it five, Lieutenant."

Nodding (and biting his tongue), Tom stepped around the first officer. He was headed for the turbolift door when the deck seemed to abruptly spasm under his feet, pitching him headlong into midair.

Proximity alarms blared in tandem with the red-alert Klaxon. Janeway picked herself up off the deck and felt the metallic tang of blood in her mouth. *Bit my tongue,* she thought while wiping her mouth on her sleeve. Pressing herself back into her chair, she felt the ache of a torn ligament in her shoulder, but forced the pain from her mind. All around her, the bridge crew was responding to emergency calls from around the ship, every member of the command center skillfully dealing with the most pressing situations, alternately reassuring rattled crewmen and barking orders. Meanwhile, at the security console, Tuvok was performing quick scans and feeding data to Janeway's command station.

Pulling up the status report, *Voyager*'s captain confirmed what her instincts had told her only moments after the event: The ship's sensors had suddenly detected an object on a collision course, and, reacting faster than a human could have, the navigational computer had engaged the thrusters to shove them out of the path of whatever it was. Glancing up from the display in her chair, she saw that the main viewscreen was trying to resolve an image, but the thing—the object, the intruder, the whatever-it-was—was too near for a clear view.

Reviewing the raw data, Janeway glanced over at Tuvok, who, not surprisingly, was looking directly at her. She raised an eyebrow, an expression her old friend would correctly interpret as *Am I reading this correctly?* The Vulcan nodded.

The only thing Janeway knew for sure from the readings she was seeing was that her ship had barely avoided ramming (or being rammed by) a gigantic object. But where had the object come from? Seconds ago, space in every direction had been clear. *A cloaking device?* Janeway wondered, but speculation without data was worse than useless; it was a waste of time. Janeway wanted facts. "Tuvok, launch a remote! We need to see what . . ."

"Launched, Captain. We will have a feed in three, two, one . . ."

The main viewscreen shimmered, and an image abruptly snapped into focus. A hush of awe fell over the bridge, and in the sudden silence Janeway became aware that Chakotay was kneeling over the prone figure of Tom Paris, muttering and apparently administering first aid. Then she heard Paris speak, and that moment of reassurance was enough that she could tear herself away from the prospect of an injured crewman and again try to take in the astonishing sight upon which they all gazed.

Shining like an opal in the lower left-hand corner of the viewscreen hung a tiny dot that, Janeway knew, would be no wider than the tip of her thumb if she lifted her hand and held it before her at arm's length. An icon floating near the dot told her that this fragile blip represented the shell that held her life and the lives of her 156 crewmen.

The other ninety-eight one-hundredths of the screen was filled by . . . what could she call it? Could it, as the preliminary scans said, truly be an artificial object? The most rational part of Janeway's mind said, yes, of course it could, but some more primitive part rebelled at the idea. However, as her eye focused first on one part of the vessel, then on another, scale became less and less important. Janeway began to perceive the sense of the builders' design and found that she was admiring its cool elegance. Awe gave away to curiosity about the vessel's makers.

A flattened sphere as large as an orbital starbase was foremost, and as the image resolution became sharper it became evident that the hull was composed of large, uneven metallic plates welded in overlapping curves one on top of another. The bow curve was peppered with dozens of shallow openings that Janeway quickly decided must be some form of ramscoop for collecting interstellar hydrogen. The hydrogen would be processed somewhere in the hull, then fed to the . . . she counted quickly . . . seventeen massive engines mounted on the rearmost curve.

Ramscoops. Hydrogen. She pondered. These people, whoever they might be, were propelling themselves through the void by blowing up small hydrogen bombs and riding the concussive blasts. *What could motivate them to do such a thing?*

The answer dangled behind the main hull: dozens of blocky containers, each attached to the vessel with a cable that had to be as thick as *Voyager*'s primary hull. For a moment, Janeway found herself wondering if the ship's creators had been inspired by the thought of some unimaginably gigantic hot-air balloon carrying aloft tiny gondolas. "Tuvok," she said. "Life signs?"

"Sensors are still collecting data," Tuvok said, "but current estimates are in the range of fifteen thousand individuals."

In a hushed whisper, Knowles, at the navigation station, croaked, "One moment there was nothing there. I swear, Captain. Nothing! And then . . . *this* . . . !"

Janeway looked to Tuvok for an answer, but the Vulcan said only, "Unknown, Captain."

Janeway settled back into her chair, adjusted her uniform jacket, and, feeling a grin of anticipation creep across her face, said, "Then I guess we had better just ask. Send a hail, Mr. Tuvok."

Chapter 2

"Mr. Paris, wake up."

Tom did not wish to obey. The throbbing ache behind his eyes made opening them sound like a terrible idea, but he felt himself compelled to listen to the voice despite the fact that the speaker sounded irritated, impatient, and persnickety. Sure signs that Tom was in the tender care of the Emergency Medical Hologram.

Tom opened his eyes and saw red emergency lights glowing softly on the polished dome of a hairless pate. The frown, ah, the frown, crowning achievement of Dr. Zimmerman's work—all those little lines and folds, reproduced from Zimmerman's own dour visage with painstaking effectiveness. "Hey, Doc," Tom said, and felt helpless as a glad smile stretched across his face. "Good to see you."

"A pleasant enough sentiment," the Doctor said. Tom could hear the muted sounds of people and machines exchanging information. *I'm still on the bridge,* Tom thought, and the idea pleased him out of all proportion. The Doctor explained why. "But I suspect it is motivated primarily by the compound I just administered—a little something to enhance blood flow to the brain."

Tom said, "Great!"

"Perhaps the formula requires some rethinking."

"Fine!" Tom said. And it was. Truly. Fine. Everything was fine.

"Keep your voice down," the Doctor scolded.

Tom felt part of him wanting to cringe, but the precise combination of muscles was nowhere to be found in his body's current vocabulary, so instead he whispered, "Sorry."

The Doctor patted Tom reassuringly. "Corpsmen will arrive shortly and take you to sickbay. Until then, try to be silent. The captain is about to make contact with the alien ship and we cannot afford to distract her at this time."

Tom did not attempt to respond, but adjusted his position so he could see the viewscreen over the Doctor's shoulder. Above him, he heard Tuvok say, "The alien vessel is returning our hail, Captain."

"On the main viewer, Mr. Tuvok."

A moment later, the image resolved and Janeway had her first sight of a Monorhan. She knew they called themselves Monorhans because the universal translator had plucked this information from the hail, but it was experiencing difficulty with almost everything else, including the name of the ship and its captain.

The face staring down at them was bilaterally symmetrical—an arrangement that evolution seemed to find favor with the galaxy around—but the alien's jaw was much longer than that of most humanoid species, with oversized canines in the front and a ridge of molars up each side. The nose was broad, flat, shiny, and ringed with stubby sensory organs whose use Janeway could only guess. Infrared? Ultrasound?

The Monorhan captain's eyes were structured with familiar features—white, iris, and cornea—though the pupil was large and appeared to be very sensitive, shrinking and growing as the alien turned his head. Wide-set, the eyes were rimmed with thick lashes that would be ideal for keeping out fine particles of grit, leading Janeway to speculate whether the Monorhans had evolved in a turbulent atmosphere. A bulging forehead was framed by thick, curly hair pulled back in a braid over short pointed ears.

Opening his mouth to speak, the Monorhan lifted his head, unfolded a long neck, and ululated, vibrating a long, flexible tongue against his palate. Several seconds passed before the translator caught up and delivered a humming, growling approximation of his speech: "Difficult," the Monorhan said, the voice low and guttural. "And difficult. Who is your tribe? You appear . . . Damage . . ." But the next sentence was lost in a thick buzz and hum.

"Mr. Tuvok," Janeway asked. "Has the universal translator been damaged?"

"Negative, Captain. However, Monorhan speech is unlike anything we have encountered to date. It may take a few exchanges for the translator to develop algorithms. My advice would be to speak slowly and ask the Monorhan to do the same."

Janeway glanced briefly at Chakotay, who quirked an eyebrow at her. His look said, *Interesting,* and she could not disagree. Aware that she frequently spoke at a very rapid pace, the captain took a deep breath and, in measured tones, said, "My name is Kathryn Janeway and I am captain of this vessel, which we call *Voyager.*" She briefly pondered whether she should introduce the subject of the Federation and their long journey home, but decided that this was a topic better left for when the translator was up to speed. "The near collision was unintentional. Was anyone on your vessel injured? Can we offer aid?" Though, truly, if even a small percentage of the Monorhan's crew or passengers were injured, how would *Voyager* be able to help them? Still, Janeway was convinced that the accident had done more damage to the aliens than to her crew. If she could offer any kind of restitution, she was ethically bound to do so.

The Monorhan tilted his head and narrowed his eyes as if concentrating. Finally, several seconds after the captain finished speaking, the alien spoke again, tongue and palate clicking. The translator labored, then produced its best approximation: *"Ziv, my name. Captain? Yes. Vessel is . . . <untranslatable thrum>. Casualties? No. You?"*

Deciding that the last question concerned casualties, Janeway said, "No casualties." *At least, no fatalities.*

In response, Ziv spoke rapidly. *"Good,"* the Monorhan said. *"Relief. This ship . . ."* Several thrums and clicks later, Ziv held his meaty hands wide apart, then pointed at Janeway. *"Your ship . . ."* Then, he held up two narrowly parted fingers.

Janeway smiled, then nodded. Ziv had no way to know that with her shields up, even moving at sublight speed, *Voyager* would have left a very large hole in one side of his main hull, and a second, much larger one in the other.

Beside her, Chakotay cleared his throat and pointed at the upper right-hand corner of the main viewer. He had opened up a second window and had posted data collected by the sensors. Skimming the statistics, Janeway quickly realized what her first officer wanted her to see. "Captain Ziv," she continued. "Our scans indicate your ship has been stationary for at least the past several hours. Is that correct?"

Ziv nodded. *"We began having engine <thrum, click> problems later yesterday and have been trying to diagnose its trouble. . . ."* Behind him, at least two other Monorhans began speaking in rapid pops and clicks. The translator's buffer was overwhelmed, and several seconds passed before Janeway could make sense out of what anyone was saying.

Pupils dilated, Ziv barked a sharp command, and the voices abruptly fell silent. Twisting his neck from side to side, his ears flattened against his head, Ziv murmured, *"My apologies, Captain. My crew is . . . frustrated. Our engines are not functioning as we expected."*

"Neither are ours," Janeway said. "We believe it may be the nature of space in this area. Perhaps we can pool our knowledge and find a solution together. Failing that, we may be able to give you a tow to an area of space where your engines will function better."

The Monorhan released a sharp clack. Then, recovering himself, Ziv said, *"Did I understand you correctly? You think your < untranslatable > ship can move mine?"*

Folding her arms over her chest confidently, Janeway said, "We can. Our engines are quite powerful."

"Forgive me, Captain, but I find this difficult to accept."

Janeway glanced at Tuvok, who (as she knew he would) accurately interpreted her look and nodded. *Yes,* his look said. *They may come aboard.* "Perhaps you would feel better if you sent someone over to study our engines, review schematics. If nothing else, we would enjoy the opportunity to meet you. There are few things we find so satisfying as an opportunity to make contact with new races, and you may have important information to help us resolve our mutual problem."

Ziv turned and looked at various points around him, thrumming and clicking, then listening to responses from several points around his bridge. As he talked, the translator labored to make sense of the sounds, but was unable to provide any meaning. Finally, straightening his neck, Ziv said in what Janeway took to be a formal tone, *"My* hara *and I would be pleased to visit your impressive vessel."*

Janeway waited for a moment to see if the translator would provide a synonym for *"hara,"* but when none was forthcoming, she asked, "And how many would a . . . a hara be, Captain?" Trying to be helpful, Janeway held up her hand then moved her fingers to indicate a question: *Two? Three? Four?*

Ziv studied the gesture, then held up his own large hand, four thick fingers and a thumb spread wide. The captain noted that each digit ended in a thick claw that had been carefully filed down to the tip of the finger and that Ziv's wide palm was covered in a ragged, not entirely sterile-looking bandage.

"That would be fine, Captain. A *hara* it is. Do you require transportation? We could send a shuttle or . . ." She glanced at Tuvok. Checking the status board, Tuvok shook his head. Transporters were not up. Again. She would need to speak to B'Elanna about that . . . or, better still, have Chakotay speak to her. Janeway knew herself well enough to know that if she went down to the engine room now, she might not emerge for several hours. Her energies would be better spent working with Seven and Harry on the nature of local space.

"We have a craft, Captain," Ziv said. *"It is small enough to fit inside your launch bay, assuming the large volume of space we detect inside the aft portion of your ship is what it appears to be."* When Janeway confirmed that it was, the alien continued, *"We would require only that you broadcast a beacon for us to home in on."* He tapped a control on the panel in front of him. *"On this frequency."*

"Received, Captain," Tuvok said. "Transmitting the beacon." From his tone, Janeway could tell that Tuvok approved of the arrangement. The Monorhans would be more comfortable knowing that their craft was available, and having their small craft inside *Voyager* would give security an opportunity to study their technology more carefully.

"Then, Captain Ziv, I believe we should continue this conversation face-to-face when you're aboard. Janeway out."

The Monorhan nodded, and the viewscreen once again showed the mammoth vessel. Speculative chatter filled the bridge; Janeway let it build for several beats, then cut it off with a chopping motion. "Senior staff meeting in ten minutes. We don't have much time before the Monorhans arrive, and I'd like some answers before they do."

Senior staff—Captain Janeway, Commander Chakotay, Seven of Nine, Ensign Kim, Chief Engineer Torres, Neelix, and the Doctor—all assembled promptly, much to Tuvok's satisfaction. Only Tom Paris was absent, though the Doctor explained before the meeting began that his wound had been repaired and he would be allowed to leave sickbay after a brief period of observation. However, since their current dilemma did not involve where to move, but rather *how* to move, the security officer felt it was acceptable to proceed without him.

"All right, people," Janeway said, rising, "we have two problems on the table. One, we dropped out of warp without explanation. Initial assessment is there's something unusual about this area of space. In support of that thesis, we have another vessel that also seems to be having trouble, but with a very different propulsion system. Question: Is there a relationship between this problem and the fact that we did not see the Monorhan vessel until we were right on top of them?" The captain looked around the table, making eye contact with each of the meeting's participants. "Another question: Could we be responsible for the change to local space? I'm thinking of the subspace rift created in the Hekaras Corridor."

"But that rift was caused by the old-style warp engines," Torres said. "With our variable-geometry nacelles, that can't happen."

"Don't rule out any possibilities until we've checked all the facts," the captain said. "Though for what it's worth, I agree with you. It's unlikely that we caused the problem, having just arrived, but the Monorhans have to be wondering."

"Which accounts for why you invited them over here so quickly," Neelix said. "To reassure them we have nothing to hide."

The captain nodded once, then continued. "Which brings us to problem number two. Or perhaps I should say project number two: a first-contact situation. The Monorhans will be here soon, and we all need to know everything we can about them as soon as possible. Let's begin with tactical. Tuvok?"

Having already prepared his comments, Tuvok tapped a key on his padd and brought up the image of the Monorhan vessel. "Scans indicate a level of technology roughly equivalent to late-twenty-first-century Earth technology. They do not possess faster-than-light drive. Given the amount of radiation we are finding, my assessment is they are employing a crude nuclear drive. I have not been able to confirm this with a visual scan, but I believe they are carrying several score atomic bombs. Periodically, they deploy one through this large cone in the stern, detonate it, then ride the explosion's wave front."

Torres groaned audibly. "A comment, Lieutenant?"

The engineer shook her head slowly. "Not really. Just . . . how desperate must these people be to do such a thing?"

"We do not know yet, Lieutenant. Perhaps when they arrive, you can ask."

"What about the containers?" Commander Chakotay asked. "Passengers?"

Tuvok brought up an image of a cluster of the units tethered to the drive unit. "Correct. These are little more than shells. Each unit has several interconnected levels, some for passengers, some for cargo. All are stocked with food, water, atmosphere processors."

"They can't be very comfortable," Ensign Kim observed.

"No," Tuvok said. "I believe Lieutenant Torres's observation is correct: They are motivated by desperation."

"Any theories as to why they're constructed this way, Tuvok?" the captain asked. "Why a drive unit drawing the containers?"

"Yes," the Vulcan said. "Analysis indicates the containers are all based on a similar design, but none is precisely identical. Various groups—perhaps the passengers themselves—built the containers, probably in an orbital work yard. Then, as each unit was completed, it was tethered to the drive unit."

"So whoever could pull together the resources to create a container could go along for the ride?" Chakotay mused. "That's rather cutthroat."

"An emotional supposition, Commander. I could suggest other interpretations."

Chakotay subsided and the captain interjected. "How about weaponry, Tuvok? Can they defend themselves?"

"The drive unit is equipped with several small missile launchers, probably to be used against large asteroids if they should encounter one. Their ship could not steer around such objects should they encounter them."

"Any guesses about their destination?"

"I have computed a simple course based on their trajectory. Currently, they are pointed at a small main-sequence star with a Class-M planet in its orbit less than a light-year away. Logic dictates that it is their goal."

"At their current speed," Ensign Kim calculated, "it would take them more than three years to get there. Is there any chance they would all make it?"

"Some," Tuvok judged. "Their resources would have to be carefully managed. But not all."

"How many are there in the containers, Tuvok?" the captain asked.

"With the level of background radiation from their engines, it is difficult to be precise. Some of the signals we're reading may be livestock."

"How many, Tuvok?"

"Seventeen thousand, five hundred and sixty-three life signs. These are mostly adults, though some signals are smaller. I estimate approximately one-fifth of the passengers are children."

"But no elderly?" the captain asked.

"I cannot say for certain, but, no, I think not."

"They would all stay behind," Chakotay said. "Let the children go and their parents to care for them."

"Not passengers," Neelix said in muted tones. "Refugees."

His recitation completed, Tuvok returned to his seat. Janeway turned to Seven of Nine, who had been uncharacteristically silent throughout the meeting. Normally by this point, Seven would have interrupted and, drawing on the huge database of information about alien species at her disposal, explained everything there was to know about the situation. "So," Janeway said. "Your assessment."

Seven shook her head once. "I believe everything that can be said about the Monorhans to this point has been said, Captain."

Everyone at the table—even Tuvok—turned to stare at Seven, which, apparently, did not bother her a bit. "Really?" Janeway asked. "No additional information about Species . . . whatever they are."

"The Monorhans are not in the Borg catalogue, Captain, and thus have not been assigned a species number. Would you like me to create one?"

Janeway remained silent while waiting for more information, but when she sensed there was no more to come, she said, "No, Seven, that's all right. I know we left the densest part of Borg space behind us, but I thought they had mapped this area in some detail. The Monorhans *must* be from nearby, from this system, in all likelihood."

"Your suppositions are logical, Captain, and your assessment correct. Borg probes have been through this sector within the past decade, but they did not detect this species."

"Because they only recently became space travelers?" Harry Kim asked uncertainly.

"Unlikely. A probe would have detected any form of electromagnetic activity."

"What about if the white dwarf was putting out a lot of radiation at the time a probe came through?" Kim asked. "Would that have masked the planet's electromagnetics?"

Seven considered the idea, then concluded, "It is possible, but there is no way to know for certain."

A new thought struck Janeway. "The trace radiation you detected, Seven. You said it was similar to the Borg transwarp conduits. Maybe the Monorhans used an ancient jumpgate and are only passing through this area."

Seven shook her head. "A transwarp conduit is detectable across vast distances. Even the radiation from the white dwarf would not mask it. If such technology existed here, the Borg would have invaded this system immediately."

Janeway's combadge chirped, interrupting the conversation. "Janeway here."

"Captain, this is Knowles. The Monorhans just launched a shuttle. At their current rate, they'll be here in fifteen minutes."

"Acknowledged," Janeway said, and signed off. "All right, people. We have five more minutes and then we have to go down to the shuttlebay. Let's set aside this issue for now. Captain Ziv will probably be able to fill in all the holes for us anyway. Now, what about the warp engines? B'Elanna, can you tell me what's happening?"

"Not yet, Captain. Diagnostics say the engines are functioning properly, but we can't form a stable subspace bubble. Every time we try, the field collapses. Your mentioning the Hekaras Corridor got me to thinking there might be damage to local subspace."

"The white dwarf," Kim said.

"There are lots of white dwarves out there, Harry," B'Elanna responded. "I've never heard of one affecting subspace before."

"And I've never heard of complex life forming so close to a white dwarf," Harry countered. "This can't be a coincidence."

"Begin your investigation with that theory, Harry," Janeway said. "You and Seven start working on the problem in astrometrics. I'll join you after I greet our guests." She turned to Chakotay and Neelix. "Gentlemen, I'm going to put you in charge of the Monorhans. Find out what you can from them. Be diplomatic, unless diplomacy isn't getting you anywhere. Then . . . be less diplomatic."

"Understood," Chakotay said.

"Tuvok, I want you to continue monitoring their drive section and the containers. If you start to see problems with life support, get repair crews over there. Ask Captain Ziv if you can beforehand, but if a disaster is about to occur, don't wait."

Tuvok nodded.

"Captain?"

"Yes, B'Elanna?"

"You told Captain Ziv we might be able to give him a tow."

"Yes."

"Have you considered what trying to move something that big might do to our engines, to the tractor beams?"

"I didn't say everything all at one time, B'Elanna."

"But *still,* Captain," B'Elanna said, rising to her feet, her tone sharpening, "I think you need to rethink . . ."

"Stand *down,* Lieutenant," Chakotay snapped. Then, more softly, he continued, "We can discuss this later."

The corner of Torres's eye twitched, but she slowly sat back down in her chair. "Yes, Commander. Sorry, Captain."

Janeway smiled softly. "Not necessary, B'Elanna. I'm not worried. I would never promise anything I didn't think you could deliver."

B'Elanna nodded, but Janeway could see from her demeanor that the engineer wasn't convinced. Unfortunately, she didn't have time for a discussion now. As a concession, she offered, "I'll drop by engineering later and we can spec out some options. All right?"

Torres nodded again, but this time the lines around her mouth were smoothed out.

"Any more questions?" Janeway asked. "No? Then, go to work."

Chapter 3

Captain Ziv was pleased with how quickly his *hara* had coordinated their activities, both on the ship and in the shuttle. In times of extreme stress, even the most disciplined group found it difficult to maintain a link, but the bond between Ziv the *harat* and his four *haran* remained strong. After strapping himself into the uncomfortable shuttle seat, Ziv folded his arms, closed his eyes, and felt peace descend as his companions fell to their assigned tasks. The only distraction was the sore on the palm of his hand, which, despite the medic's ardent attention, still itched and oozed a thin stream of yellow pus. The urge to scratch was almost overpowering.

Beside him in the pilot's couch, Jara, his second, sat up straight, passed a hand over the control console, nudged the thruster lever, and guided the tiny craft out of its slip. Ziv pressed his chin against his chest as the shuttle nosed into space. He disliked traveling in small ships. Cramped confines were troubling to most Monorhans, especially those with more than three in their *hara*.

The proximity sensor told Jara that he was clear of the slip. Jara fed the directional thrusters a small burst, and the shuttle lurched forward with a sputter. Rattling his tongue against his palate in annoyance, Jara muttered, "I'm out of practice."

"We have to wonder about your determination to collide with the stranger's ship," Ziv remarked, for it had been Jara at the pilot's console when the alien vessel appeared from out of nowhere. "If you try again, they might think we do not like them." Behind them, Mol, Diro, and Shet all clicked with amusement. Jara popped his tongue against his cheek—a rude sound in such a small place, but acceptable given his rank, both as an officer and in the *hara*.

Moving out of the shadow of the transport's hull, Ziv found himself thinking about the thousands of souls packed into the ship's containers. Had his announcement that they had temporarily halted made its way down into the deeper recesses? More important, would knowing what was happening—even the small amount of information he had released—relieve any of the stress they must all be feeling, or only make their lives more miserable? The very thought of those cramped quarters, of being so unnaturally pressed shoulder to shoulder in the echoing holds, made Ziv shudder. Even with the tranquilizers every passenger had been issued, he wondered how the *hara*s could continue to function.

How would his passengers—even his crew—react if they knew the ship's engines had stalled, that they were now reliant on the goodwill of strangers to get them on their way? He would like to think that most of them would understand, that they had always understood, how slim their chances of success really were, but only Ziv and his *hara* knew the entire truth. Most of his passengers believed they had only to be patient, to remain calm, and they would be delivered to a new world, a clean world, where they could begin their lives anew. *If only this were true,* the captain thought.

Jara adjusted their flight path so that they were now pointed at the alien vessel and skillfully guided the shuttle into a smooth, slow, unthreatening arc toward the rear of the ship's large primary hull.

"What do you think?" Ziv clicked to the *hara.*

Jara, preoccupied with his task, had no words to spare, but made an appreciative noise. Mol, ever the most verbose of the quint, said, "It looks more like a living thing than a vessel, like something that should live in deep water."

Shet asked, "Their captain said this tiny thing could tow our ship?" He shook his head in wonder. "I am not sure I believe them, but why would they lie to us?"

"To lull us into a trap?" Mol wondered aloud. "To trick us into letting them on our transport and plundering it?"

"Plunder *what?*" Shet asked. "Dried beans? The kilotons of steel and plastic we'll use as shelters when we land?"

"If they were going to fight us," Shet observed, "they would have done so by now. If their ship is as powerful as its captain claims, they could have destroyed us ten times over already. These people are not warriors—they are explorers."

"And now they wish to explore us," Ziv said, then turned to Diro, the youngest of the *hara*. "You have been silent, Diro," Ziv said. "Nothing to offer?"

Stirring in his chair, uncrossing then recrossing his long legs, Diro remarked, "I was thinking about how calm we all are being. We are . . . these are visitors from the stars and we act like the *hara* down the lane has dropped in for a light lunch and a swim."

"There have been other visitors from the stars," Shet said. "They are not the first."

"They are the first in a very long time," Diro countered. "And the first who lived."

"We will not speak of this to the aliens," Ziv said sharply. Then, softening his tone, he said, "As *harat*, I ask that none of you speak to them unless I give permission." He was certain the rest of the quint was already in agreement, but he felt that the formality was required. Each of the *hara* clicked their assent.

With agreement reached, Diro asked, "Did you contact the *rih-hara-tan* with details of our situation?"

"I sent a message," Ziv said, secretly glad that the time lag made conversations impossible. Sem—the tribe's spiritual leader—would undoubtedly have taken the opportunity to insinuate that the problems Ziv's ship was experiencing were entirely the captain's fault. "The *rih-hara-tan* will contact the Emergency Council. It will take time for them to reach a consensus and respond. By the time they do, I hope we will be back under way."

"And if these strangers wish to visit our home?" Diro asked.

Turning to look at his youngest *haran,* he held up the hand with the sore and asked, "Why would anyone wish to visit Monorha?" Diro reached up and touched the bandaged patch on his own throat and, beside him, Shet unconsciously touched the still-raw scar tissue on his face.

"I see your point," Diro said.

Jara guided the shuttle closer to the ship's curved primary hull and skimmed close to the skin. Ziv detected a faint blue glow at the upper range of his vision and wondered what he was looking at. "Do you see it?" he asked the others.

"A forcefield of some kind," Shet said.

"But so well-modulated. No distortion effect at all. And look how close we are to the hull."

"Impressive. Frighteningly impressive." The hull was made of metal—Ziv could see the seams between the plates—but the surface was smooth and, in sharp contrast to the hull of the transport, unpitted by any kind of micrometeor strikes. *Who are these strangers?* he wondered. *And why, with such marvels at their command, have they stopped here? Simply to aid us?* Ziv hated to admit it, but he did not believe in altruism.

"Locked on to their beacon," Jara said. Pressing a final series of controls, he pushed himself away from the console, saying, "Surrendering the conn." The shuttle bounced once, like a wagon rolling over a bump, and the engine's hum faded.

The launch bay doors of the strangers' ship loomed in their viewport. Moments later, a thin crack appeared at their center and the doors parted. A bright blue light surrounded the opening and, despite himself, Ziv gasped when he realized that in addition to the expected ships and machinery within the cavernous space, he was also looking at five tall, lanky beings, none of whom seemed in the least fretful that they were exposed to hard vacuum.

Diro said, "An atmospheric forcefield . . ."

Ziv relaxed back into his chair. *Of course.*

"Incredible." Shet, normally very difficult to impress, was leaning out over the control panel to get an arm's-length-closer look. "Such control! And it must be permeable to allow ships to pass without compromising the atmosphere."

Unable to fight off the urge, Ziv flinched as their craft's nose touched the blue field.

"Think of what we can learn from them!" Diro whispered.

"Best not to speak of such things," Ziv said. "Best not to hope too much." He spoke these words knowing that they were wise and sensible, that he was fulfilling his role as the leader of the *hara* and the captain of his vessel. Deeper in, down past wisdom and common sense, Ziv was shouting to a god he was no longer certain he trusted, *Do not make a fool of me! Do not let me hope too much!*

The moment the Monorhans stepped from their vessel, Neelix was struck by how different they were from any species *Voyager* had encountered. Though shorter than an average human (most of whom Neelix had to look up at), the Monorhans were half again as wide at the shoulders, with torsos that tapered down into narrow hips. Their arms were quite long in comparison with their legs and so thickly muscled that he was not in the least surprised when the first one to exit the hatch leaned forward and rested his gigantic hands on the deck.

"Gorillas," Chakotay whispered behind him.

"What?" Neelix asked.

"Sorry. Terran primate species. They're built like that: short, but broad." He clenched his fist and flexed his upper arm. "Powerful. They nearly became extinct."

"Interesting," Neelix said, and meant it. He considered asking "How did that happen?" but bit his tongue. Humans tended to be sensitive about this kind of thing and he made a small, cryptic note on his padd to look up the topic on the library computer at a less busy moment.

As soon as the five Monorhans were clear of their ship, they arranged themselves into a wedge with their leader at the point, then shifted their weight so their heads were held high, shoulders back, eyes forward. They were, Neelix decided, standing at attention. While moving, they held their heads close to their shoulders, but as soon as the leader had settled into place, he relaxed, revealing a neck longer than Neelix was expecting.

Their baggy uniforms were drab and utilitarian, each one distinguishable only by strips of color around the forearms and small metallic squares on the collars, which Neelix decided were rank insignia. The leader—Ziv, according to Tuvok's report—also wore a thin scarf around his shoulders, though Neelix judged that this had nothing to do with his military service. An indication of religious affiliation, perhaps? Neelix made a note on his padd. These were the sorts of things he knew he tended to notice that the others sometimes missed. *The trader's eye,* he thought proudly.

Stepping forward, Captain Janeway extended her hand to Ziv and said, "Captain Ziv, I'd like to welcome you and your *hara* to *Voyager.* I'm Kathryn Janeway. May I present some members of my senior staff?" But even as the first word was out of the captain's mouth, the Monorhans collectively lowered their heads down to their shoulders, startled. Captain Janeway immediately froze, and Neelix watched Tuvok and Chakotay shift into stances of readiness. After a trio of heartbeats had passed without anyone moving, the captain asked solicitously, "Is something wrong?"

The Monorhan leader flinched again, but not so dramatically. After a moment, he straightened his long neck and twisted his head from side to side as if listening. Neelix heard—or rather, *felt*—a stream of low clicks and thrums. Watching the Monorhan carefully, he realized the sides of the captain's throat were vibrating ever so slightly in time to the tones. A second later, his lips twitched and Neelix heard the translation through his combadge. "How odd," Ziv said. "I hear my words in my language at the same time I hear them in yours."

"It's a device we call the universal translator. These badges on our shirts are networked with the translator so we can understand what you're saying."

The Monorhan cocked his head and studied the captain's combadge. "Fascinating. Previously, when we spoke through the communication system, I did not experience this . . ." He waved his hand over his ears. ". . . this doubling effect." One of Ziv's companions lifted his head, and again Neelix both heard and felt the deep bass thrum. Ziv responded with a nod, then turned to Captain Janeway and said, "The device does not seem to work with the second speech."

Captain Janeway grasped Ziv's meaning. "Interesting," she said. "This is probably because neither we nor any of the races we deal with have this ability, this second speech."

Ziv stretched his neck to the side—Neelix interpreted this as a sign of mild surprise or amusement—then replied, "Then we both have something new to learn."

The captain smiled and once again extended her hand. "As do I, Captain Ziv. Please allow me to welcome you aboard my ship. May I present my first officer, Chakotay?" Beside him, Neelix felt Chakotay relax as he stepped forward. Once again, the captain had skillfully negotiated a tricky moment in a first-contact situation. Less than five minutes later, the Monorhans appeared to be at their ease and understood that he and Chakotay would be their escorts for the balance of their visit.

Before they left the shuttlebay, Chief Clemens, the

perpetually grease-stained deck chief, asked the captain if the Monorhans would like him to take a look at their vehicle. "Chief Clemens loves his work," Neelix offered.

"I'd have to on this ship, wouldn't I?" Clemens asked.

Ziv turned to one of his companions and let loose with a series of short clicks. Then he turned back to the chief and said, "My pilot says you should feel free to inspect our craft if he may later in turn examine one of yours."

The chief grinned, obviously pleased at the prospect. "Absolutely!" he said. "I just finished patching one back together! Best you come around before they let Mr. Paris fly her, though. You never know if you're going to see one again when he takes it out."

"That's enough, Chief," Neelix said, smiling indulgently. "No reason they should be afraid of Tom any sooner than necessary."

Looking slightly baffled, Ziv allowed himself to be led away, then fell in easily beside Captain Janeway in an odd loping, rolling gait. Three other Monorhans fell in behind the pair, followed by Chakotay and Tuvok, clearly intent on engaging them in conversation. The smallest of the five Monorhans lagged behind the rest and, when everyone else had passed, slowly knuckled over to the shuttlebay forcefield and studied the blue glow raptly. Twisting his head to regard Neelix, the Monorhan asked, "Can I touch it?"

"Yes."

The Monorhan reached out and tentatively felt for the edge of the field. Neelix heard a faint angry buzz, which grew louder and more insistent as the Monorhan pushed forward. Finally the field reached its tolerance and the Monorhan's hand was expelled. Wiggling his fingers, the visitor asked, "Could I push through if I tried?"

"I don't think so," Neelix said. "Though I confess I've never tried. Would you want to?"

The Monorhan did not answer, lost in thought. "But the vessels—ours and yours—can go through."

"That's controlled by the computers," Neelix explained. "I won't pretend to understand it. Somehow it knows the difference between a person and a ship. Ships go through; people don't."

"Remarkable," the alien sighed, and Neelix thought he detected a trace of sadness in his voice.

"*Voyager* is home to many remarkable things," Neelix said, "and remarkable people."

"The way you say that," the Monorhan said, "you don't sound like you feel you are one of them."

Surprised by the words, Neelix briefly considered the idea, then admitted, "Sometimes I feel like I am and other times, not so much. I was not part of her original crew. They rescued me . . . and a companion . . . several years ago and allowed me to join them on their journey."

"So you've traveled far from your home?"

"Quite far."

Looking out into the void beyond the forcefield, the Monorhan asked, "Do you think you will ever return?"

Neelix shook his head and felt a deep sadness creep

into his voice. "I can't. My home was destroyed many years ago." Then, remembering his responsibilities, he said, "But *Voyager* is my home now. Someday, perhaps somewhere else, but for now, I try to always keep in mind that there are much worse places to be."

"Yes," the Monorhan said in a matter-of-fact tone. "You could be on my world."

"Ah," Neelix said, and though he was unsure where the conversation was going, he wanted his guest to feel like he should speak his mind. "So you prefer to be out here in space."

"This is my first trip into space. So far, I have found it . . . terrifying."

"Oh. Well . . ." He knew he should try to find something else to say but was baffled by the young man's candor. Noting that they were alone in the shuttlebay but for the flight crew who were examining the Monorhan's craft, Neelix said, "The others will be wondering what happened to us, and we need to stop in sickbay to make sure there's nothing in our environment that's harmful to you." Extending his hand, he said, "My name is Neelix, by the way. And you are?"

"Diro," the young alien said, grasping his hand. "And I wouldn't worry about there being anything harmful in your environment." Pointing at the bandage on his neck, Diro said, "I doubt it could be anything worse than what we dealt with on Monorha."

Guiding Diro toward the exit, Neelix asked, "I noticed several of your friends were wearing bandages. Then these are not injuries?"

"No. A blood disease many of us have. Not fatal, but we're easily injured and heal slowly."

"Our doctor may be able to help you," Neelix said, hoping he wasn't promising too much.

"We would be grateful," Diro said touching his throat, "though I doubt he could aid everyone who suffers with this."

"Possibly not," Neelix agreed, as the shuttlebay doors shut behind them, "though I'm sure he'd try if asked. He's that sort of fellow."

Chapter 4

Tom Paris sulked.

No grilled cheese sandwich.

He hated being sick or, at least, a patient. For a nurse, sickbay was a fairly interesting place in which to hang out; for a patient, it was deadly dull, especially now that the Doc's pain medication was wearing off.

Unfortunately, the medication hadn't worn off when B'Elanna had come by for a visit, and Tom knew his spacey demeanor had as much to do with her leaving so quickly as her continuing angst about the engines. He seemed to recall her saying something about Chakotay ordering her to relax, but Tom wasn't sure that meant she had to relax with him.

"L'amour est enfant de Bohême," howled the Doctor from his office. With no patients other than Tom to attend to, the Doctor had given free rein to his opera-buffery. *"Il n'a jamais, jamais connu de loi . . ."*

"Doc."

"Si tu ne m'aimes pas, je t'aime . . ."

"Doc!"

"Mais je t'aime, prends garde à toi!"

"Doc!"

The Doctor poked his head out of his office, wiping his hands on a cloth. "Yes?"

"When can I go home?"

"How are you feeling?"

"My head hurts and I'm cranky and I don't think anyone is bringing me a grilled cheese sandwich."

"This is not a mess hall, Mr. Paris," the Doctor said, flipping open his medical tricorder.

"Precisely why I want to go home."

Waving the device over Tom's head, the EMH frowned. "Hmmm . . ." he hummed while consulting the display. "Self-absorbed. Churlish in a moderately amusing manner. Concerned only with your own feelings." He snapped the tricorder shut. "You're cured. Go home."

Tom flipped the thin blanket off his legs and swung them off the side of the biobed. "Thanks," he said. "Can you do anything about my headache?"

"Take two analgesics and call me in the morning," he said, and returned to his office.

As Tom was sliding on his boots, sickbay's doors parted and Harry stalked in looking unusually agitated. "Hey," he said. "Feeling better?"

"I'm all right," Tom said. "Just another sharp blow to the rear of my head."

"That's quite a collection you're amassing. What is it about you that you're always getting hit?"

"I assumed," Tom said, lightly touching the still-tender spot, "that it has something to do with flying into the face of danger at a moment's notice."

"Or, possibly, being clumsy."

"The Doctor has suggested as much," Tom said. "Are you here to see me or to talk to the Doc?"

"Neither," Harry said. "I was hoping B'Elanna was here."

"She was here for a few minutes," Tom confirmed, "then had an idea and wanted to go check it out. I suspect she doesn't want to be bothered until she's had a chance to work all the angles. Is this about the physics of the local space?"

"Yeah," Harry said, distractedly skimming some notes on his padd. "I'm supposed to meet Seven down in astrometrics and begin working this problem, but wanted to check a couple things with B'Elanna first."

"Because she's so much more reasonable . . ."

Harry snickered appreciatively. "Depending on her mood, yes. If nothing else, she's a touch less condescending."

"True." Glancing over Harry's shoulder at his padd, Tom tried to make sense of the notes. "How could a planet's magnetic field look like that?"

"Usually from extreme volcanic activity, but I haven't seen any evidence of that so far. I'm telling you, Tom, *nothing* here makes any sense."

Tom grinned. "So you're enjoying yourself, then?"

Kim tried to hide his smile, but had to surrender. "Enjoying? That might be a bit extreme, but, is it *interest-*

ing? Yes. And to think we almost flew past here without a backward glance."

"And then you had to open your mouth."

Before Harry could reply, the door opened and sick-bay was suddenly packed full of broad-shouldered, thrumming, knuckle-walking Monorhans. Hearing the commotion, the Doctor emerged from his office and attempted to assert control, but it wasn't until the captain was at the center of the room calling for quiet that Tom had a chance to study the guests. At first glance, all five Monorhans appeared very similar, but as he examined them more closely he detected subtle differences in face shape and hair color. Their leader, Captain Ziv, was the tallest and gave the impression of having the most self-control. The other four (the last one, accompanied by Neelix, joined the group just as the captain was explaining the examination procedure) were fidgety and nervous. Tom decided that the hollow clacks and thrums he heard were some sort of unconscious subvocalizations.

Once everyone was settled, Neelix and Chakotay took over and escorted first the Monorhan captain, then the others into the examination room. The tests were basic screenings and DNA scans, the sort of thing the Doctor would run on any visitor who arrived on a shuttle to make sure they weren't carrying some dodgy virus or microorganism that *Voyager*'s environmental filters couldn't handle.

As soon as the Doctor finished taking his readings, the Monorhans were hustled away, followed by the captain and Harry, who were already discussing theories about the nature of the fabric of local space-time. Realizing that B'Elanna was not going to be in her quarters and seeing that the ship was still at yellow alert, Tom suggested he stay and help process the test results, an offer the Doctor accepted without any of his usual sarcasm.

As they settled down to work, the Doc hummed merrily, occasionally singing a line in German or Italian under his breath. As time passed, though, his countenance grew more and more grave until finally Tom had to ask, "What is it, Doc?"

The Doctor did not respond directly, but, staring at his medical tricorder intently, asked, "Could you pull up the scans of local space for me, Mr. Paris?"

Without replying, Tom turned to the computer, tapped into the sensor logs, and piped the data to the Doctor's work station. "Coming up on your screen," Tom said.

The Doctor thanked him, then immersed himself in the data. Finally, after several minutes of intense study, the Doctor looked at Tom and with a furrowed brow asked, "Did the captain say how long we'd be in this area?"

"I'm not sure," Tom said. "I would imagine not for very long. I think her primary goal is to help these people, then continue on our way. Why?"

In reply, the Doctor pulled up a model of a molecule that Tom quickly identified as a strand of DNA. Several chains in the strand were blinking ominously, diagnostic data flashing in boxes beside them. Pointing, *Voyager*'s chief medical officer said, "Because our guests are not very healthy," the Doctor said softly.

"You saw the bandages they all wore," Tom said. "You must have known there was something wrong with them."

Shaking his head, the Doctor replied, "That is nothing. Compromised immune systems. But this . . ." He indicated the display. "This is quite another story."

"Is there anything we can do to help?" Tom asked.

The Doctor looked up at him then and said, very bluntly, "No, Mr. Paris. I do not think there is. And if we don't leave soon, I won't be able to do anything for us, either."

After leaving the medical area, Janeway's second, the one named Chakotay, asked Neelix to escort Ziv and his *hara* to living quarters. The commander was required to visit the engine room, he said, but would find the Monorhans again shortly. Though the opportunity to rest was enticing, Ziv also felt strongly that he should see as much of the vessel as he could and asked Chakotay if he could join him. The second hesitated only for a moment, then acquiesced graciously. The *hara* whistled and clicked unhappily about being separated from their *harat*, but Ziv chastised them and ordered them to be on their way.

The walk to the engine room was short, but Ziv tried to absorb every detail he saw and smelled. He was astonished by how wide and clean the corridors were compared with the narrow, poorly lit passages on his own vessel. He asked how many crewmen were aboard, and the second answered, "Only about one hundred and fifty, though we could easily accommodate more if we needed. How many are aboard your vessel?"

"The drive section?" Ziv asked. "Approximately twelve hundred."

"That's a lot of room for twelve hundred," Chakotay said, walking swiftly down the hall. Ziv had to swing himself along on his knuckles in order to keep up. He was mildly uncomfortable moving this way in front of a stranger, but the Voyager did not seem to care. Even the crew members who walked past in the opposite direction paid Ziv only the scantest attention. Obviously, these were a jaded people. "Couldn't you move some of the passengers from the . . . the containers?"

"No," Ziv said. "The rear third of the ship, closest to the engine, is uninhabitable because of radiation. And besides, we don't have any way to move passengers. There is only one shuttle, and the containers, as you call them, do not have airlocks."

"Then how will you get the passengers off when you arrive at your destination?"

"Each container is outfitted with lifeboats. When we find a world on which to settle, the containers will be left in orbit after we remove all the items we can use. My hope is that we will be able to program decaying orbits that will bring the containers down in locations where we may be able to reclaim some of the raw materials, though this is many steps into the future."

"Do you know whether you can settle on the world you're aiming for?" Chakotay asked as they boarded one of the small elevators.

Ziv reluctantly admitted that they were not certain. Their observations of the target world indicated it may be habitable, but there was no way to be sure.

"We performed only cursory scans as we passed it," Chakotay said casually as the elevator door opened, "but I think you'll be all right. The oxygen/nitrogen ratio is a little off, but there's water and the life-sign indicators were good."

Ziv stopped short just outside the elevator. "You know all this?" he asked.

Chakotay turned to look at him. "Well, like I said, these were cursory scans, but, yes. I'm fairly confident the scans are accurate."

Staggered by the news, Ziv clacked loudly, though he immediately recognized that the Voyager did not know what the exclamation meant. "You have no idea," he said, "what this will mean to my passengers and crew."

The corners of the alien's mouth curled up, and Ziv sensed his pleasure. "Happy to help," he said. "This is the engine room. Please don't touch anything without asking, but otherwise feel free to look around. I'll only be a moment."

Ziv found the entire ship astonishing, a marvel of clean, rounded edges and efficient design, but nothing amazed him as much as the engine room. Where his vessel's engine bay was a cacophonous cavern of clattering, rattling moving parts watched over by clicking, stuttering, frantic *harai,* this place was like a temple overseen by slow, solemn acolytes who served an altar of coruscating blue light.

Studying the scene with reverent awe, Ziv's peace of mind was shattered when a small, lithe figure abruptly planted herself before the alien commander and began barking sharp, staccato sentences. For a brief, confused moment, Ziv thought the newcomer might be some kind of priestess cursing them for their insolence, but, focusing on her words more carefully, he finally understood: she was an *engineer.*

The commander, to his credit, seemed immune to the engineer's scathing tone and said simply, "Captain Ziv, our chief engineer, B'Elanna Torres."

The engineer simply stared at Ziv for a moment as if mildly surprised to find him there, then said, "How are you?"

Ziv knew that she did not particularly care, but having met enough of these creatures to know it was a good idea to stay on their good side, Ziv said, "Dazzled. Before I came here, I had doubts that this tiny ship could draw the great behemoth we travel in across the heavens. But now, seeing this, my doubts are banished."

Looking around her, the engineer threw back her shoulders, and Ziv felt a great swell of pride emanate from her. "Yeah," she said, "it's pretty impressive. Glad you could come see it."

"The honor is ours," Ziv said, then took a step back, allowing the commander to speak to his subordinate. Though he could not hear their words, Ziv could tell from their posture that Chakotay was placating the engineer, perhaps even reassuring her.

". . . Tractor beam generator isn't . . ." Ziv heard the engineer say as her voice rose above the pulsing conduits.

". . . Wouldn't ask anything of you or the engines that . . ." the commander rebutted. ". . . Just have to get them moving and then Newton's driving . . ."

One of the passing acolytes nodded to Ziv as he approached a control surface and asked if he had any questions. Ziv thanked him politely, then nodded toward the engineer. "Is that one your *haras?*" he asked.

"Our . . . what?" the acolyte asked.

"Your . . ." Ziv searched for a word that came close to the meaning. "Is she your group's organizer, primary planner, your . . ."

"Oh! Yes!" the acolyte said, comprehension dawning. "She's the chief."

"Chief," Ziv said, savoring the flavor of the word and feeling its meaning in his mind at the same moment. "Ah, excellent."

By the time the captain (trailed by Ensign Kim) arrived in astrometrics, Seven of Nine had completed modeling local space and organized her thoughts. Knowing she would have the captain's attention for only a few minutes, Seven knew she must transfer the critical information as efficiently as possible. When she had been part of the collective, data distribution had been effortless, instantaneous, and universal; such was not the case with her crewmates on *Voyager.*

As much as she had come to cherish her individuality, Seven was frustrated by the feeling of isolation it provoked. There were things she *knew,* important information locked away in her Borg databases, and she wanted very badly to share those things with others, but it seemed to her that Captain Janeway—all of them, really, but the captain more than any other—was always fomenting obstacles to her distributing that information under the guise of helping her become more "human." When opportunities such as this one arose, when the captain set aside time in order to allow Seven to help elucidate a situation, she deeply resented distractions.

Lieutenant Torres was being a distraction.

No sooner had Seven begun her recitation than Torres hailed Captain Janeway with irrelevant questions about tractor beam performance in heavy inertial situations. This was *precisely* the sort of query engineering databases had been created to answer, but Torres could not be bothered with such a simple solution to her problem, especially if asking the captain also gave her the opportunity to *again* voice her opinions about the wisdom of assisting the Monorhans in the manner Captain Janeway was considering.

Unfortunately, the captain seemed to be *enjoying* the discussion about tractor beam specs; her face was radiant with what looked like joy, though Seven knew she sometimes misinterpreted emotional states. Five minutes of inane chatter later, Janeway was agreeing to meet Chakotay and the Monorhans on the bridge so that the engineer could test their ideas. Seven felt her agitation growing, but bit back the desire to comment. Torres was an important, if annoying, member of the community. Straightening her back, Seven inhaled deeply and attempted to clear her mind.

"I'm sorry, Seven," the captain said as soon as she signed off. "I have only a few minutes now, but I want to hear what you've found out."

"Two things of note, Captain," Seven said, beginning her recitation. "There is an eighty-one percent likelihood that the Monorhans are from a planet in the white dwarf binary system."

"Yes, Seven. Captain Ziv confirmed that while we were walking to sickbay."

"Of course, Captain. Though, of course, he could have been lying. I am merely saying that, statistically speaking, it is very likely."

"Why would he lie?" Ensign Kim asked.

"Why does anyone lie, Ensign?" Seven asked. "I am merely observing that sometimes they do. In this case, there is an eighty-one percent chance the Monorhan is being truthful."

"All right, Seven. What else?"

Seven touched a control and brought up a display on the main viewscreen. "This is a three-dimensional model showing the density of the local subspace layer. Of course, a fourth- or even fifth-dimensional model would be more accurate, but there are limits to what I can accomplish with this equipment in a compressed time frame."

"Seven . . . I have three minutes."

"Of course," Seven said, and internally chastised herself for falling prey to the same editorializing she had mentally accused Torres of committing. "Please note the extreme irregularities," she said while highlighting a spiky patch. "Subspace can usually be described as a homogeneous layer. This section I've indicated has the white dwarf at its center."

The captain and Kim studied the display for several seconds before either of them commented. Finally, Kim asked, "But what does it mean?"

"It means," the captain said, "that whatever we're dealing with here, it's not the same sort of subspace instability seen at the Hekaras Corridor. I studied those subspace density models for that area—every captain in Starfleet did—and they looked nothing like this." She contemplated the model for another moment, then turned back to Seven. "So then what are we looking at?"

"I do not know, Captain, but something has profoundly affected the texture and density of subspace in this area. The energies required to do such a thing are . . . I would like to say 'inconceivable' . . ."

"Except here we are discussing it," the captain said. "Do you think this represents a threat to the ship?"

"I have been pondering that very question, Captain, but so far I have come to only one conclusion: The Monorhans have collectively placed themselves in a situation of great risk to escape this system."

Captain Janeway responded, "And there may be wisdom in their decision."

Seven nodded.

"All right then. Thank you, Seven. Continue working on this problem. I would like to know a little more about what we're seeing here, though I'll gladly do it from a distance."

"There's more, Captain," Seven said. "I believe I understand why we did not see the Monorhans until we almost collided with them."

Before the captain could respond, her combadge beeped again. "Captain Janeway to the bridge, please," Commander Chakotay said. "We're ready to move."

After responding, the captain asked, "Is that information critical to our current situation?"

"Perhaps. I believe the extreme folds in subspace are affecting the curvature of space-time in our continuum."

"Which means?" Harry Kim asked.

"Which means, Ensign, that when the ship begins to move, we will likely be in for a rough ride."

Janeway permitted her guests to move around the bridge escorted only by Neelix. Now that they were all together again, the Monorhans seemed to prefer to remain no more than an arm's length away from each other, all except for the youngest, Diro, who seemed more easygoing than the others. She wondered what else Chakotay had observed about their guests in the time they were together, but knew she could not leave the bridge for a private consultation. Catching her first officer's eye, she indicated he should join her near Tuvok's station. "Tell me what you think of our guests," she said.

"If I were speaking as a xenologist," Chakotay remarked, wearing a small grin, "I'd say that we should spend a year with them. We've encountered some fascinating species since we've come to the Delta Quadrant, but I'd have to put them near the top of the list."

"They are quite something, aren't they?"

"Have you noticed how they orient themselves around the captain, how he's always in at least their peripheral vision?" Chakotay asked, some academic fervor creeping into his voice. "And the subvocalizations? I don't think they even realize they're doing it sometimes. The sounds are as subconscious to them as a blink or finger twitch to us."

"Why can't the translator understand them?"

"Because they're not using words, Captain," Chakotay said softly. "The sounds are expressions of emotion. And there's something else going on, too. I'm not sure what. I can't quite put my finger on it."

"Pardon my intrusion, Captain," Tuvok said, leaning forward slightly. "But I believe I have something to add."

"Go ahead."

"I have a headache," Tuvok said.

Janeway and Chakotay looked at each other, both struggling to maintain neutral expressions. Janeway turned back to the security officer and prompted, "And?"

Tuvok pointed at his temple. "Here," he said. "My frontal lobe. Typically, this part of my head aches whenever I overtax my psionic abilities. On several occasions when I worked with Kes, I experienced this unique form of pain. And I experience it whenever the Monorhans communicate subvocally."

Chakotay asked, "You think they're communicating telepathically?"

Tuvok shook his head. "Not necessarily. But the Monorhans possess some form of psionic ability, and it is related to their subvocalizing."

Janeway pondered this for several seconds, then offered, "A hunting language?" Tuvok's eyebrow shot up. "Just something I was thinking about on our way up here from sickbay. The way they move, the way they stay so they always sense where the others are. They remind me of descriptions I've read of primitive peoples who coordinate hunts with whistles and clicks."

"The Yamamato of Earth," Tuvok cited, nodding. "Or the Ki'tai of Severus VI."

"Exactly."

"And this could have developed into some kind of psionic ability?" Chakotay asked.

"More likely the other way around," Janeway said. "They survived and became a successful hunting species *because* of the psionic ability." She gave her security chief an approving nod. "Thank you, Tuvok. Good work."

The human captain and two of her *hara*—her *crew*—were standing at the opposite side of the bridge discussing Ziv and his *hara*. Not just his *hara,* but his entire species. While their conversation did not bother him, he was surprised that they should converse in such close quarters. He was even a bit insulted, until he considered that these aliens might not possess hearing as acute as his people's.

Another, more disturbing thought hit him then: Perhaps she knew *precisely* how good a Monorhan's hearing was. Perhaps she *wanted* Ziv to hear what they were saying. *Psionic.* The word held a very specific meaning for the aliens, especially the brown one with pointed ears; Ziv grasped the general concept, though the specifics were vague. Simply put, the aliens knew that he and his *hara* could bind their minds in a way that the Voyagers could not.

"Captain?" The voice came from over their heads, and for a moment Ziv thought one of his *hara* was contacting him subvocally.

"Go ahead, B'Elanna," Captain Janeway said. "We're all here."

Ah, the engineer.

"We're ready to lock on with the tractor beam and try this out. I can't promise how fast we'll go under the circumstances, but even with just the impulse engines . . ."

"Understood, B'Elanna. Do your best. And, B'Elanna?"

"Yes?"

"When we get out of the disruptive area, do you think you could extend the warp field to include the Monorhan vessel?"

The engineer did not respond immediately, and Ziv imagined her consulting the oracle of her engines. Presently, she said, *"We'll have to move at a leisurely pace, Captain. Nothing more stressful than warp two, I'd say."*

Captain Janeway glanced at the pilot, who appeared to be plotting a course. "Agreed, Captain. Warp two point one, to be precise. Should take us about four days at that speed."

Ziv thrummed involuntarily and felt his *hara*'s responses in his inner ear. *Four days!* Their collective exhilaration threatened to hammer him into unconsciousness, and he had to signal them all to silence. The Voyagers were staring at them all intently, and the one named Tuvok was massaging his forehead. When he had his thoughts under control again, Ziv looked at Captain Janeway, who asked, "Would that be acceptable, Captain Ziv?"

Ziv stared at her in stunned silence for several seconds, then settled on what he felt was an appropriate response. "We are all in your debt, Captain. I do not know what turn of fortune brought this encounter, but I am eternally grateful. I could not be sure how many of these passengers would survive the crossing, but now *all* will."

"We're happy to help," Captain Janeway said, and Ziv could see in her eyes that these were not merely words. All around them, he could feel the goodwill of her crew. Bowing his head, Ziv wondered what he had done to deserve such kindness, then cast aside the question as unworthy. The Blessed All-Knowing Light taught that this life is fraught with difficulty and that compassion is a gift that should never be refused.

Quoting the Texts, Ziv said only, " 'The universe is kinder than any of us has any reason to expect.' "

This seemed to please the captain, and she turned away from Ziv smiling. "B'Elanna?" she called. "Ready when you are."

The pilot put the image of Ziv's ship up on the large viewscreen. Through his feet and deep in the pit of his gut, Ziv sensed the first of a series of deep throbs, the vessel's great engines coming to life. *And not the translumi-nal engines,* he thought, shaking his head in wonder. *The things we could learn from these people . . .* The bridge light-ing changed subtly, and then Ziv saw that it was because the image on the screen had changed: his transport was sheathed in deep blue.

"That's our deflector—a shield," the captain said. "To protect us as we travel."

"I understand." Then the wonder of the moment faded and he recalled the people deep in the vessel's holds. "Captain," he asked. "May I speak with the trans-port. My crew may be alarmed . . ."

"Of course," Captain Janeway said, "though we have been in touch with them. They know what is about to happen in general terms. But hearing it coming from you . . ."

"Precisely." The image of his transport shrank into the corner of the viewscreen and his second-in-command appeared. "Mateo," Ziv said, then paused while his XO made the gesture of acknowledgment. "All is well?"

"Well and truly well, my captain. We will be under way soon, I understand, and moving very quickly."

"You have no idea, Mateo. I only regret that you have not been able to see this extraordinary ship."

"There may still be time," Captain Janeway said. "If you permit it."

On the viewer, Mateo beamed happily. A talented of-ficer, his second-in-command was also one of the few of his senior staff who saw their flight as some kind of great adventure. Yes, a visit to this alien vessel would be a fitting reward for his service. "We will discuss it when I return to the ship, Mateo. But for now, relax and tell the crew and passengers to do the same. Have you informed everyone what will be happening?"

"Word is filtering down through the holds, Captain. It is difficult, but I think most of them have the sense that something wonderful is about to occur."

"More wonderful than even they know, Mateo," Ziv said, not able to keep the joy from his words. "But perhaps it would be best to keep that between us now." Mateo, sensing his captain's keen excitement, grinned and agreed. "I will see you soon," Ziv finished, and signed off.

"Let's be on our way, then," the captain ordered.

The pilot took this as permission and pressed a series of controls. "Tractor beam activated, Captain. We have the drive unit." Pausing, Knowles checked her instruments. "All green. One-quarter impulse, Captain," she said. Chakotay felt the ship lurch slightly under his feet. "Sorry about that," the pilot said. "I must have miscalculated the mass a little."

Chakotay checked the sensors, frowned at what he was seeing, then said, "Understood. Check your acceleration curve."

"Will do. Acceleration normal." Again, the ship shuddered.

"Ease off the throttle there, Knowles," Chakotay said. "I don't like that."

"Me, either, sir," the pilot said. "It's not the engines. We're encountering some kind of turbulence."

"Harry," Chakotay said pointing at the feed from the main sensors. "What am I looking at here?"

"I think we've reached the edge of normal space, Commander."

"That can't be right," Chakotay said. "We shouldn't be here so soon. Seven's charts clearly show . . ."

"It could be that navigating this system is more complicated than we thought."

"But we don't know for sure."

"Not unless we stick around for a little while to map."

Chakotay glanced at Janeway, silently asking whether she wished to do what Harry suggested. The captain shook her head once: *No.* "I don't think that will be necessary, Harry. Let's be on our way, Ensign."

Once again, *Voyager* eased forward, then shuddered along her beam like a long boat hitting the crest of a wave. Knowles looked over her shoulder questioningly, and Chakotay urged her on. In a moment they would be clear of the turbulence, and after a quick check they could be in warp. Later, he and Kathryn would have a conversation about helping wayfarers and what that did to crew morale, but for now he had to admit that he was enjoying watching Captain Ziv. How often would *Voyager* be able to perform such a great favor at so little cost to themselves?

The ship shuddered once more, the deck trembled, and Chakotay saw in his mind one of the great salmon of the American Northwest leaping up a waterfall. *Of course,* he thought, *not many salmon leap up a waterfall dragging a giant bottom-feeder behind them.* Not the kindest image he could conjure, but the Monorhan vessel was a great, ungainly thing. Comparing it to any kind of fish was almost a compliment. Glancing up at the screen, Chakotay saw the blue containment field flicker once, then grow dark, then flash and disappear. The Monorhan drive unit slid away behind them, inertia keeping them moving at almost twenty percent of light speed.

"All stop," Janeway ordered. "What the hell is going on?"

"Engine room," Chakotay called. "What happened to the tractor beam? We lost the transport. She's slicing off to the starboard side."

The main viewscreen flickered then, and for a brief moment Chakotay thought he saw Mateo staring at them, an expression of hopeless dread etched on his features, but the image disappeared before Chakotay could be sure what he had seen.

The view switched back to the external cameras and all of them watched as the great wallowing drive section broke in half like a glacier calving an iceberg. For a split second, the sight was inexpressibly beautiful as the transport shattered into millions of pieces, each shard as sharp and shiny as precious gems, as if a giant had scattered a handful of diamonds, rubies, emeralds, and opals across the face of the heavens. A moment later, the first gondola began to disintegrate, followed by another, then another and another . . .

Chapter 5

Disaster plus 1 minute

From her workstation in astrometrics, Seven of Nine coolly watched the Monorhan drive unit and the passenger units dissolve into what she judged the naked human eye would perceive as slivers of ice. Alone as she was, Seven did not feel the need to do anything to acknowledge the phenomenon other than to ask the computer to select one of the larger pieces and perform an analysis. While the computer worked, Seven adjusted the sensor arrays she controlled from her station and projected a long-range view of the scene.

In the lower right-hand corner of the data display she marked a pinprick of light that was *Voyager*. Backtracking, she marked the spots where the transport disintegrated. Farther back along their course, she marked the coordinates where both ships experienced tremors. She noted the distance between the disturbances and their relative distance from the disaster. Quickly overlaying the scene with readings from all of *Voyager*'s sensors, Seven attempted to find a direct correlation, but found none.

Background radiation from the nearby white dwarf was very high, but she had already known this. She had also already found some exotic high-energy particles in nearby space, but nothing so unusual as to warrant attention.

Seven required less than five minutes to complete this handful of operations, during which time the remains of the Monorhan vessel began to disperse in a predictable Newtonian spray. If they encountered no obstacles, the pieces would continue on their current courses until the universe expired, several billion years hence. Seven idly calculated the percentage of particles that would likely intersect another object while watching indicators flash on her console that told her *Voyager* was performing emergency maneuvers.

As new data rolled in, Seven catalogued the likely questions Janeway and her advisors would ask when the inevitable meeting was called, and began scripting replies. Seven worked diligently, her outward demeanor unblemished by a ripple of concern. An idle question flitted through her mind: What percentage of the debris from the Monorhan vessel could be attributed to an organic source? Her spectroscopic scans said that the chemical nature of the wreckage was homogeneous, but she might be able to fine-tune the scans. Another thought intruded: *Why would I want to do that? What difference does it make?*

Setting the thoughts aside, Seven returned to her preparations. She noted that the corner of her mouth was twitching slightly and, subconsciously, Seven's system manager ordered a small contingent of nanoprobes to massage and repair the muscles. Twitching would not do. Twitching was inefficient, and, more important, imperfect. It would not do at all.

Disaster plus 5 minutes, 40 seconds

Chakotay had never heard a sound like the one that erupted from the Monorhans when the transport disintegrated—a shrieking howl that spiraled in and out of the ultrasonic, making his sinuses and eardrums ache. His first fear was that the Monorhans would think that *Voyager* had devised the disaster, and, indeed, the youngest had turned toward Janeway and assumed what Chakotay had interpreted as a threatening stance. Tuvok must have agreed, because he drew his hand phaser and pointed it at the youth, who did not even seem to notice. Fortunately, Captain Ziv *did* and called to his crewman in a series of sharp rasping clicks. The young man backed away from the captain immediately and joined his fellow crewmen, who had fallen into a ring around their captain.

Captain Janeway recovered more quickly than Chakotay, calling to the helm to stop, then ordered a sweep of the sector for survivors. Chakotay didn't see how there could be any. He kept staring at the main monitor, the sensors locked on to the spreading field of . . . what was it? Debris? Could they even call it that? The ship hadn't exploded or even broken up; in his Maquis days, Chakotay had seen more than his fair share of ships die that way. But this . . . It made no sense. The Monorhan transport had simply disintegrated.

Shaking himself, feeling the sense of shock receding, Chakotay climbed the three steps to the secondary scanning station beside Tuvok's and began replaying the sensor logs. Tuvok was doing the same, but his attention was focused primarily on sweeps of the area. *Gods of my father, the idea of an attack didn't even occur to me.* "Anything?" he asked.

"Nothing," Tuvok said.

"So it wasn't an attack?"

"I would not presume to make such an assumption. Let us just say, the probability is growing lower with each passing second that we remain alive."

As he studied the sensor logs, pieces began to click into place. "We have to get back into their system."

"Agreed," Tuvok said, "but bear in mind that we do not know how this area of space will affect us if we stay too long."

"I have to speak to the captain, make sure she understands what's happening."

"Will she not be preoccupied with our guests?"

Glancing across the bridge, Chakotay saw the captain and Neelix herding the Monorhans toward her ready room and silently agreed with their decision. Better that the grieving aliens should try to absorb what had just happened in relative privacy. How many refugees had Ziv said were on the transport? Twelve thousand? Did that include crew? He shook his head. Did the number even matter? He looked around the bridge and tried to guess what *Voyager*'s crew might be thinking. *Is this our fate?* he wondered. *All because we slowed down for a minute at a binary star, and that was just precisely long enough to put us in precisely the spot where we almost collided with a wandering refugee?* What were the odds? In the entire great galaxy, what were the chances these two ships should encounter one other? Chakotay shook his head again and tried to recall which of the Great Spirits had such a sardonic sense of mischief. *Why, Coyote, the Trickster, of course.* Then, in a moment of cross-cultural referencing that Chakotay could only ever attribute to stress, he recalled that in Greek legend the warrior Odysseus was often referred to as the Trickster. And what was another word for one on an odyssey?

Voyager.

Disaster plus 7 minutes

Don't call me, B'Elanna Torres thought as she raced from station to station, checking readouts and consulting with her experts. *Don't call down here and ask me to explain what just happened because you know, you already* know *I don't know!*

B'Elanna's combadge chirped, but she ignored it as she studied the data coming in through the sensors. The shields had momentarily collapsed when *Voyager* had encountered an energy surge, but came back up again almost immediately. Readings showed space around them was closer to "normal" than anything they had found since approaching the binary system.

Her badge chirped again, this time followed by a voice. *"B'Elanna? Can you hear me?"*

Harry. B'Elanna considered answering. Harry would know better than to ask stupid questions.

Tapping her badge, B'Elanna said, "Torres here. Things are a little tense down here, Harry, so make it quick. I'm busy."

"We're all busy, B'Elanna," Harry snapped. *"I just watched a transport disintegrate with the captain standing about three meters away. Don't you think that might introduce some tension into my life?"*

B'Elanna winced. There weren't many people she was less likely to become friends with than the optimistic, career-oriented young Ensign Kim, but life on *Voyager* had produced many stranger pairings. (*Like you and your boyfriend,* B'Elanna thought sardonically.) The words came hard, but she knew she should say them: "Sorry, Harry. Go ahead."

"Never mind," Harry said, his voice sounding less frayed. *"I just wanted to let you know what we've found so you don't make yourself too crazy."*

"Well?"

"The problem wasn't in the shields," Harry said. *"The problem was with the subatomic structure of the transport and everything and everyone on it. I ran my scans past the Doctor and he agrees with my theory: All of the matter in the system has subtly different properties. As soon as we got outside the range of the white dwarf, conditions were too different. The forces that held the atoms together collapsed."*

B'Elanna held her peace for a count of five, then said,

"You call *me* crazy? That's the most bizarre thing I've ever heard. How can the laws of physics be so different in such a localized area?"

"I don't know," Harry rasped. *"And I don't know how long we can be here and not be affected. We need to explain this to the captain. . . ."*

The word "captain" reminded B'Elanna that Ziv and his *hara* had been on the bridge when their ship had crumbled into shards. "What happened to the Monorhans on *Voyager*? Did they . . . ?"

". . . Disintegrate? No, they're all right. We stopped before we crossed completely into normal space. Captain Janeway has them in her ready room, trying to calm things down, explain. . . ." He paused, collecting himself. *"I don't even know what to tell her. I've never seen anything like this."*

"None of us has ever seen anything like this. That's what we say every day around here until we do see it. And then we deal with it." Harry did not reply, and B'Elanna feared that she might have overwhelmed him. Reeling herself in, she said, "I haven't seen all the sensor logs yet. I can come up in a little bit so we can run them together."

"Yeah," Harry said. *"Sure. Do you want to rendezvous in astrometrics and use the big screen?"*

"Will Seven be there?"

"Probably. It's her domain."

"Then, no," B'Elanna said. "I don't."

"You shouldn't be so hard on her, B'Elanna. She tries."

"She tries to be *annoying*," B'Elanna spat. "And smug and superior. And she succeeds. You should stop treating her like she's a human being, Harry. She's not. She's a machine in the *shape* of a human being."

"And you're an engineer," Harry said. *"So you should really get along."*

"Shut up, Harry. I have work to do."

"We all have work to do. Come up when you have time."

Disaster plus 10 minutes

"Gentlemen, fellow sapients, my friends . . ." The Monorhan's clicking and thrumming was almost deafening in the relatively close quarters of Captain Janeway's ready room, but Neelix doggedly continued to try to get the aliens' attention. "I don't know what we can do at this time, in the face of such a tragedy, but if there's anything . . . anything at all . . ." But it was no use; the Monorhans had drawn into a tight circle around their captain, each one facing inward, chirping madly. Helplessly, he offered, "Perhaps a nice cup of tea?" then almost smacked himself on the forehead. Who would want tea at a time like this? He realized the answer in an instant: *I do.* Deciding he could do nothing else for the Monorhans until they decided to calm down, Neelix slipped around the group to the replicator.

"Oolong tea," he said into the pickup. "Hot." The mug of tea appeared a moment later, and two seconds after Neelix lifted it clear of the replicator, the youngest Monorhan, Diro, shuddered, dropped his shoulders, and pivoted to face Neelix.

The Monorhan's face convulsed and he covered his nose, saying, "That smell! What *is* it?!" A moment later, the other four Monorhans were holding their broad noses and backing away into the corner. One of them retched and gagged.

"Neelix!" the captain shouted. "Your tea! The smell is making them sick!"

Hastily, Neelix replaced the mug of pungent tea on the replicator and punched the Recycle button. The air above the pad wavered and the drink was once again reduced to its component molecules. "Sorry about that! I should have thought to ask. There are more than a few humans that don't take to oolong."

The captain was holding her forehead and wearing one of her *I'm going to hurt you, I just haven't decided how* expressions. Possibilities began spinning through his mind, but Neelix decided his time would best be served trying to placate the Monorhans. "My friends, I must apologize! I had no idea this substance was so offensive to you. It's hardly common here on *Voyager,* but . . . but . . ." He knew he was making a complete fool of himself, but he didn't know what else to say. Despite his vast experience in dealing with individuals of other species, he knew how easy it was to make mistakes of this sort. "Perhaps I should just take my leave for now. . . ."

"Perhaps that would be best," the captain said, again calm. "But could you ask Commander Chakotay to step in as soon as he has a few minutes?"

"Yes, Captain. My friends, again . . ." Neelix moved closer to the Monorhans, hoping that he could convey his concern. To his relief, Diro stood and briefly clasped hands with him. "If there's anything I can do," he murmured one more time, but he knew that the sad truth was that there was *nothing* he could do. At times like this, there was nothing to do but pull your grief to you and try to make an accommodation with it. Neelix believed he knew that better than anyone on *Voyager,* but he also knew it was something no one could teach another.

Out on the bridge, all was relatively calm, though Neelix could feel the undercurrent of tension. No one understood what had just happened. Neelix had boundless admiration for the crew of *Voyager,* had seen them come together as a team on countless occasions to battle opponents that appeared unbeatable. But it was one thing to ready yourself to fight Species 8472 or the Kazon, and another thing entirely to, figuratively speaking, escort a pleasant stranger on a stroll and then have the stranger explode on his front lawn. *Everyone,* he decided, *is going to be hungry.*

Pausing only briefly to pass on the message from the captain to Commander Chakotay, Neelix scurried to the turbolift, all the while running through the list of ingredients for tonight's menu.

Disaster plus 14 minutes

Janeway was overwhelmed by the need for a cup of coffee, but did not dare approach the replicator. Who knew what the Monorhans would think of Colombian dark roast? How many different alien species had been aboard *Voyager* in the past four years? Ten? Fifteen? Had there been a series of disasters *anything* like those that had plagued her ship and crew in the past . . . what was it? She glanced up at her chronometer and saw that less than five hours had passed since Harry Kim had first mentioned the anomalous readings. She wondered how much longer they would be here in the Monorhans' system, then fell to thinking about whether they would ever be able to leave at all. *Best to deal with the problems at hand.*

"Captain Ziv," Janeway begin. "Gentlemen . . . My sincere condolences on the deaths of your crewmates, your passengers, and no doubt what must have been your friends and members of your families." She watched as the Monorhans, all of whom had been trying to regain their dignity since Neelix exited, sagged down into themselves. Yes, obviously, there had been members of their families in the disaster. "Please let me assure you that no one on my ship was responsible and that we'll do everything we can to uncover the reason for this disaster. If there is an outside agent responsible, I will do everything in my power to bring that party to justice. If nothing else, please let me put you in contact with your government so you can inform them what has occurred." A thought suddenly struck Janeway. "Could they have been watching us from your world? Is it possible they saw everything and are already trying to formulate a response?" *Like a large bomb that we won't see coming in this strange, warped region of space?*

Ziv inhaled deeply, then exhaled, visibly collecting

his resources. "I do not think so," he said, then fell silent and lowered his head. Ziv's *hara* moved closer until they were wrapped tightly around their captain, one or two dropping their heavy hands onto his shoulders. Finally, Ziv raised his head, straightened his shoulders, and continued. "I formally request that you transport me and my *hara* back to my homeworld."

"Of course," Janeway replied. "As soon as possible."

"Further, I accept your offer to investigate this disaster. With your technical resources, I believe you will be able to help us understand what has happened if for no other reason than to explain it to the loved ones of the dead."

"Also agreed."

"And finally, I request that you allow me to contact my *rih-hara-tan.*"

"I will ask my second-in-command to arrange for the transmission and pipe it in here. Please stay as long as you need." Rising, Janeway indicated her chair and viewscreen. As she walked around the desk, Chakotay entered the room. "Excellent. Commander, please speak to Mr. Tuvok and ask him to find the correct frequency to contact Captain Ziv's homeworld."

"We're working on it, Captain," Chakotay said. "There are difficulties, but Tuvok thinks that, as we get nearer, the problems should be resolved."

"Fine. I think we should give the captain and his . . . his *hara* some privacy until Tuvok makes contact." With that, Janeway walked out the door, never so grateful to be leaving her sanctum.

Disaster plus 25 minutes

Diro knew he was expected to say something, say *anything*, but he did not know what it should be. In just the short time since Captain Janeway had left the room, all the others, all his fellow *haran*, had said something heartfelt about the loss of the transport, expressing their sorrow, their anger, their incomprehension, but Diro had remained silent. When the others turned to him, his tongues were as dry as ashes. He felt his *haran* close to him, felt the link ready for him should he need or desire it, but Diro could not respond. He was isolated.

Staring out the long row of windows in Captain Janeway's ready room, the only words that came to mind were *I'm sorry*. If he said the phrase aloud, though, he knew he would repeat it over and over again ... how many times? Fifteen thousand? He felt that trying to express his sorrow and horror in one all-encompassing statement would demean the dead.

But were sorrow and horror all he was feeling? He wished that they were, but he owed the dead honesty if nothing else. So, instead of being heartfelt or eloquent, Diro chose to be truthful. Staring out the window, looking at the pinprick stars, he said softly, "I'm glad I'm not dead." The others waited for more, but Diro was silent.

Finally, Ziv said, as if to bring his remarks to a conclusion, "We're glad you aren't dead, too."

Diro turned to look at his *harat*, disappointment in his weakness tearing at his soul. "I'm sorry, Ziv," he said. "I know I should be mourning—I feel their deaths here within me—but more than anything, I'm thinking about what it would be like to die that way, so suddenly, without foreknowledge. Could anyone in the holds have known what was about to occur?"

Rising, Ziv shook his head sadly and joined Diro by the window. "No, my *haran*. There is no way they could have known. Even Mateo could not have known. I watched the transmission, and the change, whatever it was, was so quick . . . They were gone before any of them knew what happened. Was this just or merciful? I do not know."

Pointing at the blue glow the windows emitted, Diro asked, "Did the forcefields protect us? Or was it all just chance?"

"No," Ziv said with certainty. "I refuse to believe that. I chose to believe we were spared for a reason. We must return to Monorha, tell the *rih-hara-tan* what we have seen, and hope that these miracle workers, these Voyagers, can aid us."

"And if not?"

Ziv shrugged, his eloquence at an end. "Then consider this question when your end comes: Would you like to see it coming or not?"

Turning back to the window, Diro stared long into the darkness between the stars, searching for an answer.

Chapter 6

"Can the shields take it, Tuvok?"

Tuvok knew the answer to Captain Janeway's question, but hesitated to give it too quickly. Tuvok had long ago learned that with humans one could not simply dispense information, especially when the answers carried so much emotional weight.

He knew precisely how much radiation the white dwarf would produce, assuming the readings he had been taking over the past several hours were an accurate baseline. He also knew how much punishment *Voyager*'s shields could take, and that those shields could survive many hours of exposure, *assuming nothing else changed*. But there was the problem: Conditions rarely remained constant.

And so a moment's hesitation seemed a sensible precaution. Captain Janeway would remember this later and factor her tactical officer's reluctance into her decisions. He looked out over the top of his station at the officers clustered around him—the captain, Chakotay, Kim, Torres, and the Doctor—and considered releasing a scowl. Holding a meeting on the bridge, while not a security risk, might mean that those who did not currently need to would hear certain facts better left uncirculated. He understood the captain's motivations: Staying on the bridge meant she could respond quickly to an evolving situation. Staying close to her ready room was both respectful of their guests and prudent. While overall he was impressed with the Monorhans, he could not know what their guests might do when they recovered from the shock of watching thousands of their people wiped from existence so suddenly.

"Taking readings from the white dwarf has been difficult, but I believe we have captured enough data to make reasonable assumptions about its behavior. Despite the significant output of X-rays and other forms of hard radiation, we are not currently in any danger."

"But as a precaution," the Doctor inserted, "I recommend a course of hyronalin for everyone on board. It will protect the crew from the worst of the radiation damage if the shields should fail."

"Very good, Doctor. Chakotay, inform all hands."

"Yes, Captain."

"Doctor," Torres asked. "What about the Monorhans?"

"What about them, B'Elanna?"

"Are you going to give them the treatment, too? Their sores—those are caused by the radiation, aren't they?"

"They are," the Doctor said. "But the damage is far beyond anything that could be cured with a simple hyronalin treatment." He shook his head remorsefully. "Of course I can help them—I *will* help them—but what will happen to them when we return them to Monorha? We don't have the resources to treat an entire planetary population." He looked at the captain. "Do we?"

"Not the symptoms," Captain Janeway said. "But perhaps the cause. We'll know more when we reach the planet and can study the white dwarf at closer range."

The group began to disperse, each returning to his duties. The door to the captain's ready room opened, and Captain Ziv and his associates shambled out, then settled into the now familiar wedge formation. "Have you been able to contact my *rih-hara-tan,* Captain?"

"Not yet, Captain. Conditions in this area are very unusual. We have just now decided our ship's shields can withstand the radiation from the white dwarf and so we will be pressing ahead at higher speed."

The *hara* exchanged glances and a quick burst of burbling clicks. Finally, Ziv turned back to the captain and said, "On several occasions you have made reference to a 'white dwarf,' but we do not understand what you mean. At first, I thought it was a failure of the translator as before, but my *hara* all hear the same words. What does it mean?"

Now it was *Voyager*'s crew's turn to exchange looks. Finally, all faces turned to Tuvok to explain. Straightening, his hands clasped behind his back, Tuvok recited, "When small or medium-sized stars begin to run out of hydrogen and the fusion reaction has slowed, the forces of gravity within the star will compact the remaining mass. This results in a relatively small, relatively cool body known as a white dwarf. A white dwarf's outer helium and hydrogen layers are thin and the X-rays that were always created by the hotter inner layers are free to escape. Thus, your planet's problem."

"Oh," one of the Monorhans said. "They're talking about the Blue Eye."

"The what?" Kim asked.

"The Blue Eye," Captain Ziv said. "That's our name for the dead star that orbits the central sun."

"Ah," Captain Janeway said. "We call that dead star a white dwarf."

One or two of the Monorhans clicked at each other, and their long necks undulated in what, to Tuvok's eyes, appeared to be their version of a shrug. "A peculiar name, Captain, but we understand now."

"In any case, the whi . . . the Blue Eye makes communications difficult. We will continue to work at the problem as we move through this transitional zone around the system. It may take time, so you might be more comfortable in your quarters. . . . Neelix *did* assign you a suite, didn't he?"

The Monorhan nodded. "We would appreciate the opportunity to refresh ourselves and . . . to speak more among ourselves. How long do you think this process will take?"

"Tuvok?"

"Perhaps another hour. No more."

Ziv nodded. "An hour then."

Moments later, the Talaxian, responding to the

captain's hail, returned to the bridge, then hustled the Monorhans onto the turbolift. As soon as they were off the bridge, the captain said softly, "Keep watch over them, Tuvok."

"I intend to, Captain."

"They have no reason to believe that we're not responsible for the destruction of their vessel."

"None whatsoever."

"I think the Monorhans are a people who are slow to anger, but if they do, they may do something desperate."

"They may try, Captain, but they will not succeed."

Captain Janeway nodded, satisfied that her message had been understood.

Cleared of all the disruptive elements, the noise level and the mood on the bridge soon returned to its usual efficient, businesslike hum. Chakotay asked, "Ensign Knowles, how long to Monorhan orbit?"

"At our current rate, sir, sixteen hours."

Chakotay glanced over at the captain. "Is that acceptable, Captain?"

"It is. Try to give us a smooth ride, Ensign."

"Aye, Captain."

Kathryn looked at Chakotay and said, "Commander—a moment of your time. Tuvok, you have the bridge."

Entering the ready room, Chakotay noticed a pungent though not unpleasant odor. "The Monorhans?" he asked.

"When they get stressed, I think," Kathryn said as she

knelt down by the small hutch beside her desk and began to open and shut cabinet doors. Finally, after the fourth or fifth slam, she said, "Ah!" Turning back to Chakotay, she held up a cloth-wrapped bundle in triumph. "Here we are."

"What's this?"

"Get two coffee cups," she said as she unwrapped the bundle.

He rose to obey, but asked again, "But what is it?"

"Something Mark gave me before I left Earth. He told me, 'Keep this tucked away in case of a bad day.' " Kathryn finished unwrapping the package and said, "This has been a pretty bad day, hasn't it?"

Chakotay put the cups in front of her and said, "We've had worse."

"We've had many worse and much more deadly. I wouldn't consider doing this if I felt we were in any danger . . . any more than usual . . ." She placed a bottle on the desk, then held her hands to either side of her head about four inches away from her scalp. "As my mother used to say, 'I have a headache this big.' You pour. Not too much, though; it's potent."

While carefully working the stopper out of the bottle, Chakotay studied the label. Not being a drinker, he didn't recognize it, but the name had a nice Old Earth flavor to it: Jameson Irish Whiskey. When the stopper popped out, the rich, peaty aroma immediately overwhelmed the lingering musky smell of the Monorhans. "Woo," Chakotay said. "That's really something."

Pouring a modest amount, Chakotay asked, "You've had this for more than four years?"

"I forgot about it until earlier this year and since then, well, when would I have wanted a drink?"

"I can think of fourteen or fifteen occasions. Easily." Chakotay swirled the liquor around in his cup and inhaled. Generally, he did not much care for spirits, preferring wines or ales if he was going to drink, but if Kathryn was willing to offer something so rare, he was happy to partake. He sipped, and the whiskey left a trail of liquid fire down his throat as warming vapors rose up into his nasal passages. "Wow," he said.

Leaning back in her chair, Kathryn lifted her feet up onto her desk, something like a smile on her lips. "Indeed." She shifted her gaze to the view out her window. "Over fifteen thousand beings died just a little more than an hour ago, Chakotay, and here I am having a drink. Do you think I'm being callous?"

Surprised by the question—almost as surprised as by the drink—Chakotay thought for a moment and said, "No." Reflecting further, he said, "I think you tend to take things much too much to heart sometimes. Not everything that has gone wrong on our trip so far has been your fault."

Kathryn looked askance at him and raised an eyebrow. "Oh. Thank you," she drawled.

"You're welcome," Chakotay said, settling back as well as he could into his chair. He briefly considered putting his feet up onto the desk, but decided that might be pushing the situation too far. "Here's how I see it: We just stepped up to the edge of the abyss and now we're savoring a moment of reflection. The Monorhans should mourn; maybe at some point we should even mourn with them. But just for now, I say let's be glad we're alive."

Smiling sadly, Kathryn lifted her cup in salute and said, *"Slainte."*

Chakotay lifted his in response, then asked, "We are off duty, aren't we?"

"If I say we are," Kathryn said, "then we are. I'm the captain."

Though savoring the moment of quiet companionship, Chakotay couldn't ignore the question that had been growing in his mind. "Then if we're off duty, I'm going to ask you this as a friend and not as your first officer."

Kathryn sighed deeply. "Which means you're really being my first officer, but you're trying to be diplomatic about something."

Chakotay snorted. "Maybe a little."

"Go ahead," Kathryn said, then sipped some more of her drink. "Or, no, wait: 'Permission granted.' What's your question?"

Pausing to think, Chakotay realized suddenly how hard the whiskey was hitting his system. He was going to need to find the Doctor before the next crisis occurred and acquire something to sober himself up. Rallying, he asked, "How much do you think we owe these people?" he asked. "What do you think we should be doing for them?"

"An interesting question," Kathryn asked. "Why do you ask?"

"Because of a discussion I had with B'Elanna earlier."

"A *'discussion'*? With B'Elanna? I don't believe you."

"A tirade. B'Elanna assaulted me with a tirade."

"You see? Now I believe you. What was her point?"

"Distilling it down for you?" Looking into his cup, he saw that he was almost finished with his drink. *Ask for more?* he wondered. *No, probably a terrible, terrible idea.* Then, thinking back on his last statement, he chuckled feebly at the use of the word "distilling." *Absolutely no more.* "She worries about 'her' ship. This is our home, she says, and the only way we're going to make it back home—for those who want to get home, she added carefully—is if we take care of her. Sometimes, B'Elanna says, you are . . . careless."

Twisting her legs, Kathryn half-turned toward her windows so she could watch the stars slowly slide past. Her words came slowly, as if she was thinking about each one as she said it. "Meaning," the captain said, "that I stick my nose into other people's business sometimes." She shrugged. "What can I say? She's right. But these people, the Monorhans—we dragged their ship into a spot in space where it was shattered into millions of pieces. Doesn't that mean we owe them something?"

"I don't know, Kathryn. The ship was probably going to be destroyed anyway. At least we saved Ziv and his *hara*. We can take them home."

"But no more than that?" Kathryn asked. "What if we know something that would spell the difference between their entire civilization being wiped out or saved? Don't we have a responsibility?"

"Perhaps," Chakotay said. "But how far can we go before it's too far? These people haven't developed FTL technology yet. And while I don't think we could have abandoned them, we might have to consider carefully whether General Order One allows us to do more than take them home."

"And then watch them die in our monitors as we fly away."

"We might not be able to prevent it, Kathryn," Chakotay said. "We may appear to have unlimited resources to these people, but you and I know that isn't true. How much are you willing to expend in order to try to fix a situation that can't be fixed?"

"I don't know the answer to that, Chakotay," Kathryn said. "But I'm not ready to give up."

"No one is asking you to give up, but if the time comes, I'm going to step in and remind you. Are you going to be prepared to listen to me?"

"Of course. That's why I give you whiskey." She raised her glass in salute, then tossed off the remaining liquor. Chakotay raised his glass in response, but knew there was no more to drink and he wasn't going to ask for more. He decided then and there that if the captain ever again asked him if he wanted a drink, he would politely refuse. Though he knew his job was to tell the captain everything she should know in order to make a decision, telling her everything he felt would set a dangerous precedent.

~

Sem, the *rih-hara-tan* of the Eleventh Tribe, was not pleased. Even though Ziv could not see her, Ziv heard it in her voice, in the pauses between sentences. He knew her moods well, better than anyone in the universe. *Even better than she knows them herself,* Ziv reflected. She was not, however, giving in to her displeasure, her anger or suspicion. Sem had listened to Ziv's report and understood all the implications, spoken and unspoken. She knew that he and his *hara* were being treated as honored guests, but were, in fact, only a whisker's breadth from becoming prisoners. Ziv had no doubt that the weakest of his *hara* could break any of the Voyagers in two with the merest blow, but he also had seen their forcefields. If Sem ordered them to attack the Voyagers, to try to take possession of their ship, he and his comrades were honor-bound to obey, even knowing they could never succeed. Fortunately, Sem was not that stupid. *Crazed, sometimes,* Ziv thought. *Amoral. Remorseless. But stupid? Oh, no, never that.*

"So," she said after pausing to consider his report, "*this explains what happened to the ships that preceded yours.*"

Ships that preceded mine? Ziv thought. Most of his crew had heard that the city of the Twelfth Tribe had been working to launch a ship, but he had no idea that they— or someone else—had been successful. Glad that Sem could not see him, Ziv replied flatly, "Yes, though there can be no way to know for certain."

"*But we have no other theories at this time.*"

Ziv inhaled and tried not to let his thoughts run too

far ahead of him. *Ships!* "The aliens say that the interference from the Blue Eye is strong enough that even their communication systems could not pierce it until we were this close. Perhaps they survived."

"Yes, perhaps," the *rih-hara-tan* said. *"Perhaps. We have no way to know. But would you gamble on the outcome, seeing what you have seen?"*

Nearby, Ziv felt his *hara* stir uncomfortably. He knew what they would say if pressed to the point. Though a *harat* cannot actually read his *haran*'s thoughts, only a fool would ignore their mood: they would elect to dissolve their fellowship rather than risk their fates in space again.

"But if the aliens are able to pierce this mystery," Ziv said. "What then? Their captain—I think we may ask her for aid. She is driven by her conscience."

"A sharp goad," Sem said, then fell silent for several moments. Finally, she continued, *"Ask their captain to contact the Emergency Council. Better the planetary authority ask her for help than the leader of your tribe."*

"I understand."

"And learn whatever you can about their propulsion systems and their shields."

"We'll try, but it will be the work of many days to even begin to understand it."

"True, but we must begin somewhere. We would not even have made it off Monorha if our tribe did not display a talent for unraveling complex technical puzzles."

Ziv knew this was true and took some pride in the historical fact that his grandsire had been one of the technical team that had disassembled the alien craft that had landed near their city. If only the aliens who piloted it had survived long enough to explain some of its mysteries or possessed the universal translator the Voyagers treated with such casual disregard. "We will do what we can, my *rih*," Ziv said. "Though I do not know what chances we will have. According to my hosts, we will be in orbit in approximately fourteen hours."

"And what will happen then?"

Near a state of complete mental exhaustion, Ziv almost snapped at the *rih-hara-tan*, *What do you mean what will happen?! We will return to our city! We will lie down and die with all our families and friends! Our ship is destroyed and we cannot flee this world even if we wished without risking being turned into slivers of glass!* But he was a good *haran* (or, at least, a fearful one) and did not speak these words. "What would you like to happen?"

"Ask the aliens to accompany you to our city. If necessary, tell them you are worried about the state of your shuttle—not an entirely unrealistic concern."

"If I can, I will."

"You can, Ziv, my shi-harat."

Ziv squirmed at the use of the term, as Sem no doubt knew he would. He felt his *hara* stir behind him as they all mentally withdrew from him. He wanted to shout at her, to curse her, to call down the condemnation of the Blessed All-Knowing Light, but instead he said, "Thank you, my *rih*. I will do what I can."

Six hours from orbit, after Neelix had conveyed a message from Ziv that he would like the captain to speak to the Monorhan Emergency Council, Janeway had asked Chakotay to bring Lieutenant Dandibhotla to her ready room so he could talk to him about their social structure. Dandibhotla, the only crewman versed in both anthropology and linguistics, had, at Tuvok's request, been watching and listening to all the recordings made to date and was chomping at the bit to discuss his observations.

Clustered around the conference room table, Janeway and Chakotay and Neelix gave the small, dapper anthropologist their undivided attention. "Judging from what Neelix has told me and what I've seen," Dandibhotla said, "the Monorhans were divided into tribes or possibly city-states. The *hara* groupings suggest a modularly hierarchical society. They work in groups, but the groups can be disassembled when necessary. A leader of one group can be a subordinate in another. The fact that Captain Ziv is the *harat* of his group, but refers to his tribal leader as a *rih-hara-tan,* makes it sound like we're talking about someone who performs the function of *harat*—or, in the case of a female, *haras*—for perhaps a large group of *harai,* may be an entire tribe. Just a guess, but there's probably some kind of religious power backing that up."

"So, they might be a religiously organized society?" Janeway asked.

"Possibly," Dandibhotla said. "But in the recordings I've seen, I've only heard Ziv mention what might be a god once or twice. No, more likely, their religion was once much more important than it is now. When a society is placed under the sort of stress the Monorhans are under, old models tend to collapse."

"Unless they're prohibited from mentioning their god's name in front of outsiders," Chakotay suggested.

Dandibhotla nodded. "He's got me there, Captain. It's a possibility."

"Okay," Janeway sighed, massaging her temples. "I'll try to keep all this in mind, but how much of it do we really know is true?"

Chakotay and Dandibhotla both were silent for several beats, and then the latter shrugged. "None of it. Without time to do a survey or even monitor their electronic broadcasts—assuming they have any—we're completely making this up as we go along."

"Hardly an ideal first-contact situation, Captain," Chakotay echoed. "But keep this in mind: We're not coming here with any intention in mind except returning their citizens."

"And offering help," Janeway added.

"If we can," Chakotay said.

"There's always something we can do."

Chakotay met her eyes, and Janeway could see he was still thinking about their earlier talk. *This conversation isn't over,* his gaze said.

Perhaps not yet, she thought, *but in the end, the decision is mine.*

Chapter 7

"Shalla Kiiy is from a different district of my city-state, Captain," Ziv explained shortly before the meeting was scheduled to begin. "And speaks a different dialect. I have found I have difficulty understanding her, and your translator may experience the same problems." His long neck curled to one side in a movement Seven of Nine now recognized as the Monorhan equivalent of a human shrug. Seven had decided some time ago that the shrug was an eloquent gesture and had practiced the necessary movements in private, though thus far she had not found an opportunity to try it. The one who shrugged, she knew, was attempting to communicate a degree of uncertainty, which was a condition Seven rarely experienced. She had considered *feigning* uncertainty just to see how effectively she could perform, but ultimately could not bring herself to be so duplicitous.

"We appreciate the warning, Captain Ziv. Just to be certain I understand the circumstances, she is *not a rih-hara-tan?*"

"No. Shalla Kiiy is a member of the Emergency Council, the body that organizes the efforts to save the people of my planet."

Seven watched Captain Janeway give Tuvok and Chakotay a sidelong glance. *This is new information,* she thought.

"A planetwide organization?"

Ziv's head bobbed, his long neck waving back and forth. "Citywide, yes. There are only thirteen cities. Perhaps it would make a difference if you understood there are less than six million people left on Monorha."

This, too, was a surprise to the captain and her advisors, though Seven didn't understand why. How could they have missed the signs?

"What was your population at its peak?"

Ziv looked at Jara, the only member of his *hara* to accompany him to the meeting. Jara responded with a brief burst of tongue clicking. Ziv clacked back, then said, "I am not an expert on these things, Captain, but my guess would be, at its peak, perhaps sixty million."

"You've lost nine-tenths of your population in a century?" Janeway asked.

Ziv nodded impassively.

Chakotay whispered a word Seven did not recognize and filed it away for later research. *Likely the name of some deity,* she decided.

"My sympathies, Captain," Janeway said. "I don't know what else to say."

"You've already helped us more than anyone could have expected," Ziv said. "As my *rih-hara-tan* pointed out, we would not even know what happened to ships sent out by the other cities if not for you. Now, perhaps, we can develop some method for protecting ourselves when we cross the threshold out of Monorhan space."

Seven privately doubted that this would be possible unless something was done about the radiation from the white dwarf, but she kept this opinion to herself. A minute and forty-five seconds later, the image of a Monorhan female appeared on the main viewer. Without anyone else nearby to compare her with, Seven could not judge how tall Shalla Kiiy was, but her body seemed more slender, with smaller forearms than Captain Ziv or any of his *hara*. Her hair was not so thick as Ziv's, nor as curly, and Seven saw streaks of gray, perhaps indicating advanced years. Alarmingly, though not unexpected, Kiiy also had a generally unhealthy appearance: pallid skin, rheumy eyes, and a large, irritated red patch on her left cheek. When she spoke, Seven noted, her left eye occasionally twitched spasmodically.

Like Ziv and his associates, Kiiy's clothes were utilitarian and without ornament, though the midsection was not so tightly fitted as the males'. Evidence of reproductive organs? It seemed likely, though Seven had not as yet accessed the medical scans. For all she knew, the Monorhans budded like potatoes to reproduce. A quick consultation of the Borg database she retained showed that fewer than one-tenth of one percent of the known sentient species reproduced in this manner.

"Captain Ziv," Kiiy said with a peculiar buzz in the

words. *"Introduce me to your friends."* *(Introduzzze me to your frienzzz.)*

"Shalla Kiiy," Ziv said, touching his knuckles to the ground and lowering his head formally. "This is Captain Janeway of the Federation starship *Voyager.* They name their ships, Councilwoman. The word means . . ."

"I hear the meaning of the word in my head, Captain," Kiiy said, bowing in return. *"Quite a remarkable devizzze. How long did it take for you to become comfortable wiz it?"*

"Not long, Shalla. In a short time, you will not even notice the difference."

"Azztonishing. And what is a Federation, Captain?"

Janeway assumed her most bright, diplomatic tone to answer. "The United Federation of Planets is an alliance of worlds in my region of the galaxy that works for the mutual protection and advancement of its members. Currently, the Federation includes approximately one hundred and fifty planetary civilizations and their colonies, all of them a considerable distance from Monorha."

"Yes, you have been out of touch for some time, haven't you? Ziv says your ship was thrown across almost the entire width of the galaxy."

"That's correct," Janeway said. "Although the exact circumstances that brought us that great distance are beyond our ability to duplicate, our vessel is capable of limited transluminal velocity."

"We understand that idea here on Monorha, Captain, but were given to understanding that light speed was an absolute, that nothing could travel faster."

"In normal space, no," Janeway explained. "But there are ways around these absolutes."

"And is this something you could teach us, Captain?" Kiiy asked. *"You know of our plight, do you not? Traveling to another world at faster-than-light speeds—we would be saved. Do you understand?"*

Seven saw Janeway sag slightly, shoulders drooping forward. "I understand, Shalla. May I call you that? What does it mean?"

This was a clever ploy, interrupting the flow of the conversation. Kiiy was temporarily thrown off her stride for politeness' sake and to respond to the captain's question.

" 'Shalla'? *It means . . ."* She turned to Ziv. *"Captain, help me. What is another word for shalla?"*

Ziv mouthed a couple of words that the translator rebroadcast as "overseer" or "boss."

"I understand," Janeway said. "I can call you Shalla, then?"

"Of course. It is not a title many have, but I am far from the only one. Not so much an honor as a burden, eh?"

Janeway smiled. Seven could see that the captain was coming to like this Shalla Kiiy. *Potentially a dangerous decision,* the Borg decided. "But to get back to your question, yes, we could possibly teach you the theory behind faster-than-light travel, but there are laws concerning such exchanges in my culture."

"Laws?" Kiiy asked, raising her arms. *"Who cares for laws here? You are far from home. Who would know?"*

"We would know, Shalla, and we police ourselves, but

that's beside the point. Even if we had time to teach you even the basics, they would do you no good. Building the drive would require years, special materials, and even more specialized tools. We don't have them here with us on *Voyager.* The crystalline substance we use to control the extremely powerful energy generated by our engine core is very rare and we have no evidence that there is any on your world or those nearby. Worst of all, there is something about your system, about the dead star, that inhibits the formation of the field that allows us to make the jump to transluminal speeds."

"So you are trapped here with us, then?" Shalla Kiiy asked, her voice evincing what Seven took for genuine concern.

"No," Janeway said, and Seven was surprised that she was being so honest. If anyone had asked her, she would have advised the captain to keep some information private. Though they appeared peaceful, the Monorhans might turn violent at any moment. Though few in comparison to one hundred years ago, there were forty thousand Monorhans for every member of the crew of *Voyager,* which were not good odds. "We could get out of the system and then engage the engines in a short time. We're not trapped. In fact, I do not wish to stay long if we can avoid it. The radiation from the dead star, what you call the Blue Eye, is the problem. Or part of it, anyway. We do not understand every aspect of the problem yet, but continue to investigate."

"Sem," Kiiy continued, *"Ziv's* rih-hara-tan, *told me that the ships launched before his may have been destroyed, too. Can you confirm this?"*

"No," the captain said. "Again, the radiation from the Blue Eye makes this difficult; however, what we have learned about the unique physical properties of your system makes it unlikely anyone else survived." Captain Janeway hesitated for a moment, a sign that Seven recognized and that meant she was about to shift to a difficult topic. "You'll forgive me for bringing up a delicate topic, Shalla, but I must ask . . ."

"Why we launched more than one ship without knowing the fate of the first?"

"Yes," the captain said. "And without telling Captain Ziv."

Seven noted that the buzz in Shalla Kiiy's voice had almost entirely disappeared, a sign that the translator had mastered her accent. *"What else would you have us do, Captain?"* Kiiy asked. *"We have no other options at this time. If it had been up to me, everyone would know everything, but it is not. I am only one of thirteen on the council—one for each city."*

"We can see them now that we're in orbit," Janeway said. Seven glanced at her scanner and saw the Monorhan world map stretched out flat, each of the cities a tiny jewel nestled along one of the coastlines of Monorha's four minute continents. Though sixty million was a tiny number compared with the billions on Earth, the planet could not have supported much more. Much of the world was covered in shallow seas, another factor that accounted for how the biosphere could absorb so much radiation. If the landmass-to-water ratio had been higher, Monorha would have died long ago.

"So now that you are here," Kiiy asked, *"what will you*

do? Ziv has indicated that you might be able to help us in some other manner. If not by giving us the transluminal drive, then how?"

"First," the captain said, "by examining the Blue Eye. Perhaps we can learn something about the link between its properties and the other peculiarities we're finding here in this system."

"You do not think it is a causal relationship?" Kiiy asked, a question Seven found to be insightful. Obviously, the *shalla* was not a simple, self-centered politician.

"It seems likely," Captain Janeway replied, "but we've learned not to make assumptions about such things. A closer examination is required."

"Very well," Kiiy replied. *"But are there any other, more practical recommendations you can make?"*

"On a more practical level," the captain continued, "we would like to send some engineers down to your planet so they can study the energy shields you've erected around your cities. We may be able to offer some suggestions that would make them more effective."

"Ah," Shalla Kiiy said. *"Then I take it that Ziv has already told you about our shields."*

"He has not," Captain Janeway said. "But as soon as we were in orbit we detected them with our sensors." Though she did not need to refamiliarize herself, Seven pulled up the scans in case the captain wished to review them. The shield generators were, in a word, ineffective. Given the general level of technology the Monorhans exhibited, the design was clever, perhaps even inspired, but against the radiation levels the Blue Eye emitted, the citizenry might have been just as well protected if they were walking around sheathed in metal foil.

"*Of course,*" Kiiy said, raising her arms in a gesture Seven interpreted as a sign of gratitude. "*We would welcome any help you can offer, Captain. How may we aid you in your investigations?*"

"Tell us where to have our shuttle land," Janeway replied. "The sooner we get started, the sooner we'll know where we stand."

Very diplomatic, Captain, Seven thought approvingly. *Very efficient.*

Shalla Kiiy seemed just as capable of moving events along. "*We will send coordinates as soon as possible, Captain. How many people will be landing?*"

"That depends," Captain Janeway said. "On whether Captain Ziv and his associates would like to come home or go with *Voyager* to visit the Blue Eye."

Ziv was visibly surprised by the idea, but responded quickly, "My *hara* and I would like to accompany you, Captain. We wish to know more about the radiation."

"*And may I suggest, Captain,*" Kiiy inserted, "*that we request the assistance of some Monorhan experts? An astrophysicist, perhaps, and another who has knowledge of the history of our system and the Blue Eye in particular?*"

Captain Janeway looked at both Chakotay and Tuvok for a brief instant. Each must have, after his fashion, offered his assent in a manner Seven could not detect, because the captain agreed to Kiiy's suggestion. "We accept," she said. "We'll send my team down in one shuttle and pick up yours with a second."

Kiiy nodded politely. *"May I know the names of the individuals who will be aiding us, Captain?"*

Obviously, the captain had been thinking about this, because she replied without hesitation, "I'll be sending down my chief engineer, Lieutenant B'Elanna Torres." Seven approved of the decision. As difficult as Torres could be, she had an astonishingly good grasp of deflector and shield technology. "And to assist her, I'll be sending along *Voyager*'s resident expert in all manner of esoteric technology. . . ."

"She's sending *Seven?!*" B'Elanna roared, and threw her microspanner against the office wall. It bounced off, then landed point-side down in a slap of temper-foam packing.

"Nice throw," Chakotay said. "If that's broken, I'm taking it out of your pay."

B'Elanna hastily retrieved the tool and carefully inspected the tool. "We don't get paid," she said absently.

"Then I'll bust you down to ensign."

"Good, then I won't be chief engineer anymore and the captain will have to send someone else."

"Then I'll bust *Tom* down to ensign."

"Don't do that," B'Elanna said, and set the tool back on the worktable. "He'd pout."

"Fine. Then just get used to the idea that you've got to work with Seven sometimes."

B'Elanna sighed hugely. She had half-expected this when the captain had consulted with her about the Monorhans' shield generators. Even in orbit, it was difficult to determine much about them except that they weren't doing the job, and as much as it pained B'Elanna to admit it, Seven was probably the best person to send along. She had a flair for analyzing these kinds of problems. "Fine. But I'm in charge, right?"

"You have the rank," Chakotay said. "Unless you want to be an ensign again."

"Not that she'll listen," B'Elanna said grumpily.

"She will," Chakotay said. "In her own way, she respects you."

"Oh, someone engrave those words on my tombstone." She rubbed the bridge of her nose, then said, "I've been in here for more than twelve hours. I'm starting to get fuzzy."

"I told you to visit Tom in sickbay and take it easy hours ago, but you couldn't do it."

B'Elanna stopped massaging her nose and said, "Sickbay—that reminds me—what do we do about protection from the radiation?"

"The Doctor will want to see you before you go. More injections. He'll give you scanners, too, so you can monitor your exposure. He says he'll be able to reverse any damage you take when you get back."

"All right. How much time do I have to get ready?"

"The captain wants us to get moving on this, but I say take a couple hours; make sure you've got the right supplies with you. Also, we need to give Chief Clemens time to prep two shuttles."

"Not transporters?" B'Elanna asked. "And why two?"

"One is to take you two down and the other is to pick up the Monorhans. The captain decided we might not want to tip our hand about the transporter just yet."

"Ace up her sleeve, huh? Well, I can't fault her for that." B'Elanna sighed and sat down on the corner of the worktable, then picked up the microspanner again. "Did you talk to her about keeping our noses out of everyone else's business?"

"I did."

"And what did she say?"

"In a nutshell, she said she understands your position, but that we have responsibilities."

B'Elanna rolled her eyes. "What responsibilities?" she asked irritably.

"As sentient beings, B'Elanna," Chakotay said flatly. "As decent, moral individuals in a cold, indifferent universe."

For several seconds, all B'Elanna could do was toy with her microspanner. "I *hate* that argument," she said. "There's no refuting it."

"None that I've found so far."

"Fine," she said replacing the tool again. "I'm going to get shots and kiss my boyfriend."

"A good plan. Go do it."

Just as the door to the office was opening, Chakotay's combadge chirped. *"Commander?"* it said. *"Chief Clemens here."*

Chakotay tapped the badge. "Go ahead, Chief."

"We have a bit of a problem down here on the hangar deck. I

could use some clarification. I got one functioning shuttle down here right now. I'm figuring it'll be a couple hours until I can get the other one together."

"No problem, Chief. B'Elanna and Seven aren't leaving for a couple hours."

"But you want to send someone down to pick up the local dignitaries now? I figure we got a lot going on around here, so why wait?"

Chakotay pondered the request for all of two seconds. "Finish prepping the shuttle, Chief. I'll be down in ten minutes. See if you can find me a copilot."

"I'll ask around, Commander. Thanks."

"And, Chief?"

"Sir?"

"Why do we have only one shuttle that can fly right now?"

"Because you all keep breaking them."

There weren't many people on *Voyager* who were permitted to be quite so forthright, but Chief Clemens was one of them. Chakotay nodded. "Point taken, Chief. Thanks."

"See you in ten, Commander."

After Chakotay signed off, B'Elanna asked, "You're going to go get the Monorhans?"

"I haven't flown for a while," he said.

"But you're not leaving yourself enough time for injections and lectures from the Doctor."

"The privileges of command. And, besides, I'll only be down there for a few minutes."

"Famous last words," B'Elanna said, but let the topic drop. Chakotay was a cautious fellow.

"Commander Chakotay has departed to retrieve Shalla Kiiy's experts," Ziv reported. "And Lieutenant Torres and Seven of Nine will be leaving shortly."

"Excellent," Sem replied. *"This has gone as well as could be expected. If anything should happen to you or the Voyagers, at least we have their engineers and the shuttle to examine."*

Ziv accepted the compliments, though he did not like knowing his *rih-hara-tan* had pondered what to do if his hosts left the system without returning. He was glad the rest of the *hara* had gone to the mess hall for a late dinner. They did not need to hear any of this. "Do you know who Shalla Kiiy asked to come to *Voyager?*"

The *rih-hara-tan* checked her notepad, but Ziv knew she was making a show of it. Finally, she said, *"An astrophysicist named Morsa. Do you know him?"*

"No."

"And her historical specialist is . . ." The show continued as the *rih-hara-tan* twisted her face into an expression of mock surprise. *"I hope this won't present any problems, but Kiiy has sent someone named Professor Sem. I believe you know her?"*

Ziv closed his eyes and involuntarily contracted his neck muscles. *Of course. Because this day hasn't been difficult enough.* Aloud, he said, "Yes, my *rih.* I await your arrival."

"Excellent, Ziv."

"But Captain Janeway," Ziv said, his mind racing. "Might she not wonder why such an important person would be risking herself in such an endeavor?"

"She might," Sem said. *"Or she may think I am a responsible leader, just like she is. I wish to be on the scene, to lend aid in any manner I can, especially since so many of my people have died this day. Is it really so unlikely that I would be a historical expert, too?"*

Especially since you are, Ziv thought. "Not unlikely at all, my *rih*."

With a nod and a sly smile, but no other comment, the *rih-hara-tan* signed off.

Monorha may have always been like this, Chakotay thought as the shuttle dropped down below the cloud layer, *but I hope not.* Hectares of barren rock bordered by roiling sea slipped beneath the shuttle's prow. There were no signs of green vegetation, though here and there he saw patches of gray that might have been some kind of fungus or hardy lichen.

While the atmosphere was not actually corrosive, breathing it for any length of time would make him feel like someone was scrubbing his bronchial tubes with chemical abrasives. Scans showed that the seas still lived, the Monorhan version of plankton still able to survive, but microscopic anaerobic organisms were proliferating, coating the waters in large gray slicks. The deeps of the ocean were dying, with several dozen species of large predators and game fish failing. Chakotay began to wonder about their earlier assessment that the Monorhans

were a predatory species. How could they have evolved
from pack hunters when there was so little landmass?

Ensign Smothers, the copilot Clemens had found for
him, announced, "Coming up on our coordinates,
Commander." Twenty kilometers ahead, Chakotay spotted the curve of the lead-colored hillside that Shalla Kiiy
had described. Behind it, the same dull color, rose what
might have been another hillside, except that this one
sketched an impossibly precise curve against the russet
sky. "How much power do you think their shields take,
sir?"

Chakotay couldn't even begin to guess. If the
Monorhans had some form of matter-antimatter generator, this wouldn't be a problem, but the scans they had
made of the transport hadn't shown anything more sophisticated than crude fusion reactors. *Impressive in its
way,* Chakotay decided, struggling to be fair. *If not for Ze-
fram Cochrane and the arrival of the Vulcans, Earth might have
ended up looking a great deal like this.*

Two minutes later, Smothers pointed out the curved
airlock door. "There it is, sir. Just where they said."

"I see it, Jim. Hang on. I'm going to go in slow so
everyone can have a look." Switching over from impulse
engines to a-grav, the shuttle shimmied slightly.

"The shields are still up, sir."

"I know, Ensign."

"Yes, sir," Smothers said. "It'll just make the landing a
little . . ." Nearing the ground, the shuttle bucked once,
then again, as the shields readjusted for the proximity of
the ground. "A little bumpy, sir."

"Yes, Ensign. Duly noted."

The shuttle touched down with no additional dramatics. After powering down the engines, Chakotay pushed his chair away from the console and put his hands behind his head. Smothers looked at him questioningly, but did not speak.

"Say what's on your mind, Ensign."

Smothers swallowed, then nodded. "We're not going in?"

"No," Chakotay said. "We're waiting right here until our guests come out to meet us. I have no desire to be exposed to any more hard radiation than necessary."

"Fine by me," Smothers said. "Those shots the Doc gives us make me bloat." He gave Chakotay a sidelong glance. "But that's not the only reason, is it?"

"Good observation, Ensign," Chakotay said. "Maybe I'm getting a suspicious nature in my old age, but I've seen too many of these little errands go wrong."

"Don't you worry the Monorhans will think we're being rude?"

Chakotay shrugged. "Who knows what the Monorhans consider rude? I'd prefer not to take any chances." In actuality, Chakotay was fairly certain the Monorhans *would* find his actions rude, but B'Elanna's comment had stuck in his craw. *Time to listen to some of my own advice and be cautious.*

Five minutes later, his caution was rewarded. The airlock cycled open and two broad-shouldered figures loped out, both wearing what Chakotay would have found to be heavy, uncomfortable environment suits, but to the Monorhans were probably no more than a minor annoyance. "Wait until they're five meters away, Smothers, then lower the shields and open the hatch."

"Got it, sir."

"Are you watching the airlock?"

"Yes, sir. Are we expecting to see something?"

"No. Just being careful."

The Monorhans, too, were being careful, both of them taking their time picking across the broken concrete outside the airlock.

"Can you run a scan on the forcefields, Smothers? And anything you can tell me about their environment suits would be useful."

Smothers attempted to coax useful information out of the shuttle's small sensor package. "Not much on the shields, sir. I'm reading about twenty gigawatts, a lot of heat radiating into the atmosphere. If their planet wasn't already such a mess, I'd say that these fields weren't doing them much good. Otherwise, there's nothing revolutionary about what I'm seeing: they're the great-great-grandfathers of *Voyager*'s shields."

"And the suits?"

"Again, nothing too interesting. These might be the short-range version, because they're not recycling water or atmo. Just a small air bottle on the back, some decent linings in the hoods to keep the rads out. That's it, really."

"All right, Ensign. They're close enough. Drop the shields and open the hatch. Let's get out of here as fast as we can."

The Monorhans knuckled into the shuttle—the first one's shoulders were as wide as the hatch—then waited patiently while Chakotay and Smothers helped them remove their bulky hoods and packs. When they were uncovered, Chakotay was surprised to find that the second figure was a female. Though shaped like Ziv and the others, she was a third smaller and wore the same shapeless tunic Shalla Kiiy had. Fortunately, Tuvok's patch to the universal translator worked with the shuttle's smaller unit, and they were able to communicate.

A thought struck Chakotay suddenly, one that he realized should have occurred to him hours ago. "Only two of you?" he asked.

The female replied, "Yes, just two. Did Shalla Kiiy indicate there might be more?"

"No," Chakotay said. "We don't know much about this yet, but Captain Ziv's *hara* is larger. It never occurred to me that a *hara* could be only two."

"We are not a *hara*, Commander," the woman said. "There is no formal link between us. Not all Monorhans choose to be in *hara*, sometimes for personal reasons, sometimes professional. Some occupations make the *hara* link quite impractical. Others are simply congenitally incapable—a small, sad minority. For myself, my life has taken me down many paths. I have been in *hara*, both as *haran* and *haras*, but today I travel only as myself, as Sem, *rih-hara-tan*."

"Sem?" Chakotay asked. "Aren't you Ziv's leader?"

"The *rih-hara-tan* of Ziv's tribe," Sem said. "Yes."

Chakotay studied the small figure for several seconds, trying to read something in her expression, but finally had to give up. She was, after all, an alien. He could not know what was in her heart by what he read on her face. *Not any more than I could with most humans,* he concluded, but there was something . . . something about her that made the skin on the back of his scalp itch. "All right," Chakotay finally said. "If you'll just strap yourselves in, we'll be on our way."

Settling into the pilot's chair, Chakotay softly asked Smothers if the shields were back up. "Just as soon as the door shut behind them, sir."

"Good job, Ensign. Get us back home. I'm going to mind the sensors as we fly."

"Yes, sir."

Chakotay kept a careful watch on the sensor output, finding nothing unusual as they traveled, but only really letting out his breath completely when he picked up *Voyager* on the short-range scopes. Just as they slipped into the shuttlebay, the second shuttle, with B'Elanna at the pilot's station, was lifting up off the deck. B'Elanna even waved and smiled as they slid past and through the forcefield.

Maybe I've been letting my sense of caution get the best of me, he thought as the shuttle's pads clicked against the deck. *Maybe everything will be fine.* But it was hard to shake B'Elanna's comment out of his head.

Famous last words.

Chapter 8

And everything had been going so well, too. B'Elanna thought.

The Doctor had let Tom out of sickbay duty so there was time for a proper goodbye before B'Elanna headed down to deck ten and the shuttlebay. When she got there, Clemens was just finishing refastening his preflight and did *not* give her one of his *Why don't you send your people down here to help me with these things?* looks. The engines powered up on the first try, and all the diagnostics looked good. Seven showed up on time (no surprise there, really), but she *didn't* recheck all the shuttle's systems before strapping in. The shuttle's nav computer successfully downloaded Chakotay's sensor logs as they passed each other, and, hey, Seven was even fairly quiet and unannoying except for the standard entirely understandable system reports. The ten-minute flight into Monorha's lower stratosphere was utterly, completely predictable.

Humming something cheerful and tuneless, B'Elanna had just begun to bring the shuttle in below the cloud layer, leveling off, their airspeed just over six hundred klicks per hour, when every single system went into catastrophic failure. Suddenly, the only light in the cabin was the rosy glow of the sun through the port windows. B'Elanna's pupils snapped open so fast in a frantic attempt to absorb all possible light that she thought she heard them pop. Her bowels contracted, and the adrenaline surge hit her like a brick to the back of the head. Time dilated and slowed.

"Seven . . . ? " she began, and then bit off the word. *No point in asking questions,* she thought as she pressed the first switch in the restart sequence. *Don't think about what just happened. Don't think about how you're in a brick losing altitude damn fast. Don't even think about the hole that you're going to make in the landscape. Just* start the engines. She touched the second switch in the restart sequence. Time crawled. *Why is this taking so long!?* One more switch and she would know if the engines were going to fire up. Emergency lights flickered on around her. *At least the batteries are working.* If the engines didn't start . . . well, they had a couple of other options, but, again, no point in getting too far ahead of herself.

Beside her, Seven said, "Lieutenant . . ."

"Not now, Seven!"

The shock wave crashed into the shuttle like a tsunami rolling into a paper boat. G forces crushed B'Elanna toward the stern, forcing her hands away from the console. Around her, lights flickered as the shuttle began to spin, sun flashing past the viewports. B'Elanna's internal organs were smashed up against her trunk's interior walls, and she would have vomited if the centrifugal force hadn't been shoving everything down. *I'm going to black out,* she thought.

The shuttle stopped spinning as suddenly as it began, jerking B'Elanna painfully against the harness straps, making her gag and retch.

"Inertial dampeners on," Seven announced. Somewhere behind B'Elanna, a panel burst apart in a shower of sparks. She looked back over her shoulder to see if the fire-control systems were functioning. Chemical extinguishers deployed out of the walls and two seconds later shut off.

"Battery couplings," B'Elanna said. "You just blew them out."

"It was that or die, Lieutenant."

Glancing out the window, B'Elanna could see that they were still spinning, but with the inertial dampeners on, they were not subject to the effect. Switching the dampeners on had been a brilliant idea, but such systems weren't designed to turn on without having the engines turning over. She didn't reply to Seven's comment, but said instead, "We're falling up."

"The shock wave," Seven said, calmly checking her systems console. "We will begin to fall again in fourteen seconds. I suggest you restart the engines."

Biting back a suggestion of her own, B'Elanna began to work the console again. The shock had rescrambled all the shuttle's systems, so she had to begin the sequence from zero. This time, she made it through, but when she hit the last control, every light on the navigation console flashed, then died. More showers of sparks behind her. *Damn, damn, damn! Not good!* B'Elanna thought. *Why isn't* Voyager *beaming us out?* Maybe the radiation was blocking sensors again. . . .

Scanning the board in front of her, B'Elanna noted that the computer was rerouting power away from nonessential systems and trying to restart for her. Risking queasiness, she glanced out the window again and saw that they must have reached the peak of their arc and were beginning to fall again. "Any idea how high up we are?" she asked.

"Not far enough up that gravity isn't an issue, Lieutenant."

Right, B'Elanna thought, then added, *Smartass.* More lights on the panel were green, but the autostart wasn't working. The batteries were shot. *Reroute power from life-support,* she thought. *Those systems are on a separate power source.* Of course, that would mean losing inertial control. "Brace yourself."

Not waiting for Seven to respond, B'Elanna pressed herself back as firmly as she could into her chair, mashing her head against the support, then touched the switch that would shunt power from life-support to the thrusters. Her last coherent thought was *I hope we're not pointed at the ground.*

Ready to scream, ready to bellow to the universe how unfair it was that she should die here and now, B'Elanna Torres saw her world turn red, then black.

~

Then there was white. The white was pain felt first behind the eyes, as if someone were touching the backs of
the sockets with a white-hot welding torch. Opening her
mouth so wide she heard her jaw crack, B'Elanna tried to
scream, but couldn't get air into her lungs. Another
white-hot coal touched her neck, and B'Elanna tried to
swat it away, but her arms were either too heavy or tied to
the chair's armrests. *Seven! She's pierced me with those damn
tubules! She's turning me into a Borg!*

"Lieutenant! Stop struggling!" Seven shouted. "We
have little enough supplies as it is!" The white-hot coal
hissed as it touched her again, B'Elanna's skin charring
and curling away from the brand.

The pain receded. Everything felt lighter and
B'Elanna's arms floated up into the air over her head.
White light turned pinkish and shapes came into focus.
There was a blob in front of her and it was saying, "Can
you hear me, Lieutenant?"

"I'm fine," B'Elanna said, though her mouth felt
numb and her tongue was sandpapery. "Do we have any
water?"

The Seven-shaped blob disappeared, and B'Elanna
heard rustling sounds. Illogically, B'Elanna found herself
thinking of the kitchen cabinets in the house when she
was a girl and her dad shifting objects inside while looking for something to make for supper. Neither he nor
B'Elanna were particularly fussy eaters, so "cooking" was
often a matter of juxtaposing items until they found two
roughly compatible foods. *Tomato sauce and beans?*

B'Elanna thought. *Sure! Nothing wrong there! Replicated chicken and cucumbers? Both good so they're good together!*

"What happened?" B'Elanna groaned.

"You were unconscious when we landed," Seven said. "The shuttle's medical tricorder recommended I treat you for shock. We were without inertial dampeners for almost two minutes while the computer struggled to regain control of the shuttle."

"No," B'Elanna said. "Before that. What happened? What knocked us out of the sky?"

"I have not been able to access the sensor logs yet, but I believe we were struck by a shock wave."

"Well, obviously," B'Elanna said testily. "But a shock wave from *what*? A weapon? An industrial accident? Some other kind of explosion? Was it directed at us or were we simply caught in the blast?"

B'Elanna heard Seven sigh. "I repeat, Lieutenant, I have not had time to check the sensor logs. The discharge, whatever it was, disrupted our electrical systems, which suggests some kind of electromagnetic pulse."

Considering the options, B'Elanna asked, "Atomics? Could the Monorhans be using nuclear explosives? That would be insane."

"The Monorhans strike me as a desperate people. Desperate people do foolish things."

Cupping her forehead, B'Elanna collected her thoughts and considered Seven's observations. She was right about the last thing: The Monorhans were desperate. But could their desperation drive them to start lobbing nuclear weapons at each other? And if that was the case, could she and Seven have absorbed a lethal dose? Well, not that Seven would worry about that. . . . Likely her nanoprobes had already converted the rems into useful packets of energy that the drone could live off of for centuries to come. She looked up at her companion and was annoyed to see that her outline was still fuzzy. "What's wrong with my eyes?" she asked.

"Your corneas were damaged by g forces," Seven replied crisply, "but the drugs I have administered will deal with the worst of that effect. Your organs may also be bruised, but that will not be fatal. Merely painful."

"Yeah," B'Elanna said as she tried to sit up. "Painful. Yes." After struggling into a seated position, she felt so exhausted she wanted to lie back down again. "This has been another awful day."

"Really?" Seven asked. "I cannot say that I have noticed it is any worse than most of your days." The comment confused B'Elanna. *Is she saying that all my days are bad or that this one hasn't been worse than most of them?*

"What do you mean?" B'Elanna asked as she surveyed the shuttle's interior. The lights were on—a good sign—but the bulkheads were extensively charred and supplies had tumbled out of every cabinet onto the deck, a bad sign. *Rough landing,* she thought. *Glad I missed it.*

Seven was checking the supplies in the emergency medical kit. "I have observed that you complain a great deal, Lieutenant, so my assumption is that all your days are bad."

"Shut the hell up!" B'Elanna exclaimed much too

loudly. "OW!" Her ears rang and her eyes throbbed. "I thought you gave me some kind of analgesic."

"I did," Seven said. "But not very much. We must ration supplies as we cannot be certain how much longer we will be here."

"What time is it now?" B'Elanna asked, wrestling the chair back into an upright position. "And how long has it been since we left the ship? Have they contacted us yet? I was surprised when there was no emergency beam-out. Maybe it's better that we didn't because, yow, Clemens is not gonna be happy." She squinted at the navigation console. "I'm having trouble focusing. Is that supposed to happen?"

Seven inhaled deeply, then sighed heavily and answered in rapid, clipped tones. "It is seventeen hundred hours and forty two minutes. No, *Voyager* has not attempted to contact us and I have been preoccupied with other matters, so before you ask, no, I have not attempted to contact *them*. I, too, was surprised when there was no beam-out, but perhaps that speaks to the situation with regard to *Voyager;* that they were affected by the shock wave, too. Yes, Mr. Clemens will no doubt be angry, but his anticipation of trouble is what motivated him to install the emergency restart software packages, which saved our lives. And, last, yes, I am not surprised you are having trouble focusing; the damage to your corneas was extensive. It may take a few hours until they are fully repaired." She inhaled again, then said more softly, "If you think you are feeling slightly . . . hyperactive . . . it may be a result of the mild stimulant I added to the hypo. I thought you might be feeling sluggish after the accident."

B'Elanna had wondered why the top of her scalp had been tingling. "Ah," she said, but decided not to make an issue of it. *Too many other things to do.* "What's our status? Do we have power? Sensors?"

"Yes and yes. The engines are functional, though I fear the shuttle may have taken damage during reentry."

Another thought suddenly presented itself. "How are you, Seven? I seem to have taken the worst of it."

"Several of my ribs are broken, Lieutenant, and one of them pierced my left lung," Seven said calmly. "Also, I strained my wrist and my hand was burned when I attempted to put out a small electrical fire."

B'Elanna squinted at her. Though fuzzy, Seven appeared more or less as she always did: composed, unflappable, serene in a cranky sort of way. "How can I help?"

She shook her head. "The nanoprobes in my system are already at work repairing most of the damage, thank you." She held up her hand and B'Elanna saw a small, gradually fading pinkish patch.

"Must be nice," B'Elanna commented, but did not add *having a bunch of little robots crawling around in your bloodstream.*

"It has its advantages" Seven acknowledged. "We should attempt to contact *Voyager.* I find it troubling that they have not hailed us yet."

"Agreed." B'Elanna checked the shuttle's comm system. Green bars on all displays. She smiled. All things considered, the shuttle self-repair systems were doing their job. Chief Clemens would be pleased. *"Voyager,* this is the shuttle *Montpelier.* Please respond." No one replied. She checked the system again, but found no problems.

Seven was already working the sensors, but her knit brow told B'Elanna she was getting no satisfaction. "We're approximately seven hundred kilometers from our intended destination," she announced. "We've landed in what appears to be a dry lake bed and the sun will be setting locally in approximately twenty-two minutes."

"Wonderful. What exactly does this have to do with *Voyager?"*

"Nothing, Lieutenant. I just thought you'd enjoy some irrelevant chatter while I worked. I assumed you would find it soothing."

B'Elanna closed her eyes and rubbed them, realizing she must still be in some light form of shock, because the only thought going through her head was *Please, Tom. Please still be out there, because if she's the only one left I may just have to kill myself. Or her.*

Seven continued to work for several more minutes until she finally announced, *"Voyager* is not there."

"Can you tell where she went? Did she leave orbit? If so, why? Did she attempt to land? Or . . . did something else happen?"

Seven shook her head. "There is insufficient information, Lieutenant. Also, the local radiation levels . . ."

". . . Make it very hard to scan. Right. But is there any evidence of a matter-antimatter explosion? That would show up no matter what."

"None."

"Well, that's something. She didn't blow up."

"The *core* did not blow up," Seven corrected. "The ship might have been destroyed without the core being damaged."

"All right," she snapped. *"Fine.* It could have happened. But probably not. So let's focus on the most likely possibilities. What are they?"

"That *Voyager* was forced to leave orbit in order to avoid the shock wave is the most likely scenario," Seven reasoned. "A secondary possibility is, as you said, the ship was forced to land, perhaps on some other part of the planet. If that happened, communication may be difficult to achieve without an orbital relay—"

B'Elanna pointed at the Borg, then turned back to the communication console. "Good!" she said. "Very good! I should have thought of that!"

"We do not have communication satellites, Lieutenant. Unless Chief Clemens has been working overtime."

"Was that a joke?"

"Not intentionally."

"Didn't think so," she said, and pulled up a map of the sky directly overhead. Squinting to keep her eyes focused, B'Elanna scanned the heavens for several minutes. "Hello," she said at last.

"You have found a communications satellite?"

"Not exactly. It's some kind of low-orbit surveillance drone, I think. Somebody obviously doesn't trust somebody else. Maybe it recorded what happened to *Voyager.*"

"What leads you to believe it was not pointed at the planet?"

B'Elanna paused to stare at her. "If an alien starship suddenly appeared in the sky above your world, what would *you* do with your spy satellites?"

Seven considered, then said, "I concede the point."

Wow, B'Elanna thought as she absentmindedly punched through the spy satellite's laughable encryption software and accessed the playback routines. *Something is finally going right today.*

Harry Kim bent double, gently touched his forehead to the long-range sensor console, and begged, *begged* his stomach to continue to play nice with the tomato soup he had for lunch. *Please,* he thought. *I do not want to have to explain to B'Elanna why she needs to disassemble the whole console and clean every component.* The thought of his friend's ire gave him the necessary resolve, and Harry felt his nausea recede. Glancing up over the console, he was moderately gratified to see that he was not the only person the energy wave had distressed. With a grace and composure Harry did not think he could ever possess, Clarice Knowles at the pilot's station quickly turned her head to the left, spat up something into an empty coffee cup, then turned her complete attention back to her board. Ensign Grench, who had been manning the security station, abruptly became as stiff as a board and fell face-forward onto the deck.

Startled, Harry looked around the bridge to make sure that no one else was tumbling over, saw that no one was, then realized that no one else had seen Grench collapse. Knees rubbery and wobbling, Harry staggered the three steps across the deck to where Grench lay and began a cursory examination. "Grench?" he said, and tried to turn the Bolian over. "Can you hear me?"

Grench's eyes were open and his lips were moving, but only incoherent sounds emerged. A moment later, his entire body began to jerk and spasm and a thin yellow foam oozed from the corners of his mouth, clashing garishly with the Bolian's blue skin. Harry pulled away, inexplicably frightened that the Bolian might have a horrible new disease, but then his training caught up with his fear. "He's having a seizure," Harry said aloud, more to get his own brain started than to inform anyone on the bridge.

"Make sure he doesn't swallow his tongue," Knowles shouted over her shoulder. A lifetime of first-aid classes came flooding back, and he pried open Grench's mouth to make sure his airway was clear. Satisfied that the Bolian was breathing, Harry leaped up, found a padd, and yanked the heavy stylus from the clip. Hoping that Bolians didn't have extra-powerful jaw muscles, he inserted the stylus between Grench's teeth and watched for several seconds to make sure he wouldn't accidentally swallow it. Harry tapped his combadge and called sickbay, but was answered by the Doctor's automated triage program.

"Please state the nature of the medical emergency. Give as much detail as necessary, your location, and steps being taken to treat the patient."

"It's Harry Kim, Doc, on the bridge. Ensign Grench is having a seizure. He's breathing and I don't think he's in any immediate danger. I, uh, shoved a stylus between his jaws."

When he stopped talking, the program parsed Harry's report and replied, *"Thank you, Ensign Kim. Your emergency has been assigned a B priority. Your treatment for Ensign Grench is acceptable. Please call again if Ensign Grench's condition appears to grow worse. Someone from sickbay will contact you as soon as possible."*

Great, Harry thought as he rose. *Sickbay must be swamped. Still, that triage program seems to be working. That was a good idea. . . .*

"How is he, Harry?" the captain asked.

Harry hadn't seen her come onto the bridge, but his attention had been fixed on his patient. "He's okay, I think. Are you all right, Captain?"

Captain Janeway instinctively touched her stomach, smiled wanly, and said, "Fine," but then her expression became stern. "What happened? Where are we? Give me information, Harry."

Kim looked up at the main viewscreen. Either something was wrong with the exterior cameras or they were being blocked by some kind of forcefield. Where only moments before there had been a field of stars and the burnt-umber arc of Monorha in the screen's lower edge, now there was only a black field occasionally broken by pinprick flashes of white. "The planet's gone," he said, but felt inane as soon as the words were out of his mouth.

Without excusing himself, he stumbled to his station and began checking the sensor logs. Data flowing back to him was a confused jumble. Only minutes earlier, Harry had been cataloguing radiation from the Blue Eye, hoping he could send some useful information to B'Elanna about how to modify Monorha's shield generators, but now there was virtually no radiation at all, but only energy sputtering and arcing without any discernable pattern.

"Were the engines engaged?" he asked.

"Negative," Knowles shouted back. "Nothing. The engine room reported we were in standby mode. Impulse only."

None of this makes any sense, Harry thought, and shook his head. *Something's wrong with me.*

"What hit us, Harry?" Captain Janeway asked, but her words were slightly slurred. "What can the sensor logs tell us?"

Sensor logs. Good idea. "Checking, Captain," he said. "Scans say that four minutes ago . . ." *Four minutes? Only four minutes?* "Four minutes ago we were hit by an energy wave that emanated from the surface of Moronha. . . . Sorry, Monorha . . . The surge covered most of the northwestern hemisphere. I can't make sense of what the scans are saying. There was a shock wave in the atmosphere, but none of that reached us up here."

"A shock wave caused by what?" the captain asked. "In the atmosphere? On the surface? How powerful? Was anyone on the surface injured?"

Harry shook his head in frustration, his thoughts sluggish. "I can't tell, Captain."

"An underground test, perhaps?"

"Possible," Harry said. He knew that they used to do underground nuclear tests back on Earth before someone figured out the effects such blasts had on the biosphere.

"What about the shuttles?"

Shuttles? Harry shook his head again and was tempted to smack his own face. "Shuttles," he said aloud. "Wait. Sorry, Captain, let me check."

"We're all feeling it, Harry," she said, "but shake it off. I need you to focus."

The turbolift doors snapped open and two crewmen and Tuvok stepped off the car. Pointing the crewmen at Grench, Tuvok called, "Is everyone else all right?"

"None of us is great," the captain said, "but we're still here. Take care of the ensign."

The Bolian was already on the stretcher and was floating through the doors guided by the crewmen. Harry was glad to see him getting help, glad that sickbay had been able to respond so quickly.

"Shall I stay on the bridge, Captain? I am not as disabled by the problem plaguing the ship as some others." But Harry could see that "not as disabled" didn't mean "unaffected." There were dark circles under Tuvok's eyes, evidence of the strain he was experiencing.

"Stay, Tuvok. Harry is examining the sensor logs, but I want you to check the shields. If this disorientation is caused by something external . . ."

Tuvok didn't even respond, but stepped up to his station and began checking shields.

"The shuttles, Harry."

Shuttles. Right. He did the simple thing first and checked the shuttlebay logs. "Commander Chakotay and his party were on board when the energy surge hit, Captain. Looks like he's okay, though the bay forcefields flickered. Some debris got sucked out."

"No crewmen though?"

"No, everyone is accounted for."

"What about B'Elanna and Seven?"

Harry searched the logs for a sign of the second shuttle's fate. *There they are approaching the atmosphere. Here's their signature crossing into the daylight side of the hemisphere. And then . . .* "I don't know, Captain. I see them getting tossed by the same surge, but I can't tell what happened. The shuttle didn't break up, but I can't determine what else might have happened after we were hit."

"But hit by *what,* Ensign?" Captain Janeway snapped, rising from her chair. "Where are we? Where are the *stars?!*"

Dumbstruck, staring, Harry ran his hands over the control panel, trying to make sense of what was happening. *The captain is shouting at me,* he thought. This wasn't the first time it had happened and Harry knew that he wasn't so thin-skinned that a shout should bother him so much, but he was all too conscious of the fact that he was close to breaking into tears. *It's this space,* he thought. *There's something wrong with it. But the scanners can't scan it.*

A new idea struck him: Maybe the scanners were out of calibration. Maybe the energy surge blew out the configuration files and all he needed to do was do a reset. *I'll do that,* he thought. *I'll reset them and everything will work and I'll figure this out and the captain won't yell at me anymore.*

The shuttlebay forcefield *dropped.* Just minutes earlier, Chakotay had settled the shuttle onto the deck, shut down the engines, and was seconds away from touching the control that would have opened the hatch. Then, for no reason that he could name, Chakotay looked out the bow viewport and watched as every loose item in the bay abruptly began to tumble and fly across the deck toward the main door. Klaxons sounded and the handful of technicians who had been working on shuttles either quickly shut themselves into their vessels or managed to seal themselves in the safety pods that lined the walls for exactly this sort of situation.

Chakotay heard the hurricane rush of air even through the shuttle's walls and wondered if he should strap back in and restart the shuttle's engines. If *Voyager* was being attacked, he might be able to do more good outside the ship. *Or I could get the environment suit out of the locker and try for the airlock,* he thought. *All the atmosphere is going to be gone in a minute.* The solid bay doors would already be sliding into place—he couldn't see from where he was standing—but the flight deck was a large, open space and would take time to repressurize.

"Smothers," Chakotay said. "Restart the engines. We might need to get out of here."

Smothers wasn't listening. Chakotay turned to see what he was doing and saw his copilot staring back into the passenger section at the Monorhans. Chakotay looked back at them, too, and they stared in response, both leaning into the center aisle, polite, but curious.

"Smothers," Chakotay repeated. "Respond. Restart the engines."

Nothing.

Chakotay shook his shoulder, but the ensign was completely unresponsive.

"Commander Chakotay?" Sem asked. "What is happening?"

He shook his head, and with his tongue feeling thick in his mouth, Chakotay said, "The forcefield door failed. An accident maybe. It's all right, though."

"Your crewman is all right?" Sem asked. Behind her Morsa rose and seemed to fill the entire rear third of the shuttle.

"I'm not sure," Chakotay said, leaning over to get a closer look at the glassy-eyed Smothers. "I think I should call the bridge and find out what's happening. It may turn out to be safer for you if we return to the planet."

"We hope not," Sem said. "We came to assist. If something has gone awry, we wish to stay and offer our services."

Chakotay nodded. "I appreciate the offer, you dog-faced alien. If I can think of anything that needs fetching, I'll . . ." He felt his own eyebrows sliding up his forehead and his mouth hanging open. *What did I just say?*

Sem looked at him curiously, her long neck snaking to the left, then right. "Something is wrong with your translator devices, Commander. I could not understand what you just said. What does 'dog' mean?"

"Yes," Chakotay replied. "I heard it, too. Something is wrong with the translator. Maybe it's related to what's happened to the hatch." *Nothing is wrong with the translator,* he thought. *That was me, though they have no way of knowing it. What's happening to me?*

"Commander?" the second Monorhan (what was his name?) asked, his voice rumbling loudly in the small space. "What is wrong?"

"The light," Chakotay said, shutting his eyes. Suddenly, the overhead lamps began to strobe fiercely. Chakotay heard a series of brief, sharp popping sounds from inside the bulkheads.

"Commander," Sem asked. "What was that? I felt something."

Smothers whispered, "Yes, the light."

"Commander?" Sem asked. "What light?"

"Over your heads," Chakotay said. "Can't you see it?"

"I see nothing," Sem said, a note of worry creeping into her voice. "Except what was here only a moment ago. Perhaps you are ill?"

Perhaps I am, Chakotay thought. *Could the shuttle be leaking atmosphere?* But, no, that was ridiculous. How could they have made it to the ship if it was? He tried to open his eyes against the glare, but quickly spun away. Unclenching his eyes for a moment, Chakotay looked at Smothers, but was baffled to see that his features were not, as he had expected, bathed in light. Instead, oddly, tears were running down the ensign's cheeks, though they did not appear to be tears of pain, but rather of some rhapsodic joy.

"The light," Smothers whispered.

"What light?" Sem asked, her voice sharp with impatience. "Is this some game, Commander? Are we your prisoners now and this is how you will torment us?"

"No," Chakotay shouted in reply. "Whatever is happening, we're not doing it."

"He's right," Morsa said, his voice now surprisingly soft. "There's a light." Chakotay heard a thump as if something heavy had fallen to the ground.

The next thing he heard was Sem saying, "Morsa, get up. Get off the deck. Morsa, look at me. *Look at me!*"

But Morsa, apparently, did not or could not. Facing the viewport, Chakotay thought it was safe to open his eyes, but the urge to look back over his shoulder was almost overwhelming.

"She disappeared," B'Elanna said.

"Play it back again slowly."

"I'll try," B'Elanna said, "but the scan rate is low. Look how grainy the image is." A moment later, she had the tiny silhouette of *Voyager* back on the monitor and ran the recording forward as slowly as the satellite's playback would permit. "See?" she said. "It happens practically between two frames: one second there; the next, gone."

"And no evidence of debris."

"None. They weren't destroyed."

"A cloak?"

"Did *you* build a cloaking device? If you didn't and I didn't, then I'd say no cloak."

"Then where are they?" Seven asked.

Harry completed his check of the sensors, pleased with what he had found. He had been right: The whole system had reset when the energy surge hit. Now all he had to do was recalibrate and he would be able to answer the captain's question again and she would like him again. He smiled goofily. All would be well.

With what he felt was an appropriate amount of flourish, Harry pressed the control sequence that would bring the sensors back online. When he touched the last control, his arm sank into the console up to his elbow.

"Put him on the examination table, gentlemen," the Doctor said to the crewmen as Paris finished closing the wound on Ensign Chilkis's forehead. Chilkis had said he'd "come over all funny," only one of a couple dozen similar complaints Tom had heard after returning to sickbay.

Tom was glad to be useful, though he wasn't sure precisely how useful he was being. He was fumble-fingered and he was finding it difficult to remember formerly well-practiced routines. Even now, closing a scalp wound, Tom had difficulty keeping the stud on the skin regenerator depressed while running it lightly over the wound. The worst part was that he *knew* he was being stupid, but wasn't precisely certain how much smarter he usually was.

Fortunately, whatever was affecting Tom (and, apparently, most everyone else on the ship) *wasn't* affecting the Doctor. He was his typical prickly, officious self. "Ensign Grench, my, my, what have you done to yourself?"

More than anything, Grench looked abashed and confused, as if he wasn't completely clear why he was in sickbay. Or anywhere, for that matter. "Don't know, Doctor," he said. "Just feel . . . funny."

"Mr. Paris—my tricorder, please. We must find out why Ensign Grench is feeling so humorous." The Doctor smiled as if he had just said something funny. Tom knew enough to smile, then remembered that he was supposed to be getting a tricorder.

"Here you go, Doc," Tom said, then realized that he was handing the doctor his skin regenerator. "Oops. Sorry. Let me get it."

"Mr. Paris, is it possible that you are being even less useful than usual?" the Doctor asked. "It hardly seems likely, yet here we are facing the question."

"Sorry, Doc. I said it once before and now I'm saying it again: Sorry." The surprising thing was that Tom felt genuinely aggrieved, his cheeks unexpectedly flushed.

The Doctor regarded him curiously as he removed the medical tricorder from Tom's hand. "Never mind, Mr. Paris."

"I'm okay," Tom said, embarrassed, but trying to sound businesslike. "Can Chilkis go now?"

"Did you sterilize the wound after sealing?"

"I think so."

"You *think* so?"

"I mean, I'll check."

The Doctor frowned. "A somewhat more satisfactory reply, though by this time I would have expected the answer to be 'Yes, he's ready to be released.' "

"Sorry." Tom hung his head and turned back to his patient, hoping and praying the conversation was over.

Hearing the medical tricorder purr, he knew it was, at least for a while. "Let's see what we have here, Mr. Grench. The report says you collapsed and had a bit of a seizure. Is that correct?" the Doctor asked.

"I think so," Grench said. "I don't remember. Is that why everything looks so funny?"

"Funny? Funny how?"

"Kind of bright and glowing. There's a prism around everything, like colors, but glittering."

"Very descriptive, Mr. Grench."

Tom finished with Chilkis, then looked to see who was next and was surprised to find that he was finished. "No more patients, Doc."

"Yes, the last few were frightened away. . . . No, please don't look like that, Mr. Paris. I cannot abide another long face. What's wrong with everyone today?"

Tom and Grench said in chorus, "I don't know."

"Of course you don't. This is why I'm the doctor. Oh."

Tom didn't like the catch he heard in the Doctor's voice.

"Something wrong?" Grench asked.

"What? Oh, no. I think Mr. Paris may have miscalibrated the tricorder. Yes, that must be it. . . ." Tom turned to the Doctor, wondering what he might have done, and was shocked by his sour expression.

Afraid to hear the answer, he asked, "Did I break it, Doc?"

"Something did. Something must have or I don't understand what I'm seeing. . . ."

Abruptly, Grench let out a sharp gasp and went rigid, arms stiff by his sides, toes pointed, and eyes staring wide.

The Doctor shouted. "Mr. Paris! Quickly!"

Tom ran to the biobed, sick with worry that his clumsiness with the tricorder may have created a problem. "What? What do you want?"

"A stasis field!" the Doctor shouted as he spun to the drug dispenser. "We may only have seconds! I'll see what I can do with . . ."

But they were already too late. His face fixed in a grimace of pain, Grench inhaled once so deeply that Tom thought his sides might burst, then released it in an explosive grunt. His stiffened arms fell over the sides of the biobed and Tom watched in fascinated horror as first one and then the other stretched out like ropes of maple syrup. The elongated limbs folded over onto themselves, then dribbled away from Grench's shoulders. A moment later, the Bolian's body wobbled, then lazily oozed away from the center of the bed in rubbery sheets until the only thing left was a sticky residue.

Tom and the Doctor stared at the viscous mess spreading around their feet, both of them rendered speechless for a count of one, two, three seconds. Then, without looking away, the Doctor said, "Computer, this is the chief medical officer, requesting a voice verification."

The computer replied blandly, *"Verified."*

"Quarantine."

Chapter 9

"We should stay."

"We must go."

"Stay."

Seven refused to reply. *Stupid Borg,* B'Elanna thought. *Doesn't even know how to have a decent argument.*

"The shuttle's self-repair routines will only go so far, Seven," B'Elanna said, trying to sound persuasive, abandoning the much more satisfying prospect of verbal combat. "If we stay, the two of us working together can have *Montpelier* off the ground inside a day."

"By which time any chance of assisting *Voyager* will have long passed," Seven replied tersely.

"How do we know we can help her? Especially dirtside. If we can get airborne, we could go inspect the site where she disappeared, maybe get a better idea what happened."

Seven sat down heavily in the copilot's chair, cradling her side cautiously. "And if we contact the Monorhans, we may be able to persuade them to let us use a space-craft."

"We don't even know if they *have* any more space-craft," B'Elanna said. She was eyeing the tool locker, itchy to do some real work. The sitting-and-talking was beginning to grate. "This isn't Earth, you know. No shuttle in every garage."

"Humans do not have shuttles in their garages," Seven said.

"My *point* is, these people just aren't that technologically advanced."

"Someone was sophisticated enough to produce the energy wave that brought us down and is probably responsible for *Voyager*'s disappearance."

Or destruction, came the grudging thought. B'Elanna rubbed her eyes and successfully resisted the urge to scream. While shouting at Seven would be satisfying, she knew it wouldn't produce any useful results. Logic might, though. "The city we were heading toward is probably still hundreds of kilometers away. We'll never get there without the shuttle."

The tiny lines around the corners of Seven's mouth turned downward—her version of a grimace—and she pointed at the sensor readout. "I have already shown you this," she said. "Using the data collected before the sensors failed, I have determined that there is a ninety-two percent chance that the energy wave was centered not ten kilometers from here. We could walk there in a matter of hours."

"Yes, you explained that," B'Elanna relented. "What you haven't explained is why we would want to go to the epicenter of the blast. What if it was a bomb? What if they were using nuclear weapons? Can your scans tell us that?"

Seven lowered her arm. "I cannot," she said. "However, if the shock wave was the result of an atomic blast, you would be showing signs of radiation sickness by now."

"Not with all the drugs the Doc pumped into me," B'Elanna said, hoping it was true. "And you *still* haven't answered the most important question! What could *be* there?"

"The device that affected *Voyager*," Seven replied coolly. "She was not destroyed, but the energy from the blast somehow pushed the ship out of phase. It is the only possible explanation."

"And I maintain that if we can get the shuttle off the ground, we can find the answers in space."

"Our journey to and from the epicenter will require less than twelve hours if we leave now. Would the shuttle's self-repair systems be able to finish their work before then?"

B'Elanna sighed resignedly. Seven had finally found the best argument: Even with both her and Seven working constantly, they would still have to wait for the shuttle's automation to repair key systems. She clenched her hands and shut her eyes. *I don't want to go explore a mystery with you!* she wanted to shout. *I want to stay here and fix things! That's what I do!* "We don't know what we're going to find," she finished weakly, the only other defense she could offer.

"Of course we don't," Seven said flatly. "But we may find our way back to *Voyager.* Or, at least, we may find a way to contact her."

B'Elanna nodded, but deeply resented her acquiescence. She hated the fact that Seven could find a way around her argument. She hated it when Seven was right.

Too many things were happening at once.

"Captain," Tuvok said. "The shields have dropped . . ."

"My hand!" Kim said with rising alarm. "Did anyone see what just happened to my hand?"

"Bridge, this is sickbay," said Paris from the intercom. *"Captain, the Doctor has just placed us under quarantine. And Ensign Grench, ma'am . . . I don't know how to say this . . ."* Janeway heard a staccato burst of small explosions in the bulkhead nearest the science station. A new set of alarms blared.

Another channel cut off Paris. *". . . Is the shuttlebay. The doors are shut, Captain, but Commander Chakotay just . . . I don't know how to say this, but he blew himself out of the shuttle and shot himself across the bay to the airlock. I think he may have hurt himself and I don't know what's happened to the Monorhans . . ."*

"Captain," Ensign Knowles said about every ten seconds, "what's our heading, ma'am? Where are we going? Which way, ma'am?"

Janeway's head hurt worst than it ever had. Once, long ago when she was eight or nine years old, she had come down with some kind of flu, something her father had accidentally brought home with him from a mission that the usual decontam screenings hadn't caught. She remembered lying in her bed for three days with the house automek constantly pinging at her, giving her such a headache that she could barely contain her rage. When she had finally been well enough that she could sit up, the first thing young Kathryn had done (after her mother was out of the room) was swat the awful device a shot with her pillow. Of course, it immediately beamed a message to her mother about what she had done, but that wasn't the point.

But what was the point?

The point was *her head hurt*. Janeway was certain it would stop hurting if everyone would simply be quiet for thirty seconds and let her collect her wits, but, no, everyone was talking, talking, talking to her, asking her things, pleading, demanding. Why wouldn't they just do what she wanted?

"Everyone!" she shouted, and everyone turned to look at her. Janeway wanted very, very badly to say simply, "SHUT UP!" But training ground so deeply into her being that it had virtually become part of her genetic code took over and she said, "One at a time." Turning to Tuvok, she asked, "Shields are down?"

"Yes, Captain."

Janeway almost yelled at him then, her oldest friend and advisor. She almost shouted at him the same way that she was fairly certain she had shouted at Harry Kim a few minutes earlier, but she stopped herself. Instead, she asked, "How are you feeling, Mr. Tuvok?"

The question caught the Vulcan off guard. He cocked his head to the side, thought for a moment, then replied, "Peculiar, Captain. I do not feel fully in control of myself."

"Neither do I, Mr. Tuvok." A chorus of me-eithers ran around the bridge. "No one does. Think about what you need to do to get the shields back up, Tuvok. Remember the sequence?"

Tuvok looked down at the console and laid his hands on the controls. "Yes, Captain."

"Do it, Tuvok."

Tuvok pressed a series of controls, and a moment later, the fog that had wreathed Janeway's mind thinned and the headache eased. She heard audible sighs all around the bridge.

"Better, Tuvok?" she asked.

The Vulcan stretched the muscles in his neck, first one, then the other, then arched an eyebrow at her. "A distinct improvement."

Janeway turned to Ensign Knowles, who was glancing back over her shoulder every ten seconds, though the expression of panic she had worn twenty seconds earlier was gone. "Hold this heading, Knowles, whatever it is. We'll try to figure out where we are in a moment."

"Aye, Captain."

"Bridge to sickbay," Janeway called, tapping her combadge.

"Sickbay. Paris here."

"Where's the Doctor, Tom?"

"I'm not sure you want to know, Captain."

"Tom!"

"He's scooping up what's left of Grench into a tub!"

"Put him on, Tom," Janeway said. "I need him."

Thirty seconds later, the Doctor came on. *"Captain,"* he said in clipped tones. *"I've placed sickbay in quarantine. There may be a disease agent on the loose that is fatal to Bolians."*

"I don't like to argue with you, Doctor, especially about medical matters, but I believe we have an entirely different kind of problem. Scan sickbay for radiation, please."

Over the comm, Janeway heard the distinctive whine of the medical tricorder and the Doctor muttering, *"Oh, dear."* Another minute passed.

"Doctor?"

"Another round of hyronalin, Captain. Bolians first. I've scanned Ensign Grench's, uh, remains and it would appear his people are particularly susceptible to the radiation permeating the ship."

"Understood, Doctor. Please get right on it. After you take care of the Bolians and get the process under way, come to the bridge. Oh, and check on Commander Chakotay in the shuttle hangar. I think he may have injured himself."

"Understood, Captain. And I will be calling off the quarantine."

"Thank you, Doctor. Now hurry, please." Janeway

marshaled her resources and turned back to Tuvok. "I'm going to the engine room to see what I can do to give Joe Carey a hand with more power for the shields. You have the bridge."

Heading for the door, she caught sight of Harry Kim, who was staring intently at his hand. "What's wrong, Harry? I know you can still feel it, but it's not as bad now, is it?"

"No, Captain," Harry said, his voice little more than a hoarse whisper. "But, Captain, a minute ago . . ." He pointed at the console before him, then reached down beside him and fumbled for his tricorder.

"What is it, Harry? Did the sensors go offline, too?"

"Yes," Harry replied. "But that wasn't the problem." Flipping open the device, Harry clumsily scanned the console, then his hand, then turned the display toward the captain so she could see the results. "Look," he said softly, as if he were afraid to speak too loudly. "Molecular cohesion tables."

Janeway studied the tables for several seconds, then tentatively tapped the console with her index finger. Looking Harry in the eye, she said, "Whatever it was that happened to Grench . . ."

"Yes, Captain?"

"I won't let it happen to you."

After a moment's hesitation, Harry nodded cautiously.

"Continue your scans, Ensign. See if you can find out what caused that Klaxon to go off. That was the bioneural circuitry alarm, wasn't it?"

"Yes, ma'am."

"And find out what happened to the stars."

Ziv, Diro, and Jara stepped aside to let the pair of human medics enter the airlock and tend to their injured comrade. The second airlock door that led into the shuttle hangar was still sealed, but Ziv watched the atmospheric indicator on the wall climb toward normal. Soon Morsa and Sem would be able to leave the shuttle and then, well, things would unfold as they would unfold.

"Commander?" asked one of the medics as he waved a device over the fallen human. "Can you hear me?"

Chakotay, the captain's first, opened his eyes and nodded minutely. His eyeballs were dark with blood and the flesh around them was bruised. Liquid was dripping from his nose and ears. Ziv had seen depressurization damage before and knew the human would probably live if he was at least as tough as a Monorhan, though he would be in terrible pain until the bubbles in his blood subsided.

The second medic worked silently and skillfully, first injecting what must have been an analgesic because Chakotay's painracked frame visibly relaxed. Even as they worked, the bald-pated doctor from the ship's hospital bustled up and inserted himself into the process. "Commander Chakotay?" he asked. "Can you hear me?"

"I already said, 'Yes,' " Chakotay said.

"It is me, Commander, the Doctor. We're treating you for exposure to vacuum, sir. You should be fine in a few minutes, though you'll be weak for a time."

"Understood," Chakotay croaked. "The Monorhans?"

"All fine, Commander. They had the sense to stay in the shuttle."

"And Smothers?"

"Still in the shuttle, too, sir, though he appears to be unconscious. Commander, what happened? Why did you leave your ship? Didn't you know the bay had no atmosphere?"

Trying to push himself up, Chakotay groaned. "Yes. . . . It just didn't seem important."

"Most of the ship has reported feeling muddled and confused, though I myself have no idea what you're talking about."

Ziv listened carefully to the exchange. He had gathered from the ship's status reports (Diro had figured out how to get the ship's computer to give them regular updates) that most of the Voyagers had been ill, but were better now. One of them had died in a peculiarly gruesome fashion and others were concerned the same might happen to them.

"You were in sickbay?" Chakotay said.

"Of course."

"Deep in the ship," Chakotay muttered, as if thinking aloud. "Sickbay and engineering are the best-shielded areas on the ship."

"Correct," the Doctor said.

"That might explain it. And the shuttlebay . . ."

"The least shielded," the Doctor agreed. "I understand now." The two medics had opened a pair of packs and assembled a stretcher. Now they wished to lift their injured commander onto it. "We're taking you to sickbay now." He glanced at the atmospheric indicator. "I'll go check on Ensign Smothers."

"Be careful," Chakotay said softly, then moaned as he was lifted onto the stretcher. "The light . . ."

The Doctor's eyebrows rose as he said, "Yes, Commander. Of course."

Moments after the commander and the medical technicians disappeared into the lift, the airlock indicator turned green and a bell chimed softly. The doors parted and Ziv stood face-to-face with Sem. Behind her, the one called Morsa stood with a human—presumably Smothers—cradled like an infant in his massive arms.

Sem looked at the Doctor and asked, "Where would you like him?"

The Doctor, temporarily without a stretcher, said, "Please come with me," and began to examine the unconscious human as Morsa stomped down the corridor toward the lift. Catching the look in their *harat*'s eye, Diro and Jaro followed.

As soon as they were out of earshot, Sem said, "They are all insane."

Ziv decided that it might not be an entirely bad thing that she thought this . . . for a while, at least. "Perhaps," he said. "Though they are also very powerful. I recommend . . . restraint."

Sliding her arms into the opposite sleeve of her garment, Sem brushed past Ziv and began looking around her. "What is happening here, Captain Ziv?"

"I do not understand precisely, though I believe we can find out quickly enough. They are very free with information."

Sem strode three paces down the corridor and looked up and down the intersection. "No guards?"

"In some areas," he said under his breath. "And I believe they have automated defenses, too, if you were planning to order us to take the ship."

Turning to him, then wrapping the long sleeves of her robe around her body, Sem said, "I'm here to advise the captain of this vessel, Ziv, and to lend moral support to my *hara*. You have all suffered a devastating loss, haven't you?"

"More than you could ever understand, Sem."

Ignoring the jab, Sem continued, "The humans . . . they said they saw some kind of light. Morsa did, too, though now he says he doesn't remember it. Do you know what they were talking about?"

Ziv shook his head. "No, though it concerns me that whatever was affecting them did not seem to affect either me or my *hara.*"

"Worries you? Why? That would seem a good thing to me. Though I have to confess I felt *something*. A strange tingling, like I feel when I am linked to a large *hara*. Then there was a sound and the sensation stopped. Do you know what it was?"

"No, my *rih,* but I have been thinking about this radiation, if that's what it is. We may already be accustomed to it. We may be so full of it that there is no room for any more."

Sem took a step closer, then reached out and touched Ziv's cheek lightly. "You were always the cleverest *shi-harat*, Ziv. I have never felt completely safe since you left. Why *did* you do that?"

Ziv flinched away from his *rih-hara-tan's* finger, not out of fear of Sem, but because of how desperately he desired her after one simple touch. "Sem," he said. "For the sake of all those who died today, I beg you . . ."

"Ah, yes," she said, lowering her hand. "How could I have forgotten? The excitement of my arrival has affected me. I should speak to your *haran*, reassure them."

For a moment, at the thought of Sem touching her mind to that of his *haran*, he considered reaching out, catching her by the neck, and simply snapping it. He could, Ziv knew. The universe would be a better place for her passing. But what of Diro? What of Jara and Shet and Mol? They would be made to pay for his moment of weakness. With a wave of his hand, he indicated the exit from the shuttlebay. "After you," he said, but thought, *As if I would give you the opportunity to be at my back.*

"Do you want to stop and rest?" Torres asked for the fourth time in an hour.

"No, Lieutenant. Do you?"

"No," Torres replied, her voice faint with exhaustion. "Not if you don't."

"I have already indicated I do not wish to rest," Seven said, though she allowed her pace to slacken as she spoke. She would never admit it to Torres, but her resources were becoming depleted. Though the planet's terrain was not particularly demanding, the arid atmosphere and the haze of fine particulate matter made breathing difficult. Also, the pain in her side where the ribs were slowly knitting did not make the process any easier. Her last complete regeneration cycle had been more than twenty-four hours earlier, so Seven was certain the nanoprobes in her bloodstream that repaired and maintained both her biological and cybernetic systems were slipping into dormancy.

"Are you sure we're going in the right direction?" Torres rasped.

"We are," Seven said. "I'm sure." Stopping briefly, she pretended to rub grit from her eyes. For a brief moment, the thought of assimilation crossed her mind. Imagine how much more . . . *compliant* the engineer would be. Who would know? The answer, of course, was simple: She would know. And if Captain Janeway asked her what happened to her chief engineer, Seven would respond truthfully. While Seven was confident that some on *Voyager* would understand the desire (she had noted that Torres was considered *abrasive* by many), the captain would be displeased, and keeping Captain Janeway pleased with her was very important to Seven.

Sighing, she became aware of the coating of fine silicate particles in her mouth and trachea. Seven willed nanoprobes to lubricate her throat, but their resources were needed elsewhere, so she chose an alternative method to alleviate her discomfort. "May I have some water?" she asked.

"Are we . . . Oh, sure," Torres said and handed her

the canteen. "I thought your suit reprocessed sweat and other fluids and kept you rehydrated that way."

"When all is working optimally," Seven replied, "yes. But I was injured and have not been able to regenerate."

"Hmph," Torres said, taking the canteen back and replacing the cap. "Interesting." Looking up at the sky, she asked, "Sun will be up soon. If it's this bad now, we'll want to be under cover by the time it rises. How much farther do we have to go?"

"Approximately three-quarters of a kilometer," Seven replied.

Torres smiled. "That's not bad. We can do that in a half-hour if we keep up this pace."

"Yes," she said, surprised at how reasonable Torres sounded.

"As long as we're going in the right direction."

"If you're so afraid I'm taking us in the wrong direction, please check your tricorder."

"I don't want to waste the batteries," Torres said, starting again. "And it's okay. I trust you. Well, your nanoprobes. But, wait, didn't you say they were getting tired?"

"I said nothing of the sort," Seven said, following the engineer.

"I'm going to power up the secondaries now, Captain," Joe Carey said, but before he did, he walked up behind the captain and tried to draw her away from the couplings. "I'd feel better if you stepped away from them."

The captain started when he touched her, but other-

wise did not move. "I'm okay here, Joe. The coupling
will hold."

Carey sighed and backed away. She was probably
right. Hell, not *probably*. Of course she was right. In all
his years in the service, he had never known a commanding officer who knew so much about her ship's engine
room. While most captains had a working knowledge of
their ship's power plant, few, if any, knew their way so intimately around the engine's guts as Kathryn Janeway. If
Carey hadn't known for a fact that she had been a science
officer before she was a captain, he would have bet
holodeck time that Janeway had been a microspanner-
wielding, atom-crunching, antimatter-pushing, lubri-
cant-stained engineer.

"It's just the way this radiation is degrading the
bioneural systems, Captain," Carey said, then let the
thought trail off. He was finding it difficult to focus,
though the captain had explained that was due to the rads
coming in through the shields. Refocusing, he finished,
"If another circuit blows out, we're going to lose the secondaries again."

"I know, Joe," the captain said, not taking her eyes off
the coupling. "Harry told me half the packs on the bridge
and the *Montpelier* burst. But if we get shields up to full
power, the bio-neurals won't be vulnerable." She flicked
her eyes up to Carey's. "So throw the switch."

"Aye, Captain," Carey said and was grateful when she
broke her gaze away. When she was like this, looking into
the captain's eyes was like staring into the engine core
without filters: beautiful, yes; thrilling, even, but the fire

would burn right through you. He turned back to the console—another one of Chief Torres's jury-rigged masterpieces—and triggered the sequence. A moment later, indicators showed power pulsing through the secondaries.

"How's it looking, Joe?"

Carey studied the flow and, even as he worked, felt the fog that had been impeding him lift a little. Sensor readouts that he had struggled to understand only minutes ago were now looking like old friends. "Good, Captain. It looks good." He straightened, pleased, but suddenly feeling every ache in his body. "We're dumping more power into the shields than the specs say we should. . . ."

"But B'Elanna and Seven have altered the shields extensively over the past year," Captain Janeway said. "With some of the Borg modifications."

"Right," Carey said. "The only problem with that is we don't have a baseline. We don't know how long the system will continue to function because we've never pushed it to failure."

"Give me an estimate," the captain said as she shrugged back into her uniform jacket. A loose strand of hair fell over her eyes and she blew it away with a puff of air from the corner of her mouth.

Carey hated this kind of moment. In the end, he knew, this was why B'Elanna Torres had been made chief engineer instead of him. Working with Torres for four years, he had learned more about line engineering than he had in the previous fifteen, and one of the most important things he had learned is that a chief has to occasionally pull answers out of thin air. He shook his head and felt his eyes go out of focus. "If we were dealing with standard Starfleet systems, I'd say eight hours. Maybe ten. This is a Torres/Seven special, though. I'd give it fourteen hours."

"And then?"

"Then either the primaries or the secondaries blow out and the core system cascades down into failure."

The captain smiled grimly. "Come on, Joe. Give it to me straight. . . ."

Carey grinned in response. "That's the only way I know how, Captain."

Janeway nodded. "All right. Stay here. Babysit it. Read it stories if you have to, but keep the shields up. I'll go figure out some way to get us out of here . . . wherever here is."

As she strode from engineering, Carey heard Commander Chakotay summon the captain on her combadge. "Janeway here. I'm on my way, Chakotay, but we have to keep this short. . . ." To Carey's eyes, she looked as fresh and focused as she had when she'd strode into his inner sanctum two hours earlier. He checked his chronometer and calculated that the captain had been on duty for over twenty-four hours. *And here I am feeling like I'm ready to collapse onto the deck.* Pulling himself up straight in his boots, Carey went in search of techs to watch over the core system. And a cup of coffee. It was going to be a long night.

~

Last to arrive in the conference room, Janeway was surprised to find most of the seats occupied by Monorhans. Not only were Captain Ziv and his entire *hara* there, but also the two newcomers, Sem and Morsa. The *rih-haratan* rose and introduced herself briefly, but she seemed to sense the tension in the captain's demeanor and kept her comments short and simple. "Wishing to understand as much as we can, Captain, we asked Mr. Neelix if we could listen to your discussion. We will remain silent unless one of us has to offer a comment that has a direct bearing on our situation." When Sem said, "We will remain silent," Janeway knew, she meant, *"I* will remain silent." None of the others would speak unless their leader spoke first.

Harry Kim, Tuvok, the Doctor, and Chakotay were in the usual spots, the latter looking battered and weak from his misadventure on the shuttle deck. Janeway nodded to her first officer as she slipped into her customary spot, though she did not seat herself. If she sat, she knew, she would begin to feel precisely how tired she was. "All right," she said. "Let's get started. We're working against the clock, so keep your statements brief. Harry, you first. What can you tell us about where we are?"

"We're in a subspace fold, Captain."

Janeway held up her finger for Harry to halt, then looked at Sem. "Do you understand what he means?"

Sem nodded. "Before you arrived, Ensign Kim delivered a brief lecture on the nature of subspace. I cannot say I understood it all, but the concept is clear: We are trapped in a layer that exists under what we consider 'normal' space."

Janeway dipped her head, impressed with Sem's grasp. "I couldn't have put it better myself. How did we get here, Harry? And how do we get out?"

"The energy wave from Monorha's surface triggered a subspace inversion. I found references in the library computer to similar phenomena near the Bajoran wormhole. Once every fifty years . . ."

"No history lesson, Harry," Janeway warned.

"Right. Sorry, Captain. The energy wave tore a hole in 'normal' space. As soon as that happened, within point one zero zero one seconds, the system restabilized, but in that blink of an eye, *Voyager* was swept into the pocket. Normal space and subspace found equilibrium and we were left in between."

The captain shook her head in wonder. "I've never heard of *anything* like this, Harry. How is it possible?"

"Anywhere else in the universe, Captain, and I don't think it would be. I've been able to work my way through some of the sensor logs from our trip to Monorha. The fabric of local space is riddled with weak areas, spots where inversions could occur."

"We didn't spot them before?"

Kim shook his head, frowning. "I don't have an explanation for that, Captain, or an excuse."

"Except," Chakotay offered, "no one has ever seen anything like this before."

Lowering his head, Kim refused to take the proffered excuse.

Janeway didn't press the point, but neither did she support Chakotay's justification. Nothing she could say at this point would alleviate his self-recrimination. "All right then," she continued "If I'm getting this right, we're in a pocket of subspace that's very similar to the subspace bubble we create around ourselves to go to warp speed. Correct?"

"Correct," Harry said.

"So what will happen if we engage the warp engines?"

"We'd substitute our bubble for the fold."

"But there's a reason why we shouldn't do that, isn't there?"

Tuvok spoke up. "Correct, Captain. If we engage the warp engines, we will emerge from this fold, but we do not know precisely where. It may be in the Monorhan system or halfway across the Delta Quadrant."

Janeway felt herself nodding, comprehension settling into her bones. "Because we didn't have the navigational computer recording our coordinates as we entered the fold." She pondered their situation for a moment, then asked, "Can we map this fold, get some sense of its size and topography?"

"There are no landmarks in the fold, no stars or other bodies," Tuvok explained, "so we have begun to drop markers. Unfortunately, the radiation begins to affect them almost immediately."

"Then we need to rig small, powerful shield generators for them. That's our top priority. We'll need to know as much about the fold as possible."

Tuvok nodded. "That would be logical, Captain. I will begin work at once."

Turning back to Harry, Janeway asked, "If we need to go to warp, could we do it? Could we find a way to give the navigational computers the information we need to emerge where we want? And whatever it was that affected us in the Monorhan system, is it in here, too?"

"I don't know. I need more time . . ."

"We don't *have* much time, Ensign," Janeway snapped, slapping the table with the palm of her hand. "Fourteen hours maximum. Then the shields go down and the core blows."

Harry's head snapped back like he had been slapped. "Yes, Captain," he said. "Understood."

"We need to know if we can get out of here," she said. "I don't want to leave B'Elanna and Seven behind. I'll stay here just as long as you tell me I can, but not one second longer. Is everyone clear about their jobs?"

Everyone, even the Monorhans, nodded, all of them grim-faced.

"Then get to work."

Chapter 10

"This is what we've been looking for?" B'Elanna asked in a whisper.

"It is the spot from where the readings emanated," Seven replied also in hushed tones.

They were lying flat on their bellies, their heads level with the swell of a hillside, both B'Elanna and Seven facing into the east, where they could see the rim of the sun rising. Below them was a low, long building perhaps a hundred meters on the short side and two hundred on the long, made from corrugated steel and adobe bricks. No windows, only one door. Fifty meters out from the building stood a high fence topped with razor wire. A series of tall lamps threw watery pools of light across the courtyard. Just at the edge of every circle of light, B'Elanna saw a guard armed with a heavy rifle. She counted four on the side of the building they faced and guessed there were at least that many on the other. No roads approached the site.

"Doesn't exactly scream 'officially sanctioned government outpost,' does it?"

"I would not walk up to the gate and knock to be let in."

"Then what do we do?"

Seven pulled out her tricorder and ran a brief scan. "Utilizing our superior technological resources," she said, "I will devise a plan that will permit us to evade detection."

"Or," B'Elanna said, "we could just shoot them with our phasers."

"A waste of resources," Seven said. "We may need the batteries later."

Was that a joke? B'Elanna wondered, but only said, "To shoot our way out?"

"My method is more efficient."

"But it will waste time. We need to contact *Voyager* as quickly as possible."

"And what if one of your phaser shots inadvertently damages their equipment?" Seven asked. "Or someone inside hears our shots and deliberately destroys what we seek?"

Hefting her phaser, B'Elanna considered their options. She was really beginning to hate Seven's being right all the time. "All right," she said. "Stealth. If stealth fails, then we shoot."

"That is how these situations tend to unfold," Seven replied and began to creep down the side of the hill. "Especially when you are involved."

~

Tom wished he had thought to bring a hot pad. The heat from the bottom of the plate was singeing his palm. "Harry? C'mon, Harry. Open the door. I'm burning my hand." Tom pressed the buzzer to his friend's quarters again. "Harry? I know you're in there. The computer told me." The omelet smelled good and he was tempted, *very* tempted, but there had been enough mushrooms left to make only one and, well, a promise was a promise. He'd try one more time. If Harry didn't answer, he'd have a nibble. Just to make sure it was still good. "Harry? Really. Flesh burning now. I'm going to leave if you . . ."

The door slipped open. Tom poked his head in and inhaled the rich smell of loamy earth. *Guess we should have done a better job of insulating those mushroom-growing racks,* Tom decided. The room was dark except for a single lamp next to the library computer station. "Harry? You there? I brought you some supper. Omelet, Harry. Mmmm. Mushrooms!"

"Just put it down" was the response. Tom could see Harry in the pool of light. The top of the desk was littered with a half-dozen other padds and a jumble of data cubes. "I'll eat later."

"If it gets cold," Tom said, "it will take on the consistency of plastic foam. I refuse to sacrifice the only usable mushrooms in the crop because you're having a bad day."

"I'm not hungry."

"How can you not be hungry? According to Neelix, you haven't eaten since yesterday."

"Tell Neelix to mind his own business."

"I have," Tom said setting the plate on the low table near the desk. "But he's constitutionally incapable."

Without looking up from his work, Harry asked, "What are you doing here, Tom? I thought you and the doctor were inoculating everyone on the ship."

"Right," Tom said, opening the medpack at his hip and pulling out the hypospray. "You'll be pleased to know you're the last. Could it be because you ignored all the calls from sickbay? Possibly."

"I'm working on something, Tom. The captain needs to know if the radiation in this fold is going to prevent us from going to warp."

"Yeah, I heard. Neelix told me about the meeting. Sorry she tore into you like that."

"It's okay," Harry said. "She was just trying to get me to do my job. . . ."

"Harry, there isn't anyone on board this ship who works harder than you do."

"Except the captain," Harry countered.

Tom reflected on that, then nodded in agreement. Pressing the hypo to Harry's forearm, he injected the drug. "If you feel queasy later, it's probably the drug, not radiation sickness. Having something in your stomach would help."

Harry looked up at his friend in mild confusion. "All this mothering is getting on my nerves."

Tom shrugged. "With B'Elanna off ship, I have a lot of extra mothering to burn off."

"Were you able to pull up sensor data for the shuttle?"

Tom nodded and felt his face go numb. "Some. It

didn't look good, but we didn't see the end. She might have been able to regain control. B'Elanna's a good pilot."

"Or they could've beamed out," Harry said, trying to sound positive.

"Maybe. Either way, they're probably not in great moods right now. Monorha isn't what I'd call a convivial vacation spot." Tom scanned the debris on the desk, but wasn't really looking at anything. He knew the best thing he could do was stay busy, stay focused, and not let his mind wander to worst-case scenarios. "Until you science whizzes explain where we're going, the best use of my time is to hand out injections." He pointed the empty hypospray at Harry's computer. "You figured this out yet?"

"No," Harry replied tensely. "I'm still just getting my head around it. Preliminary scans say that this fold is flooded with the same radiation that permeated the Monorhan system, which doesn't make sense."

"Why not?" Tom asked. "If we were sucked in here when the fold cracked open, wouldn't the radiation come in, too?"

"Sure," Harry said. "Some, but not the amount I'm detecting."

"So no going to warp."

"No, we can go to warp. I've determined that for sure. We just won't know where we're going."

Tom had heard this grim assessment from Neelix earlier. His chest grew tight as he pondered the idea of going to warp and emerging in a random corner of the universe. Not only would they be leaving Seven and

B'Elanna to fend for themselves, there was absolutely no way to know where *Voyager* would appear. What if they ended up back at the beginning of their journey or, worse yet, smack dab in the center of Borg-controlled space? He didn't want to think about it. "Maybe the space contained by the fold is very small and it's concentrating the radiation."

"I considered that. But then I checked the topographical survey Tuvok is building." Harry turned the library computer screen so Tom could see. "See, it's big."

Studying the diagram, Tom saw that Harry was right. Based on what Tuvok had mapped so far, the fold was quite large. As he watched, several more blinking dots appeared: more probes. Tom cocked his head, then pointed at the line formed by the points. "It's curved," he said.

Harry cocked an eyebrow and turned the monitor back so he could see what Tom meant. "You're right," he said. "I hadn't noticed the arc."

"It's very slight," Tom said. "If it weren't for those last couple of probes, I probably wouldn't have noticed it. Does that mean anything?"

"I don't know," Harry said staring at the monitor while tapping the tip of his chin with a stylus. As they watched, another half-dozen probes blinked on. "Tuvok is working fast."

"How is he marking the perimeter?" Tom asked.

"The probes are emitting small amounts of warp plasma particles. They react with the edges of the fold."

At that moment, Tuvok must have fired another volley of probes, because the edge they had been watching form suddenly grew several hundred kilometers longer. The slight curve became more radical.

Harry tapped his combadge. "Kim to Tuvok."

"Tuvok here."

"Tuvok, I'm looking at the map of the fold you're creating and wanted to know if you could quickly launch a few more. I'm interested to see where that curved edge goes."

"Very well, Mr. Kim. Please stand by."

Several minutes ticked by before another cluster of lights appeared on the screen. The curve of the line grew radically tighter, then disappeared into a corkscrew spiral.

"Is that sufficient, Mr. Kim?"

"Can we map some more?"

"Not at this moment, Mr. Kim. We have used up our compliment of probes for now. I am in the process of assembling more, but our resources are low. It will require time."

"Understood. Kim out." Harry continued to stare at the peculiar curved shape. Tom watched his friend and was surprised to see that a slow grin was creeping onto his face.

"What is it, Harry?" Tom asked. "What are you seeing?"

Harry did not respond to Tom, but rather tapped his combadge and said, "Kim to Captain Janeway."

"Janeway here."

"Captain, could you meet me in astrometrics right away? I think I have something."

~

In truth, sneaking into the compound turned out to be almost fun, and the electrified fence was no match for any of B'Elanna's tools. Tricorder scans got them through the guards. Locks opened with no resistance, and less than six minutes after B'Elanna cut through the fence, they were inside the main building.

Checking her tricorder, Seven said softly. "There are no internal alarms. We may move—cautiously, but without fear."

B'Elanna's wrist lamp illuminated banks of primitive (to her) computer equipment and generators. At the center of the main floor, they found a stairway that led down into what her scan said was a deep underground chamber filled with water and lined with photomultiplier tubes. "What is this?" B'Elanna asked. "A reservoir? Emergency supplies?"

Seven shook her head. "I do not think so. I believe we have stumbled onto a research station. This appears to be a neutrino observatory."

"A what?"

"You know too little of your own history, Lieutenant. Four hundred years ago, humans first theorized the existence of neutrino particles. Researchers hit upon the idea of building or adapting large chambers like this one, filling them with pure water, and lining them with very sensitive light detectors. Primitive engineering, to say the least, but functional, to a point."

"What does this have to do with the energy wave we felt earlier?"

"Probably nothing," Seven said. "Subatomic particle research of this sort is highly theoretical work—'pure science,' as you would call it. I am intrigued that the Monorhans, a people enmeshed in such difficult circumstances, would expend resources in the pursuit of abstract knowledge."

"Maybe not such pure research," B'Elanna suggested. "If you lived this close to a white dwarf, wouldn't you want to know as much as possible about exotic particles?"

Seven considered this, then nodded. "Though a moot point in our current investigation. This apparatus has not been used in several years."

"Meaning what? The Monorhans abandoned their pure research in favor of weapons research?"

Shaking her head, Seven said, "I do not think the energy wave was meant to be a weapon. This installation does not look like a weapons lab."

"For something that wasn't meant to be a weapon, the energy wave did a hell of a job."

"We require more information," Seven said, then indicated a cluster of consoles in the center of the main room. "I believe we can find out more by checking that data center. Readings indicate it was used most recently."

"All right," B'Elanna said, pointing her lamp down at the stairwell one more time. The idea of the large water-filled chamber below made her skin crawl. Maybe the idea reminded her of one of the death traps the heroines in Tom's silly serials always seemed to get trapped inside.

~

"Harry thinks he has something," the captain said, still leaning over the latest batch of sensor logs scrolling up onto the science officer's station. Studying her face in the glare from the monitor, Chakotay saw the dark circles under her eyes. *She hasn't slept in over a day,* he realized. "I'm going to meet him in astrometrics."

"What about Captain Ziv and the *rih-hara-tan?*" Chakotay asked. "You told them we would meet with them."

When she rose from the chair, Kathryn's knee joints popped loudly. "Agh!" she said. "I need to stretch. What I said was 'Someone would meet with them.' You're my officially anointed 'someone.' Find out what they want and then try to find out what they *really* want. I don't trust Sem. The way she and Ziv act around each other—there's something wrong there."

Chakotay nodded in agreement. Even in their short encounter in the conference room, he had sensed the tension between the pair. "Try to join us later," he added. "I get the feeling Sem thinks the rest of us are . . . beneath her."

Even as Kathryn disappeared into the turbolift, Chakotay heard her say, "It's good to be the queen."

After a moment's reflection, Chakotay asked Neelix to throw together a quick meal. Kathryn wouldn't have done such a thing, but she had put him in charge of the Monorhans. As was his wont, the Talaxian put a little too much effort into "a quick meal." When Chakotay arrived in the conference room, the table was laden with an abundance of "typical" food items, everything from peanut butter sandwiches and fried tofu to Rian pickled eggs (Chakotay knew better than to ask where they came from) and a lovely replicated roast chicken, which was one of the very few foods everyone agreed tasted just as good replicated as real. Chakotay supposed this latter had something to do with the fact that *all* replicated food basically tasted like chicken.

As soon as everyone sat, Chakotay realized his observation about Sem was correct: the *rih-hara-tan* wished only to speak to the captain and neither Chakotay nor Neelix would do. She stewed and fumed while Ziv half-heartedly attempted to make conversation. The hulking Morsa helped himself to every food on the table, then methodically and meticulously chewed every bite into paste before swallowing. Chakotay hadn't heard him speak a word since the shuttlebay. *What was that about? And why does he deny remembering it?*

Finally, when food was no longer a distraction, Chakotay asked, "You had questions?"

Sem responded impatiently, "Will the captain be joining us?"

"Eventually, yes. Until then, ask me whatever you'd like."

Sem clicked indignantly, but finally said, "Do you know how to get out of the fold?"

"The captain is working on that problem as we speak."

"Does your captain always spend so much time working on these sorts of problems?"

"The captain," Chakotay said flatly, "possesses one of

the finest scientific minds in the service. If anyone can guide us to an answer, it's Captain Janeway."

"Hear, hear," said Neelix.

"She asked me to get additional information about our situation," Chakotay continued. "Perhaps we can cover some of that until she joins us."

Responding (perhaps) to Chakotay's tone, Sem straightened her back, but gave him her undivided attention. "What would you like to know?"

"Tell us more about the Blue Eye—scientific data, history, even legend. Anything you can tell us might be useful."

"All right," Sem said, her voice becoming formal. "The Blue Eye is the most prominent feature in our sky except for Protin herself."

"Protin?" Chakotay asked, then guessed, "The main star?"

"So we call it in my tribe. Among the fourteen tribes, it has other names."

"The fourteen tribes?"

Neelix inserted himself into the conversation. "All Monorhans identify themselves as being a member of a tribe, Commander. Each of the cities on the planet is the origin point of a tribe, though according to Mr. Dora, members from many tribes live in each of them."

"I have a very good memory," Chakotay said, addressing the comment to Sem. "When we saw your planet from orbit, I saw thirteen cities. Was there once a fourteenth?"

"A fourteenth," Sem said. "Yes. And many smaller

towns, but as the population has dwindled, most of our people have returned to the cities, where they can be better protected."

"That's avoiding the question. Fourteen tribes?"

Sem stirred uncomfortably, then settled again. "Yes, fourteen."

"What happened to the fourteenth tribe?"

"That is a very long story, Commander, and not relevant to your first question. The Eye has not always been as we see it now. Historical documents tell us that it was once a pale red."

"When did it turn blue?"

Sem spoke a phrase that the translator deciphered as "Twenty-five hundred years."

"Is Protin the Blessed, All-Knowing Light?"

Shaking her head as if Chakotay had asked a childish question, she said, "No, Protin is a name out of legend— a hunter, I believe. I don't know the story in any detail."

"When the Blue Eye changed color, did its behavior change?"

"It is difficult to say. We know for a fact that the Eye began to emit more harmful radiation approximately one hundred and fifty cycles ago. Our environment began to degrade at the end of the previous century. At first, our scientists thought it might be part of a process we had not previously perceived, that the cycle would end shortly after it began, that our atmosphere could protect us. . . ." She shook her head slowly. "Sadly, none of this was true."

"When did your scientists determine this?"

"Some say they knew as long ago as forty cycles, but I was only very young then. Certainly it has only been during the past ten that any concerted effort has been made to protect ourselves."

"The shields over your cities?" Chakotay asked.

"Yes, of course."

"What about the energy pulse that put us here? What do you know about it?"

"Very little," Sem said. "Those who did it were . . ." She searched for a word. "Outlaws? Outcasts? I hear the correct word in my head, but neither of those is correct. The Emergency Council believes they are trying to find a way around the inevitable."

"The inevitable?" Chakotay asked. "What do you think is inevitable?"

Sem looked first at Ziv, then at Morsa, still quietly eating. "That our planet will die. That we must find a way to leave it or die, too."

The words hung in the air for several seconds and Chakotay considered trying to find something reassuring to say, but before he could say anything, someone else broke the silence.

Ziv said, "And tell them the last thing, Sem. Tell the whole truth. Explain how we already know that not everyone will escape. Explain how you and the other *rih-hara-tan* have decided who may be allowed to quietly perish."

"That's *Voyager*," Torres said, pointing at a tiny blip on the monitor built into the console. "They knew she was up there. Not a very friendly thing to do, shooting off their little cannon."

"Just because we found *Voyager* in their scans," Seven retorted, "does not mean the Monorhans knew she was there. Researchers frequently have tunnel vision." She was surprised when the engineer let the comment pass without a response. Likely, Torres did not consider herself a researcher and so did not perceive the statement as an insult.

"We need to get this panel off and take a look inside," Torres said, addressing the immediate problem. She pointed at the quick scans she had performed on the console and the large array on the roof. "Is it just me, or does this remind you of a deflector dish?"

The similarity was slight, but Seven had to admit these sorts of intuitive leaps frequently baffled her. "Perhaps," she said. "Do you believe the Monorhans were attempting to upgrade their shielding technology?"

"I don't know," Torres said while opening her tool kit. "It's a possibility. We may need to talk to some of these people later and find out what they think they're doing."

"They will probably not want to talk with us," Seven said. "I am under the impression that they are not affiliated with the planet's emergency planning council."

"Which suggests another question," Torres said, feeling around the edge of the panel. "Here, hold this light so I can see." Carefully running her fingers along the seam of a console, she found a recessed catch. "If these guys aren't part of the Emergency Council, why hasn't anyone come looking for them?"

Seven had also been wondering about this and decided there was only one possible conclusion. "If this is some kind of deflector array, the energy wave may not affect their technology, but only ours."

In the shadow cast by the lamp, Seven saw Torres make an unhappy face. "Seems unlikely," she said. "More likely the officials detected the wave, but don't have the resources to do anything about . . . Oh, wait, I got it." The panel popped off the console with a quivering twang.

The shadows disappeared from Torres's face in a blaze of white light. Seven's ocular implant attempted to parse the event and capture every moment, but the result was only a sputtering mélange of images: Torres's eyes snapping shut as her hair flew back; tiny bits of steel and plastic flying out from the console; a belch of smoke bleached white by the bright flash. All these images assaulted her, overlapping, then faded into a pinpoint of contracting darkness.

Chapter 11

B'Elanna awoke in darkness, hearing nothing but the sound of water dripping—a disturbing noise for a spacer, as bad in its way as the hiss of escaping atmosphere. Recognizing that she was in a pool of icy water, she sat up quickly and rolled awkwardly to her knees. Sniffing, she smelled mold, rust, and a musty chemical aroma. She lifted her hands and rubbed her arms briskly, then groaned with pain. Cramping muscles? Injury? Probably the former. That fit with the cold and the wet, anyway.

B'Elanna passed her hands in front of her face to make sure her eyes weren't bound and, finding nothing, tried to be still and listen carefully. For the first few seconds, the sound of her own breathing filled her senses, but she was soon able to focus past the whoosh of air and make assessments about her surroundings.

A drop splashed into a pool, and the echo reverberated through the air. *Large room,* she decided, and a chill not caused by the cold ran down her spine. *Cavernous.*

She inched her hand carefully along the floor by first her right side, then her left. To the right, she encountered a callused and pitted metal wall damp with condensation. The floor to the left, also metal, went on for her full arm's length, until her fingertips found a steel mesh barrier.

I'm on a walkway, she concluded, though there was no telling how old it was or how strong.

Groping carefully, B'Elanna found a small chunk of crumbled concrete, which she lifted, then tossed toward the mesh wall, careful not to put too much force into the throw in case the concrete bounced back at her. A moment later, she heard a gentle plop. She had been pretty sure where she was, but this clinched it. "Great," she said. "I'm in the neutrino-detection chamber."

"Correction," Seven said. "We are *both* in the neutrino-detection chamber."

The voice made B'Elanna gasp, equally surprised and annoyed that she hadn't detected her traveling companion. *How can she be so quiet?*

"I see," B'Elanna said, attempting to conceal her surprise. "Except I don't really. Not yet, anyway." She knelt and felt around her waist to see if their captors had inadvertently left them any useful equipment. "Do you have anything we can use to see with? Even the light from a tricorder display would be good."

"I do not," Seven replied. "Whoever searched us was most thorough."

"And even enhanced Borg senses can't see in total

darkness?" B'Elanna asked, glad to finally find some flaw in Seven's array of special enhancements.

"In fact they can," Seven said. "Or would if we were in total darkness."

"Then we're just going to have to be careful and feel around until . . ." Seven's last comment registered. "Wait. What are you saying?"

Seven paused, and B'Elanna could sense her struggling to think of the most efficient manner to explain the situation. Finally, she settled on "You cannot see anything."

"Nothing," B'Elanna said, trying not to let panic creep into her voice. "Are you sure your Borg enhanced senses aren't just in overdrive?"

"Quite sure."

B'Elanna sagged back against the wall. "Oh, crap."

Her mind raced. *Blind? Blind?!* How could she be blind? What good would she be to anyone now, especially to Seven? The Borg would surely figure some way out of the trap, but B'Elanna was useless now, so she'd be abandoned down here in the dark where her captors would either torture her or leave her to starve or drown or . . . *Stop! Enough!* Holding her breath, B'Elanna clenched her fists and then punched the concrete at her feet. *None of this!* she thought. *Hold it together! There's a way out of this. There's always a way. If I have to find a stick and put a leash around Seven's neck, I'll find a way.*

For just a moment, she let her thoughts stray to Tom, wondering what his predicament might be at that moment. Was he dead, or were they right in their assumptions that *Voyager* had been forced to flee? She had to know. And if he needed help, if they *all* needed help, she, B'Elanna, would be the one who made certain they got it. *No trusting the Borg,* she decided, and as soon as the thought came, she knew it was unfair. Seven wouldn't abandon *Voyager* or, at least, the captain. And once they found the ship, the Doctor would be able to help her. For all she knew, the injury was temporary. Her vision might return at any moment.

"Is there anything else you wish to say?" Seven asked.

B'Elanna exhaled sharply. "Not at this moment, no." She felt for her combadge, and found it missing.

"Mine is gone as well," Seven said.

"They might be able to understand us, so we should try to talk as softly as we can."

"Agreed."

B'Elanna waited, but she didn't hear sounds of someone moving. "So why don't you come over here? That way we won't have to talk too loudly."

"I cannot," Seven said dully.

"They bound you?"

"No. I am simply unable to move. I am paralyzed below the waist."

B'Elanna muttered a Klingon phrase so caustic it probably removed rust from a nearby wall.

"I concur," Seven said.

"But we still need to keep our voices down," B'Elanna said. "How far am I from you?"

"Less than three meters," Seven said. "And there are no obstacles in your path, though you should be careful to stay near the wall. The guardrail is in poor condition. If you rested your weight against it . . ."

"I won't. Just hold on. This is harder than it looks." B'Elanna rose carefully, both her hands pressed firmly against the wall, then inched toward the sound of Seven's voice. Her boots scuffed against the floor, dislodging small pieces of grit and debris, every tiny piece sounding like a tumbling boulder in the cavernous chamber.

Finally, Seven said, "Stop there. I am less than ten centimeters away."

B'Elanna slid gratefully to the floor, her boot touching the Borg's leg. She jerked it away, then remembered that Seven said she was paralyzed. "Can you feel that?" she asked.

"No."

"Are you in any pain?"

"No." She felt dry, cool fingers against the flesh beneath her eyes. "Are you?"

The thought hadn't crossed her mind. "No," B'Elanna said. "Which is strange when you think about it."

"I detect a faint astringent odor," Seven said, keeping her voice low. "I believe we have been given first aid. Our captors may have saved our lives. We should consider that as a factor in our negotiations."

"Negotiations?" B'Elanna asked, struggling to keep her temper. "What do we have to negotiate with? We're prisoners."

"Possibly. But knowledgeable prisoners. Between the two of us, we know a great deal."

The thought was reassuring, though B'Elanna believed Seven was being optimistic. "Maybe. We'll see. Do
you remember what happened?"

"I remember everything that happened up until the
moment I lost consciousness. Some element within the
console detonated."

"Rigged?" B'Elanna asked. "Or just sloppy work?"

"We cannot know until we ask."

A thought struck B'Elanna. "Shouldn't your nanoprobes be repairing you?"

"They should. Unfortunately, I have not regenerated
in more than a day. Many of my systems have lapsed into
dormancy."

"Being unconscious doesn't do it?"

"No. Nor sleep. Without the regeneration chamber,
my Borg implants will ultimately fail. The nanoprobes
are merely the first to fail."

From somewhere above them came a piercing, grinding sound. "A hatch," Seven said under her breath. "In
the ceiling. A male with a large weapon is descending a
ladder. He is followed by five others, all armed." She
paused. "It would be a mistake to do anything . . . impul-
sive."

B'Elanna wished she knew precisely where the
Borg's head was so she could give her a thwack on the
side of it. "I'm blind," she said. "You're crippled. You
think I'm going to make a break for it?"

"I have noted that you can sometimes act quite . . ."

"Impulsively?"

"Yes."

"But stupidly?"

"There are degrees of impulsiveness."

"I might just have to push you off into the water."

"Thereby proving my point."

B'Elanna listened as first one, then four more heavy figures dropped onto the walkway and marched toward them. As they approached, she heard several short, sharp clicks and trills, the nonverbal language Chakotay had mentioned. Would they have the combadges with them? If not—or if their captors had made the mistake of trying to disassemble them—this would be a very short interview.

The first figure stopped less than a meter away. B'Elanna could hear his heavy breathing—climbing down a ladder with a heavy rifle must be difficult—and caught whiffs of wet hair, some kind of machine oil, and the ozone tang of an old, overtaxed power pack. *Some kind of energy weapon*, B'Elanna figured. *Probably unreliable as hell, hard to use, and so poorly shielded the guy who's carrying it is already dying of cancer, but just as effective as a phaser in its way.* The rest of the gang stopped short, obviously not wanting to crowd the boss too much or get too near the aliens.

The boss said, "You'll answer questions now."

Seven, predictably, spoke up before B'Elanna could say a word. "We have nothing to hide. There has been some kind of mistake. We are here to help."

They have the combadges, B'Elanna thought. *One piece of good news, anyway.* Feeling she had to add something so she wouldn't be excluded from the conversation,

B'Elanna added, "Someone is going to be really ticked off that you stopped us."

Behind the boss, B'Elanna heard the other Monorhans burst out in astounded chatter. "It works!" one said. "Amazing!" another replied. "Are they speaking the same language or does each of them have their own and they use the device to communicate?"

They don't talk like kidnappers or thugs, B'Elanna thought. *Who the hell are these people?*

"Quiet," the boss snapped, and the gaggle of commentators grew quiet. "Who are you? Who do you think you are helping and why did you break into this facility? Where do you come from, that you don't know about private property?"

Seven said, "Lieutenant, would you like to answer? The captain said you were in command."

Surprised but pleased, B'Elanna said, "My name is B'Elanna Torres. My companion is called Seven of Nine. We're from a vessel named *Voyager.* As you may have surmised, we're not from around here."

"Thank you for crediting us with rudimentary observational ability." The boss made a clicking sound that B'Elanna interpreted as laughter. "Where is your ship, B'Elanna Torres? Why are you here alone? Please try to be brief, for I fear we may not have much time together."

What does he mean by that? B'Elanna wondered. Partly to relieve a cramp and partly to play for time, she adjusted her legs. *This boss doesn't sound quite as threatening as he did a moment ago.* Deciding that honesty was the best policy, she said, "We're here because your Emergency

Council asked us to come help with the shields that protect your cities. We know a lot about shielding technology where we come from, and my commanding officer decided we should try to do something while they investigated the star that is creating all the radiation. You do know that, don't you?"

One of the mob behind the boss let go of a sharp exhalation and said, "Of course we know."

"No offense meant," B'Elanna said. "I just need to know who I'm . . . who *we're* dealing with."

"Be quiet, Bria," the boss said. "We agreed I'd do the talking."

"Sorry. Right," Bria said apologetically. "Carry on."

Less and less like thugs all the time. "So, to continue," B'Elanna said, "we were on our way to a city—did we ever get its name, Seven?"

"No."

"The city to the north of here, anyway, when this energy wave bounced us out of the sky. Our ship—a shuttle—landed a little way from here and we decided that we would attempt to figure out where the wave came from."

"Why didn't you just go back to your vessel in orbit?" the boss asked.

"The shuttle was damaged in the crash and something happened to *Voyager.* We can't contact her and we think you might know something about that."

"Why do you say that?"

"Because your machine—the one we were looking at—had an image of *Voyager* in its databank."

A new voice—a high-pitched, fast talker—spoke up. "Kill them now!"

"Hey!" B'Elanna said. "We're here to help! Why would you want to kill us?"

"They know too much," the fast talker chattered in a rapid burst. "They were looking at the generator! If these aliens make it to Araxs and tell the *rih-hara-tan,* she won't be able to ignore us anymore! Soldiers will come no matter how much she wants to pretend we don't know anything!"

"We *don't* know anything," B'Elanna protested.

"Kill them or they will betray us!"

"I don't even know what you look like!"

"I do," Seven said, her only contribution to the conversation.

"Shut up, Seven!"

"You are not affiliated with the Emergency Council, are you?" Seven asked.

"Kill them!"

B'Elanna felt the boss shift his weight and heard the low whine of the portable generator grow more shrill. "No," he said slowly, "we're not part of the Emergency Council. And you," he concluded, "might very well be spies."

Sem clicked loudly twice and every Monorhan in the dining room sat up straight, spines rigid. As one, the Monorhans stood up and pushed their chairs away from their seats, though Morsa maintained his grip on his plate of lasagna. Sem said formally, "Thank you for the meal, Commander, and for the conversation. We will be returning to our quarters now. My people have had a difficult day and require rest."

Chakotay stood and moved to block the exit from the conference room. "I think I need to know what Captain Ziv meant by his last statement."

"Captain Ziv," Sem said flatly, "is overwrought. You, of all people, must understand what it means to lose a ship and a crew. He does not know what he is saying."

The mountainous Morsa took a half-step forward, but Chakotay crossed his arms over his chest. "I want to know," he said slowly, "what Captain Ziv meant."

Sem stared at him for several seconds as if slightly puzzled by his response, then turned her gaze back to Ziv. Voice pitched high, as if she were speaking to a child, she asked, "Ziv? Do you have anything else to say?"

Ziv appeared to struggle to tear his eyes away from Sem's, but could not. Haltingly, he replied, "No. Not . . . I . . . have nothing . . ." Gasping, he finished, "Good night!" Then, Ziv and his *hara* briskly filed out of the room. When the doors closed behind them, the two remaining Monorhans relaxed, though Sem appeared taxed and woozy.

"I'm going to have to report this to Captain Janeway," Chakotay said.

"Do as you please, Commander," Sem said imperiously. "After all, we *are* in your power."

"You're our guests," Chakotay said. "But no one enjoys having their hospitality abused."

Sem considered this, then looked up at Morsa, then down at the plate still held in his hand. "I believe Morsa would enjoy more of your hospitality. Is that right?"

Morsa nodded, then sat. A second later, the sounds of chewing once again filled the small room. "There you are," Sem said to Chakotay. "Someone to interview." With that, she pushed her own chair under the table and swept out of the room. Chakotay and Neelix watched her leave, but as soon as the doors closed behind her, their eyes were drawn to the sound of relentlessly grinding jaws. A very long minute passed while the Monorhan finished chewing and swallowing.

Slowly, Morsa lifted his napkin to his mouth and daintily patted his lips. Then, lowering his hands into his lap, he locked eyes in turn with Neelix then Chakotay and, speaking slowly, in a low, unexpectedly gentle voice, he asked, "What would you like to talk about?"

Seven of Nine pushed herself up on her elbows and addressed the group's leader. "We could be spies," she said. "But consider this: If we come from a superior culture, why resort to spying? You have seen our technology: the translators and our scanning devices. I suspect you have attempted to use our weapons. Correct?"

The leader pulled a phaser out of one of his many pockets. "This, you mean? We could not operate it."

"A safety device prevents anyone but Lieutenant Torres or myself from operating it; however, carelessness could damage the power supply, which might result in the destruction of this structure."

The leader clicked softly, then slid the phaser with respectful care back into his pocket.

Satisfied that she had made an impression, Seven continued. "We admit we were trespassing, but only because we did not understand the nature of your relationship with the Emergency Council. If you were affiliated with the organization that asked us to come to Monorha, then we were entirely within our rights to be cautious, seeing as your device knocked our vessel from the sky. Since we now understand you are not, the next logical step would be to determine your status and ascertain how you fit into the larger picture. Can you help us? Can we help you? Most importantly, what precisely is the device you have constructed?" Satisfied with her recitation, Seven shifted her weight and propped her back against the damp wall.

In response, the leader shifted his weight, resting the butt of the large weapon against his hip. The hum from the rifle's power unit echoed ominously.

"She's trying to trick you," the small, shrill one said. "If we kill them, we can take their devices and maybe even find their spacecraft!"

The leader turned to his small companion and said, "Quiet, Pad. Nobody's killing anyone. Besides, I strongly suspect that if she wanted to, she could kill you without trying very hard." Touching Torres's shoulder, the leader asked, "Is she always this way?"

Torres, though clearly surprised by the question, was not too surprised to answer: "Pretty much all the time."

He shook his head, then beckoned at them to rise.

"Well, come on. We need to talk and there's no reason we should all be uncomfortable. It's damp and cold down here."

Torres said bluntly, "I can't see you."

"And I cannot walk," Seven added.

The leader sighed. "Well, that's what you get for playing with machines you don't understand."

"We understood it perfectly," Seven replied. "You arranged for it to explode if someone tampered with it."

The leader turned and stared at the one named Pad. "I told you *not* to set that. We're all under too much stress as it is. What if someone had gotten caught by the explosives?"

"Someone *did* get caught by the explosives," Torres protested.

"Someone who was *supposed* to be there."

"You don't listen to anything I say," Pad said. "They're going to come for us now! The Emergency Council can't ignore us any longer, especially after the test! We have to be ready for them!"

"Your companion is correct," Seven said. "The effect of your device was felt all over the planet. You must explain to us what you are attempting to do."

"Why?" the leader asked. "Why should we tell you anything?"

"Because we can help," Seven said.

"You came to help the Emergency Council," Pad said accusingly. "You said that."

"We came to help all Monorhans," Torres said.

"But now we need to help ourselves, too," Seven

added. "We will help you because we need you to help us."

The leader slipped the power pack off his back and set the rifle against the wall. Leaning forward, he pulled Torres to her feet. "That," he said, "is a very convincing argument."

"The first thing you must understand," Morsa began in a reasonable tone, "is that until a short time ago the *rih-hara-tan* of the thirteen cities were the ruling authority of my world." He had not been willing to answer the most obvious question—what had Ziv meant by his comment?—but was more than happy to discuss the origin of the energy pulse responsible for their current predicament. Chakotay settled back into his seat, calmed by the Monorhan's resonating bass voice. "When it became obvious that the Blue Eye would be our collective death, the thirteen *rih-hara-tan* appointed a council to study the problem and make recommendations. There was a problem with this course, however."

"Scientists are not an esteemed class on your world," Neelix inserted, speaking for the first time in many minutes.

Morsa stretched his neck toward the Talaxian, then tilted his head. "Correct. May I ask how you came to that conclusion?"

"Of course," Neelix said. "The *rih-hara-tan*'s authority clearly has its roots in the worship of the Blessed All-Knowing Light. Your world is scientifically advanced in many ways, but the technology we've seen could be described as defensive in nature: reflective or inward-looking. I'm guessing that a central authority, which keeps a close watch on innovation, funds the sciences. This would certainly be possible given the hierarchical nature of the *hara.*"

Morsa blinked once, opened his mouth once, closed it, then said, "Yes." Turning back to Chakotay, the Monorhan continued, "For most of the history of my world, individuals who displayed exceptional scientific talent were closely monitored, their abilities funneled into activities deemed worthwhile by the *rih-hara-tan.*"

"And what if an individual does not wish to be monitored?" Chakotay asked. "What if they wished to pursue ideas wherever they went?"

"From what I understand, for many years individuals of the sort you describe would simply disappear. Eventually, however, the *rih-hara-tan* came to understand that this was not necessary. Any scientist who does not wish to have his work reviewed can refuse. Of course, they also understand that they would be cut off from sanctioned resources."

"And there are no unsanctioned resources," Chakotay said.

"Very few, though in the past several years, the *rih-hara-tan* and the Emergency Council they created have not been able to control resources as effectively. Two years ago, a group of unaffiliated scientists began work on a forcefield system that they said would better protect the cities. When they had a working model, the researchers brought their designs before the Emergency Council."

"Wasn't this a risky thing to do?" Neelix asked.

"Under different circumstances," Morsa said, "definitely yes. But the researchers very understandably felt they had nothing to lose. The most likely outcome, they knew, was to end up in an Emergency Council research enclave working on their designs in a sanctioned manner. At worst, they would be sent away."

"So, what happened?" Chakotay asked.

"The council found too many problems with the design. Some of their comments were specious, since it was clear the council did not understand the underlying concepts the researchers were using. Other comments were understandable. Several of the researchers saw that the council had legitimate concerns about the energy shield disrupting the planet's magnetic envelope, potentially as dangerous a problem as the radiation from the Eye."

"And what happened next?"

"The research group was co-opted. The council took in those they felt could be useful and sent away the others. Separated, the council believed, the scientists could cause no mischief."

"And you know all this because you were one of the co-opted researchers," Chakotay concluded.

Morsa twisted his neck from side to side, a gesture Chakotay interpreted as embarrassment. "As you may have noticed, Commander, I have a large appetite. The Dissenters were not able to keep me well fed."

"The Dissenters?" Neelix asked.

"That is the name the council gave us . . . them. And since I have been working for the council, we *have* made progress with the design of the shield generators. The type used to protect the cities now is twenty percent more efficient than the previous generation."

"Which is nowhere near enough," Neelix said.

"No," Morsa admitted. "It is not. But it is something. If I had stayed with the Dissenters, we would have even less."

"And you would be thinner," the Talaxian concluded.

Chakotay continued, "But now you think the others have built the shield generator despite the warnings from the Council."

"Quite possibly. The Emergency Council has been consumed with gathering materials to build ships. Watching a small group of scientists was not a priority."

"Did you stay in touch with your old colleagues?" Chakotay asked. "Do you know anything about their recent work?"

Morsa wagged his head back and forth. "They were not interested in speaking to me. Perhaps if you could show me your readings from the energy wave, I could say if it was modulated in a manner consistent with their research."

Chakotay considered, then concluded this might be a good idea. If nothing else, they would know who all the players were when they got out of the subspace fold. He was rising from the table when a wave of nausea and confusion hit him. As he sank back into his chair, doubled up over his gut, the red-alert alarm erupted. The klaxon sounded for several seconds before Chakotay could muster the energy to tap his combadge and shout, "Bridge! What's happening?"

Abruptly, the sickness lifted, and moments later the klaxon fell quiet, but the red alert lights did not cease to flash. Chakotay rose groggily but swiftly and raced to the door, Neelix at his heels. Just before he exited, Chakotay saw Morsa pulling another plate of food in front of him.

Chapter 12

Climbing up the ladder to the hatch, B'Elanna had to keep reminding herself that she had been in many worse situations that involved utter darkness and precarious circumstances. She could recall several occasions where she had been crawling down a Jefferies tube when the power had gone out and she'd been forced to scale a narrow incline, never knowing if she was about to lay her hand on a live power source. What difference did it make that she was climbing straight up a (by the feel of it) rusty metal ladder with no other handholds anywhere nearby. None at all. She comforted herself with the thought that at least she could move under her own power. Judging by the grunts behind her and Seven's periodic admonishments, the Borg was being carried up the ladder slung over someone's back.

The climb took a few minutes, but she was profoundly grateful when she heard the Monorhans in front of her push up on the hatch cover. The echoes diminished, the air grew warmer, and B'Elanna suddenly found she was out of ladder. A pair of strong hands grasped her forearms and half-lifted, half-dragged her through the hatch. Moments later, she heard two Monorhans click in an aggravated manner as they pulled Seven up, then felt a heavy thump as the hatch slammed back into place.

"You can walk all right?" the leader asked, touching B'Elanna's shoulder.

"As long as someone steers me in the right direction."

"Too bad you're not strong enough to carry the other one. She seems to like telling people where to go."

B'Elanna laughed despite herself. She still didn't know if she believed what these people were telling her, but she trusted the leader. "Yeah, Seven's like that."

She felt the leader shift his weight suddenly. "I can't get used to the sounds in my head being different from the sounds of the language. Is the other's one name really a number?"

"Yes. Her name is actually Seven of Nine, Tertiary Adjunct of Unimatrix Zero One. She used to be a Borg, which, apparently, all get easy-to-remember names like that."

"A Borg?"

"Yes, a group you haven't encountered. If you had, we wouldn't be having this conversation."

"I've heard of them," the leader said.

"You're kidding. How? Ziv said your world has never been visited by other races."

"Then he lied. We should discuss this, but let's do it where we can sit and get something to eat. Pad, Quel—

tell the others we're going upstairs. Sora, see if you can find some kind of trolley to bring Seven."

"That's everyone's name except yours," B'Elanna said.

"Was it?" the leader asked. "You're a good listener." He patted her on the shoulder with a gigantic hand and said, "Kaytok. I'm Kaytok."

B'Elanna reached out and felt Kaytok's arm, which was covered with a stiff, wiry fur. "Good to meet you. Now tell me about meeting Borg."

"What?" Seven asked. B'Elanna heard heavy wheels moving on squeaky bearings. Sora must have found a trolley.

Pleased about knowing something Seven did not (however briefly the exclusivity might last), B'Elanna said, "That's what Kaytok said."

Walking slowly so that B'Elanna could keep up, Kaytok replied, "I did not say I had met one; I said I heard of them. About forty years ago, a pair of spacecraft landed on Monorha near the third city. I did not see them with my own eyes, you understand, though I have spoken to those who have. Their vessels, my source said, were not in good condition, nor were the occupants. They died shortly after they arrived."

"Radiation sickness," B'Elanna said. "If we hadn't taken drugs before coming, I would be sick by now, too. Your race seems to have some developed natural defenses because you can tolerate rems that would kill most other species."

Ignoring B'Elanna, Seven asked, "What does this have to do with the Borg?"

"The aliens—the other aliens, I should say—they didn't have your translators, so we couldn't understand what they were saying, but 'Borg' was one of the few words they said over and over that anyone remembers. We've always wondered what it meant."

"It means death for most people," B'Elanna said.

"Assimilation," Seven corrected. "A new form of existence."

"A form of life where everyone would prefer to die," B'Elanna retorted. "Not much to brag about."

"I am not bragging, Lieutenant. I merely wished to point out the inaccuracies in your statement."

"I wasn't being *inaccurate,* Seven. Editorializing a little, maybe, but . . ."

"So you two travel together a lot?" Kaytok asked.

"No!" B'Elanna and Seven answered as one.

"Imagine that," the Monorhan commented dryly. "Dip your head down here," he instructed B'Elanna. "Low doorframe."

Chakotay stepped out of his turbolift car onto the bridge and found the captain already there, though she could have only just arrived because Dan Fisher, the gamma-shift bridge officer, was snapping to attention and issuing his report. "The shields came down, Captain. Only for a few seconds, though." Chakotay slid into the science station and began checking sensor data. To his right, he heard Tuvok running a roll call of all the security stations. Glancing at Kathryn, he saw a flash of the anger she must be feeling. Fisher must have seen it, too, because he stepped away from the CO's chair and said, "Engineering is standing by, Captain."

The veins in her temples popping, the captain snapped, "Engineering, this is the captain. Report—and *don't* tell me you don't know what happened."

"Engineering, Chief Jango here." Chakotay was pleased to hear Jango's voice. He was one of the older, more seasoned members of B'Elanna's team, a Starfleet vet who had formed a personal attachment to the captain because (he told Chakotay once) she bore a striking resemblance to Jango's oldest daughter.

Kathryn smiled, the stress lines around her eyes softening. "Good to hear you're down there, Bill. Give me a status report."

"You're not going to like this, Captain," Jango said. *"But we really don't know what happened. We've been monitoring a slow drain on the core over the past couple hours, but it wasn't enough to make anyone really nervous. Figured the baby was just missing its mam."*

Chakotay almost laughed aloud. Not many people got to talk about B'Elanna that way, though he knew there was a myth among the engineers that the main core always ran better when B'Elanna was on board, even if she was nowhere near the engine room.

"Then, about five minutes ago," Jango continued, *"the main board shot out an alert that the coolant injectors were offline and scrambled the entire core. We tried to keep everything run-*

ning off secondaries until we figured out what was wrong, but the shields were drawing too much. Mr. Carey says you two were working on these. Is that right?"

"That's right, Bill. Check the radiation levels in the core if Joe hasn't already."

"He's crawling around the injectors right this second with a radiation scanner, trying to figure out which seal is going to pop."

Kathryn rubbed her forehead. "How much time do we have left, Bill?"

"Going by what I've seen, you're going to want to get out of here in the next five hours, Captain. Maybe a little more. Depends on how much guidance control you'll be wanting."

"All right, Bill. Keep us posted. Let me know if you get a better estimate."

"Will do."

As soon as she signed off, Tuvok signaled to the captain that he wished to speak to her privately. Janeway stalked to her office, indicating that Chakotay and Tuvok should follow. She didn't even sit down when they entered, but only walked around behind her desk and stood with one hand resting on the back of the chair. "Make this quick, Tuvok. Harry and I were working on something . . ." The Vulcan stood stock-still, arms folded behind his back, and looked straight ahead. Sensing his mood, Kathryn stopped speaking, and nodded once stiffly.

Tuvok said, "Ensign Platt is dead."

Melissa Platt had been one of Chakotay's, a Maquis who been drawn to the group on ideological grounds. A student at Mars University, she had been so incensed by the plight of the Juhrayan colonists that she had quit school to join the Maquis. Though she had been too physically timid to help in armed conflicts, Chakotay had been glad to have her in his group because Melissa had been one of the warmest, most caring individuals he had ever met. Also, she had shown an uncanny knack for repairing weapons systems, likely born out of the same patience and attention to detail that had made her a first-rate student. Tuvok often told Chakotay that he had been glad to have Platt in security. Some altercations were better addressed with a quiet word than a phaser set on stun.

"What happened to her?" Kathryn asked.

"She walked into a doorway expecting the door to open for her. It did not, though it was temporarily immaterial when our shields dropped."

Chakotay closed his eyes, not wanting to picture what must have happened next. Kathryn said, "And then the shields went back up."

"Yes," Tuvok said. "If it is any consolation, the Doctor said she died instantaneously."

Kathryn nodded, her face ashen with grief and anger. "All right. See that her body is put into stasis so we can have a service when we're clear of subspace."

Tuvok cleared his throat, then continued. "They are having some trouble recovering the body. I told them to simply cut away the door and put Ensign Platt in a closed casket."

"Oh, God," Kathryn said softly, then gripped the edge of her desk and stood for several seconds with her eyes tightly shut, her chest rising and falling sharply. When her breathing calmed, she opened her eyes and Chakotay saw they were once again clear and filled with a fierce, cold light. "All right, Tuvok. You did the right thing. Thank you."

Tuvok nodded, spun on his heel, and paced to the door. Stopping a centimeter short of the electric eye, the Vulcan turned and looked back over his shoulder at his commanding officer. "Captain, I would be remiss if I did not point out that the next time this happens, it could be a primary bulkhead or a section of hull containing an energy main."

"I understand, Tuvok."

Tuvok hesitated for only a moment, as if he had something else to say, but then nodded once and exited. When Chakotay turned back to Kathryn, she said, her voice full of iron, "Come with me to astrometrics. I think we've found a way out."

Ziv stood with his head thrown back, his arms straight at his sides, his wide nostrils flaring in anger. "I cannot believe," he said, "that you would shame me—that you would shame *all* of us—in such a manner." His *hara* stood arrayed around him like sheets of polished steel around a fire, his rage reflected back and increased a hundredfold.

Sem dismissed them all with a wave of her slender hand. "These Voyagers do not understand shame, Captain, at least not in any meaningful way."

"I am pleased to see that some things never change," Ziv said scornfully. "Quick judgments with no real understanding of what you dismiss. Have you seen nothing? Don't you understand the *power* these people wield?"

"They have power," Sem said, gliding gracefully to the large window. "I'll grant you that, but they don't understand how to wield it. Else why would they have put themselves in this predicament?"

"Because they are good," Diro said, unasked. It was a terrible breach of etiquette for the youngest to speak, but Ziv allowed it because it was as if his *haran* had read his *harat*'s thoughts. "They seek no gain for aiding us other than the knowledge that if they had done otherwise, it would have lessened us all."

Sem stared at Diro incredulously, as if a piece of furniture had suddenly begun to dance and sing. Turning to look at Ziv, she asked, "You allow this?"

"Times must change, Sem. And he speaks the truth. These Voyagers, their philosophy is not so different from things I've read in some of the ancient texts." Speaking from memory, he quoted, " 'For each of us must go out into the world and drink in all there is to see and to hear and to taste.' In the end, each of us must sit by the right hand of the Blessed, All-Knowing Light, tell the story of our life, and be judged."

Sem rolled her eyes in disgust. "And even if I still believed this tale told to children, I would at least know that I spent my life trying to help my people. Can you say the same, Ziv?"

"*Some* of your people, Sem. And which ones? Tell me, how did *you* become the judge?"

Sem retracted her head down to the level of her shoulders and scowled at him. Abruptly, she clacked her tongue twice against her palate, then whistled sharply. Under her robes, Ziv saw stirrings like the ripples made by a breeze over the surface of a pond. His mouth went dry. *No,* he thought. *I will not be a slave to this again!* "Tell them to leave, Ziv," she said.

Ziv struggled against her will. *I will not be a slave to this again!*

His *hara* all stood as if to file out the door, the programming that controlled their movements older than the language Sem spoke in. Small slits near the waist of her garment parted provocatively and pheromones began working their ancient magic.

Marshaling his will, Ziv turned his eyes so he could look at his *hara,* all of whom, he assumed, would have their gaze averted. To his surprise (and mild embarrassment), Ziv found that all of them had their eyes locked on him, as if they were willing him their strength the same way that he, the *harat,* could sometimes lend them his own. Their eyes did not accuse or shame him and one—Ziv would never know who—clicked once softly, a note of sympathy and compassion. Ziv clenched his eyes shut, and though he could not stop thinking about what was beneath Sem's robes, he said, "No."

"No?" Sem said, surprised but amused.

"No," Ziv said. "Leave here. You shamed me once and took my life from me. I will not let you do it again."

Moving very close to him, so close that Ziv could feel her warm breath on his cheek, Sem asked in a whisper, "I took something from you? And here I was thinking I *gave* you something."

"I did not want what you gave me," Ziv hissed.

"Then what is it you *do* want?"

"I wish to be something I can never be again."

"And you think I could not arrange for you to be my *shi-harat* again?" Sem asked. "We could say your resignation was simply a mistake, a misunderstanding. Who would dare doubt me?"

The desire to succumb, to agree to anything Sem asked, was overwhelming, but Ziv kept moving his eyes from Diro to Shet to Jara to Mol, then back again. "Leave," he whispered, but even Ziv was not certain if he spoke to Sem or to his *hara*. No one moved for several seconds until, finally, Sem took a half-step away from him, sighing as her robes settled back into place.

"Fine," she said as she exited. "A wonderful time and place for you to develop some character, Ziv. What else will I find to do to amuse myself before the end?"

Uncharacteristically, it was Mol who broke the silence after Sem left. "I'm sure," he said softly, "that she will think of something."

"You two were sent to help," Kaytok said. "So what can you do? What were you doing to our scanners?"

B'Elanna could hear the crackle of wood and felt the heat from a low fire on her knees, but did not smell smoke, so she assumed they had outfitted some kind of stove in one of the laboratories. The warmth was a comfort after the damp cold of the underground tank, and the rations from her kit had done a lot to bring her back to full consciousness. "We can't do much now," she said, picking at a bit of food wedged between her teeth. "Not until we can contact our ship and get these wounds healed. Just before the, uh, accident, we saw something in your scanners that might help us get back in touch with her."

"You mean the scanner that was severely damaged in the explosion you caused?" Kaytok asked. "Wonderful idea. Think of another one. Is there any way you could explain to us what you need?"

"Possibly," Seven said. "But we have a limited amount of time. Before the explosion, we learned that *Voyager* is trapped between two layers of subspace."

"We did?" B'Elanna asked.

"*I* did," Seven said. "It is the only explanation for the readings I saw."

B'Elanna resisted the urge to snarl. There was no point to arguing about data that she had not read. "All right. Then what's their status?"

"It is difficult to say," Seven said. "Borg vessels trapped in similar circumstances were never imperiled for the short term. The danger comes if they attempt to escape. Fortunately, we should be able to contact them with subspace radio."

"Then speed is important, but there's no way we can create the communication system we need from what's here."

"What about your ship?" Kaytok asked. "Do you have what you need there?"

"Yes," Seven said. "Some of it would have to be adapted. Using materials from your shield experiments, we may be able to free them."

"Who said anything about shield experiments?" Pad asked, his voice sharply suspicious.

"No one," B'Elanna said. "But we saw the array on the roof and got a look at the equipment downstairs. It's the only explanation that makes any sense." One question still nagged her, though. "But why are you out here in the middle of nowhere doing this work in a lab that looks like it was deserted months ago? Who are you hiding from?"

Kaytok made a sound that the translator interpreted as a dry chuckle. "We're not hiding," he said. "We're just not important enough that anyone would come look for us."

"That makes no sense," Seven said. "You are attempting to save your people. Why would the authorities not care what you do?"

"Because they've given up on saving everyone," Pad said. "Didn't you know?"

"We knew that someone is building evacuation ships," Seven said. "We encountered one on the way into the system." She decided it was best not to reveal the fate of the transport. Someone in the room might have had a relative or friend on the doomed vessel.

"And how many of those do you think the Emergency Council will be able to build?" Pad sneered. "Ten, maybe twenty if they're incredibly lucky? How many people can they get off? One hundred thousand? Two hundred thousand?"

"So the council has no intention of removing your entire citizenry?" Seven asked.

"Just the ones whom they consider necessary to survive on a new world: engineers, pharmacists, teachers, farmers, and, of course, capable administrators."

"Those are all reasonable choices," Seven replied soberly. "Someone must make the decisions."

"Maybe," Kaytok said. "But shouldn't everyone get the chance to make their case? What about artists and writers? What about children who haven't shown what they can do yet? And even if you don't let everyone have a say, shouldn't the council at least tell everyone what's happening? Almost no one in the thirteen cities knows they're likely going to die before another year has passed."

"A year?" B'Elanna asked. "How can you be so sure? And for that matter, how do you know all this when no one else does?"

"We have sources inside the council," Kaytok said. "Someone who was once part of our group went to work for the council. We trade information. That's how we know that though most of the council disapproves of what we're attempting to do, a couple members believe we should get a chance." His voice suddenly dropped low in disappointment. "Unfortunately, our resources dried up a little while ago and we've been struggling to complete the prototype. The experiment we performed yesterday—that was an act of desperation. Nobody thought it would really work."

"What were you trying to do?" B'Elanna asked. "I still haven't pieced it together. Obviously, you were trying to enhance your shield generator, but I still don't understand what happened that *Voyager* disappeared into . . . wherever she is."

Kaytok replied, "You're right, we were trying to enhance the shield generator. The new wrinkle we figured out was a method to power the shields with the radiation that's been poisoning our planet. We've engineered a collector that absorbs the emissions from the Blue Eye and transforms them into power. Or so we thought. . . ."

Pad chimed in. "The transformer didn't alter the radiation enough. We ended up pumping out altered energy rather than a shield. Blew out the collector and the transformer."

"We may be able to help with that," Seven said. "If we can bring *Voyager* out of the subspace fold, we can use all her resources to help you repair your prototype. The idea has merit."

"She's right," B'Elanna said. "Now that I know what you were trying, I think I can suggest a couple changes that might help."

"The only problem being that that one is blind," Kaytok said, "and you can't walk. So how exactly do you plan to proceed?"

"I have a proposal," Seven said. "Though I strongly believe it will find little favor with Lieutenant Torres."

~

Seven understood the concept of understatement and knew that many of her shipmates thought it a form of communication she practiced intentionally. This was not the case. Suggesting Seven employed understatement (or any of the other forms of wordplay including sarcasm, irony, and cheap ridicule) meant they believed there was a better way to communicate other than clearly stating facts in a simple, unadorned fashion. Seven found this idea baffling.

Though she appreciated the fact that Torres's initial response to her suggestion had been succinct, she was troubled by the flat refusal. "There is absolutely no way in *hell* I'm going to let you stick any of that Borg crap in me! Your little bugs—swimming through my bloodstream? Make me a part of the collective? Forget it!"

"You would retain your individuality, Lieutenant, not become a member of the collective. You *couldn't*, because there is no collective here." She stopped then and considered, realizing she was not being completely accurate. "Actually, that is not true: *we* would be the collective: a collective of two."

Torres stared into the middle distance, her jaw slack. Gathering her wits, then shaking her head, the engineer said incredulously, "You say that like somehow I'd find it reassuring. Amazing. No, Seven. Absolutely not. I won't even consider it."

Kaytok and the others watched them argue, their heads swinging back and forth on their long necks.

"Then quite likely all these people will die."

"Agreeing to this is no guarantee they'll live."

"You'll never see your friends again."

"I will if the ship finds us."

"But they *won't* find us unless we can contact them and help them escape the subspace fold," Seven said reasonably. "And we cannot do that unless you can see and I can walk. And neither of those things will happen unless you agree to this procedure."

Rage—B'Elanna's old friend—was rising up within her, choking her, clouding her thinking. She knew she was being unreasonable, even irrational. Seven did not wish to make B'Elanna into a drone any more than B'Elanna would want to be one. The idea of their becoming linked was probably as repugnant to the former Borg as it was to her. She had been turning over possibilities in her mind for the past hour, trying to figure out some way to contact the ship, but she kept running into the same obstacles: She was blind, Seven was lame, and there was no way the Monorhans could do the delicate technical work they required. And here was Seven proposing a possible route out of their dilemma and all B'Elanna could do was imagine how violated she would feel having nanoprobes swimming through her blood, into her muscles, brain, and nerve endings.

Grimmer memories began to filter into B'Elanna's mind. She found herself remembering the names and faces of her former Maquis allies, all of them now slain if she was to believe the news from the Alpha Quadrant. Thinking of them, she felt her rage begin to condense and cool, to become something like a black hole in the center of her being. What about the sacrifices they had made? What about the *ultimate* sacrifice? If Seven thought she knew something that would save *Voyager* (and as much as B'Elanna hated to admit it, Seven was usually right about these things), then she owed it to her shipmates, to her friends, to do anything, to surrender anything to save them. Lowering her head, she hissed softly, "How long will it take?"

"Not long," Seven replied. "But it would be best if you were unconscious for the first part of the procedure. Some of the nanoprobes will need to construct an ocular implant to enable you to see."

"Only one?"

"Two would not be wise," Seven said. "There would be complications."

"Great. No depth perception."

" 'In the kingdom of the blind, the one-eyed man is king.' "

"But he still would have no depth perception."

Seven sighed, a response that only Torres could tear out of her so frequently. "You are a very difficult person, Lieutenant. Lie down now."

"I know," Torres said, lying back on the floor. "It's just that I really don't like you at all. No offense."

Seven leaned down over Torres and unconsciously flexed a muscle in her forearm. A minuscule gap opened between Seven's wrist bones just above the cuff and an assimilation tubule snaked out from it like a tiny black tongue. Seven touched the tube to Torres's neck and the engineer grew quiet. "None taken," Seven said.

Chapter 13

When Kim had asked to meet her in astrometrics, Captain Janeway had thought he had found an answer to her question about going into a controlled warp in the fold. This was not the case. Instead, Kim had seen something in the map of the fold Tuvok had been creating that he wished to discuss. At first, she had been impatient with the ensign, almost angry, but as he had talked, Janeway had begun to see the idea toward which he had been driving. Now, having fleshed out Kim's idea, she wanted to get Chakotay's opinion before proceeding. "Explain it to him, Harry," she ordered.

Kim brought Tuvok's incomplete map up onto the lab's big monitor. "This all started when Tom and I were looking at Tuvok's map and we noticed this curved line," Kim began.

Janeway read the consternation on Chakotay's face and even heard a note of annoyance in his voice when he said, "I don't follow you, Harry. So it's curved? So what?"

"Which is precisely what I said," Janeway admitted. "Why wouldn't a fold have a curve?"

"And I conceded that," Kim said. "But there was something about the shape that nagged at me, so I asked Tuvok to send out more probes and complete the line. He did, and then we got this." The line became appreciably longer, but the curl of the curve was more extreme. "Up at this end, the curve spiraled in on itself. I had to ask myself why it would do that."

Chakotay stared at the diagram for several seconds, then rubbed his eyes. "I'm not following you, Harry."

"Show him what we think the rest of the curve looks like," Janeway said.

"Right," Kim said and worked the controls. "I think I saw the beginnings of it because of a topography class I took in high school." He dropped his eyes. "Unfortunately, I didn't do very well in the course. The captain saw the answer right away."

When Harry was finished, the rest of the shape emerged and Janeway saw the light of understanding dawn in Chakotay's eyes. "We're not in a fold," he said.

"Right," Harry said. "It finally made sense when the captain reminded me about the radiation in the space around us. Where is it coming from? It couldn't have all come in when we did." The diagram on the screen showed *Voyager* in a space that looked remarkably like a paper bag whose mouth had been twisted into a corkscrew shape. "It's leaking in through the top of the bag."

Chakotay slowly nodded, then looked at Janeway.

"All right. I get it and I agree. It's the only explanation that fits the facts. What do we do now?"

"We have to uncurl the top of the bag."

"Any ideas how we're going to do that?"

"Yes," Janeway said. "One."

She briefly outlined her plan, after which Chakotay sagged back against one of the stools along the wall. "Suddenly I'm glad B'Elanna's not on board. She isn't going to like what we're about to do to the engines."

"So you agree?"

"We're running out of options, Captain."

Feeling every muscle in her lower back protest, Janeway straightened. "Then assemble the senior staff in the briefing room," she said. "Everybody needs to know exactly what their job will be."

"Lieutenant, wake up. You must open your eye."

Eye? B'Elanna thought. *Right. Only one. Which did she pick?* Her eyes shut, B'Elanna reached up and touched her left cheek, then gently probed the socket, finding unfamiliar ridges and bumps. She felt her skin suddenly grow clammy. *An implant,* she thought. *I have a Borg implant in me. I'm going to hate this.* Fighting down panic, she inhaled and exhaled slowly, then tried to assess her condition. *All things considered,* she decided. *I feel fine.* If Seven had performed some kind of surgery on her, the Borg had worked very skillfully. But, wait, no, of course not. Seven had not grafted the implant into her; she had injected preprogrammed nanoprobes and the implant had *grown* in her. B'Elanna fought back a second shudder. *No time to be squeamish,* she decided. *The sooner we get this done, the quicker I can get home and have the damned thing removed.*

"Lieutenant?"

"I'm here," B'Elanna said, her throat raw and scratchy. Struggling to sit up, she opened her eyes. "How long have I been out . . . Oh!"

"Be patient, Lieutenant," Seven said. "Your brain is attempting to process a new level of data. Frankly, I'm not entirely confident that it will be able to do so, but there are adjustments we can make. Here," she said when B'Elanna did not reply. "Let me . . ."

B'Elanna brushed her hand away. "No," she said. "Don't touch . . ."

Light. Everything was made of light. Her glowing hand moved back and forth in front of her face, tiny pinpoints of luminescence sprinkling down from her palm like pixie dust. Looking past her hand, B'Elanna saw a galaxy of pinpoint stars flicker and dance, shivering down from the sky, twirling in whorls and Brownian waves.

"Lieutenant?"

B'Elanna turned toward the voice and gasped in wonder. "Oh, my . . ." she said. Seven's face and form were picked out in infinitesimally tiny beads of color, subtle hues shading one into the other, all glistening, all vibrating with life.

"Lieutenant?"

B'Elanna tried to speak, but her throat was constricted, so overcome was she by what she was seeing. Finally, she choked out, "Seven?"

"Yes, Lieutenant?"

"Is this how you see the world all the time?"

The glimmering goddess that was Seven of Nine reached up to touch her own temple, making B'Elanna gasp and grow weak with a wondrous sensation that she imagined must be what religious people meant when they spoke of ecstasy. "Let me see . . ." Seven sighed and then said, "No, Lieutenant." Abruptly, the galaxy shifted. All the lights and colors dimmed by half, then half again. Details receded and shapes grew hard edges. Nothing sparkled anymore. "The magnification and spectral analysis modules were set too high. You were looking at microscopic life-forms, dust mites, nematodes . . . nuisances, really."

"But, but . . . they were so beautiful."

Seven cocked an eyebrow. "Yes, Lieutenant. If you say so. How do you feel otherwise?"

B'Elanna performed an internal audit and was surprised to find that she felt . . . fine. *I feel good,* she thought. *Really quite good.* "What the hell is wrong with me?" she asked, but couldn't work up a genuine feeling of aggravation. "I don't feel right. I mean, I feel . . . calm." *Almost happy, even.* "What did you do to me?"

"I have done nothing, Lieutenant. Nanoprobes are monitoring your physiology. It is possible that they are adjusting some of your functions for maximum efficiency."

"You mean they're drugging me?" B'Elanna knew she should be upset by the idea, but was not. Apparently, she could not be if the nanoprobes would not permit it.

Seven shrugged. "This is what I believe you would refer to as hair splitting."

"I'd prefer they didn't do it," B'Elanna said. "Make them stop."

"*You* make them stop, Lieutenant. They are *your* nanoprobes."

B'Elanna considered the idea: *her* nanoprobes. Hers. How could she make them obey her? More important, what was the point of ordering them to let her be the agitated and inefficient B'Elanna of old? Why not maintain this calm, cool clarity? She looked at Seven and for the first time found that the Borg's icy tranquility did not annoy her. Indeed, she found it admirable. *What am I thinking?* she wondered, and shook herself out of her reverie. A moment later, she felt the nanoprobe-induced serenity lift. Blood moved into her face and B'Elanna knew she was pink-cheeked with fury.

Obviously observing this, Seven nodded briefly, then rose from B'Elanna's bedside. "We must make plans. How can we contact *Voyager*?"

"You're walking!" B'Elanna said. "What happened? I thought you said your spine was damaged and your nanoprobes couldn't complete the repair."

"Ah," Seven said. "But using your nervous system as a guide, the nanoprobes were able to replicate the necessary tissue. It is easier to trace than to create."

"My nervous system was the guide?" B'Elanna asked. "How . . . ?"

"The process of injecting you with nanoprobes was not one-way," Seven said. "As with any such process, there is always a mingling of essences. I did not think you would mind."

"I . . . don't," B'Elanna said. She thought she should, but had to admit to herself that she did not. She could see again; Seven could walk again. Both of them were restored and they might now be able to help their crewmates. What could be wrong with that? Still, she couldn't shake the feeling that somewhere underneath it all, she *should* feel violated, but that the nanoprobes were nullifying any opposition she might have to the idea. *How can I trust anything I'm feeling? How can I ever know if anything I'm doing is because it's something I want to do?* Then the clincher—the final thought on the subject—came: *How did I know if that was ever true before?*

"Very well," Seven said. "To continue, then . . ."

B'Elanna nodded, rising slowly. "Right. *Voyager.* Kaytok's people were able to find the ship with their equipment; whether that was intentional or not is immaterial. We'll need the subspace radio array from the shuttle to . . ."

". . . Pierce the veil and speak to *Voyager.* But a closer examination of their equipment . . ."

". . . Would be useful," B'Elanna continued. "Where's Kaytok? We'll need to . . ."

". . . Make arrangements," Seven said. "He is downstairs waiting for us. I believe he understands that we wish to aid him. However, he also fears this installation will be investigated in the near future. We must move quickly. If the authorities . . ."

". . . Confiscate their shield generator, we're screwed."

"And so are the Monorhans," Seven concluded.

Both women paused and looked intently at each other. "Did we really just do that?" B'Elanna asked.

"I believe we did," Seven said and made a face that on anyone else B'Elanna would have had to describe as a wry smile. "Hmph," she said. "The feeling was almost . . . nostalgic."

"So, we're in a bag?" Tom asked. "And you want me to fly us out through a tiny opening you think might be near the top? An opening big enough that it only lets in sub-atomic particles, but nothing else?"

Harry nodded. Tom looked around the conference table and noted that everyone (except for the Doctor, naturally) appeared exhausted. Just before he had come up to the meeting, Tom had stopped in his quarters to change into a fresh uniform and had been surprised by what he saw in the mirror. Being up for more than twenty-four hours would account for the dark circles and the pasty complexion, but not the red eyes and the broken blood vessels around his nose. A check with the medical tricorder confirmed his suspicion: the shields were letting in radiation, so the hyronalin injections were wearing off sooner than the Doctor had predicted. "Oh, okay," he said. "Any other miracles you want me to pull off?"

"Tom," Chakotay said, his tone warning Paris to ease off the sarcasm.

"Sorry, Harry." He dipped his head toward the captain. "Apologies, Captain."

"It's all right, Tom," Captain Janeway said tolerantly. "Fortunately, it won't be as difficult as that. We're pretty sure that we can use the deflector and quantum torpedoes to widen the opening."

"But we're not sure exactly how much," Tom said.

"Correct. It may be a very narrow opening, which is why I want you at the helm."

"All right," Tom said, pleased despite himself. "But if I understood everything else you and Harry were saying, there are other problems."

"There are," the captain said. "First, we don't know precisely what's going to be on the other side of the opening. It might be normal space. The 'top of the bag' might be the way we came in."

"But you don't think so," Tom finished for her.

"No, I don't. I think we came in through a rent in space precisely as we discussed . . ." The sentence trailed off. "How long ago was that? Only yesterday?" She shook her head in mild disbelief, then resumed. "I think we're going to find ourselves somewhere else. We have a theory, in any case, but that's not important right this second. The other factor that will complicate this process is."

"The shields," Tom said.

Tuvok said, "We do not have enough power to keep the shields at their current level *and* employ the navigational deflector as the captain described. We will be affected by the radiation. I will arrange the shields so that the bridge is as protected as possible, but we will need to program the autopilot to see us through in the event Mr. Paris cannot."

"And what about the rest of the crew?" the Doctor asked.

"We're moving everyone into the center of the ship," Chakotay said. "You said earlier that you didn't feel the effects in sickbay, so we're going to put as many people as possible down there."

"Lovely," the Doctor grumbled. "Company."

"You can sing to them, Doc," Tom said. "That'll keep them settled."

The Doctor's eyebrows shot up as he considered the possibility of a captive audience.

"And Neelix?" the captain said. "I'd like you to stay with the Monorhans. Their section of the ship is well protected, but I think they'll feel more reassured if you're nearby."

"Captain Ziv said that he did not feel the effects of the radiation last time," Neelix pointed out.

"No, but Morsa did," Chakotay said. "Probably because he was in the shuttle hangar. The Monorhans may have some resistance to the effect, but there's no guarantee they're completely immune."

"One last question, Doctor," the captain said. "Will another round of hyronalin help?"

"It would," the Doctor said, "if we had time to synthesize enough for the entire crew. However, with all the power going to the shields . . ."

"Is there enough for Tom and the rest of the bridge crew to have a dose?"

The Doctor nodded. "Barely."

"Then do that." The captain looked around the room and asked, "Are there any more questions? Comments? Does everyone know what they're doing?" All around the table, heads nodded in acceptance. Tom was briefly struck by how strange it felt to have everyone acquiesce so quickly, then recalled that neither Seven nor B'Elanna was present. One of them, of course, would have found a reason to disagree. Not for the first time he wondered how the pair were getting along.

"Mr. Neelix?"

The Talaxian looked up from the padd he had been studying and was surprised to find the *rih-hara-tan* standing before him. Had he been so absorbed in his work that he hadn't heard her enter the dining hall? Neelix doubted it, but he had to admit he had grown accustomed to the clamor humans made when they moved around and had forgotten that many races could be much quieter. Kes, he recalled, could walk across a sand-covered floor and barely stir a grain of sand. He sighed, remembering his lover and companion, and was then startled to realize he had not thought about her for many days. Shaking aside such thoughts, Neelix rose and said, "Yes, ma'am. My apologies. I was lost in thought. What can I do for you?"

"It is I who should apologize to you, Mr. Neelix," Sem said, her voice low and sweet. "I don't wish to distract you from your work, but Captain Janeway told me I should contact you if I need anything . . ." She hesitated, seemingly confused and a little flustered. "And there's so much here I don't understand. Could you help me?"

"Of course!" Neelix said, pleased to be of service. His primary role during the kind of emergency *Voyager* was currently embroiled in was to monitor the crew and make sure they ate and rested regularly. Neelix knew he was well suited to the role, but the situation had not evolved to the point where he needed to exercise the authority the captain had invested in him, so he was, as a consequence, slightly underemployed, especially since Captain Ziv's *hara* had sequestered themselves in their quarters. He was surprised to see Sem, but despite the earlier unpleasantness, he was determined to assist her in any way possible. "What can I do for you, *rlh-hara-tan?*"

"Well," Sem said, "first, I was hoping you could help me find something to eat. Commander Chakotay explained how the replicators worked, but I must be doing something wrong. The machine doesn't seem to understand what I'm asking for."

"It wouldn't," Neelix said, escorting her to a small table. "Especially if you're asking for something it doesn't recognize. What did you want?"

"A beverage. Something hot, I think. On my world, we drink a kind of infusion called *nualla*. It's slightly bitter, but calming. Do you have anything like that?"

"Ma'am," Neelix said, laughing and pulling out a chair for Sem, "thousands. We should sample some items to see if you can find something close."

Settling into her seat, Sem emitted a small trill that Neelix took to be a sound of merriment and pleasure. "Where do we begin?"

"With some green tea, I think," Neelix said, rubbing his hands together with anticipation. "Something mild." Speaking to the replicator, he ordered a cup of jasmine and waited as the device assembled the beverage from its component molecules. "You understand, this won't be as good as something I could make from fresh ingredients, but the kitchen isn't open during yellow alerts. Too much danger of fire or . . ." He waved his hands vaguely. "Collateral damage."

"I understand," Sem said as he set the cup down in front of her. "Though I hope I'll have the chance to try more of your cuisine before we leave. I thought the food you prepared for the banquet was quite lovely."

"Oh, *that?*" Neelix exclaimed. "A *banquet?* That was *nothing*. Pretty much just cleaned out the refrigerator."

"I'm sure that's not true," Sem said as she picked up her teacup and sniffed the brew. She jerked her head back slightly at the faint aroma, but then inched closer to it again and inhaled carefully. "This is interesting," she said. "Not what I was thinking of, but interesting." She took a small sip, then quickly set the cup down.

"Too hot?"

Sem nodded rapidly.

"Not to your taste?"

"I'd like to let it cool," Sem said, then coughed slightly as if to clear her throat.

"Is there something else I can get you?" Neelix asked.

He found he was feeling ever-so-slightly protective of her. Wondering if perhaps his earlier judgment had been too harsh, he asked solicitously, "Hungry?"

"No," Sem said, then rubbed her forehead with the back of her hand. "Exhausted, though. It has been a trying day."

"You should try to rest," Neelix said. "I'm sure you'll have a lot to do when you get home."

"I'd like to," Sem said. "I've tried to sleep, but the humming is oppressive. I don't notice it so much when I'm awake, but when I'm trying to relax . . ."

Neelix regarded Sem curiously. "Humming?" he asked. "What do you mean?"

Sem clicked once, a sound of impatience, and waved her hand past her left ear. "You don't hear it? It's ever present."

Neelix cocked his head and strained to listen carefully. "No," he said. "When did you start hearing it?"

"First on the shuttle," Sem said, her tone growing irritated. "I thought it was the engines or some piece of equipment, but then I heard it in the hangar and have ever since. You really don't know what I mean?"

"I'm afraid not, ma'am," Neelix said. "None of Captain Ziv's *hara* mentioned a humming."

"Really?" Sem asked, surprised. "How odd. It's been . . . pervasive. I assumed you all heard it."

"No," Neelix said, "and I have particularly acute hearing." This was an interesting puzzle, one he felt bound to solve. The constant irritation a disturbing noise would produce might explain some of Sem's behavior.

"Well, not entirely pervasive," Sem said, correcting herself. "There was a short time in the hangar when the sound disappeared."

"Really? When?"

"During the period when your shields were down," Sem said. "I remember there was a sound, a soft thud. Several in a row, in fact."

Searching his memory, Neelix tried to remember what might have happened in the shuttlebay while the shields were down. Of course, Commander Chakotay had his small misadventure and the forcefield had collapsed briefly. What else? He usually reviewed the damage control reports after every such incident so he could keep track of which crew members might require some special attention later. Fortunately, none of the shuttle crews had been hurt in the incident, though he *had* heard Chief Clemens was aggravated that B'Elanna hadn't been able to assign a damage control team to replace the bio-neural gel packs that had burst. . . .

"Ah!" Neelix said, standing up. "I believe I have an answer! Come over here, please," he said, leading Sem back to the replicator.

"I don't think I want any more tea, Mr. Neelix."

"Not tea. I'm not going to prepare anything. I just want you to stand here. Wait." He bustled back and brought a chair. "Sit," he said. Though Neelix couldn't account for it, there was certainly something about the Monorhan that made him feel solicitous. "Just in case this makes you feel poorly."

"What are you going to do?"

"*Voyager,* I'm told, possesses some fascinating technology." Touching a pressure point under the replicator, the maintenance panel snapped open.

"I should say," Sem said.

"My friends tell me that the most innovative is this." Reaching into the replicators depths, Neelix pulled out one of the gel pack modules. The case was sealed, but he could tell from the way the Monorhan shied away from the unit that this was the source of her discomfort. "This module contains bio-neural circuitry—a kind of neural tissue that's used to process data faster than any inorganic substance could."

Sem lowered her head down to her shoulders. "You mean," she said, "the ship is *alive?*"

"Not precisely. The neural tissue is artificial, but it simulates neural tissue's ability to process data very efficiently."

"Ah," Sem said. "Then the hum I'm hearing is the sound of the ship thinking."

Neelix grinned, delighted by the idea. "I suppose. I understand you possess psionic abilities beyond those of your *hara.* That would account for your sensitivity."

"As a *rih-hara-tan,* I can touch the minds of every member of my tribe," Sem said. "If I understand what you're saying correctly, I believe you are correct." Pointing at the gel pack, she asked, "Could you put that away now? In such close proximity, the noise is disconcerting."

"Sorry!" Neelix said and gently replaced the module

in the maintenance bay. "The good news is that I believe we can now solve your problem. I can ask the chief engineer to shut down the circuitry near your quarters."

"He can do that?"

"If he can reroute all the critical systems, certainly. We're trying to conserve energy anyway."

"Does the circuitry run throughout the ship?"

"Oh, yes, everywhere."

Sem rose then and bowed slightly. "Thank you, Mr. Neelix. You've been so helpful. I will be sure to mention your kindness when next I speak to the captain."

"Oh, that's all right," Neelix said, delighted. "I'm glad I could . . ." Behind him, he heard a small popping sound. Turning back to the replicator, he immediately saw that the small indicator light that meant the system had failed was blinking. "Oh, dear," he said.

"What's wrong?"

"I must have jostled the circuitry when I replaced it." He grimaced. "It's very fussy."

"Will your captain be angry?"

"I . . . I don't think so," Neelix said, but then he thought of B'Elanna and mentally winced. "But I should report the problem as quickly as possible. Is there anything else I can get for you, ma'am?"

"No, you've been more than helpful. Please speak to your engineer as soon as possible. I would like to get some sleep soon." Leaving barely a ripple, Sem turned and swept out of the dining hall, the only sound to mark her passing being the swish of the door.

Interesting woman, he thought, and was suddenly

struck by how she reminded him in some ways of Kes. *Not as kind or as gentle,* he concluded. *But there's something . . .*

Seven of Nine was irritated. Having shaken off the calming influence of the nanoprobes, Torres was now being as difficult as ever, insisting on making all the decisions concerning the repairs to the shield control generator. Apparently, Pad, the Monorhan who had attached the explosive charge to the panel, had used more than he knew. His intention had been to surprise, not to injure meddlers or damage their work. When Seven had observed to Kaytok that a simple alarm may have been more effective, he had ducked his head and said, "You don't know Pad."

"Bring that lamp over here," Torres called. "I can't see what I'm doing."

"As I explained earlier," Seven said, "you must will your eyes to use the available light."

"I don't like how everything looks then. There's a kind of shimmer around objects."

"Because you let the spectral analysis bleed in. Learn to control yourself."

"Hey, how about you just hold the light over here and then I won't have to." Unbelievably, Seven found she was being drawn away from where she had been working toward Torres.

"Stop!" Seven called and dragged herself back. "I will not be *violated* in this manner."

"What the hell are you talking about?" Torres bellowed. "Just get over here. The sooner we finish this, the sooner we can get moving."

Seven continued to resist the compulsion to approach Torres. "Why not allow the Monorhans to do their own repairs?"

"Because they might screw it up."

"It is *their* machinery!" Seven insisted, taking a step back to where she had been working.

"And it's going to have to merge with *our* machinery." Seven's foot slid back toward Torres.

"Please *stop* that!"

"Ow! Hey! I pinched my hand! And, hey, what are you doing?! I can't move my hand!"

Ah! Seven thought. *What's good for the goose is good for the gander!* She stopped and looked at the tool in her hand and wondered at the alien thought. *Where did* that *come from?*

Backing out of the panel, Torres appeared to be ready to throw the microspanner at Seven's head and was only confounded by the fact that she did not appear to be able to unclench her fist from around it. "What's going on? How are you controlling me like this?"

Seven stood her ground when Torres approached, but only barely. "It is not me," Seven said. "We are both responsible. The link makes it difficult to be in disagreement."

"Then how the hell do Borg even . . ." She held up her hands in surrender. "Never mind. I already know the answer. Borg never disagree about anything, right?"

"A collective mind cannot argue with itself."

"But we can," Torres said, studying her hand as she flexed the fingers. "I knew I was going to hate this."

A surge of rage climbed Seven's spine. "*You* hate this!? *You!?* What about me? What about . . . ? " And then she stopped, aware that she had clenched and raised her fist above her head. With her augmented physiology, a blow to the engineer's head would certainly render her unconscious, if not outright kill her. A small voice in the back of Seven's head said, *Good!*

"Go ahead," Torres said. "Try it." Seven looked up at the engineer's flinty gaze and was surprised—actually *surprised*—by what she saw there. Torres knew what Seven was thinking—if not in detail, then certainly in broad strokes. "You might be fast enough. I know you're strong enough. But keep this in mind if you miss." She held up her tool in a manner that Seven found genuinely intimidating. "I know how to take machines apart."

Feeling the unaccustomed rage subside, Seven said simply, "I am not a machine." Then, focusing her gaze on the ridges of the appliance around Torres's left eye, she said, "At least, no more than you are."

With her free hand, Torres reached up and touched the flesh around her eye socket, her mouth in a surprised *Oh!*

A voice spoke from the shadows: "Are you two just about through?" Kaytok stepped from the gloom, a large chunk of circuit board carried effortlessly under his right arm. "Because if there's something you want to settle, please try to do it far away from my shield generator. You have a bad habit of damaging it."

Seven asked, *"Your* shield generator? What do you mean? I have observed that Monorhans frequently use collective possessive pronouns."

Kaytok gently lowered the circuit board to the ground, lead wires jingling against the concrete floor. "I might not say it if any of the others was around, but, yes, I consider it my own. I designed it, built most of it."

Torres and Seven exchanged glances, then Torres said, "We assumed that this was part of a larger government project, that the shield generator was based on the models being used to protect the cities. That's not true?"

"The Emergency Council giving us a shield generator to play with?" Kaytok laughed, his large head snaking back and forth. "No, not really something they would do."

"Then you built this yourself?"

"That's what I said."

Torres and Seven looked up at each other again, their movements perfectly synchronized. Seven heard herself say, "Wow."

Torres murmured, "Indeed."

Kaytok knelt down next to the circuit board and began clipping leads to the damaged panel. "Amazing what an individual can accomplish, isn't it?"

Walking down the corridor back to her room, Sem lightly touched the walls as she passed and permitted herself to feel a modicum of delicious satisfaction. *I can hear you singing, little minds,* she thought. *And you can hear me, too, can't you?* These Voyagers—so smug in their superiority. Could any of them do what she could? She knew the answer, but enjoyed asking the question anyway, especially because she was the only one who knew the correct response. But now there was a new question: knowing what she knew, what should she do next?

Feeling the urge to exercise her will once more, Sem concentrated, listened for the song of an unimportant little mind, then chirped a countertone in response. A moment later, nearby, she heard a small pop. Nothing else terribly overt occurred except for the overhead lights dimming. She clicked her tongues together in pleasure. *Excellent*, she thought. Now her goal would be to find *important little minds*, and she was certain where she could find some.

When this is all over, Chakotay decided, *I'm going to bunk down for a solid twenty-four hours.* If he couldn't arrange that, what was the point of being the commander? Patrolling the bridge, he examined the crew and assessed their preparedness. Fortunately, not everyone on the ship had needed to remain awake for the duration of the crisis. Tom Paris must have found time to sleep for a few minutes, because when they caught each other's eye, Paris gave him a goofy half-smile, half-smirk. Once upon a time, Paris's hijinks had irritated Chakotay, but now he knew that the pilot's cavalier attitude was his way of coping with stress.

Kathryn sat straight-backed in the center seat, alert but quiet. Having told her crew what she expected of them, the captain had subsided into a state of watchful readiness, marshaling her resources. Chakotay tried to figure out when she might have slept in the past thirty-six hours, realized that he couldn't think of a time when she might, and decided that instead of going to his quarters when this was all over, he would make sure she went to hers. *And* that, he concluded, *is* really *the point of being the commander.*

Completing his round, Chakotay stopped at the tactical station and cocked an eyebrow at Tuvok, who nodded once. "Status, Harry?" Chakotay said.

From his station, Kim said, "Engineering asked for five more minutes to 'batten down the hatches.' "

Chakotay smiled. It was good to know Bill Jango was down there. "That should give you just enough time to get down to sickbay then."

Kim cocked his head, the question implicit in his expression.

"The captain said she'd like you down there in case something goes wrong, Harry," Chakotay said. "You know as much about our situation as anyone."

"Except for Tom," Kim said, grinning slyly. "But he has to push a button."

"Never underestimate the importance of button pushing," Paris retorted.

Chakotay glanced at the captain, who was not smiling, but not frowning either. Her expression said, *Let them blow off some steam if it helps.* "The important thing is having the right man for the job," Chakotay said. "Get your finger ready, Mr. Paris." Turning to Kim, he said,

"Go to sickbay. If everything works, you'll be back here in ten minutes."

Kim nodded once and headed for the lift. "Aye, Commander."

A minute later, the comm piped and Joe Carey called, *"Captain?"*

"Joe."

"Ready to go?"

Kathryn settled back into her chair, gazed around the bridge at her crew, then glanced briefly at the all-too-conveniently lost Sern. She inhaled deeply, then sighed. Looking over to Chakotay, she asked, "Do I have time to get a cup of coffee?"

"Not really, Captain."

"Then go ahead, Joe. Deflectors to full."

"Aye, Captain."

"Tuvok, shields around the bridge to maximum. Launch torpedoes on my mark. Mr. Paris . . ."

"Aye, Captain."

"Get your button finger ready."

Chapter 14

"Are you sure we're headed in the right direction?"

"Sure," B'Elanna said. "I remember that dead tree."

"If you say there's a dead tree over there," Kaytok said, "then I believe you. The first question I have is, how can you see that dead tree? And, second, how can you tell that the dead tree you're looking at is any different than the twenty other dead trees we saw before the sun set?"

Kaytok, B'Elanna noted, liked to complain. Sure, he might very well be a brilliant individual, even a being of exceptional personal strength, but, goodness, a complainer. And he didn't like walking. He didn't like carrying a backpack—an empty backpack. He didn't, in fact, seem to like being outside his lab. The farther they got from it, the more Kaytok grumbled. And now he was moaning about the damned dark when it wasn't really that dark in the first place. Maybe Monorhans' eyes were poorly adapted to night vision, which certainly didn't seem sensible considering how large . . .

Then B'Elanna remembered: She was looking at the world through nanoprobe-enhanced eyes. Well, eye singular. With an ease that mildly worried her, she mentally commanded the implant to return to human-normal mode and watched as the world turned dim and faded to black. Then, experimenting, she slowly increased the lens aperture until the scene before her was as bright as a summer's afternoon, though the absence of shadows was weird and disconcerting.

"Are you all right?" Kaytok asked.

"Sorry," B'Elanna said. "I was playing. So are you saying it's too dark for you to travel?"

"Not if we're careful, but I like feeling I know where I'm going. Are you sure this is the right way?"

Pulling out her tricorder, B'Elanna checked their position. She had set the device to automatically record the route she and Seven had taken, then programmed it to ping if she wandered too far off course during the return journey. "Yes," she said. "We're about three-quarters of the way there."

Kaytok peered at the backlit screen, then glanced up at B'Elanna. "That's a wonderful little device. May I see it?"

B'Elanna had an engineer's disinclination to share tools, especially items that could not be easily replaced, but she trusted Kaytok. The closer she had examined his shield generator, the more convinced she had become that she was in the presence of a certifiable genius-level intellect. She handed him the tricorder without comment.

Kaytok adjusted the display, touched several controls, then walked around in a small circle while carefully observing the changes in the scans. After flipping through a variety of screens, he clapped the device shut and handed it back. "Lovely," he said.

"You seemed to pick up the controls pretty quickly."

Kaytok shrugged. "Good design."

B'Elanna nodded and clipped the tricorder to her belt. "You mind if I ask you a question?"

"You can if I can," Kaytok said. Without either of them saying anything, they fell into a slow careful stride, walking side by side where previously they had been in single file.

"You first," B'Elanna said.

Kaytok nodded. "That was quite a fight you and Seven of Nine had back there before you left. She really didn't want you to leave for the shuttle so soon. Why? It strikes me that right now every minute counts."

B'Elanna chuckled. Without knowing it, Kaytok had cut precisely to the core of the problems she and Seven had been having over the past year. "Seven has a very precise mind," B'Elanna said. "She doesn't like haste and has a very low opinion of what human beings can accomplish."

"If she thinks you can't make this trip, then why didn't she do it?"

"Because she *knows* she can't do it. Seven is very aware of everything that happens in her body. There's a little meter somewhere in her that says, 'Here's how much energy you have. Don't go beyond this line.' "

"But not you?"

B'Elanna smiled. "I have one. I just ignore it."

"How do two people with such different personalities get sent out together?" Kaytok asked.

Chuckling, B'Elanna replied, "I wonder about that myself. Sometimes, I think my captain is blind to the problems some people have getting along. Other times, I just think she has a strange sense of humor." She smiled to herself, surprised that she was saying such things to a relative stranger. "And then there are the other times where I think the captain is trying to make sure we all learn to get along because we might be together for a very, very long time."

"I don't understand."

B'Elanna sighed. "It's difficult to explain," she said. "My ship, *Voyager*, we're not out here just for exploration or for, I don't know, for fun. We're trying to get home, but home is a very long way off, even moving at multiples of the speed of light. We've had a couple lucky breaks, made some jumps, but at the current rate of speed, we're still many, many years from the edge of an area we call the Alpha Quadrant."

"Home," Kaytok said.

"Right. And the way things have been going, we might not ever make it. Or maybe our kids will if we're allowed to have kids. It's one of those things we don't talk about very often because the captain . . . she doesn't like to admit it might take that long."

"And yet she stops to see how she can help a group of aliens living on a planet that she's never seen before."

"There's something to that," B'Elanna said. "I know there are some in my crew who feel that way, but not everyone. My concern is more that she sometimes doesn't seem to think about how her decisions might affect our home, our way of life."

"And you've never told her how you feel about this?"

"Not precisely. It's not easy to talk to her about this kind of thing. She's my captain. She outranks me."

"It sounds to me like she's your *hara-tan,* but not a very sensitive one if she does not hear your thoughts."

"A *rih-hara-tan* can read minds?"

"Not precisely," Kaytok said. "But a *hara* can sense the well-being of his *haran* through their bond, or so I am told."

"You've never had a *hara?*"

Kaytok shook his head. "I have never been able to form the bond."

"Oh," B'Elanna said, uncertain what was appropriate to say next. She considered saying, "I'm sorry," but instead settled on, "Is that unusual?"

"Fairly," Kaytok said, and his wistful tone told B'Elanna what she needed to know: Here was another outsider. "But not unknown. Once, a child who could not form the link would have been allowed to die. Today it is treated as a sad thing, but not an evil. Certain avenues are closed to one, certain opportunities. Many of my colleagues are like me, as you may have noticed."

"I did," B'Elanna said. "I didn't spend much time around the Monorhans on my ship before we came here, but I saw that they tended to stay close to each other and speak in the whistles and clicks . . . What do you call that?"

"Second tongue."

"Right. You and your group don't so much."

"There are some *hara* among us, but the groups are small," Kaytok explained. "And they try to be discreet. Those like me, the *na-hara,* as we are called, we tend to cluster together. It helps that we are all engineers, too."

B'Elanna felt a twinge of kinship. "Right. Engineers. We're always kind of on the edge of things."

"Indeed."

"And you end up working out in the middle of nowhere on a project that no one wants despite the fact that it might save the world."

Kaytok clicked his tongue in a manner B'Elanna took to be a laugh. "Yes, precisely. This is what happens. Except the project doesn't really work and so I need help in the form of funny-looking visitors from the sky."

B'Elanna rolled her eyes. "You have no idea how many times I've heard that. It gets kind of old."

"Seriously?" Kayok asked. "You've been in this situation before?"

Shrugging, B'Elanna said, "Saving the world? Yeah. I've been here before."

"And that does not give you a good feeling? You are not gratified?"

"Of course. It's great. Only . . ."

"Only what?"

B'Elanna hesitated. She rarely would consider discussing such feelings, especially with someone she barely knew, though there was something about Kaytok. "Only that sometimes I wish someone would save me."

They walked several paces in silence and B'Elanna began to wonder whether she had broken some kind of taboo. Just as she was thinking of trying to offer an apology, Kaytok suddenly halted in his tracks.

"Kaytok?" B'Elanna asked, leaning down over him, one hand on his shoulder. "What's wrong? Are you all right?"

Kaytok's right arm shot out and closed around B'Elanna's ribcage, instantly cutting off her air. She tugged uselessly at the Monorhan's grip. Caught completely by surprise, B'Elanna had no breath in her lungs as he pulled her to the ground and the dark instantly began to creep in around the edge of her vision, until it closed completely.

Sickbay was crowded, but Harry managed to make a spot for himself in a corner near a computer station so he could watch the sensors. The Doctor stood nearby, fussing over his medkit, probably mildly resenting having his sanctum turned into a shelter. Harry noted with approval that the Doc was wearing his holoemitter, though when he thought about it, he realized they had no reason to assume the twenty-ninth-century technology was any more immune to the radiation.

Listening to the captain's orders through his combadge, Harry watched the sensor feed as the deflector came online and the first of the torpedoes hit the twisted end of the bag. Then, without warning, a crippling, numb sensation enveloped Harry's mind like a sodden blanket. Feeling the panel under his hands, he was vaguely aware that he was supposed to be doing something, watching something, but he couldn't remember what or why or even how to keep his eyes focused.

"Mr. Kim?" Harry heard the Doctor speak, but could not lift his head to look around. "The shields must have collapsed. It's much worse this time, isn't it?" Harry's knees buckled and his chin collided with the top of the panel. "My readings show sickbay is receiving twelve times more . . ."

Harry heard a clatter as something heavy fell to the deck. Dropping to his knees, he forced his eyes open and scanned around himself. There—to the left of his hand—something blocky and familiar: a medical tricorder. To his right he saw the Doctor's feet shuffling around and around in tight circles. Emergency klaxons began to blare while beneath his hands, Harry Kim thought he felt the deck growing insubstantial.

In their assigned quarters, Ziv and his *hara* writhed on the deck, their minds roiling in torment. The Voyagers had warned them this might happen. The captain had even sent Neelix down to stay with them, and the *hara* had settled down to wait, Ziv at the center of a circle, all wishing they had something to do. The first time they had been exposed to the subspace radiation, none of the *hara* had felt anything worse than a mild tingle, but this, *this* was much more than anything Neelix or the others had described. The Talaxian fell to the floor, instantly unconscious. Jara and Shet cried out incoherently while Mol vomited. Ziv felt each of them drop out of the link, their minds swallowed up by an inarticulate hum until he was left desolate, trapped within his own mind. He curled around himself, ready to tumble into the void because anything, *anything* would be better than the wretched isolation.

Without warning, Ziv felt a voice in his mind, the special twinge that meant the *rih-hara-tan* was communicating with him. *But how?* Ziv asked, struggling to focus his eyes. *She's not here.* Even considering the special bond a *rih-hara-tan* shared with her *shi-harat,* mental contact from outside a room was impossible. And yet, he heard Sem in his mind. She had done something—something she had been pleased about, but now regretted as a mistake.

This is very bad, Ziv thought, pushing himself up off the deck. She did not like to make mistakes.

"What is wrong with all of you?"

Janeway heard the words despite the fact that she had her head down between her legs. She was vaguely aware that the lift doors had opened, and that someone had entered the bridge, but could not summon the will to look up. The exposure to the radiation in the subspace fold on the two previous occasions had been wrenching and unpleasant, but this time the effect manifested itself as a blinding, searing pain set directly behind her eyes and at the roots of her teeth. She started to count just to keep her mind working, marshalling all her resources to keep the numbers in order. *I can take this,* she thought. *I can.*

"Tom," Janeway shouted. "Are we moving?"

No answer. Janeway forced her eyes open and saw that the pilot was slumped over the helm console, his fingers feebly gripping the top edge so he wouldn't slide out of his chair. Brilliant lights flashed on the main monitor as another of the preprogrammed array of torpedoes burst against the twist in the subspace fold. *Dammit!* she thought, and pushed herself up out of her chair.

"What is wrong with you?" Janeway heard again.

Someone—some *idiot*—was speaking to her. All around her, Janeway heard groaning and muttering, the sounds of men and women grappling with their agony.

In the periphery of her vision, Janeway saw that Tuvok was unconscious on the floor. *Whatever is happening here is harder on him than it is on us.* To her left, Chakotay was still moving. He was looking at her. No . . . past her. Janeway finally turned and saw only . . . light.

"Captain Janeway," said a voice from the center of the light. "I demand you tell me what is happening!" Janeway felt another hand on her other shoulder. Both hands gripped hard and small bones crunched. Pulled up sharply, the voice from the light snapped at her impatiently. "Is this some sort of trick?"

How can a ball of light scream at me? Janeway wondered. The voice. She knew the voice. Janeway squinted against the glare and tried to shield her eyes, but could not lift her hands.

"And the *noise!*" the voice shouted. "Why does it have to be so loud?"

The klaxon was sounding again. *How many times is that in the last twenty-six hours?* she wondered. *Three? Four?*

The voice was still shouting: "You're not listening! *Tell me what is happening!*"

How absurd, Janeway thought distractedly. *A petulant ball of light.* The idea that Q might have come for a visit slogged through her mind, but she dismissed it. *No, the voice is wrong.* Everything was wrong. She was so very tired, and her shoulders ached horribly where they were being gripped. Pain overcame exhaustion and she decided she had to break free. Kicking out feebly, she felt contact and heard a sharp "Oof!"

That worked, Janeway thought and decided it felt so good she would do it again. Setting one foot, she planted the other, half-turned, and jabbed, but felt her leg caught at the ankle and held in place. "Not there!" the voice shouted.

"Warning," the computer intoned. *"Autopilot has been disengaged."*

"Let her go!" someone cried. "You've done enough damage, Sem! Get away fom that interface!"

The ball of light shouted back, "They won't tell me what's happening, Ziv! I don't think they *can* tell me what's happening. They don't know *anything!*"

Sem? Janeway thought, then lashed out with her free foot, the pain in her collarbones increasing a hundredfold. *Balls of light don't have bones,* she thought happily. Sem released her grip and Janeway crashed to the deck, her coccyx cracking painfully against the edge of the seat.

A shadowy figure rushed past her and bore the ball of light down onto the deck beside the helm station. The two figures, one light and one dark, flailed wildly at each other, both pumping and pummeling. Wild grunting noises filled the bridge and the pungent smell grew sharper and more penetrating.

Enough of this, Janeway thought and pressed herself up again despite the agony in her head and her lower back. Once she was on her feet, she allowed gravity to do its work, tipping forward, falling on Tom's back, and though she hoped she didn't injure him, she knew the welfare of one crewman was less important at the moment than getting the ship moving.

Button, button, where's the button? The near-incoherent thought swirled around in her head, and she cursed herself for her foolishness. *There!* Janeway found the correct row of switches and activated the thrusters. Fortunately, Tom had keyed the entire sequence to a macro, so what normally would have required several commands required only one. *Voyager* lurched forward, the underpowered inertial dampeners struggling to compensate for the leap to full impulse.

Looking up at the monitor, Janeway saw a gap in the unchanging white, a burst of energy, and then blackness as the overloaded sensors shut down the feed. Suddenly, the agony lifted and the captain gratefully lowered her weight onto the deck, careful not to drop onto Tom again. They had created a gap and gone through it . . . to what? She would find out in a moment. For now she was grateful to simply rest her eyes.

"Don't move, Captain," Chakotay shouted to be heard over the klaxon.

"Chakotay?" she stammered. "What happened?"

"I think Sem somehow turned off the autopilot." The klaxon suddenly died and Janeway heard Chakotay speaking into his combadge: "We need the Doctor up here." Janeway tried to sit up, but Chakotay gently pushed her back down. "The way you fell," he said softly. "I want the Doctor to take a look at you."

There was a long pause during which Janeway had a moment to reorient herself and recall everything that happened in the past few minutes. Struggling to see around Chakotay, she spied two crumpled Monorhan bodies to the left of the helm: Sem and Ziv. Was either still breathing? She couldn't tell for certain, but she thought they both were. Finally, she heard Harry Kim say, *"Bridge, this is sickbay. I'm sending up an auxiliary med team."*

"Is the Doctor busy?"

"Not exactly, Commander. There's a problem with the holomatrix. He's missing . . . parts."

"Parts?"

"Important parts."

Chakotay frowned, but did not let the anxiety in his face creep into his voice. "Okay, Harry," he said. "Stay there and coordinate. I expect you'll be seeing patients soon."

"Understood. Is the captain there?"

"Yes, but she can't respond . . ."

"I'm here, Harry. What is it?"

"Captain, I'm reading that the main monitor is down. Could you try to bring it up? I'm looking at something through the sensor feed I think you'll want to see."

"Help me up, Chakotay," she said under her breath. He sighed, but did as he was asked, then helped Janeway settle into her chair. "Tom," she asked. "Are you all right?"

"Yes, ma'am," Tom said, rubbing the back of his neck. "Sorry about not . . ."

"Belay that, Mr. Paris. Get the monitor up."

"Aye, aye, Captain." Tom's fingers danced over the console and a moment later the main monitor lit up. The background noise on the bridge died down as everyone stared up at the image.

"Harry," the captain asked. "What are we looking at?"

"It's what you told me we might see, Captain," Harry said. *"It's the Blue Eye."*

Before she opened her eyes, B'Elanna was aware of the scent of clean sheets right out of the 'fresher, a smell that people made a big deal about, but she honestly didn't care about one way or another. Except this time. This time it was wonderful, special, the most delightful aroma she had ever experienced. She rolled forward and, eyes still shut, pressed her face into her pillow. *They found us,* she thought. *They got us and I'm back on the ship . . . back home.*

This last thought struck B'Elanna as funny, what with all the complaining about *Voyager* she had been doing of late, but where had she ever lived that was any more her home than this ship? Back on Earth with her savage mother and emotionally damaged father? At the Academy? Even in the Maquis? None of these places had ever really felt right. B'Elanna Torres had never found a home because she didn't know what home *meant. But maybe here,* she decided, feeling the soft cotton against her cheek and nose. Catching a whiff of Tom Paris on the pillow next to hers, she smiled. *Maybe here.*

Her door chimed and B'Elanna lifted her head. The lights were set low, but not off. Tom must have put her to bed after they picked her up, then gone back on duty. Where was her clock? Not in its usual place. "Computer?" she called, but nothing replied. *Must be offline,* B'Elanna thought, sighing. *Gone for a few hours and everything goes to hell.*

The door chimed again. "Door, unlock." Again, no response. "Damn," B'Elanna said, the pleasant sensation of justifiable pique creeping into her. She threw off the comforter and was surprised how chilly the air was against her skin. *Environmental systems are off, too.* This was not good. *Voyager* must have had a rough time wherever she had been after they disappeared. Of course, whatever had gone wrong, the situation mustn't be too out of hand or the captain wouldn't have let her sleep.

Sitting up, she felt a peculiar ache in her neck and shoulders. Touching herself just under the chin, B'Elanna found a tender spot, like the new skin grown with a dermal regenerator. *Kaytok,* she remembered. *He attacked me. Why did he do that?*

B'Elanna heard a dull thud: her visitor pounding on the door. Slipping out from under the covers, she found she was wearing clean undergarments, but nothing else. She wondered absently how Tom could have managed that and smiled at the thought. *Bet he enjoyed that.* The cool air raised goose bumps on her flesh and she ran across the floor, blood pumping effervescently through her veins.

When she pressed the manual override, the door slid open and revealed a slightly peeved Tom Paris holding a tray of food. "Hey," he said. "I figured when I locked the door behind me I'd be able to open it again. Someone should fix this."

Grinning, B'Elanna took an edge of the tray and drew Tom inside the doors. Then, taking the tray from his hands, she set it on the end table and stepped into the circle of his arms. "That's breakfast," he said.

"I'm not hungry," she replied (a terrible lie, but food could wait), and threw her arms around his neck, joyful to feel his warmth against her. Arms closed around her waist and Tom lifted her so that her mouth was on a level with his own. They kissed, tenderly at first, but with increasing urgency, one of Tom's hands at the back of her head and the other stroking her spine under her T-shirt. B'Elanna curled one of her legs around Tom's upper thigh and gently bit his lower lip, a signal he knew well. Tom stooped, dropped his arm under her legs, stood with B'Elanna cradled against him, and walked to the bed.

Feeling her feet leave the floor, Seven of Nine flailed, kicked her legs, and squirmed like a small child who was being carried away to an early bedtime. Paris lost his grip and dropped her legs, but held on to her waist so that she fell awkwardly to the ground. "What's wrong?" Paris asked.

Seven half-stood and crabwalked toward the bulkhead, too confused to respond. Where was she? How had she been transported back to *Voyager* without her remembering it? And what was she doing in B'Elanna Torres's quarters? Paris approached her again, still smiling, but obviously confused. "Are you all right, hon?"

"Lieutenant Paris," Seven said, taking another awkward step backwards. "I think there's been a mistake . . ." She looked down at herself and felt her confusion grow even greater. She was wearing nothing more than a couple of pieces of thin cotton undergarments. What happened to her uniform? Looking up at Paris, she felt a cold fury rise up within her. She had always known Paris had a lascivious temperament, but this was too much. "I must report this to the captain, Lieutenant. You give me no choice."

Paris shrugged. "Report *what*?" he asked. "It was her idea."

The captain's idea? This was too much. Captain Janeway had finally gone too far. Seven tried to respect her ideas, but this, *this* was too much. Touching the wall behind her, Seven groped along it until she felt the edge of a doorway. Spinning, she lunged through the door and heard it snap shut behind her. The bathroom. This would do. She would program the replicator to give her a new uniform, then call . . . someone. Commander Chakotay perhaps. Or Tuvok. He would have no tolerance for this behavior.

The room lights blinked on and Seven found herself staring into the large mirror over the sink. *Humans,* she thought. *So vain.* Seeing that a strand of hair had fallen down over her forehead, Seven lifted it with the intent to tuck it back into place.

Something was wrong with her forehead. Leaning closer, she saw a shadow, a ridge. Reaching up, Seven touched her forehead and found . . . bumps. What had happened? Who had done this to her? Running her fingers along the ridges, she saw she now had the subdermal bony plate of a Klingon female. Fury overtook her and she punched the door control.

"Lieutenant Paris!" she shouted, the blood running hot in her veins. Paris was standing next to the tray of food, idly picking at a repugnant pile of bacon slices. Seven suddenly felt her mouth awash in saliva at the thought of cooked meat.

"What is it? Want some bacon?" Seven curled her hand into a fist and aimed at Paris's face but did not connect, and instead she grabbed the bacon from Tom's hand. Seven stuffed it in her mouth. She was almost overcome by the disgusting, wonderful texture and revolting, lovely salty tang. Closing her eyes, she savored the flavor, but then opened them abruptly when she felt arms around her shoulders and waist. "See?" Paris said. "You were just hungry."

B'Elanna squirmed, enjoying the kiss on her neck, but still more interested in the bacon. Tom's attentions quickly became more insistent and she considered letting herself become distracted. Turning, she lifted her mouth to his and touched her slightly greasy lips to his. Laughing, Tom asked, "Are you okay now?"

"I'm fine," she said, reaching up to touch his cheek. "I'm just glad to be back with you." Two thin tubules emerged from the backs of her wrists, snaked up over her fingers, and gently pierced the flesh at Tom's temples. His eyes rolled up in his head and his neck muscles grew taut. Traceries of tiny black webbing ran out in fractal threads from the punctures and his skin turned a clammy gray. The strength went out of the man's legs and he slumped forward. B'Elanna caught him easily despite his size and lowered him gently to the ground.

As she watched, the black threads became blotches. The skin over his cheekbone split open and a tiny input module sprouted.

Seven leaned down over the module and spoke softly into it, like a parent awakening a child. "Wake up," she said. "Wake up. It's time to wake up."

Chapter 15

"I'm awake!"

"Shhhh!"

"I said, 'I'm awake!' "

"Lieutenant, be quiet!"

"I'm awake!" B'Elanna croaked for the third time, her throat so parched and scratchy she felt like she was inhaling sand. "Now everyone . . . just . . . *shut up!*"

"I will if you will!"

"What?" B'Elanna opened her eyes and then immediately snapped them shut again. "Too bright!" she rasped.

"Keep your voice down," Kaytok hissed. "We don't know who's around here."

B'Elanna opened her eyes slowly, this time remembering to shield the Borg implant. Kaytok hovered over her, poised to clamp his hand over her mouth if she shouted again. Abruptly, the engineer remembered that the last time she had seen Kaytok, he'd nearly squeezed the life out of her.

She batted his hands away, rolled on her shoulder,

and tried to get her feet underneath her, but the loose soil slipped away beneath her. The roll became a tumble until she became jammed up against a rocky outcropping. Scrabbling at her belt, she searched for her phaser, but found nothing. B'Elanna looked up, expecting to see Kaytok holding the weapon, but was instead surprised to see the Monorhan squeezing himself into a cleft between two large boulders.

Quickly looking around, B'Elanna saw that they were in a stand of low, scrubby trees, all with bare branches. Several boulders, none more than a meter high, were bunched up against the tree trunks as if they had tumbled down the hillside and been stopped.

Torres twisted from side to side, searching for movement in the gray dawn. The sun could not have risen more than a few minutes ago, so the blinding glare she had seen when first opening her eyes must have been a result of the pupil being too far open. Remembering the Borg appliance, she willed the aperture open and carefully scanned the horizon for signs of movement. An idle internal question—*I wonder if I can see in infrared?*—flitted through her mind, and suddenly the world was painted in bands of red and blue.

The only living thing besides herself in the immediate vicinity was Kaytok, barely visible in his hiding place, but gesturing for her to stay low, a suggestion she completely ignored. Scaling the steep hillside as quickly as she could, B'Elanna yanked the Monorhan up by the front of his jacket and rasped, "Why did you attack me?"

Frantically scanning from side to side, more afraid of

the attackers he could not see than the one he could, Kaytok whispered, "I didn't. I was trying to protect you. I smelled patrols last night, and in my haste to pull you to safety, I may have misjudged my own strength."

"There's no one nearby," B'Elanna said, tapping her eye. "This says so. Now tell me what's been going on or I'll make you wish someone *was.*"

Visibly relaxing, sagging back against the boulder, Kaytok said in normal tones, "I don't know. I don't remember. When I awoke, you were unconscious. When I couldn't wake you, I carried you up here." He looked around. "In the dark, it looked sheltered. I thought about starting a fire, but was afraid someone might see it."

Pointing at the Monorhan's small backpack, B'Elanna asked, "Do you have my weapon? My tricorder?"

Nodding, Kaytok opened the bag and handed the equipment back to her. "I was afraid they'd fall off your belt while I was carrying you and we'd never be able to find them." B'Elanna had to concede that this sounded like a sensible precaution and not an excuse to rob her.

"Do you have any water?" she asked.

Kaytok handed her one of their two water skins and she took a long pull, clearing the dust from her mouth, then gently touching what she suspected must be bruises on her throat. "How long was I out?" she asked.

"A couple hours, I think. Hard to say since I was out myself for a while." He examined her more carefully, searching for injuries, B'Elanna suspected. "Did I really attack you?"

B'Elanna nodded. "You began to foam at the mouth. The last thing I remember is you trying to throttle me." The memory was dim, but she tried to recall the last moments before her world dimmed. "And you were talking, but not to me. You said, 'Sem.' "

"Sem?" Kaytok's neck contracted until his chin was practically lying on his chest. "I said, 'Sem'?"

"I take it Sem is not a nice word," B'Elanna said.

"It's not a word, it's a person."

"A bad person?"

"Yes. Or, at least, bad for me." He waved at her to sit down. "Don't worry, I'm not going to hurt you." Opening his own water bottle, he took a small sip.

"I'm not worried." And she wasn't. She would keep a closer watch on the Monorhan now, but B'Elanna didn't feel he was a threat.

"I'm not the only one who was talking in his sleep," he said. "What's a Tom?"

"Tom is a who, not a what. He's my . . . my partner, I guess you'd say."

Kaytok snorted derisively. "Interesting coincidence. Sem was *my* partner."

B'Elanna thought back. "The one who was part of your group, then left? And she works for the Emergency Council now? The bad guys?"

"They're not all bad," Kaytok said. "Some of them genuinely believe they're doing good. And, no, that's Morsa I was thinking about. Sem . . . Sem was never part of our group. I knew her a long time ago, back when I was still a student, still inside one of the cities."

"So, why did you say her name right before you tried to throttle me? Does thinking about her usually affect you that way?"

Kaytok's head sank back down to his shoulders. "Now that you mention it, yes. But I don't think I was *thinking* about her. It was more like, for a brief second, she was inside my head. I could feel her there, glowing like a . . . like a sun, I guess. She was angry, yelling at someone."

"Did anything like that ever happen before?" B'Elanna asked, now worried that maybe the Monorhan was not merely a bit eccentric, but mentally unbalanced.

But Kaytok clicked and shook his head. "No, never. And I mean *never*. I can't share like the others. Remember, *na-hara?*" He took another sip of water, then sealed his canteen. "What about you? Were you in communication with your friend again? I heard you talking and for a few seconds it even sounded like she was here with us."

"Never use the words 'friend' and 'Seven' in the same sentence," B'Elanna said, but hearing the name brought details of her dream.

I would also find that acceptable, Lieutenant.

B'Elanna started, sat up too quickly and cracked the crown of her head on an outcropping. "Ow! Dammit! Seven!" She fumbled at her combadge, but she quickly realized the voice did not have an external source. "Seven?" she asked.

"Who are you talking to?" Kaytok asked. "Are you all right?"

"I'm fine," B'Elanna said, then had to wonder. "I think. Shut up and let me listen. Seven?" *Seven?*

I am here, Lieutenant.

How are you doing this? Is this the nanoprobes?

Apparently, yes. I am pleased to discover that this is possible while you are awake. I would hate to have to eavesdrop on your dreams again.

You were trying to contact me while I was dreaming?

No, I learned that we could contact each other while you slept. The more . . . forceful images . . . crept into my consciousness. I had to counteract them by any means possible. I nearly destroyed a very valuable piece of equipment.

A thought struck B'Elanna. *Why don't you just call me on the communicator?*

I have tried, Seven said. *But the radiation from the Blue Eye has increased over the last several hours. Without more sophisticated scanners, I cannot say why, but I fear the situation may be growing exponentially worse.*

Wonderful, B'Elanna replied. *Anything I can do?*

Move faster, Lieutenant. The sooner you get to the shuttle and return, the sooner we can use Kaytok's equipment to contact Voyager.

So, you see, B'Elanna taunted. *It was a good idea for me to leave immediately.*

No, it was not. You've been asleep for two hours in a ditch. If you had simply rested for two here in moderate safety, you would be that much closer to your goal.

B'Elanna frowned. "Get out of my head, Seven!" *And don't contact me again unless it's an emergency.*

Believe me, Lieutenant. I take no pleasure in our mingled condition. And at this juncture everything *is an emergency. Seven of Nine breaking contact.*

B'Elanna suppressed an urge to swipe at the air.

"What is going on?" Kaytok asked, his tone wavering somewhere between fear and annoyance.

"I have bugs in my head," B'Elanna said. "And they're talking to me." The Monorhan drew back farther into the small nook where he had been hiding. "Never mind," she said. "I'm fine. Are you ready to go?"

Though she couldn't say why he would, Kaytok seemed to relax. He was, B'Elanna realized, depending on an alien who talked to thin air to save his planet. The situation couldn't be much worse than it already was. "I suppose," he said, sliding out of his nook. "Are you sure you trust me?"

"I trust you," B'Elanna said. "As long as you walk in front of me."

Kaytok seemed to find that condition acceptable and rose. "While we're walking, you could tell me more about Tom."

"Or you could tell me more about Sem."

"I'll consider it," the Monorhan said, and began picking his way down the hillside.

"And so will I," B'Elanna said, and fell in behind.

Seven of Nine sighed as her awareness of Torres's consciousness slipped away. What a strange, solitary, angry person the engineer was. Why would she protest the joining with a greater whole so vociferously? What did she gain from her behavior? Seven could not see the sense of it.

"Are they all right?" One of Kaytok's associates, Pad, stood nearby, holding a small brown paper sack.

Rising, Seven said, "They are currently undetected. How likely are the Emergency Council to have forces out in the field?"

Pad shrugged. A tiny, gnarled creature, he, like Kaytok, seemed either unable or unwilling to join into a *hara*. Though he followed in the wake of the group, Seven never sensed the soft fading of the edges of his persona that she saw in many Monorhans. The difference between Kaytok and Pad was that she never sensed desperation from the former. "Maybe not so likely. What's the point in putting a lot of people out in the field when the world's coming to an end? I figure if the council hasn't sent anyone out looking for us by now, they're not going to."

Seven nodded. She had been pondering their situation and wondered why the Emergency Council had not sent out a team to investigate the energy wave. "Why not?" she asked Pad.

"Because they're all too busy trying to figure out how they're going to live another day," Pad said. "Word of the ships breaking up has probably leaked by now. Some of the council members will try to keep panic from spreading, but a lot of the others will be looking for a crack where they can hide their . . . Well, you get my meaning." He looked down at the small bundle in his hand

and asked, "You want some lunch? I brought you something."

"No thank you," Seven said. "I do not currently require nutrition."

"I haven't seen you eat since you got here."

"I do not need to eat very often. Please give the food to someone else." Seven looked at Pad with what she hoped was a meaningful expression. "Yourself, perhaps. You look as if more sustenance would do you good."

Pad poked a single gnarled digit at the oily package. "Don't seem to matter too much whether I eat or not. What with the world coming to an end."

"Why die on an empty stomach?" Seven asked. "And who knows what tomorrow may bring?"

Unwrapping the package, Pad muttered, "Now you sound like Kaytok. Pretty soon you'll be telling us all that the Fourteenth Tribe'll be coming back to collect us all up and take us to Gremadia."

Seven had heard more than one of the Monorhans speak of a Fourteenth Tribe, usually in a manner that was meant to incite a cynical lack of belief, but this was the first mention of Gremadia.

"Gremadia?" she asked.

Pad picked at the blob of food. "Just a story some folks'll tell you. Kaytok—his people were Fourteenth Tribe—he could tell you more if you like."

"But Kaytok is not here," Seven said. "You are. And neither of us appears to be doing anything of significant value." She hated to admit this, but it was true. After Torres and Kaytok left for the shuttle, she had found appallingly little worth doing. Any adjustments she could make to Kaytok's shield generator had been completed long ago, and she could discern nothing else of value from the sensor recordings the Dissenters had taken before she and Torres had inadvertently damaged the system. When they had the equipment and tools from the shuttle, they should be able to link into Kaytok's device quickly and efficiently. Seven was pleased with this, satisfied with the work she had completed, but continued to experience an uncomfortable urge to return to the device and—she knew no other word—*tinker* with it. Sighing despondently, she attributed this to the influence of Torres's psyche on her and attempted to remain calm. They would be back on *Voyager* soon and then they could be rid of each other.

"Do you know the story of Dagan?" Pad asked. "Picked up any of this along the way?"

"Assume I have not."

"All right," Pad said and settled down on his haunches. Monorhans, Seven had already noted, seemed built to hunker down, their chairs little more than floor cushions. "This all started about three thousand cycles back, just when things started to be pretty good for most people. The tribes had finally stopped fighting and there was enough good land being tilled to feed all the people. They had a council—we have records of it—and this is where the fourteen *rih-hara-tan* got together and decided on how the stories told by all the different tribes fit together. It turned out that, you know, all the different aspects of all the gods were really different faces of one god—the Blessed All-Knowing Light. Least, that's what they said then."

Seven nodded, approving of the evident orderliness of the process.

"And everything was fine for a few hundred cycles until this farmer in the Fourteenth Tribe, Dagan by name, broke his plow blade on a rock. Except, of course, it wasn't a rock." He paused, waiting for Seven to ask the inevitable question.

Something in her almost rebelled at the expectation, but Seven fought it down, deciding that cooperation was more important at the moment. "Then what was it?"

"It was the Key," Pad said. "The Key to Gremadia."

"And what is the Key to Gremadia?" Seven was suddenly overcome by a desire to throttle the shriveled little creature.

Pad held up his hands about twenty-five centimeters apart and said, "I've seen drawings of it. About this big. Porous. Nothing special about it except that Dagan says as soon as he touched it, he started getting visions."

"About Gremadia," Seven said. She had analyzed enough of these sorts of stories to know what would come next. "An ancient city of wonders where the pious would live forever in peace and harmony."

Pad extended his neck and reared back slightly. Seven hadn't seen the gesture before and didn't know how to read it until the Monorhan said, "Not exactly. Gremadia was a city on another world or in another dimension—Dagan wasn't too clear on this—and it was inhabited by these all-powerful beings that battled for dominance.

The gods the fourteen *rih-hara-tan* had talked about weren't all one god, Dagan said, but a bunch of different fellows who all wanted to be the leader. Sometimes one person is in charge, sometimes another, and that's why things rise and fall the way they do."

Seven was intrigued. Though there were certainly cultures who had developed myth cycles that revolved around the tales of constant conflict between divinities— Earth's Norse myths and the ancient Klingon god cycles were prime examples—these were generally legends of warrior civilizations. As confusing as Monorhans were in many regards, they were definitely *not* a warrior race. "Interesting," Seven said. "And this Key—what happened when others touched it? Did they share Dagan's visions?"

"No," Pad said. "Some got sick, enough that other folks decided the gods didn't want anyone but Dagan to touch it. Of course, that doesn't explain why he died so young."

"How young?"

"Just a few cycles after he found the Key," Pad said. "Least that's what the history books say."

"But despite that he managed to gather followers," Seven said—a statement, not a question.

"He managed to convince most of the Fourteenth Tribe," Pad said, crumbling the greasy paper into a ball and throwing it into a dusty corner.

"He must have been very persuasive."

"They say he could persuade anyone of the truth of his words in less time than it took to plow a field a *chao* long." He added apologetically, "That's a small field."

"What did the other tribes—the ones who did not hear him speak—think of Dagan?"

"Nothing good. The *rih-hara-tan* were threatened by the change. There were lots of border incidents, though it never came to war." Squinting up at Seven from where he squatted, Pad explained, "We Monorhans have a hard time going to war. We get mad at each other, we fight, but large, organized aggression, it doesn't come easy to us. Something to do with the linking, the way *hara* see into each other." From his tone Seven could hear he was guessing, that he could not know for certain.

"What happened to his followers? Were they destroyed or . . . assimilated?"

"Neither," Pad said. "The Fourteenth Tribe was forced out of its lands and they wandered the edges of the civilized areas making a living as best they could. Their enhanced psionic talents made people even more suspicious. Nobody really liked them, especially because of all the troubles that started after Dagan died—earth tremors, tidal waves, changes in weather patterns."

"People attributed natural disasters to Dagan's death?"

"No, they attributed the disasters to the Blue Eye turning blue. They attribute the Blue Eye turning blue to Dagan's death."

"The Blue Eye has only been blue for twenty-five hundred cycles?" Seven asked. This was intriguing new information.

"Well, a few less than that, but, basically, yeah."

"What happened to the Key?"

"No one knows exactly," Pad said. "When Dagan

died, they figured it had something to do with his death and the earthquakes and the Eye turning blue, so they stuck it in a box and hid it. Supposedly, it got handed down from sire to child for a long time, but then the Fourteenth Tribe got pretty thinly distributed and it disappeared."

"And did the Fourteenth Tribe disappear?"

Pad shook his head. "Fortunately, Dagan had emphasized the importance of education, especially language, so a lot of the tribe ended up knowing more about math and languages than almost anyone else. Soon, it got to be that the other thirteen tribes *needed* them, so they allowed them back into the cities, but never too many and never outside the prescribed areas."

"And their numbers grew?" Seven asked.

"Yeah. Slowly. Then, round about my great-grandsire's time, there was even talk of the Dagan followers establishing their own city again. But then something else happened."

"Which was what?"

"Their *rih-hara-tan,* a woman named Klyrrhea, got the idea that if they were really serious about their beliefs, if they really believed in Dagan's visions, they shouldn't just be hanging around Monorha. Someone, Klyrrhea said, should go out into space and look for Gremadia."

"Truly?" This was an interesting twist. "Was space travel considered a radical concept?"

Pad shook his head. "Not really. People back then knew that it was possible. We'd even begun launching probes and the first ships. But what Klyrrhea proposed was doing something in a *big* way. Fortunately for her, she had Gora on her side."

"Gora?"

"Yeah, Gora. Scientist. Genius. Guy was two hundred cycles ahead of his time. There was no one like him. He knew more about engineering, about rocketry and propulsion systems . . ." His voice tapered off in awe and envy. "If we had someone like that with us now, Monorha wouldn't be having the problems we are."

"Impressive," Seven said. "So he built a ship for Klyrrhea."

"The *Betasis,*" he said. "Big enough to carry ten thousand people. I've seen pictures of her. She was a beauty. Too bad Klyrrhea didn't live to make that journey."

"Interesting," Seven said. "But I was under the impression that Monorhans did not name their ships. I believe I heard Captain Ziv say that."

Pad snorted. "No, we don't. Not after what happened to the *Betasis.* She was the first one with a name and the last. After her, naming a ship was considered bad luck."

"The ship came to a bad end."

"They managed to make it out of orbit," Pad said. "But you know I should probably let Kaytok tell you this part."

"Why?"

"Didn't I say before?"

"Say what?"

"That Gora was his grandsire."

~

The situation on the bridge sorted itself out as quickly as it could, but it was at least half an hour before Janeway felt she had a clear grasp on everything that had been happening. The exhaustion was hitting her hard now, despite the Doctor's drugs. The drugs . . . She'd pay for that soon. *Never mind that,* Janeway thought scoldingly. *Keep it together. Keep awake. Work the problems.*

But there were so *many* of them.

Two medics were carefully lifting the Monorhans onto stretchers. Both Sem and Ziv were unconscious, though neither appeared injured. "After the medics have looked her over," Chakotay told the medic, "put Sem in the brig. And make sure there's a psionic dampening field erected around her cell."

"Is that how she tampered with the autopilot?" Janeway asked. "Psionically?"

"That's our best guess." Lowering himself into his chair, he asked Janeway, "How's your back?"

Janeway rubbed her tailbone, which still tingled from the bone knitting. "Okay," she said, straining desperately to sound reasonable, then moved her hands to her collarbones. She could still feel Sem's hands around her neck. "But I could use a cup of coffee."

"I'm fairly certain," Chakotay said, "that would be a terrible idea. If you were wound any tighter, you'd disappear into another dimension."

"How would that be worse than the way things are now?"

Her first officer grinned. "I'd be all alone."

Unable to resist, Janeway smiled in return. "Okay, fine. *Tea,* then." Looking around the bridge, she saw order was reestablished, and thought, *On to the next thing.* "What can you tell me about the situation with the Doctor?"

"Only that there's something wrong with the holoemitters," Chakotay reported. "We haven't been able to track it down yet." His expression turned sour. "It's pretty disturbing. Harry says, the legs just standing there without a torso."

"Can't you just shut down the entire system?"

"We're afraid to try. Harry is concerned that we won't be able to reintegrate the . . . the parts."

"So until then?"

Chakotay shrugged. "We hope nobody trips over him. Them."

Tom Paris barely choked back a snorting laugh.

"Keep your mind on your station, Mr. Paris," Chakotay said.

"Sorry," Tom said. "Tickle in my throat."

Janeway almost chuckled herself, but returned to business. "Meet me in astrometrics in ten minutes," she said. "Get Harry out of sickbay, too. We need to consult."

"About that, you mean," Chakotay said, pointing at the viewscreen. "About how we could possibly be seeing the Blue Eye in subspace."

She nodded. "Call Joe Carey, too, and ask him if he can tear himself away from the engines."

"Yes, Captain."

"And how's Tuvok? We'll want him there, too."

"I just spoke to him from sickbay. The radiation hit him hard, but he's conscious now and wants back on active duty."

"Let him. We'll need him."

"Done," Chakotay said. "Any chance I can talk you into going to your office and closing your eyes for ten minutes?"

"Do you have a crowbar to open them back up again if I do?"

"I think B'Elanna took our only crowbar with her on the away mission."

"Then maybe just that tea."

Chakotay pointed at the ball of roiling energy on Astrometric's main screen, and said, "So you're telling me that's the Blue Eye."

"As it appears in subspace, yes," Janeway replied. She turned to look at Tuvok and Harry who, despite being near exhaustion, stared at the uncanny sight, utterly engrossed.

Tuvok said, "This is completely contrary to any understanding we have of subspace."

"Precisely," Janeway said. "But then, everything about this system is contrary. Complex life should not have developed so close to a white dwarf. Subspace should not be so warped and folded. Natural laws governing matter shouldn't be so radically different. Nothing fits right. Why is that?"

"You have an idea," Chakotay said.

"I have a suspicion," Janeway replied. "I think something unprecedented happened here a very long time ago and when it was all over, someone or something tried to patch it back together again and make it look 'normal.' "

"Why?" Harry asked. "For what purpose?"

"I don't know," Janeway replied. "Though having dealt with some of the transcendent, transdimensional beings we've met, I know their motives are often beyond our comprehension. Let's just say it happened and go from there."

"All right," Chakotay said. "A patch. And we've become trapped underneath it—caught in the threads, as it were."

"Right. The fold or conduit we're in, it's part of a web of energy that holds this system together."

"And the Blue Eye," Tuvok said, taking up the metaphor, "is a pin."

"Correct. It pierces through different levels of the universe and holds everything together." Janeway turned back to Chakotay and saw that he not only understood what she was suggesting, but accepted it.

"All right," he said, "so in order to escape, we have to loosen the pin."

"That's where I'm going. We have to shrink the white dwarf, kill it, stop the radiation."

"Which will save the Monorhans," Tuvok said, nodding his approval.

"And if we shrink it enough," Harry said, "we can slip out in the gap."

"Precisely."

Chakotay sighed resignedly. "It's a wonderful idea: shrinking a star. Any ideas how to do that?"

"There's only one way I know," she said. "We have to make some trilithium."

Chapter 16

"Gora, my grandsire," Kaytok began, "was an unusual person. Unusually intelligent, unusually persuasive, unusually . . . unusual. You could say that he was the most famous person in his generation." They trudged along in silence for several seconds and B'Elanna wondered if she was supposed to make some kind of comment.

"You must have admired him very much," she said.

"I didn't know him well enough to admire him," Kaytok replied, then snorted and kicked a small rock with the toe of his boot. B'Elanna, surprised that the Monorhan could see well enough to target a stone, let her visual receptors relax to human-normal and saw the eastern sky was beginning to grow lighter. "I won't go into all the background details," Kaytok continued, staring intently at the patch of ground a meter before them. "It's all about religion and not a little about politics. I'm really *not* the person to give you an impartial account."

"Don't worry about being impartial," B'Elanna said.

"We all have our stories." *And,* she added silently, *you only have a little more time to talk.* They were less than two kilometers from the shuttle now.

"I'm sure that's true," Kaytok said. "But there aren't many like mine. My grandfather helped convince a lot of people that they should leave the planet and find a lost city built by . . . well, that's the part they always had trouble explaining. Built by who? Built for what? And what would everyone do when they got there?" He threw his hands up in the air. "But enough people had heard this story enough times that they never doubted it would be a great idea to go there."

"That's impressive," B'Elanna said, and meant it. "How many people are we talking about?"

"Not everyone who wanted to go could go," Kaytok explained. "Space travel is difficult—I guess you know that—and the very old were asked to stay behind. Also, people in poor health, though I think Gora might have promised some of them that he would figure out a way to come back and collect them after he made it to Gremadia."

"The mythical city?"

"Right. He'd come back and get them because in Gremadia they'd be able to cure any ailment these people might have. See how it works?"

"Sure," B'Elanna said. She understood perfectly: Kaytok believed his grandfather had been some kind of trickster or confidence man. "But I'm guessing he managed to get a lot of people to come with him."

"Almost ten thousand."

B'Elanna whistled appreciatively: a ship that could carry so many people. She had, of course, seen bigger in her time, but these had been massive transports moving the immense replicators and gigakilos of raw material used to create colonies virtually out of thin air. "What happened to them?"

"Nobody really knows," Kaytok said. "They left orbit successfully. They made it past the Blue Eye, which was considerably less active than it is right now, and then the radiation from the Eye made it impossible to communicate with the ship. Not that many people wanted to."

"Not you?" B'Elanna asked. "Not your parents?"

"My sire—Gora's third child—went along. My mother stayed here with me and my sister. She didn't think going off into space with two young children was a good idea."

That may be the understatement of the year, B'Elanna thought, but kept the comment to herself. She had never thought very highly of the practice of Starfleet allowing families to travel on the *Galaxy*-class ships. They walked for several minutes while she waited for Kaytok to say more, but he seemed lost in his memories. Finally, growing impatient, she said, "You still haven't explained how Sem fits into all this."

"I've been trying to find the words to explain," Kaytok said. "This isn't something I talk about a lot." They walked on in silence for a hundred meters before he continued. "After Gora and his ten thousand departed and we didn't hear anything from them for a while, everyone who stayed behind started to pretend that nothing had happened."

"Including your mother?"

"Eventually," Kaytok said. "Yeah, her too." A defensive note crept into his voice. "You have to understand what it was like. When Gora was here, everything must have sounded very reasonable, but after he was gone, it was just . . . just . . ."

"Embarrassing?"

"Right. Embarrassing. I wasn't sure if your species understood that emotion."

"Why wouldn't we?"

Kaytok replied, "Because you can't sense each other the way most Monorhans can."

"Well, we do understand it. Some of us very well. I know something about being part of a family where one of the members was a perpetual embarrassment."

"You'll have to tell me later."

"Maybe. After you've finished the story about Sem."

"Right," Kaytok nodded. "Sem. Okay. The short version: When I met her, she was the only person who ever acted like my grandsire wasn't a complete lunatic, like he might have had some worthwhile ideas."

"But I thought that's what you'd thought."

"By that time, I'd come around a little. His ideas didn't seem so crazy, especially because by this time the environment had begun to disintegrate. Sem liked to listen to my stories about him, even asked to see some of his notes and programs."

"You said this was back in your . . . what do you call it? University days?"

"Yes, when I was a scholar, where people from different tribes, different cities, mingled freely. Sem was a special case, of course, because she was in training to be a *rih-hara-tan.*"

"That's like a priestess," B'Elanna said.

Kaytok shook his head. "I'm not sure what that word means. The translator can't find a word that means the same thing. She was in training to become the leader of the tribe. Yes, that involves religion—I get that connotation from the translation—but it's much more than that."

"How did you meet someone like that?" B'Elanna said. "Wouldn't she be kept safe, kept away from . . . ?"

"The people she would serve?" Kaytok asked. "No, it doesn't work that way here. And, besides, she wasn't the only potential *rih-hara-tan.* Each tribe has several. They're trained from birth, but no one knows who will be selected until the previous one dies or resigns."

"Oh," B'Elanna said. "I see. That's very . . . sensible."

"I'm glad you approve," Kaytok said, not without sarcasm. "So, anyway, yes, we were both young, which is the excuse I use for how stupid I was."

"Why were you stupid?" B'Elanna was beginning to regret pursuing this line of questioning. Kaytok was getting increasingly agitated as he continued his tale, but curiosity had taken hold, as well as an intuition that Kaytok's past was somehow entangled with the problem Monorha currently faced.

"Because I should have figured out that she was just using me," he said, head bobbing on his long neck. "One day, she left her dataset on and her personal log was open."

"Her personal log?" B'Elanna asked, almost amused. "You mean, like a diary? You read your girlfriend's diary?" *Some things are the same all over the galaxy,* she decided.

"I thought she meant me to," Kaytok said, struggling to sound reasonable. "You have to understand—Sem was a very *controlled* person. She didn't do things by accident."

"What did it say?" B'Elanna asked.

"I don't remember exactly," Kaytok said. "This is all a long time ago. But essentially what it was about was that she hadn't found something she was looking for, that she was tired of trying to find it and was weary of me."

" 'Something'? " B'Elanna asked. "You mean, like an emotion, an attachment, or do you mean a *thing?* It sounds like you're talking about the latter."

"When I read it, I thought she meant an emotion, but later I wasn't so sure. When I finally got over the hurt, when I saw what kind of person Sem was after she became the *rih-hara-tan,* I had to wonder. There were stories about her searching historical records for clues to the whereabouts of the Key to Gremadia."

B'Elanna's tricorder pinged as they crested a hill. Down below, in a long, flat gully that she now realized must have once been a riverbed, she saw their shuttle. A half-dozen Monorhans were stationed around it, each of them looking outward.

"Uh-oh," Kaytok said, squatting down so as not to be silhouetted against the brightening sky.

B'Elanna knelt beside the Monorhan. "Who are they?" she whispered.

"Emergency Council police." Kaytok grunted unhappily. "Any ideas?"

B'Elanna considered the situation, but before she could speak her mind, she felt another consciousness rise up inside her. *Go talk to them,* Seven said.

Why? B'Elanna thought.

Why not? They know who we are. The Emergency Council believes we are trying to assist them.

But they've been lying to their own people, B'Elanna thought.

They do not know that we know this.

What about Kaytok?

A friendly local who was good enough to feed you, then bring you back to your vessel.

B'Elanna considered her options. She did not want to leave Kaytok alone out here in the middle of nowhere if for no other reason than they still needed him to figure out what to do with the shield generator. "Do any of these Emergency Council people know what you look like?"

"No reason why they would," Kaytok replied.

"All right," B'Elanna said as she rose. "Then come on down with me. The bugs in my head say we should go talk to these gentlemen and convince them they have no reason to keep us from the shuttle."

"Are you sure you want to listen to the bugs?"

Picking a careful path over the loose stones and shale, B'Elanna replied, "They haven't lied to me yet."

"Captain? Captain Ziv, are you there? We are here, sir, but we cannot feel you."

In sickbay, Shet watched Mol from the edge of the small alcove where they had brought the captain after he had collapsed.

"Captain Ziv? Sir?" Mol continued to mutter to the captain, his words occasionally lapsing into the soft burring and humming a parent would use to speak to his child. Shet was vaguely aware that the Voyagers were excited, that their status had changed in some manner, but he could not bring himself to try to understand. Ziv, their anchor, had deserted his body, and there was very little chance any of them would ever see home again.

"Excuse me?"

Shet turned to look at the Voyager, the small, hairy one named Neelix. "Yes?"

"You'll have to excuse me," Neelix said, "but Captain Janeway asked me to find out if there's anything you need now."

Shet considered, but couldn't think of anything he truly wanted, so he said, "More than anything, my *hara* and I would like privacy."

"Of course," Neelix said. "I'll take care of it." He turned to leave, but then, bowing slightly, continued, "Another question, if you don't mind."

Shet nodded. Though he found Neelix slightly annoying, he also appreciated the creature's good manners.

"I hope I'm not breaking any taboos when I ask about this," Neelix said deferentially. "But the medics were wondering about Sem." He hesitated, uncertain how to continue.

Insight dawned. Of course they would have examined her. "She has two sets of arms," Shet said.

Neelix nodded. "This is . . . common?"

"Yes," he said. "For females. The extra set of arms is usually quite small, but they grow larger and more dexterous when a woman is fertile. Or pregnant." He held up his hands, which were considered quite large even for a mature male. "These are not good for dealing with small things."

"And I take it," Neelix said, speaking very softly, "that women do not expose this second pair of arms?"

"Correct."

Neelix looked thoughtful for several seconds, then continued, "I sense that you might not much care for Sem, but I feel obliged to tell you that her second set of arms appear to be . . . quite large, quite muscular. What do you think that means?"

"I expect," Shet said, "that Sem must be pregnant."

The guards watched B'Elanna and Kaytok as they slowly half-walked, half-slid down into the gulley. With her enhanced vision, B'Elanna could see that their collective lines of sight were fixed on Kaytok. Though she knew she must be an anxiety-provoking oddity, the guards' superiors must have told them to expect her. No one had said anything to them about another Monorhan, especially a scruffy-looking wanderer. To keep their attention focused firmly on her, B'Elanna raised a hand and waved. "Hello!" she shouted. "You're from the Emergency Council?"

As she had expected, there was a few seconds of confused clicking and thrumming between the guards as they adjusted to the translator. A minute or more passed with B'Elanna closing ever closer to the shuttle before the man before the main hatch called back, "You are from *Voyager?*"

B'Elanna halted five meters from the shuttle, hands clearly in view, then heard Kaytok shuffle to a stop a couple of meters behind her. A quick glance over her shoulder confirmed that he had wisely made certain that she was interposed between himself and the lead guard. There was no way to know for certain whether the Emergency Council had some kind of a warrant out for Kaytok, but why take chances? "I appreciate you keeping my ship safe," she said. "We went out to scout the terrain last night and got lost. This gentleman was good enough to guide me back this way."

The guard glanced around B'Elanna at Kaytok, but his interest was short-lived. "Where's the other one?" he asked. "They told me there would be two of you."

"Nearby. She was slightly injured in a fall. I wanted to get some medical supplies and go treat her." She took a step forward, hoping the guard would shift his stance in preparation for her passing, but he did not budge. He touched his hand to a black-handled tube strapped to his leg. B'Elanna stopped. "Problem?" she asked, trying to keep her voice low and cool.

"I don't know," the guard said. He rattled his tongues together and two more stepped from around the bow and stern. Neither had a weapon drawn, but B'Elanna had already noted that the straps holding the tubes along their legs were rigged to pop open under any kind of direct pressure. Behind her, she heard Kaytok scuffle the loose rocks.

Don't run, she thought. *Whatever you do, don't run.* Her phaser bumped against her hip as she adjusted her stance. "I'm B'Elanna Torres," she said, raising her hand in a generic kind of salute. "I'm the chief engineer on *Voyager.*"

The guard stared at her blankly, then his gaze flickered to Kaytok. "Where'd he come from?"

Shrugging, B'Elanna replied, "Out there in the dark somewhere." She leaned forward and pitched her voice low. "If you want to know the truth, I think he's not entirely well in the head. Keeps talking about someone named Gora and some kind of key. Does that mean anything to you?"

The guard's shoulders relaxed and his hand moved away from his weapon. "Oh," he said. "I get it. Don't worry about him. They're all a little bit . . ." He emitted a thrum noise that came from deep in his throat. B'Elanna jumped back a little bit, which seemed to please him.

"So I should just tell him to head off?" she asked. "Or

is he looking for money? I don't carry money. Is there something I can do for him to pay him back for guiding me here?"

The guard looked to his right and left, perhaps expecting a suggestion from his associates. His head bobbed on his long neck. "Have any food you don't need?" he asked. "They're always hungry."

"Not on me. I left my rations with my friend." She pointed at the shuttle. "But in there, sure. Food and water. As much as he could carry." The guard's neck tilted when B'Elanna mentioned food. Studying him, she noted that the guard was not much bigger or better-fed than Kaytok and was carrying considerably more equipment. Then there was the fact that he'd probably been standing outside for the past twenty-four hours. "Or maybe even something for you and your men?" she added speculatively.

He licked his lips, looking as if he were about to pant, but then straightened and said, "I was ordered to take you back to the city." He glanced up the other bank of the gulley. "We have a vehicle waiting."

"That's nice," B'Elanna said. "But I bet mine's faster. And don't forget I have to pick up my friend. You can all come with me." She didn't really want a half-dozen Monorhans on the shuttle, but if they did decide to join her, she would figure out her next move when they were up in the air. If nothing else, B'Elanna was fairly certain she could contain any hostile acts in the passenger area if necessary. She took another step towards the hatch.

"Stop," the guard said, and B'Elanna sensed the other two snap to alert attention. "I'm sorry, but you're not supposed to go in there."

"Why?" B'Elanna asked. "It's mine, after all. There's no reason this has to be difficult." She paused, then looked meaningfully over the guard's shoulder at the shuttle. "Unless you want to *make* it difficult." She knew the vessel wouldn't do anything without her being inside, but there was no way the guards could know this. Indeed, if they had been standing around outside the ship all night, they had probably heard all sorts of interesting, eerie noises as the self-repair modules had labored away.

"I should call my *rih hara tan,*" the guard said. "If you'll just stay here until I can . . ."

"Call him from my ship." Speaking more loudly than she needed to so the other guards could hear her, B'Elanna said, "Ship—open main hatch." A few seconds passed during which B'Elanna prayed fervently that the voice recognition systems were still working, but then the hatch slid open. "Come on," she said to the guard and swept past him. "It's fine." Looking back at Kaytok, she said, "You stay out here. I'll bring you something for your services."

Kaytok nodded, apparently happy to be be out in the open. *More room to run if necessary,* B'Elanna decided. *Not a bad idea, really.*

When she entered the shuttle, all the lights were on and the air was fresh. *Environmental systems working,* B'Elanna thought. *Good start.* She didn't pause in her march to the pilot's seat because she didn't want to give the guard an opportunity to grab her. "What's your name?" she asked, to give him something new to think over.

"Arul," the guard said, but neither loudly nor assertively. The shuttle was having the anticipated and much-hoped-for effect of impressing and awing the locals. *Amazing what air conditioning can accomplish.*

"Have a seat, Arul. I'm going to just make sure we're patched into the local comm network and then you can make your call." Quickly scanning the main status board, B'Elanna noted a couple yellow lights. Most of the self-repair routines had run perfectly, but shields, she saw, were not completely reliable. Also, the warp engines were still offline, but that was to be expected after the rattling the energy wave had given them. Besides, B'Elanna would never have trusted any repair program to recalibrate a warp core. She would do the work herself when they were home.

"I should call from my vehicle," Arul said, though he said this as he surrendered to the padded chair in the passenger compartment. B'Elanna heard the door open again as another guard entered, saw his *harat* sitting, and decided it might be time to take a break, too. B'Elanna checked the weapons repression system and saw that they were functioning, though she knew these would only work against energy weapons. If the Monorhans were using chemical weapons or—who knew?—projectile slingers, she would be in trouble. Best not to rely on such things.

"Just a minute," B'Elanna called. "Here we go. Audio-only. That's all right, isn't it?"

"No," Arul said, struggling up out of the chair's seductive embrace. "I should really go to my . . . *we* should go . . ."

"This is EC Headquarters," said a soothing voice.

"Hello?" B'Elanna said when Arul did not respond immediately. "This is B'Elanna Torres of the *Starship Voyager.* I'm here with Sergeant Arul . . ." She had no idea what rank he was, but sergeant seemed appropriate. "And we're looking for his commanding officer."

"NO!" Arul called out, finally managing to stand. The other guard was already outside the shuttle. "I had orders!"

"*Who* is this?" said the Soothing Voice, no longer sounding quite so calm. "Did you say you were from the *Voyager?*"

"Yes," B'Elanna said. "Perhaps I can talk to someone. I think Sergeant Arul is busy now. He's, yes, he's guarding my ship for me." B'Elanna punched a control that kept the rear hatch open in case Arul changed his mind and wanted to come back on board. She had no desire to make his life difficult just because he was trying to follow orders.

"Please hold," said the now-harried Soothing Voice. "I'm connecting you with the office of the . . ." B'Elanna never heard the name of the office, so quickly was the connection made.

A new voice, one with a much calmer, mature persona behind it, said, "Lieutenant Torres, this is Shalla

Kiiy. I'm delighted to hear from you. We were concerned when you did not visit us last night."

Visit? B'Elanna wondered. *Like it was a social call?* "We experienced technical difficulties, Shalla Kiiy, and then there was an accident. I'm all right, but my companion needs medical attention."

"Then you should come to the city immediately," the *shalla* interrupted. "While I doubt we have all the resources of your vessel, we could treat your friend while you begin . . ."

"We won't be coming to the city, Shalla," B'Elanna said. "We have to get back to *Voyager.*"

"This is problematic," the *shalla* said, and B'Elanna instantly understood that what she meant was "We aren't happy about this. Events are not unfolding as we expected." B'Elanna sensed that a threat was about to materialize. "We had hoped," the *shalla* continued, "to collaborate with you on resolving the current difficulties."

"I understand," B'Elanna said, and heard the strain of diplomacy sharpening her tone. "We could return after our medical problem is resolved."

"As I said, I'm sure we can help you with *any* medical problem you might have." B'Elanna knew this meant, "You are about to have a much *bigger* medical problem if you don't cooperate."

The shuttle's hull would hold up to any moderate small arm's fire, but if they had some kind of projectile weapon—a cannon or a guided-missile system—she knew she was in trouble. *Dammit!* How was she supposed to reason with . . . "If you do not permit this vessel to leave unmolested, *Voyager* will open fire on the source of your transmission." B'Elanna heard the words come out of her mouth, but didn't recognize her own voice.

Shalla Kiiy, apparently, did. A moment of silence was followed by a stammer, then, "You cannot be serious."

"I am completely serious," B'Elanna said.

"But we would retaliate," the *shalla* said. "You would be killed."

"The loss of one or two would be preferable to impeaching the integrity of the whole."

The *shalla* was silent for so long that B'Elanna began to wonder if she had cut off their connection, but finally she spoke. "You claimed to be here to aid us with your advanced technology, yet now you threaten us with the same."

"Only when provoked," Seven said through B'Elanna. "Please inform your guards that we are leaving now. If they stand ten meters away, they should not suffer any effects from our drive." Her hands punched out the sequence for a fast engine start and felt the impulse engines hum into life.

Behind her, B'Elanna heard a sound from the hatchway. Looking over her shoulder, she saw Kaytok, who looked confused, his long neck stretched out to its fullest length. "We're leaving," she said, and heard her own voice again. When she pointed at a seat behind her, the Monorhan slid into it with a grateful sigh.

Can I take control of your voice that way? B'Elanna thought.

You may be able to, came the reply. *Have you tried?*

No. *Maybe I just respect other people's privacy more than you do.*

And maybe you are just afraid.

Chapter 17

"Trilithium is a banned substance," Chakotay said, still struggling with his shock. "It *collapses* stars."

"It collapses *living* stars," Kathryn responded. "This is a white dwarf. It's already collapsed about as far into itself as is possible, but we need a little bit more."

Silence descended while everyone marshaled their thoughts. Chakotay was finding it difficult to believe the captain was even considering the idea. Everyone in Starfleet had heard the story of how Tolian Soran had collapsed the star Amargosa, and would have done the same to Veridian if not for the intercession by Jean-Luc Picard and the *Enterprise*. Even as Chakotay was composing his arguments, the deck spasmed so sharply that all four officers were nearly thrown off their feet.

When the shock wave had passed, Tuvok flipped open a tricorder and linked it into the ship's sensor grid. A moment later, he reported, "Gravimetric waves from the Blue Eye, Captain. Our shields have eroded twelve percent in the past three minutes."

"Will backing away help?"

"I do not believe we have anywhere to back up to," Tuvok said. "The gap we created has reclosed behind us."

"So it's forward or nothing," Kathryn said. Tuvok did not reply, his silence speaking volumes. Beneath them, the deck plates rumbled as a second spasm rippled up the ship's beam. "Do I have your support?"

"What if we're wrong?" Chakotay asked. "What if the star doesn't collapse? What if it goes nova or there's a shock wave like at Amargosa?"

"Then we're dead," the captain said flatly. "The Monorhans will die, too."

"Can you live with that idea?"

"It could be argued," Tuvok said, "that the Monorhans will die no matter what happens. If we succeed, they will live." He looked directly at the captain. "We must try, Captain."

Kathryn nodded her thanks, then looked at Kim. "Harry, get down to engineering. Talk to Joe Carey about how we can extract the dilithium resin we'll need."

"Aye, Captain," he said, then turned to leave.

"Tuvok, go with him. I need you to keep our shields up until we can try this."

"Yes, Captain." The pair left together, which left Chakotay standing alone with Kathryn.

"You don't think this is a good idea," she stated.

"I don't," Chakotay said. "But I don't have any better ones and you have a knack for figuring out these sorts of problems."

Smiling for what seemed like the first time in a

month, the captain replied, "I do, don't I? There's one more thing, though, and I think I'll need your help with this one."

"Name it."

"I think we're going to need another burst from the whatever-it-was that put us into the fold in the first place."

"Why?"

"Just because we have the subspace version of the Blue Eye in front of us doesn't mean we'll exit into the Monorhan system. I believe the Blue Eye is actually punching through multiple levels of reality . . ."

"Not just subspace and our universe?"

"Correct. If we're going to appear in the correct universe, I'd like to have a beacon. Since it's the frequency that put us here, then I think we should use it to get us out."

Chakotay said, "Then we'll have to try to contact whoever sent out the energy wave. Do you think subspace radio will work here?"

"I've been thinking about that, too," Kathryn said. "And I think . . ."

"*Captain Janeway?*"

Kathryn tapped her combadge. "Janeway."

"*This is the bridge, Captain. We've just been contacted by Lieutenant Torres. Shall I patch her through?*"

I guess that answers that question, Chakotay thought.

Four minutes after they left the ground (and approximately two minutes after Kaytok's stomach reascended from out of his lower abdomen), B'Elanna began to speak to the air again, but not (this time) to the bugs in her head.

"Torres to *Voyager.* Torres to *Voyager.* I have a locator signal from you. You're out there somewhere." She tapped a pair of controls on the panel before her and the vessel banked sharply to the left. If Kaytok had eaten any breakfast that morning (or dinner the night before), most of his food would have ended up on the right wall. *I was not meant for this sort of travel,* he concluded.

A new voice spoke from a speaker on the ceiling, a voice deeper and richer than either of the two Voyagers' he had met so far. *"This is* Voyager, *Lieutenant. Please state your current location and status."*

"I'm back in the *Montpelier* and on my way to picking up Seven. We've had an interesting day, Tuvok. How about you?"

"It has not been without its complexities, Lieutenant, though hearing your voice at so propitious a moment is most welcome. Seven of Nine is not with you then?"

"No. She's working with the locals to figure out what happened to you. So, tell. What happened to you?"

They talked for several more minutes, and though Kaytok considered himself a clever individual, he understood very little of what was discussed. The gist of the conversation was that B'Elanna Torres's ship was trapped in some kind of cross-dimensional fold and they needed her help not only to coax some dangerous substance out of the engines, but also to fire the shield generator a second time. "By now," B'Elanna said, "I expect Seven will have altered the shield generator so that it's more efficient, which means it won't produce precisely the same wave pattern."

"Then contact her and tell her to change it back," a new voice, a woman's, responded.

"She probably already knows."

"What?"

"Never mind, Captain. I'll explain later."

"So you're clear on what you need to do?"

"Yes," B'Elanna said, touching several switches in quick succession and plunging the shuttle back toward the ground. "Shrink the sun. Save the ship. Et cetera."

"Very good."

"Is Harry ready to listen to my instructions on how to get trilithium?"

"I'm here, B'Elanna."

"Harry!" And here B'Elanna broke out into a wide grin. "This is the craziest idea I've ever heard! And that includes all of Tom's!"

"Tell the captain when you see her. Start talking."

Kaytok had been confused before when they were talking about spatial anomalies, but now B'Elanna and her comrade were on the more familiar terrain of engineering rooted in the real. Well, semi-real. When they began speaking of matter-antimatter mixing technology, they passed into realms Kaytok had never imagined. Listening, the concepts began to seep into his mind and Kaytok began to grasp some small part of what they were discussing. The only way to harness the incredible energies mixing matter and antimatter would unleash was to inject them into a substance with some kind of fourth-dimensional matrix properties. The dilithium they spoke of seemed to be such a substance; however, if the residue of spent dilithium was mixed with other unspecified substances, the product was an explosive compound that could halt atomic processes in a fusion reactor, even a sun.

How can they stand such responsibility? Kaytok wondered, and yet B'Elanna discussed these matters with the same ease he, Kaytok, would bring to . . . to . . . to his own work on the shield generator, which many of his countrymen considered an insane, even illicit project. The Monorhan sighed. Judgment would have to be suspended.

"Have you got all that?" B'Elanna asked.

"Yeah, I think," Harry replied.

"You *think?*" She threw the shuttle into another sharp banking turn. She had taken the long route to the station in case the Emergency Council was attempting to follow them, but while they had been flying, she had coaxed the main computer into dumping some more analysis and maintenance time into the shields. While they weren't up to full, they were capable of deflecting a radar signal, which, Kaytok had assured her, was basically what the Monorhans used.

"I've got it. Basically, you want me to pump trilithium resin into a magnetic bottle, but first we have to disable most of the sentry systems Starfleet built into the engines to prevent exactly what I'm trying to do."

"Only one sentry system really."

"Why only one?" Harry asked.

"Because I disabled all the others months ago."

Harry did not reply for several seconds, then finally said, *"By various hand gestures, the captain has conveyed her desire to speak about this when you're back on the ship."*

"Well, *now* I'm motivated."

"I wouldn't worry about it too much. This probably won't work anyway."

"Don't be pessimistic, Harry. I think this is fabulous. Seven loves it. She's been listening in." And the weirdest part was that B'Elanna was certain Seven *had* been listening in and believed the idea was, yes, crazy, but also might be *Voyager's* only chance.

"Ooo-kay," Harry replied, but had nothing else to say. *"Then tell her that she needs to get to work on the shield . . ."*

"She knows. Already working on it. We should be ready in about two hours."

"Can you make it one? I don't think the shields will make it to . . ."

"One hour and fifteen is my best guess right now. I might be able to trim off another fifteen once I touch down, especially if Kaytok can remember some of the settings."

"I remember everything," Kaytok said.

"There you go, Harry. We're touching down. We'll call you every fifteen minutes with a progress report. Don't hurt my engines!" She signed off before Harry could reply, and B'Elanna found herself thinking how inefficient verbal communication could be sometimes.

~

After a short consultation with Kaytok's technicians, the work began in earnest. Though, as Kaytok had claimed, he remembered all the shield generator's original settings, Seven had made considerable changes to the power supply and delivery middleware. While some of these alterations had to be undone, Torres agreed that other modifications should remain as they would not change the effect, but would enhance the shield generator's performance.

Seven was pleased. She and Torres were now working together much more efficiently with thoughts and impressions flashing back and forth, words only occasionally necessary. They might not have found the level of intermingled consciousness a Borg work team achieved, but not too shabby for a couple of humans. Pausing, Seven asked herself, *"Shabby?" I have never used that word before.* She dismissed her distress. "Shabby" was a perfectly acceptable word. It had a nice ring to it.

"How much longer?" Chakotay asked. He knew he wasn't doing anything useful in the engine room. Though he knew every square centimeter of every system on the rest of *Voyager,* he had never been able to find the time to dig into the detailed specifications of the warp engines. Theory? Yes. Every graduate of the Academy had to be grounded in warp theory, but theory and practical knowledge were two very different quantum packets.

"You can't rush this kind of process, Commander," Harry said. "If you make a mistake . . ." Ensign Kim and

Joe Carey had been working for more than thirty-five minutes, and their time was running out. If Kim and Carey couldn't coax the resin out of the warp core soon, there was no way they could be ready before the shields collapsed. Paris had been doing an astonishing job of anticipating the waves and guiding *Voyager* through the worst of them, but there was no way he could avoid every one.

"I appreciate your wanting to be careful, Harry, but you're going to have to cut corners." The makeshift magnetic container was attached to Harry's belt and he had managed to squeeze under the warp core to a spot directly beneath a batch of alarmingly colored conduits festooned with warning labels and embellished with Starfleet insignia. "What would B'Elanna do if she were here?"

"Lieutenant Torres would likely just start yanking on things," Carey said. "But she knows precisely how hard to yank and which bits are likely to explode."

"Don't you?" Harry asked, his casual tone attempting to mask his anxiety.

"Sure, if everything in this room was up to Starfleet spec," Carey said. "But nothing is anymore."

Harry said, "Sorry, but can both of you be quiet for a minute. I'm about to insert the probe. If this works the way B'Elanna said it would, we should be out of here in two minutes."

Chakotay couldn't resist asking. "And if it doesn't?"

Carey said, "Then that sharp ringing you'll hear will be your molecules moving away from each other at the speed of light."

Chakotay heard Harry laugh *(Gods of my father, we're all getting punch-drunk)*, then grunted once with satisfaction. "Got it."

"Great. What next?"

"Pull me out of here. I'm afraid to move."

"How much longer?" Kaytok asked, turning his head slightly so that he was looking into a corner. He disliked watching the two Voyagers working together. Their movements were *too* coordinated, *too* effortless and smooth. B'Elanna had tried to explain earlier that Seven had once been part of something called a Borg collective and that each member of the collective was not an individual at all, but a cell in a larger organism. Given his own unusual circumstances among other Monorhans, Kaytok had initially thought this idea appealing, but then watching the mini-collective's eerie silence and flawless interaction began to prey on him. Oddly, Kaytok had noticed that Seven of Nine was smiling with beatific satisfaction, while Torres grew more quiet and grim with every passing moment.

"We will be ready in three minutes," B'Elanna said. "Have you assembled your comrades?"

"They're waiting outside. You know none of them is too happy about this."

"About our taking the generator?" B'Elanna asked. "It is to be anticipated. Many of them have devoted years of their lives to the project and they do not know if we will be doing anything to benefit either them or your world."

"Tell them to get over it," Seven said. "We'll take good care of it."

"I do not think your attitude is productive," B'Elanna said to Seven, "though I agree with your sentiment." Turning back to Kaytok, she said, "We'll be able to use the device more effectively in the shuttle. Also, if, as you suspect, the Emergency Council will track us here, then we need to move it anyway."

"You think we'll be able to move it by ourselves? The console's not so bad, but getting the dish off the roof . . ."

"We have antigrav pads," Seven said. "Once we have disconnected the dish, we'll be able to hustle it off the roof."

"Antigrav?" Kaytok asked incredulously.

"Hustle?" B'Elanna asked.

Pad scuffled into the room at the same moment that Seven's portable scanner began to sound an alert. "Company," he said. Seven retrieved her scanner and studied the display. "Two large ground vehicles—trucks—are entering the compound. There are eight Monorhans in each one, including the driver. Most are carrying weapons."

"Emergency Council security team," Kaytok said. "Trouble."

"Not necessarily," B'Elanna said. "I talked the last group of soldiers into releasing us. I believe I can do the same again."

"But you may fail," Seven replied, snapping the scanner shut. "And you are needed to complete the work on the shield generator."

"You could do it . . ."

"But not as well or as quickly as you," Seven retorted. "I believe that our recent . . . merger . . . means you have all the skills you need to finish this task, whereas I feel better equipped to kick these jerks' collective tails." She stopped, evidently surprised by her own words, but then a slow grin spread across her features. "I will return as soon as I can," she said, and headed down the stairs.

They had warned Corek that there might be Voyagers with the Dissenters. He had resolved that should this turn out to be true, he would attempt to be diplomatic. If the tales were true, the Voyagers possessed impressive technology, but the report from the other teams also noted that they were physically unprepossessing. The word "puny" stuck in his memory.

But then he caught a glimpse of his first Voyager and he concluded that the reports had omitted an important detail. They were shameless. This woman, this *creature*, marching toward him—at first he thought she was naked, but then Corek realized the blue tinge was clothing and not the color of her flesh. Were they *all* like this on *Voyager?* If so, how did they ever get anything done? And then he realized that the female only had two arms. Perhaps . . . perhaps she was some kind of special neutered gender—a drone—and the normal females were responsible for child rearing.

The giantess halted within an arm's length of Corek's vehicle and barked, "I am Seven of Nine of the *Starship Voyager.* Explain why you are here. We are performing very delicate engineering operations and your presence is disrupting our work."

Corek sensed his second-in-command staring at him, probably eager to see how his superior officer would respond to such an outrageous claim. Unfortunately, an appropriate answer did not leap immediately to mind. He had expected the Dissenters to have broken and run as they always did when they heard EC troops coming. At worst, he had expected to have a minor skirmish with whoever was inside the compound, but everyone knew that Dissenters weren't inherently dangerous as long as you kept them under control. Let them know they were being watched.

The Voyager continued to stare, fists on her hips. Corek tried to keep his eyes locked on her face. Looking at anything below her neck was distressing, though he didn't much care for anything above it either. Her small eyes and flat nose reminded Corek of an infant. He settled on the neck region and said, "I am Commander Corek of the Emergency Council police. We have been sent to investigate an electrical disturbance that our scanners tell us originated from this location approximately twenty-seven hours ago."

"Really?" the Voyager said. "We have been here for less then twelve hours, so this is no concern of ours."

"That is beside the point," Corek replied, wondering why this woman was being so obtuse. "Also, another member of my force contacted one of your crew less than two hours ago and asked her to accompany us to the city. She was very rude to the *shalla*."

"Ah, yes. Lieutenant Torres. She *is* very rude. I will make sure she is severely chastised." She paused, cocked her head as if listening to another conversation, and then repeated, *"Severely."*

Baffled, Corek stood transfixed, unsure how to respond. His second moved close behind him and nudged him in the side. "Sir?" Corek asked him what he wanted.

"Sir," the second whispered. "There's movement on the roof." He paused to let the idea sink in, then suggested, "Snipers?"

Corek stiffened and experienced a sudden desire to move closer to the vehicles. He squashed it, knowing that he could not risk showing weakness in front of his troops. Momentarily ignoring the alien, Corek lifted his field glasses to his eyes and scanned the rooftops, and instantly saw movement. If there was a sniper, he was the clumsiest in existence. Or perhaps—anxious thought—he didn't feel an urgent need to hide. "Who's up on the roof?" Corek asked.

The Voyager turned to look up, then immediately snapped around again. The creature's spine was very limber. A Monorhan would have had to take a half-step to the right or the left to look back over her shoulder that way. Watching the movement made Corek feel slightly queasy. "Technicians," she explained. "We're setting up an experiment."

"They're moving something, sir," the second said. "Do you want me to send someone around to investigate."

"No!" the Voyager said sharply. "This is none of your

concern. If you do not cease your intrusions . . ." She stopped speaking so suddenly that for a split second Corek wondered if one of his troops had lost control and fired at her. But then she said, "What?" and looked at the ground before her feet as if she were having a squabble with a small, invisible person. "Of course you can! Just hold on all the way down."

"Sir?" the second asked, taking a step back, his hand reaching toward his weapon. Dealing with aliens was one thing. Dealing with an *insane* alien something else entirely. "She's talking to someone."

"If you don't," the alien said, spinning to look up at the roof, "we're going to be here all day! Just do it!"

Of course, Corek realized. *Some kind of hidden microphone.* "Excuse me," Corek said, attempting to wrest control of the situation. "You're going to have to come with us. The *shalla* will decide what is to be done."

The alien looked up at him, her small eyes boring into his, and stepped forward. "Here's what I think of your *shalla.*"

"She punched him," Kaytok announced.

"I know!" B'Elanna shouted from the pilot's seat.

"Why did she punch him?"

"Because he made her angry." The engines hummed beneath their feet. Kaytok very much wished he could sit down, but the console was neither bolted to the floor (as he had suggested) nor lashed into the shuttle's bulkhead. B'Elanna trusted it to one of the antigravity pads, which, she claimed, would keep the machine in place. Kaytok was not so sure and had decided he should stay nearby in case it began to shift. The dish was snuggly stowed in a compartment that B'Elanna said she could open remotely when the time came.

"Remind me to never make Seven angry," Kaytok said, staring at the monitor. B'Elanna said the shuttle's systems automatically tapped into the EC's communication network so they could watch Seven, this despite the fact that B'Elanna always seemed to know what the other one was doing. Their bond was much stronger than anything he had ever seen among his own people, but Kaytok was concerned about a sort of merging or blending he was observing. "I think the commander is unconscious. Some of the other soldiers are raising their rifles."

"Emergency liftoff," B'Elanna said. "We have to get clear of the building," she added, and then, "We'll be there in a second. Don't get shot."

He was not sure what she was going to do next. Undoubtedly, the shuttle possessed some kind of weaponry, but used at such close range, an attack would be as likely to injure Seven. Kaytok's knees buckled under him as the shuttle surged into the air, clearing his lab's roof in less than three seconds.

"Hold on!" B'Elanna shouted. Glancing at the monitor, Kaytok saw that the soldiers were arraying themselves in a half-circle around Seven. Some in the back rows were suddenly distracted, one pointing up into the sky. Seven stood very erect, seemingly untroubled by any of the rifles pointed her way.

"Transporter status?" B'Elanna called.

"What?" Kaytok asked.

A pleasant but assured voice replied, *"Functioning."*

"Lock on to Seven of Nine."

"Transporter lock established."

The shuttle was not dipping down toward the ground, but continued to dash skyward. "Aren't we going back for Seven?" Kaytok asked.

"Computer, energize!" B'Elanna shouted.

Energize? Kaytok wondered. She was firing a weapon? Was B'Elanna sacrificing Seven for the greater good? He heard a whining sound and wondered if a cannon or particle beam weapon was being charged. "We're not going to get Seven?" he asked again.

"Seven is right here," Seven said, touching Kaytok on the shoulder. The Monorhan leaped away, so startled that he released his grip on the console, which did not budge a centimeter. "Though just barely." This last comment was directed at B'Elanna. "Could you have cut that a little closer?"

"It was necessary to get clear of the building," B'Elanna called from the pilot's chair. "The transporter lock was fluctuating. Something in the building's structure, I suspect." Kaytok saw that the sky through the shuttle's front windows was rapidly shifting from blue to indigo. He was flying in a vessel far above the surface of the planet and would soon be well beyond the atmosphere. Strangely, the idea induced more curiosity than dread.

"Get on the comm," B'Elanna said, sounding more like her old self. "We have to contact *Voyager* and see if they're ready for us." Through the window, Kaytok could see tiny pinpoints of light—stars, though they did not twinkle, but shone steadily. "Harry better have his new toy all ready to go."

"And if he does not?" Seven asked.

"Then this is going to be a very short trip."

Chapter 18

"What do we do first?" B'Elanna asked over the comm. No one else on the bridge spoke, afraid they would miss vital information.

"Fire the Monorhan's energy wave," Janeway said. "As soon as you do, we'll lock on to the frequency, then fire the trilithium into the Blue Eye."

"And what will be happening to you?" Chakotay asked the engineer.

"We'll probably be in free fall trying to restart the engines just like last time. I didn't have time to build in any kind of shielding, so I expect the same thing will happen."

"Couldn't you fire the shield generator from outside the gravity well?"

"We could," B'Elanna replied, *"but we want conditions to be as close to the original circumstances as possible. Besides, you can always beam us out, right?"*

"Right, B'Elanna," Janeway agreed, but something in her chief engineer's tone made the captain wonder how hard Torres would try to restart if *Voyager* failed to emerge from the fold. A shock wave coursed through the hull, rattling Janeway's back teeth. The gravitonic waves were coming more frequently, no more than three or four minutes apart, and it was difficult to think, let alone speak, when one rumbled and thrummed through the ship. An alarm bleated, but when the captain looked around the bridge she could not see any obvious problem. "What's wrong, Chakotay?"

"Nothing here, Captain. That's coming through B'Elanna's comm signal."

"Enemy ships approaching!" Seven of Nine said, her tone uncharacteristically enthusiastic. *"Energizing weapons!"*

"Patience, Seven," B'Elanna replied. *"There's no way they can catch us."*

Seven barked, *"But they were rude to me!"*

"Seven! Relax!"

Janeway and Chakotay exchanged confused looks. "Are you two all right?" Chakotay asked.

"Fine!" the pair answered in unison, but then B'Elanna took control of the conversation. *"Get ready to fire your torpedo. I've got to ditch these guys first or maybe let Seven shoot at them a little first."* Pause. *"She has a scary glint in her eye."*

Within seconds of signing off, B'Elanna realized that her problem was more complex than she had anticipated. The Monorhans, she discovered, had developed sophisticated high-altitude combat aircraft, and two were close on her tail. The desire to engage in an aerial dogfight was almost overwhelming, probably spurred on by Seven's yearning for revenge. Several confusing seconds ticked past until the sensible solution occurred to her. "Strap in, you two," she called to her passengers. "And make sure the console is secure."

"It isn't!" Kaytok said. "It's on these antigravity things!"

"Then it will be fine," Seven said, her cool aloofness reasserting itself. She helped Kaytok with his buckles and belts, then settled into the seat directly behind B'Elanna.

We are ready.

The first fighter fired an air-to-air missile, which burst harmlessly on the shuttle's shields. The sensors informed her that the second craft had a lock on them and was about to do the same, so B'Elanna did the most efficient thing she could conceive: she cut the shuttle's engines. The fighter craft cruised past the shuttle at five hundred kilometers per hour and were twenty kilometers away before either pilot could realize what had happened. By then, B'Elanna had spun the shuttle one hundred eighty degrees and was racing for the ionosphere.

"Well done," Seven said. "Though I would have enjoyed some shooting."

Tuvok was pleased with how quickly Ensign Kim assembled the torpedo mechanism, but was troubled when he saw the calculations for how much trilithium to use. "These are approximations," Tuvok observed.

Kim looked up from his workbench and slid the HUD goggles up onto his forehead. Both heard another shock wave ripple through the ship, but did not feel its effects. Tuvok made his weapons teams work in zero-gravity environments since so many of the materials used in phaser systems and quantum torpedoes were sensitive to jostling. Starfleet had made training for the technique available to crews only a short time before he had left on his undercover mission to the Maquis, but as soon as he returned to *Voyager* he had initiated his teams in the practice.

"That's true," Kim said. "All the captain and I had to work with are the rough models. It's not like this has been done very often."

"How many tests were completed?"

Kim shrugged, then glanced nervously down into the torpedo's inner workings. He had just finished infusing the trilithium compound into the quantum core. "Maybe a dozen," he said uncertainly.

"Maybe fewer," Tuvok said, "if these are all the results."

"Maybe fewer, then," Kim said irritably. "Tuvok, what's your point? That we don't know exactly what we're doing? I concede that, but I haven't heard any suggestions for better ideas. Don't you trust me?"

"If I did not trust you, Ensign, we would not be having this conversation. The question is, do you trust *yourself?* Will this work?"

The corners of Kim's face tightened and Tuvok saw how exhausted the young man was. Like most of the senior staff, Kim could not have slept more than a few hours out of the past thirty. "It has to work," Kim said tersely.

Tuvok said, "I agree."

Kim slid the goggles back over his eyes and began to seal up the torpedo.

Ziv decided that he had died when the transport had disintegrated. Everything that had happened since then—encountering the Voyagers, becoming trapped in a "fold" in space, reencountering Sem—all of these memories were elaborate constructs created by his subconscious in the infinitesimally tiny slices of a second between when his body was destroyed and his mind accepted the idea. His fear—a dread greater than the wish not to die—was that this sensation might go on forever and ever. How long could his mind continue to stretch out the millisecond? Would he continue to torture himself indefinitely if some sick, guilt-stricken portion of his consciousness decided he deserved to have his agony prolonged? Could he find ever newer, ever more horrible scenarios to torment himself?

For example, he was *sure* the Sem in his sick fantasy was pregnant. He couldn't be certain *how* he knew this was true, but there was no doubt in his mind. More, he was certain the child was his. Though their single, forbidden encounter had been many months ago, Sem's body could have held his seed in reserve.

So, Ziv realized, in this nightmare scenario, he had attempted to kill Sem and the child she carried. He was surprised to discover he had such a flair for the dramatic. What other horrors could his mind visit on him? He settled deeper into his misery, then pulled it over him like a blanket. He had only to wait a little longer and death would catch up with him.

"B'Elanna? Are you ready?"

"We're ready, Captain."

"Fire the shield generator."

"Firing, Captain."

Kaytok the engineer was very pleased about how well the generator seemed to perform. The monitors showed a regular sawtooth waveform—precisely the configuration B'Elanna had asked to see. Everything seemed perfect until the lights went out.

In the darkness behind him, Kaytok heard the two Voyagers, their voices now sounding eerily similar, speak each other's thoughts.

"Same old," said B'Elanna/Seven.

"Same old," said Seven/B'Elanna.

The shuttle, aerodynamic as a brick, dropped like a brick.

"They've fired the shield generator, Captain," Chakotay announced. "We're registering a frequency." Tense seconds ticked past as the first officer studied the display on his chair arm. "Logged and entered." He looked up at the screen and pointed toward the Blue Eye. "Tom—*now!*"

Paris touched the sequence of controls on the navigation board, and *Voyager,* like a thoroughbred racehorse that had been too long reined in, leapt forward. "Hang on, everyone!" Paris shouted. "This is going to be bumpy."

Down in the torpedo launch bay, Harry waited with his finger on the button.

The open channel from the bridge crackled, "Torpedo away."

Harry touched the button and he briefly regretted that there was no satisfying "Click!" Switches just weren't built right anymore. A green light was all the satisfaction he would receive. That, and being permitted to say, "Torpedo away."

Tom Paris knew that the timing on this run would be tricky. He had to stay far enough behind the torpedo that he didn't outrun it, but close enough that he could slip through the crack around the Eye when it appeared. None of the theoretical geniuses, not Tuvok or Harry or the captain, had been able to tell him how long the crack would remain available, so there was that problem, too. What to do, then? *Go with your gut,* Paris thought. *Feel where B'Elanna is and head in that direction.* The method hadn't failed him yet.

"Anything?" Kaytok asked. "Please."

"Not yet," B'Elanna/Seven replied. "Working."

Without power, there was no way to know what their airspeed was, but a quick mental calculation proved they had reached terminal velocity.

Whiner, B'Elanna/Seven thought.

He is frightened, Seven/B'Elanna thought. *He does not wish to die.*

I don't, either, B'Elanna/Seven thought. *But I'm not afraid.*

I'm not letting you be afraid, Seven/B'Elanna thought. *Fear diminishes efficiency.*

Agreed, B'Elanna/Seven thought. *But fear can also motivate.*

An interesting idea. We should discuss it more later.

I agree. B'Elanna/Seven pressed the restart sequence again. *After we get the engines started.*

"Torpedo contact in five, four, three, two . . ."

The countdown did not reach "one." The Blue Eye did not, as anticipated, temporarily cease to seethe and bloom. Black patches did not appear as atomic processes were momentarily halted. Nothing happened precisely as planned.

The Blue Eye burst like a balloon.

"Captain," Tom Paris called. "We still have a lock on the frequency and there *is* a gap forming." Tom watched the tenuous scarlet matter fly past on the main monitor. He decided it looked like red cotton candy or sunset clouds or sea spray or, more apt, a mixture of all three since he was beginning to see that different layers had various textures.

"The Eye is blowing off its fusionable materials, Captain," Chakotay called from the science station. "We've accelerated some kind of end-phase process."

"This shouldn't be happening," Janeway said. "The star didn't have enough mass!"

"It's collapsing," Chakotay said, and Janeway was certain she heard his voice crack. "It's going to form a singularity."

The word and the deed always seemed like one in Janeway's memory. *Voyager* had been pacing herself, moving at a steady, controlled rate at her master's command, but when Chakotay spoke his dread pronouncement, the captain gave her order and the ship, true-hearted, ever faithful, obeyed. "Helm," Captain Janeway said. *"Go!"*

Stars! There were stars on the main viewscreen, but they were limned in blue as if they were being pulled away from *Voyager* at speeds beyond imagination. The sensors were unable to process the visual data and return meaningful images. *What do you see when you look into the eye of eternity?* Chakotay wondered, but then chastised himself for permitting errant thoughts.

The ship had plunged ahead, inertial compensators briefly unable to accommodate their speed, and Chakotay had been pushed back into his seat. Unaccountable energies pulled on *Voyager:* warp engines pushing them forward, the steep incline into the deepest of gravity wells pulling on them from behind. Chakotay knew which must win if they were inside the event horizon. Worse, he knew that the moment, drawn out like a thread through a spinning wheel, might last a literal eternity and none of them would ever know the difference.

"Engineering!" Kathryn called.

"Carey here, Captain. What's going on?"

"Don't ask questions, Joe! If you've got anything that you've been holding in reserve, give it to us!"

"There's some nonstandard rerouting that Lieutenant Torres did that I think might give us . . ."

"Do it!"

"I haven't really had time to study . . ."

"Do it!"

Carey crossed his fingers and said a silent prayer. *Chief,* he thought, *I hope you knew what you were doing.*

In the torpedo launch room, Harry Kim sagged against the control board as he felt the conflicting energies release their hold on him. Resting his head on the cool plasteel, he thought, *What did I get wrong? What?* Lifting his head, Harry said, "I'm sorry, Tuvok. I thought I had it right. The calculations . . ." Tuvok was not standing by the console where he had been a moment before. The ship lurched to port and a limp weight rolled against Harry's legs. Kim looked down. "Tuvok?"

Chakotay sagged back into his seat and rolled his eyes toward the ceiling. "We got them," he said, then exhaled sharply.

Kathryn lifted her right hand and punched the air. "Yes!" she shouted, and the bridge rang with cheers and applause. Tom Paris half-rose and bowed as much as was possible without taking his hands off the navigational controls or his eyes off the main viewscreen.

The shuttle had been less than two hundred meters from the ground when *Voyager* zoomed past Monorha. Their warp field had collapsed as soon as they had emerged into Monorhan space, but the ship was still moving at a considerable percentage of the speed of light. Paris had used every trick he knew to shed momentum or *Voyager* would have raced past the planet and out of transporter range.

"Their Monorhan guest is a little worse for wear," Chakotay continued, "and the transporter chief says Seven and B'Elanna are acting very odd."

"Odd?" Kathryn asked. "Odd how?"

"They're completing each other's sentences," he says. "And Seven was cursing the transporter."

"I'd better go down there," she said, and rose.

"What you'd better do," Chakotay said softly, rising beside her, "is go to your quarters and get some sleep. The crisis is over. Now we need a few hours to pick up the pieces before we decide what to do next."

"And I need to talk to the Emergency Council," the captain protested, walking toward the turbolift, "to find out what they thought they were doing . . ."

Chakotay paced her step for step and pitched his voice low enough that no one else could hear them, but there was no mistaking the urgency in his tone. "What you need to do is go to your quarters and turn off the comm. Eight hours of sleep, Captain, or I tell the Doctor to order you."

"We don't have a doctor currently, Commander."

"Then I'll appoint myself chief medical officer and order you myself."

Kathryn frowned, and Chakotay worried for a moment that he was going to have to engage in a battle of wills—something he preferred to avoid, seeing as he was as tired as the captain. Then her combadge piped. *"Sickbay to Captain Janeway."* The voice was familiar, if not the confused tone.

Kathryn smiled. "Go ahead, Doctor. We've missed you. Well, parts of you."

"What happened to me, Captain?"

"Let's discuss that later," Chakotay interrupted. "After you go down to the transporter room and see to Seven and B'Elanna."

"Ah, they're back, then. Are we free of the fold?"

"We're not sure exactly what happened yet, Doctor. I'll be convening a meeting . . ." The muscle under Kathryn's right eye twitched and she reached up to wearily rub at the tired muscle. Seeming to realize what she was doing, the captain lowered her hand and stared at it thoughtfully for a beat. "After I've rested," she said softly. "After we've all rested."

"An excellent plan, Captain. Sickbay out."

Looking up at Chakotay, Kathryn asked, "Would you object if I at least stopped by sickbay on the way to my cabin to see how B'Elanna and Seven are doing?"

"Do you really want to hear Seven cursing?"

"I confess I'm curious."

Chakotay considered the option. "Come to think of it, so am I."

Kathryn turned back to the bridge, scanned to see who was on duty, and finally said, "Mr. Paris, the bridge is yours."

"Yes, ma'am."

"When Tuvok returns, tell him he's to relieve you so you can visit . . ." Kathryn stopped then, and Chakotay saw a look in her eyes that he knew meant, *No, wait. Tuvok would never believe that* . . . Instead, she tapped her combadge and said, "Janeway to Tuvok."

Three seconds of silence passed, two of which felt perfectly normal, but the last seemed like an eternity.

"Janeway to Tuvok," Kathryn repeated.

Another three seconds passed, and then a voice came over the comm. *"Captain Janeway, this is Kim. Tuvok is on his way to sickbay."*

"On my way, Harry."

Chakotay sighed and followed his captain, thinking, *No rest for the weary.*

Kaytok appreciated how everything on the Voyagers' vessel smelled clean. Unfortunately, this pleasure led him to wonder what these well-scrubbed others must think of his own scent. His experiences of the past several minutes—free fall followed by dematerialization—had not helped the situation. Perhaps if he asked politely, there would be time for a bath later.

For now, though, Kaytok was content to follow Seven and B'Elanna (still speaking in overlapping sentences)

through the wide, antiseptic corridors, in and then out of
tiny, humming elevators, to the sickbay. Their guide, a
roundish, hairy fellow, informed Kaytok that there
would be a surprise waiting for him at journey's end.
Kaytok hoped it was a hot meal.

It was not. Three Monorhans dressed in military
garb, all of them glaring at him, stood clustered around a
fourth who was lying on a table. This supine figure lifted
his head and stared at Kaytok questioningly, then asked
in a raspy voice, "Who are you?"

Unsure what manner of situation he had just walked
into, Kaytok took a single step forward and stopped at the
foot of the bed. Surprisingly, the three around the table
took a half-step back, opening up a space that felt like a
stage. "I'm Kaytok."

The patient struggled to rise, but the table on which
he lay was too narrow. Seeing his trouble, two of the
patient's *hara* lifted him so he could look at Kaytok lev-
elly. "I've heard of you," he said. "Sem mentioned your
name."

Kaytok watched the *hara* exchange anxious glances. A
newly honed sense of self-preservation began to jangle in
his ears. "Sem?" He looked around. "She's here?"

"On this ship, yes," the *harat* replied. "In the brig, I'm
told."

"That's like a jail, right?" The *harat* nodded. Kaytok
said, "Good!"

The *harat* smiled weakly, then said, "We should talk
later, but I have to rest now." He looked around at the

faces of his *hara*. "I'm still not convinced any of this is real."

"You and I both," Kaytok muttered.

At a third table, an erect individual with a bare pate was helping a smaller individual lift a third figure off a floating stretcher. Noting the blinking lights and readouts, Kaytok decided the tables were some kind of diagnostic device.

When the smaller individual was finished helping put the unconscious one onto the diagnostic table, he turned to look at Kaytok's companions and called out, "Seven, B'Elanna—great work down there!"

B'Elanna replied, "Your work was also exemplary, Ensign."

Seven punched him on the arm in what Kay interpreted to be a playful gesture and said, "Way to go, Harry."

The one called Harry rubbed his arm where Seven had hit him and stared at them. Leaning forward, he studied the appliance around B'Elanna's eye. "We didn't get back to the right universe," he said.

"You did, Harry," B'Elanna said. "Fear not. Some things happened on Monorha." Nodding toward the supine form, she asked, "What happened to Tuvok?"

Harry shook his head. "I don't know. Shock, the Doc says. He collapsed when we emerged from the fold. Some kind of psionic feedback maybe."

Two more individuals rushed into Sickbay, which was rapidly feeling very crowded. They, too, congratulated the returned Voyagers and complimented Harry on his work, though Kaytok also sensed some discontent with how his predictions worked out. Seeing how the others treated the newcomers, Kaytok guessed that the small female was the Voyagers' *rih*.

Wishing to remain out of the way (everyone was clustering around the stricken fellow, though the bald one was trying to push them all away), Kaytok found a cushioned seat in a small office and sat down, then leaned his head against the wall and fell asleep.

He was asleep, he thought, for no more than a second or two when someone touched his shoulder. "Sorry," Kaytok said, his tongues moving thickly. "Guess I can't sleep here."

"You can sleep later," the other said. "But I need you awake now, Kay."

Kay? No one outside his family ever called him that. Well, his family and . . . *Sem?!* Kaytok's eyes snapped open. A Monorhan stood beside him, though it was not Sem. "Why is it so dark?" Kaytok asked. "What happened to everyone?" Then, squinting, he studied the old, lined face of the figure limned in shadow and found to his great surprise that he recognized it. "Gora?" he asked.

"Yes," Gora said. "Hello. We don't have much time, and there are some things I need to tell you . . ."

Chapter 19

"We're not finished here," the captain said, looking down at the arc of Monorha from her ready-room window. From where she stood, D'Elanna could only see the white crescent of the planet's northern ice pack and a smudge of ocean. Twelve hours ago, a whole three hours after the last nanoprobe was flushed from her system, Captain Janeway had asked B'Elanna to start thinking about ways they might be able to revitalize Monorha's ecosystem. Melting the ice pack with phaser fire from orbit had been one of the few viable options that her team had proposed. The method also had the virtue of being quick, though not knowing how their efforts would pan out bothered her.

Focusing back on the moment, she replied, "No, of course we're not. We never are."

Captain Janeway turned to look at her chief engineer, and B'Elanna sensed she was being watched carefully. "What are you thinking, B'Elanna?" the captain asked softly.

Torres decided to answer truthfully. "That some might argue we don't know what happens to all the worlds we visit and leave our mark on. Others might say we have a responsibility to see things through. . . ."

"What do *you* say, B'Elanna?"

Recalling her conversation with Kaytok, B'Elanna plunged ahead. "That we need to be careful, very careful, not only for our sake, but for the sakes of the people we encounter."

Turning to look back out her window, the captain asked, a slight note of worry in her voice, "Do you think we broke the Prime Directive?"

B'Elanna pondered that one for several seconds before answering. "I'm not a debater, Captain. Or a lawyer if it came to that, but this time I'd say probably not."

"*This* time? Have there been times?"

"Yes."

"More than once?"

"Yes, ma'am. But there's something else I'd like to add."

"And that is?"

"Every time you did it, every time you broke the Prime Directive, you were right to do it. The planet where it happened was better for it." Torres had been thinking about the topic a lot over the past several hours, had even discussed it with Tom last night after their reunion, but before sleep. "Here's what I think: The Prime Directive is in place to protect planets and cultures from bad decisions being made by . . . you'll forgive the term . . . average ship captains. By people like me—people who act before they think. But there's a few, Captain Janeway, people like you or like Chakotay or, I think someday, Harry Kim, who always know the right thing to do. Or who make it right." She hesitated, wondering how much more she should say. "I can't pretend I understand all this, but there are captains and then there are *captains.*"

"And you think I'm one of the latter." Captain Janeway turned back to B'Elanna, her face softly underlit by the stars.

"Yes, ma'am. I do."

The left corner of the captain's mouth curled up ever so slightly before she turned away. "You realize, of course, that Starfleet Command would never see it that way."

"I figure that's a problem we'll deal with when we get home."

"When? Not if?"

"It might take a while," B'Elanna said, figuring she was allowed to slip in one jab. "If we keep taking the scenic route. On the other hand, I decided that home . . . home is where the *hara* is."

"And yours is here."

"Yes, ma'am." She found herself thinking of Tom and Harry, Chakotay and Neelix, and, yes, even the Doctor. *My* hara, she thought. *And there stands my* harat. *Or is it* haras? She had never quite figured out the gender assignments.

"How are you feeling?" Janeway asked, changing the subject. "Since becoming unlinked?"

"Fine," B'Elanna said. "The Doctor said all the

nanoprobes died off after Seven completed a regeneration cycle. Something about changing the resonance signature—I'm not sure I got it all. One minute she was here in my head and the next, poof, she was gone." She shook her head and smiled.

"Sounds like it was quite an experience," Janeway remarked.

"Not one I'd care to repeat," B'Elanna said, "but it was very strange feeling so intimately bound to someone . . . feeling like I *belonged*. I think I understand the Borg a little better now."

"Then I'd say the experience was worthwhile. We may need to call on that knowledge someday."

B'Elanna nodded uncertainly, thinking of that last moment before she and Seven had been severed from one another. She had not thought to say anything more, but then, somehow, she found herself saying, "There was one other thing, Captain. Something about Seven."

"What's that?" the captain ask, sounding worried in that maternal way she sometimes did.

"She's very . . . alone," B'Elanna said. "Actually, 'alone' doesn't even begin to describe it. Just before the Doctor cut us off from each other, I felt it . . . for just a second. I don't know if Seven even thinks about it or is aware of it, but . . ." She stopped, struggling to find the words to describe the sensation.

"Go on," the captain said.

"I don't know if I can. It's just a feeling. I used to think of myself as very alone, very isolated before . . ." She shrugged. "You know."

"Before Tom."

"Right. But now I know, I didn't understand what isolated meant. This is what I got from Seven: There's everything else and everyone else in the universe and then there's *her.*"

"Isn't that true for all of us?" Captain Janeway asked.

"It didn't used to be," B'Elanna said. "Not for her."

"But she chose this."

"Yes, she did, and I think she would agree that it was the better choice, but, well, I guess I just wanted to say I understand something about what it cost her."

The captain turned back to the window, reached up, and laid her palm lightly on the barrier. Speaking softly, she said, "Well, then, I guess there's another thing we all learned." She did not speak for what seemed a very long time. B'Elanna shuffled her feet slightly, and the captain came back from wherever she had gone. "Your friend Kaytok says he has something he wants to give me. Have you heard of this Key to Gremadia?"

"He told me about it . . . well, someone told Seven about it, and then after all the excitement was over, the things that Kaytok told me and the things Seven knew all coalesced. The Key was supposedly lost, but not really. Kaytok's family had it and now he wants to give it to you."

"Because his grandfather who left the planet fifty years ago came to him in a dream and told him to do it?"

"Yes, ma'am," B'Elanna said, trying not to sound too skeptical. "That would seem to cover it."

"And can you, Lieutenant, think of any reason I should accept this gift?"

B'Elanna considered, then replied, "Because I trust Kaytok. He's a remarkably sane and centered individual. And because we both know this is far from the strangest thing anyone has ever asked us to do."

Captain Janeway inhaled deeply, then sighed. "Well," she said, "you have me there."

Sitting by Tuvok's bedside, Neelix certainly had to concede that the Vulcan looked as good as ever. "Psychic shock"—whatever it was—didn't seem to have left any scars. The commander was back to being his usual irascible, punctilious self.

"Doctor," Tuvok said. "I must protest. I am completely recovered."

"Fortunately," the Doctor retorted, "I am the physician. I am not an unreasonable man, Commander. I ask only that you finish out the day of observation. If no further symptoms of your *mal de tête* become evident, you may return to duty."

Tuvok folded his arms over his chest.

"Oh, come now, Tuvok," Neelix said trying to be helpful. "Look on the positive side: a little bed rest, a chance to do some reading and meditating." Neelix observed the Vulcan's left eyebrow rise a half-centimeter. *Ah, acceptance.* "And I'll make you a *special* meal. I've been experimenting with a new kind of tortilla flour that I think would make an exceptional bean burrito."

The eyebrow rose another half-centimeter. "With guacamole?" Tuvok asked.

Neelix grinned extravagantly. "I think that could be arranged."

In their quarters, Ziv, Mol, Shet, Diro, and Jara sat on the floor around a low table set with candles, a loaf of crusty bread provided by the ever-helpful Neelix and a small bottle of thin liquor the humans called vodka. Jara had been the one to suggest the short service of remembrance and thanksgiving, and though Ziv had not felt much in the mood, he couldn't deny his *hara*. Now, though, his head spinning in a pleasant combination of drink and weariness, Ziv was glad they had done this.

Jara, ever watchful of his captain's mood, asked, "Are you all right, sir?"

Ziv clicked soothingly and replied, "Tired, Jara. Mostly just tired." He sipped a little more of the vodka, and marveled again at how similar it was to Monorhan *ahee.* He understood from Neelix that it too was distilled from a kind of grain. Smacking his lips, he savored the dry, spicy snap, then added, "And worried. When we return, we will need to speak to many sad mothers and fathers, many angry lovers and friends. Many have died, yet we still live."

"And yet there is the promise of a new life," Shet said, raising his glass slightly in salute. "Which is something you should discuss with your faithful *hara* someday." The others all clicked in agreement.

"There is very little to tell," Ziv said. "I was the *shi-*

harat, the faithful guard, but Sem was not content with that." Lowering his head, he continued, "And I was weak. I would prefer not to say any more."

"You are not the first *shi-harat,* man or woman, who weakened in that manner," Mol said, trying to reassure, though he sensed his *hara*'s disappointment.

"Nor the first man Sem has manipulated," Diro added.

"True," Ziv said. "I learned a great deal from Kaytok. He is an interesting fellow."

"Do you believe his story?" Mol asked. "Could he have spoken to Gora?"

Ziv bobbed his head uncertainly. "He believes he did, which is the important thing. And now he intends to give the Key to Gremadia to someone. 'To her,' Gora told him."

"Without being more specific about who the 'her' was," Jara said.

"Correct."

"One would think a spectral presence might be more specific," Diro said, slurring his words slightly.

The youngster has changed, Ziv thought. "One would," he agreed, then raised his glass to his lips. "But I have told Kaytok all I know of Sem, everything she has done."

"Everything?" Mol asked. "To someone outside the tribe?"

"It seemed necessary."

"And he will do the right thing?"

Ziv set his empty glass on the table. "Let us hope so, my *hara.*"

~

"So you've always had the Key?" Sem asked.

Kaytok turned away from the brig cell and looked out the large window, once again enthralled by the view of his world . . . how far below? Seven had told him at some point and the translator had done an admirable job of transforming the units so the distance meant something to him, but he couldn't recall what the number was. *A long way,* he decided. Pressing one hand against the "window," he marveled at how solid and real the forcefield felt. *The things these people could teach me,* he thought, not for the first time.

"So you've always had the Key?" she repeated.

He sighed and hung his head. One difference between windows and forcefields, he noted, was that forcefields didn't mist up when you sighed on them. "My mother gave it to me. When Gora's plans to go find Gremadia become all-consuming and she sensed that my sire would join him, she took the Key and hid it, thinking they wouldn't leave without it."

"She was wrong."

"Obviously. And by the time they were getting ready to leave, she was so terrified of what would happen if anyone discovered she had the Key that she just left it where it was."

"Out of curiosity, what does it look like?" she asked. "I thought I searched through every piece of property you owned and I don't remember ever finding anything that looked like it could be the Key."

Kaytok brushed a large knuckle against his chin, then

decided, *Why not tell her?* "It was in the music box," he said. "I kept it on my shelf next to the bed. And inside that was a small gray metal box whose top was welded shut. Do you remember?"

Kaytok could swear he saw Sem's pupils dilate at the memory of the box. "Of course," she said. "I used to play the music box in the middle of the night sometimes when you were asleep. I thought the metal box was just the workings."

"No."

"But the metal box was sealed shut. How do you know the Key was in there?"

"My mother told me," Kaytok said. "Why should I doubt her?"

If she hadn't already been sitting, Kaytok believed, Sem would have fallen over from the shock. "It could have been mine at any time," she finally exclaimed. "The greatest weapon of our age, of any age."

"Why do you think it's a weapon?"

"What else could it be?" Sem asked. "It killed Dagan. Why would anyone else be different?"

Kaytok cocked his head in wonder. "If you were sane," he said, surprised by his own honesty (it helped to have a forcefield between them), "you'd realize what a specious conclusion that is."

Sem released a thrum of anger so passionate, Kaytok felt it in his nasal passages. "I am the sanest person you've ever known," she said. "If nothing else, I'm sane enough to know you shouldn't give the Key to an alien. Or have you changed your mind?"

"I haven't. Gora told me to give the Key 'to her' so she could free him. I can't imagine you using any key to free anyone. That's not how your mind works."

Without warning, Sem rushed at him, causing the humming blue wall to buzz angrily. Though he knew she could not reach him, Kaytok flinched. Recovering, he said, "Be careful, or you'll hurt your child."

Now it was Sem's turn to be startled. Stepping away from the barrier, she wrapped her arms protectively around her midsection. "Who told you?"

"Ziv," Kaytok said, more than a little embarrassed to enjoy her discomfort. "You don't care what rules you break, do you?"

Sem took a half step back away from the barrier, but did not otherwise reply.

"He was your *shi-harat,* but you thought you needed to bind him to you even tighter."

Sem's mouth moved, but no words came out.

"How could you have done such a thing? How could you ever be trusted to free *anyone?* You should resign your position when the Voyagers turn you over to the authorities tomorrow."

Arms wrapped even more tightly around her, Sem turned away and stared at the back wall. Kaytok watched her for several moments, then turned away himself to stare out at the arc of his world. *So close,* he thought. *Yet so far away.*

"I know it might not seem like much," Kaytok said, setting the box down on Janeway's desk, "but this is

considered one of the most valuable religious arti-
facts on my world. My grandsire asked me to give it
to you."

Janeway regarded the rock with mingled curiosity
and respect. Kaytok had just returned from the surface of
Monorha after personally delivering Sem into custody.
"Thank you, Kaytok," she said. "Did he say what I was
supposed to do with it?"

"No," Kaytok said, "Not exactly. He seemed to think
you'd figure it out."

The captain lifted the box, then set it on the small
table by her desk. "In our line of work, sir, I often find we
must make things up as we go along." She unfastened the
clasp and studied the relic before lifting it from the container. Kaytok flinched. "Is there something I should
know about this artifact?"

Kaytok shook his head. "Only if you're interested in
superstitious nonsense. In my vision, Gora assured me
the key wouldn't hurt you as it did Dagan. But you
should be cautious."

Janeway extended her hand and Kaytok shook it.
When they broke their hand clasp, the captain sat down
again and said, "You may be interested to know that I
spoke with Shalla Kiiy earlier today and she also thanked
us for our efforts, though I got the impression she was
not certain precisely what happened."

"Are any of us?" B'Elanna asked. "Do we know why
the Blue Eye collapsed into a singularity?"

"Not yet," the captain said, and turned to Seven. "I

think you should put that on your list of priorities as soon as you're sure you're feeling better."

"I am fine, Captain," Seven said, glancing at B'Elanna for only a second. "Returning to a collective state was . . . nostalgic . . . but I have come to highly value my individuality."

Janeway smiled. "I'm glad," the captain said. "Then get back to work. Kaytok, again, thank you for the gift and thank you for your help."

Kaytok clicked once, but said nothing more. They made their farewells, and then B'Elanna escorted him to the transporter room for the final time.

Later, after a normal shift in engineering (during which she walked from component to component and explained all the changes she had made while Joe Carey frantically recorded and scribbled supplementary notes), B'Elanna returned to her cabin and, finding it empty, sighed gratefully, enjoying the solitude. She must have locked the door, because an hour later she awoke on the couch to the sound of the door chime. Rising, she opened the door and found Tom standing there, a supper tray in his hands. "Hey," he said. "I figured I'd be able to open the door. Someone should fix this."

"Oh, yeah?" B'Elanna asked, taking the tray from Tom's hands. "Like who?"

"Like the chief engineer maybe?"

"After she's finished eating," B'Elanna replied, heading toward the table where they usually ate their shared meals. Halfway across the room, B'Elanna stopped short, suddenly overcome by déjà vu.

Tom ran into her back and said, "What's wrong? Did I forget something?"

"No," she said and set the tray down. "I just remembered . . ." She smiled gently and turned around to face her lover. "You made me think of something . . ." Looking down at her, Tom grinned, mildly confused, but untroubled. "I missed you." Reaching up, she took his face between her hands and kissed him gently on the cheek. "You know," she said, "we're supposed to be together. Don't you?"

Tom Paris enveloped her in his arms, pulled her close, and made B'Elanna Torres feel safe, warm, and wanted. She rubbed her nose against the side of his, and was infinitely gratified when he said, "Of course we are," and returned her kiss on the cheek.

Down in her cargo bay, Seven of Nine awoke.

"Your regeneration cycle," the computer warned, "is not complete."

Seven reached up and touched her fingertips to her cheek. The sensation of a warm kiss lingered. She kept her eyes shut for several seconds as the feeling faded, something like a smile on her lips. Finally, she lowered her hand and said, "Continue regeneration."

Epilogue

"I really hate this system," Harry Kim said. He stared up at the giant display in astrometrics and struggled to make sense of the data flowing in from the main sensors. They had been at this for two days now and as each new theory for how the Monorhan system could exist in its current configuration was disproved, he found he had to reluctantly return to this flippant remark—namely, that some power created the system to its current specifications for some unknowable reason.

"Your feelings about the system have been noted and logged, Ensign," Seven of Nine said. "Repeating this litany does not bring us any closer to finding a . . ." Seven abruptly stopped talking.

Harry looked up from the console where he was working to see what was wrong. "Seven?"

Seven of Nine pointed at the holographic display at the center of the room. Far to the left of the tank was the central star, depicted as a writhing ball of gas. Arrayed at irregular intervals from the sun were the planets, three in all, then a patch of deformed space that was the tiny singularity.

Now, on the right edge of the tank, the outer edge of the system, Harry saw a new deformity, a much larger one. He asked, "Did you change the display?"

"I did not." Seven took half a step closer like she might be able to see more clearly. A very human gesture, Harry reflected absently, almost as if her mind did not want to have to try to process what she was seeing.

"And your instruments are registering correctly?" Seven took her eyes off the display just long enough to glare at Harry. "Sorry," he said, then concluded, "That's another singularity, isn't it?"

Seven nodded slowly.

"Where did it come from?"

"There is no way to know for sure, Ensign. We must play back the sensor readings from that sector."

"I think the captain would want to see this."

"Agreed. I will call her."

I really hate this system, Harry thought, then turned his attention to the sensor logs.

After the extreme activity of the past two days, every member of the crew acted like they were starved, which pleased Neelix tremendously. Unfortunately, this meant the Talaxian had to break his promise to return to sickbay immediately with the nourishment. This troubled Neelix greatly; he considered Mr. Vulcan his pet project. Fortunately, as busy as the dining hall was, sickbay seemed quiet and sedate when Neelix finally returned with his laden tray. Dark, even.

"Tuvok?" Neelix called, surprised by the low lighting. When no answer came, the Talaxian called out softly, "Doctor?"

"Please state the nature of the medical . . . Oh, hello, Mr. Neelix." The Doctor scowled. "Where was I this time?"

"I don't know," Neelix said. He stretched his neck to look about. "And where's Mr. Tuvok?"

The Doctor followed Neelix's gaze. "I don't know," he repeated.

Frowning, Neelix said, "Computer, locate Lieutenant Tuvok."

"Lieutenant Tuvok is not aboard Voyager."

Neelix blinked. "Not aboard . . . ? Computer, how exactly did Tuvok leave the ship? And how long ago?"

"Lieutenant Tuvok departed Voyager in the shuttlecraft Shoemaker one hour, fifty-two minutes, and forty-three seconds ago."

Neelix scowled and tapped his combadge. "Neelix to Janeway."

"Go ahead," came the reply.

"Ma'am, did you or Commander Chakotay authorize a shuttle launch in the last two hours?"

A pause. *"No, we did not. What's this about, Neelix?"*

The Talaxian's eyes widened. He looked at the Doctor, whose brow had furrowed in apparent confusion and concern.

"Captain," Neelix began, "I think we have a problem."

**CONTINUED IN
STRING THEORY, BOOK 2:
FUSION**

GLOSSARY OF MONORHAN TERMS

ati-harat: artisan in service to the *rih-hara-tan*

hara: group or pack

harat: male leader of a *hara*

haras: female leader of a *hara*

haran: male or female member of a *hara*

kuntafed: wild Monorhan animal

linuh-harat: seer/prophet, advisor to the *rih-hara-tan*

Protin: Monorha's primary star

rih-hara-tan: leader of an entire Monorhan tribe who can establish the same psionic link with all tribe members that a *harat* or *haras* can with his/her *hara*

shalla: head of a secular committee of Monorhans, established by the Interim Emergency Council

Shi-harat: personal bodyguard to the *rih-hara-tan*

The Blue Eye: Monorha's second star

wantain: snow

ACKNOWLEDGMENTS

First, I have to thank the *Voyager* geeks, my collaborators, Kirsten Beyer and Heather Jarman. They're the cocaptains of this particular vessel and they were kind enough to ask me aboard to play. Second, grateful thanks to Katie Fritz, without whom I never would have known enough about *Voyager* to have been in the position to be asked. I would be remiss if I didn't acknowledge the cast, writers, production team, and artists responsible for *Star Trek: Voyager.*

I wouldn't have been able to complete this project without the constant affection, assistance, teaching, and encouragement (whether you knew it or not) from Barbara Gladney, Annarita Gentile, and Joan White. Thank you, ladies. Also, many, many thanks and head rubs for my son, Andrew, and kisses for my sweetie, Helen, for their patience and love.

Last, as ever, thanks to Marco. I owe you everything for giving me the chance to do this work I love so much.

ABOUT THE AUTHOR

JEFFREY LANG has authored or coauthored several *Star Trek* novels and short stories, including *Immortal Coil*, *The Left Hand of Destiny* (with J.G. Hertzler), "Foundlings" in the DS9 anthology *Prophecy and Change*, and "Mirror Eyes" (with Heather Jarman) in the anthology *Tales of the Dominion War*. He is likely currently behind deadline on his next project. He lives in Bala Cynwyd, PA, with his partner, Helen, his son, Andrew, an irascible cat named Samuel, and a fearful hamster named Scritchy.

STAR TREK®
STRANGE NEW WORLDS

08

EDITED BY
DEAN WESLEY SMITH
WITH ELISA J. KASSIN
AND PAULA M. BLOCK

All-new *Star Trek* adventures—by fans,
for fans!

Enter the *Strange New Worlds*
short-story contest!
No Purchase Necessary.

Strange New Worlds 9 entries accepted
between June 1, 2005 and
October 1, 2005.

To see the Contest Rules please visit
www.simonsays.com/st

SNW8.01

As many as 1 in 3 Americans have HIV and don't know it.

TAKE CONTROL.
KNOW YOUR STATUS.
GET TESTED.

To learn more about HIV testing, or get a free guide to HIV and other sexually transmitted diseases, visit or call:

www.knowhivaids.org
1-866-344-KNOW

11380